AFTER THE FACTS

To Keith & Pat
I hope that you enjoy
this book.
Greetings from Missouri!

Vicco Tutertia

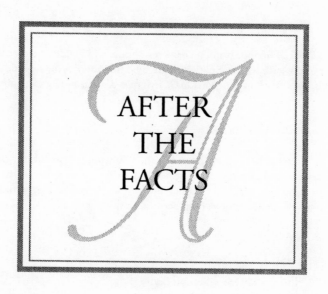

AFTER
THE
FACTS

An After Coffman mystery

VINCENT M. LUTTERBIE

Elderberry Press

Cover art by Aaron Kisner

❧ Elderberry Press

1393 Old Homestead Drive, Second floor
Oakland, Oregon 97462—9506.
E-MAIL: editor@elderberrypress.com
TEL/FAX: 541.459.6043

All Elderberry books are available from your favorite bookstore, amazon.com, or from or our 24 hour order line: 1.800.431.1579

Publisher's Catalog-in-Publication Data
After The Facts/Vincent M. Lutterbie
ISBN 1-930859-21-X
1. Literature——Fiction.
2. Mystery——Fiction.
3. Romance——Fiction.
4. Murder——Fiction.
I. Title

This book was written, printed, and bound in the United States of America.

To my mother, my wife, and to Tracy
for their faith before the fact.
To Dave and Ed
for their faith after the fact.

one

"Might just have to depend on dumb luck,"
I muttered as the shadows began to lighten in the cramped hallway
outside apartment B-23, of the Boulevard Estates apartments. The
door, scarred with years of abuse and neglect, stared back at me
without comment, shades of tan, white and an unidentifiable color
vying for prominence as they were unappealingly peeling away from
the pressboard veneer. Dumb luck was all I was having on the case
to this point, but a clue to its puzzle might just be behind the door.
Please notice that I wasn't asking for the entire puzzle, as that would
be asking for far too much.

I was struggling with my conscience, as I wondered whether or
not to pick the lock. I pulled a quarter out of my pocket, surprised
that I still had coins of that high a denomination left. I quietly said,
"Heads;" as I flipped it into the air. Of course it came down tails.
Figuring one flip was not legitimate odds, I flipped it again. Tails.
Flip.... tails. Flip....tails. Flip....heads; good enough! I took out
my picks and went to work on the door. The lock yielded its secrets
as easily as a 5-year-old caught with his hands in the cookie jar,
ready to rat on any sibling in order to avoid his punishment. Of
course the door didn't open easily, so I had to put my shoulder into
it. Knowing, however, the clientele of this elite establishment, I was
fairly certain that no one had recovered yet from the previous night's
wine binges and would not be bothered by any noises I might make.

Cheap wine too, by the looks of the bottles and cardboard boxes in the trash bin outside. How had we stooped so low as to allow wine to be packaged in cardboard? What was that all about? At least there wasn't a lot of rotting garbage in the dumpster, these people weren't into food all that much.

OK, I was in. Placing the quarter back into my pocket, I pulled some gloves on, and took the edge of my shirt to wipe off any fingerprints around the door, not that any half smart detective couldn't make a match from the grime that rubbed off onto my shirt. I was pretty sure that this particular grime would have no match anywhere else in the county. I stepped inside; pulling the door nearly closed as gently as possible. There was evidence of a chain having been forcibly removed from the door jamb at one time, but it appeared to be from a long ago time when married people may have lived here, perhaps a jealous husband breaking in on the spouse during a horizontal exercise session.

I stood inside the door, taking in as much of the room as I could. I believe that first impressions tell me more than an hour of sleuthing. This belief had never yet borne fruit, but it was a chance I was willing to take, and neither the apartment nor I had anything else going at the moment. The room was roughly 12 feet square, a worn, torn and forlorn carpet distancing itself from the walls, making an inevitable march to oblivion toward the middle of the room. There was one plastic chair sitting under the single window on the wall to my right. There was no trash to speak of on the floor, and very little dust, except for the type of very fine dust you see caught by sunlight while floating in the air. In this case, it was final proof that someone had been here long before me to clean up. Clean up what, is just what I was here to find out. There was a door on the left side of the opposing wall and an archway of sorts on the left wall, leading to the kitchen, no doubt, judging from the cracked tile floor that I could see from my vantage point. I decided to do the kitchen first.

The kitchen floor was as clean as the main room's, supporting the hypothesis that someone had been at work restoring a sense of order to the place. There was no one inhabiting this place at all, and hadn't been for days at least. There was no smell to indicate old food, or even cleaning supplies. No trace of ammonia, dusting spray or perfume. No one had been here for a while now. There was not a lot of dust in the kitchen either, and as it had been a dry summer, this Sherlock deduced it as having been a week since anyone had been here.

Nevertheless, I opened all cabinet doors, peered under the sink and looked in the small pantry built into the far wall. Nothing, not a scrap of paper, not a dollop of spilled food, not even the bones of a starved mouse. I was gratified to see a cockroach scuttle from the pantry as I opened its door, but the little fellow must have been reliving ancestral memories, as the proverbial cupboard was bare. The next thing I tried to do was look behind the trim near the floor, working my way around, searching for a place that may have been pried off, leaving a small hole to hide whatever it is I was looking for. I would be more than glad to share with you just what the object of my attentions were, if I knew myself, but my employer had not managed to inform me of this before she had met an unscheduled and untimely demise. That is a story that I will relate in a bit, allowing you to get caught up, but seriously, you know just about as much as I do right now.

Finding nothing but old glue behind the trim, I proceeded back through the archway and through the living (I use this term very loosely) room, and into the master suite. This was not a lot better. I discovered an aluminum frame bed with a lumpy mattress against the wall; a nightstand of cheap pressed wood and a lamp with a bare bulb next to the bed. No carpet on the recently cleaned floor and nothing else in the room either. There was a small closet, no rod, and no door. There was no door leading to the small bathroom. There was nothing to look for in the bedroom, but I did the obligatory lift of the mattress, looking for resown seams, feeling among the lumps for anything out of place. The nightstand had no secrets to yield, no false bottom, no paper; it had been recently polished as well. I knew there were no fingerprints to be found anywhere in this abode.

With a sigh, I approached the bathroom, expecting nothing to change here either. A funny thing, the air seemed to move a bit, the dust motes had a different pattern as I walked towards the doorless entrance. I encountered no surprises as I entered. The stool was cracked and broken under the weight of many years and countless bottoms. I lifted the top to the tank and took a look. It was somewhat dark in the room, so I turned to flip the wall switch, and barely caught a movement as the world suddenly went even blacker with a crack that I heard more than felt.

• • •

Well now, I had discovered something, what it was, I had no clue, but it was apparently a clue of some sort, and clues are supposed to be important in my line of work. I was trying to put my wits back together, one wit at a time. My first coherent thoughts were that I had a splitting headache and was flat on my back. That took awhile to sink in. I then opened my eyes, found that they were not yet ready to focus on a spinning room, and closed them again. Too late! I rolled over and vomited all over the floor near the toilet. So much for a clean apartment. Ah yes, the clean apartment! Bits and pieces began to swim about in the squishy mess that had been my brain moments (or was it hours?) before. I chanced another eye opening, but just with my right eye. Not too bad, I couldn't get any sicker anyway, unless the yellow that someone had assumed was a legitimate color for the ceiling made me sick again. Breathing a bit more regularly, I closed my right eye and opened the left. No real problem there either. Just knowing that both sides of my face were working independently was a relief, but that in itself was yielding no results. OK, I opened both eyes, and the room slowly swam back to normal, or what passed for normalcy in this little slice of hell.

Now, I had to figure out why I was in this predicament. Two options worked their way into my slowly returning consciousness. One, that I had been clubbed from behind as I was turning around; that would explain the dust moving. Someone could have entered the unlocked front door. The second option was that part of the ceiling had fallen on me. I was voting for the latter, but my vote generally does not count, and this time was no different. I pulled myself up and looked around. No new holes in the ceiling, and the doorway seemed in one piece as well. OK, I got clocked, but why? There was nothing to be found here; the place had been swept clean. Whoever conked me didn't know that though, or else I would still be looking for clues in the bathroom. Did I mention that clues are important in my line of work? They are, and unless one or two of them fell upon me (perhaps an unfortunate metaphor), I would soon be flipping burgers in the fast food restaurant down the road from my rented room for a living.

I stood up, holding the stool for support, hoping that it knew better than to move suddenly. For once, my luck held, and I made it to my feet in an unsteady fashion. Gathering myself, I slithered to the sink, wondering if the water still ran. Turning the cold water knob yielded nothing. The hot water knob did turn, and of course the water was cold, which suited me just fine. I splashed some of it on my face, and that did help a little. I looked in the mirror, which was cracked, but clean, pretty much summing up my morning. Yup, it was me, with my eyes somewhat unfocused and my right ear still lower than my left. I don't know why some people are born with perfectly symmetrical faces while others have obvious defects. My biggest flaw was that I had mismatched ears, the right much lower than the left. To make matters worse, the earlobe was bigger on the right ear, and both stood out as if they were windbreaks on a Kansas wheatfield. I remembered the kids calling me Jughead in school, and I suspected even then that there would be no Betty or Veronica in my future.

I felt that as long as I was here, I might as well finish what I came for, so I slowly and gingerly looked at the rest of the room, recovering my equilibrium as I did so. I have been hit harder, so this blow was not meant to kill or incapacitate, just get me out of the picture for a bit. I remember Gretchen White clubbing me with her purse on our first date, breaking my nose and sending me to the hospital, where my stepfather of the moment came to get me with a bemused look on his face. I don't know if he was bemused because I had actually had a date, or because I had dared to do something that would make a girl hit me like that. Actually, all I had done was suggest that Patty Boyle was a pretty good looking girl, and that had been enough to get me clobbered. Apparently Gretchen felt a bit sorry for me, as a few days later, she apologized and suggested that we give it one more try. Two hamburgers, a couple of sodas and some fries later, she dumped me immediately, and without any appearance of conscious thought or remorse when local stud Mike Worthy came into the burger joint, and asked if she would like to take a spin in his new Thunderbird convertible. She readily agreed, and after explaining to me how things, "Just sorta happen, y'know?"; she flipped her ponytail and popped out of my life forever. I didn't mind too much, as I had barely enough money for that date, and no future funding in line for another hot time. What got to me was the fact that she got into the car, and it already had 3 other girls in it. Had she no pride? After realizing whom she had shared her most recent repast with, I realized that she might not!

Anyway, as it appeared that I was going to live a bit longer, I finished checking out the bathroom, finding nothing at all. Working my way back through the apartment, I saw nothing out of place, but as I was still just a bit woozy, I sat on the plastic chair by the living room window, trying to figure it all out. I felt the back of my head, and found the tender lump recently deposited there, and wondered how noticeable it would be. Probably not too bad, as people rarely got beyond my ears before giving up at looking at my face.

As I sat at the chair, trying to figure where I would go next, I noticed a very slight movement. It was a large black ant working its way up the windowsill. A sign of life being rare around here, I watched idly as it crept around, exploring for a way out, no doubt. It wasn't long before the ant went through a place in the window frame where the wood had split and made his escape into the rarified air of 2nd floor Boulevard Estates. I peeked out the window to see how he was progressing, and noticed that I was directly above a dumpster in the courtyard between building A and building B. I had not ventured to this spot yet, not having discovered a way between the two buildings from the outside. I had noticed a locked wooden gate that probably remained that way, except for trash days. The gate and lock had been rusty and unused looking when I had first glanced at them, and I figured it had been awhile since that dumpster had been in service. A possibility came to mind that perhaps there was some trash in the dumpster that had been tossed out of this apartment in some recent time. It might come to nothing, but I decided it would be worth pursuing anyway.

Rising from my prefab throne, I tried to open the window and found it surprisingly compliant. It opened easily, revealing a dusty and dirty exterior surface, with one exception. About halfway up the interior frame, there was a clean area, as if it had been dusted by a rag. I placed my fingers on the wood and sort of played with it a bit, and to my astonishment, the wood pulled away without complaint, revealing a scrap of paper! Eagerly, I pulled it out of its crevice, and opening it with trembling fingers, read, '1:30 A.M., Green Frog....call 845-777.... ahead of time'. This was scrawled in an uneducated hand, much like mine, so I was able to decipher it fairly easily. I had two problems; the lack of a final digit to the phone number, and the fact that this scrap of paper meant absolutely nothing to me. The paper was fairly new though, there was no sign of curling or yellowing yet. Chances were strong that it hadn't been there for very long, but it must have been important enough to hide.

Satisfied that dumb luck is better than no luck at all, I considered it a well spent, if somewhat painful morning, and I slithered out the door, only slightly sorry about the deposit I had made on the bathroom floor. After all, the rest of the apartment was spotless, and would probably rent to the first person desperate enough to look at it, who would doubtless make similar deposits of his own. I locked the door from the inside, and closed it gently, going down the stairs, and out a small side door that led into the courtyard and then onward to the little used dumpster. Removing my gloves as I neared it, I realized that my earlier assumption was correct. There were weeds and trash all around the dumpster, showing that it had not been moved in some time. There were boxes and old pieces of furniture, TVs and other debris on this side of the gate, which swung inward by the look of the hinges. So, I had carte blanche to review the trash of the past few months, at least. Lucky me.

Looking around, and seeing no sign of intelligent life, I pulled myself up and over the edge of the uncovered dumpster and peered inside. As I said earlier, we have had dry weather recently and this was making the prospects of finding unspoiled paper unusually promising. The rubble was not that deep, and hardly smelt at all, so as I was still somewhat conspicuously perched on the edge, I decided to drop in for a more conclusive visit. The trash was mostly composed of paper wrappers, newspapers, bits and pieces of broken furniture, trashy paperbacks and rags, with the occasional bottle and can. I figured the rats had gotten all the old food, thus explaining the lack of odor. Even so, I knew that I was unlikely to find anything worthwhile, unless I was extremely lucky, as there was too much there to simply pack up and take with me.

I began by quickly sorting the food and bottle trash to one side, and the newspapers, books and other readable junk on the other, using the broken furniture to separate the two piles. I began sorting through the readable trash. I opened each book, shaking the pages, looking for scraps of paper. I read the headlines of the papers, trying to see if there was any theme to them. The most recent paper was dated August 4th, 10 days ago, and the other newspapers weren't anywhere near that date. Perhaps a clue, perhaps not. Someone had dumped something here 10 days ago though, and it was not food. Papers and books eliminated, I looked at the loose paper, finally spying a fairly fresh green flyer. Turning it over, I saw that the header was proclaiming the opening of a new nightclub, "The Green Frog" for the night of the 4th. It announced that the opening act was Bill Kirby and His Sound Makers" for a night of jazz. Doors open at

9:00, one drink minimum, shoes and shirt required. I felt that this was a clue for sure, and still seemingly without a case, I felt I had made progress nevertheless. A quick look at the rest of the papers yielded nothing and I rose out of the dumpster, only to find myself face to face with a very large, very upset, and very unwashed specimen of mankind. The only thing he had going for himself was the fact that in his hairy, beefy hand was a very large, and efficient looking gun.

I looked at my captor, wondering how I was going to get out of this. Trying to look him in the eye was difficult, seeing as there was about 200 pounds of metal about to be shoved into my face. The best I could do was, "Hello, how ya doing?"

He seemed startled by this, either because I had managed to sound as if I always talked while a gun was in my face, or because no one ever bothered to ask him how he was doing. Perhaps he didn't really know a response to either possibility. I decided to try an easier one, "Mind if I get myself out of the trash bin?"

Not much better, he just looked at me, gun never wavering. I chanced looking into his eyes, small and mean and black. I couldn't tell if there were pupils or not. I sensed a movement, and noticed he was moving the gun up closer to my face. I refocused on the 250 pounds of metal about to swish my life away. Beefy just kept staring at me. I stayed as still as I could, sweat dripping from my armpits down my shirt. I felt the back of my shirt clinging to me, an instant sauna. My legs were only half-straight and my knees were beginning to give out. Have I mentioned that I am not the biggest, toughest guy around? That's why my nose was broken the first time by a girl, as well as two other times I may talk about sometime in the future. Anyway, I will tell you some about my personal life after I tell you how I finally got out of this situation.

Beefy just kept glaring at me, trying to figure out what he was going to kill me with, no doubt. The gun was unnecessary; either hand would do the job easily. My legs were giving out, and I thought it was time to try something again. "I was trying to find Felix Jeffries."

I got a response, "He ain't down here."

"Oh? I thought I'd look around some."

"Lives in 23."

"I knew that, but he wasn't there, so I thought I'd come down here and wait, saw a newspaper, started reading it, and figured the sports section was here in the dumpster."

"No one uses this."

"If I would have known that, I would have just waited outside his door."

"Not here anyway."

"He's not?"

"Been gone for awhile, maybe come home soon." The gun moved back a bit, 200 pounds again.

"Do you mind if I stand up, my legs are killing me."

No response, so I slowly began to stand, and finally had regained a semblance of balance. "Listen," I said, "I guess maybe I'll just go now or something and maybe leave a phone number, then perhaps we could meet up somewhere else, not bother you again."

"Maybe," he seemed to consider this, then, "Nope."

"Why not?" I whined, at least it sounded like a whine, I cleared my throat, and tried again, "I wasn't doing anything wrong, just waiting for Felix"; definitely a whine.

"He's not here."

This was going nowhere, and really fast too, but I had run out of small talk. I tried to think of something else, but was still feeling the 200 pounds of pressure. "Ummm, can I leave a card with you to give Felix?"

He seemed to consider this, and finally lowered the gun, "Yeah, but you'll have to write yer number on it, cause I can't read or write."

Of course! I tried to appear shocked, but it was a weak attempt, at best. Then, I just nodded my head and reached for my wallet. Sonofabitch! It was gone, G-O-N-E , gone. The person who had clobbered me had taken my only form of identification, and what little money I had left. I looked at him in what I hoped was a sincere and forthright manner, shrugged my shoulders and smiled weakly. "I seem to have lost my wallet."

He took this in slowly, then very easily took my shirt in his non-gun hand, lifted me out of the dumpster as if I were a bag of potato chips and walked me over to the unused wooden gate. Looking at me with those dead eyes, he seemed about to say something, got very close to my broken nose and sort of snorted at me as if I was nothing but extra trash from the dumpster. In other circumstances, I might have been offended, but right now, he had the upper hand, and it was around my throat. I was having trouble breathing, and couldn't tell if it was from the fetid air coming from his lips to my battered nose, or if it was from the squeezing of my neck from a size 15 to a size 13. I opted to just hang there in the air, until he decided what to do with me.

He decided a lot sooner than I thought he would, which was just as well, as oxygen was becoming very, very scarce at the moment. With what appeared to be a flick of his wrist, he tossed me over the gate, where I was airborne for several seconds before landing on my walletless butt several feet from the gate.

"Don't come back."

"Maybe I should have called first?"

He turned around and left. Considering how things could have turned out, this was a reasonable outcome, and I was just beginning to catch my breath and straighten my collar out when I had another visitor.

"What's the matter, wife toss you out with the dog?"

I looked up to see one of Hustle's finest (Did I mention that I live in a berg called Hustle? Maybe later, during my life story). Now, Hustle's cops are a pretty decent bunch for the most part. You don't cause them trouble, and they won't cause you trouble. They even have a small fleet of patrolmen who actually still walk the neighborhood beat. They generally pick those who can speak in more than one syllable, are usually friendly and outgoing, and who have strong arches. This, it is believed, will foster good rapport between the men and women in blue, and the average sidewalk sitter, as I was currently occupied. Being, in general, in favor of good rapport, I laughed easily and said, "No, the landlord tossed me out."

He smiled, looking me over, and unfortunately taking me for a tenant of said Boulevard Estates, said, "You know, if you can't pay the rent here, you may not find a better deal elsewhere."

"Oh, I don't live here," I was glad to announce, "I live in a boarding house on 7th and Elm."

"Mother Teresa's?" he asked.

"Why yes," I exclaimed, "do you know her?"

"Lived there myself while going to college. Can I give you a lift home?"

Now, that was a fine offer, and I felt my heart soften in favor of our wonderful city fathers who had decided on good rapport. "I'd appreciate it immensely."

We strolled over to a blue sedan parked a few yards away and got into the car. "I thought you walked the beat," I said. I couldn't help but wonder why he was in this particular neighborhood, if he was truly off duty.

"I am, but I just got off duty and was on my way home," he replied. "I work the graveyard shift. I was looking for a friend of mine who lives here, but he appears to be out and about this morning."

"I'll bet you see some strange things during that shift." I chuckled.

"Sometimes even after the shift is over," he rejoindered.

I felt that the remark was probably aimed at me, so smiling offhandedly, I just sat back and enjoyed feeling my rump on something softer than concrete. I took the opportunity to study my new acquaintance. He was a pleasant looking young guy. Light red hair with one of those razor cuts. He had short sideburns and freckles. He wasn't much taller than I, maybe 5' 10". His uniform was still clean and starched, even after a night on the beat. He was such a straight arrow it made me quiver.

Hustle is a small town, and in no time at all, we were at Mother Teresa's boarding house, where I had a small room and a closet on the 3rd floor, sharing a bathroom with a myopic cub reporter and a demented 12 year old cat named Soot.

As I got out of the car, I turned to thank him, but I noticed that he was getting out as well, doubtless to insure I was really welcome here. We strode up the sidewalk together, actually strode is a bit strong, as I was in some pain yet from my recent fall and lumpy head, but nevertheless, we arrived at the front door at approximately the same time. Mother came to the door and seeing my companion, immediately let out a cry of glee and rushed out to sweep him up in her massive, motherly arms. "Jocko, we haven't seen you in months, where have you been?"

"Hi Mother, well, you know how it is, just married, the baby and the two jobs, hard to get away."

I was touched, this Boy Scout was too good to be true. I shuffled my feet, looking for a way past these two, and for a way back to my own safe haven on the third floor.

"That's no excuse Jocko, you know you are like my own family, so you just bring that little family of yours here to see me, I'll bake you a pie, and we'll have ice cream and sit on the porch, just like old times."

That was just about enough...JOCKO? PIE? ICE CREAM?, she never hugged me, never offered pie and ice cream to me, and never sat on the porch with me. Meanwhile the hugfest continued, with Mother alternately berating him for his faithlessness and hugging him out of sheer joy.

"Ummm, Hi Mother," I finally interjected.

"After!" she said, "And just where have you been this morning?"

"After?" Jocko looked at me quizzically.

"That's my name," I admitted. "I was born in Brooklyn," I added, as if this might explain all. Apparently it did, as Jocko shrugged and opened the door for all of us to enter.

Immediately upon entering, I made an end-run around the re-united friends, hoping to make the staircase and thus, the first step in recusing myself to my room. I thought I had made it when Jocko called me back, "After, we need to talk a bit more."

"I thought you were off duty," I got pretty close to whining again.

"I am, but there are a few questions that need answering."

Mother was thrilled, "Let me fix a lunch for the two of you, then you can talk!"

"That sounds great, Mother!" Jocko was clearly happy.

"I need to freshen up first." I grumbled.

"Go ahead, I'll just sit down here and wait," Jocko said. So much for rapport.

I trudged up the stairs, realizing what a roller coaster I had been on today, and it was only lunchtime! The stairs seemed higher and steeper than normal, and I was pretty well spent by the time I got to my room. My myopic upstairs companion, Paul, had apparently left my door open, after mistaking my room for his for the thou-sandth time, and Soot had done his bloody work again. This time, my coverlet was on the floor, all of the items on my dresser top had been thrown to the floor, and the trash can had been overturned with assorted bits of shredded paper all over the place. Luckily, as this had happened many times, I had nothing that was breakable on the dresser. I went to the bathroom, shaved again, combed my hair, put on some after shave, then went back to my room changing into a shirt that had some semblance of a normal collar.

I was ready to meet the world again, I supposed. Well, Jocko, at least. The rest of the world would have to wait until after lunch.

two

You may be wondering a few things right about now. I am prepared to clear some of them up for you. I will go over the few facts of my life that are salient, then you will be as caught up in this case as I am. You may already be way ahead of me. Anyway, the name.... I admit that After is not the usual name, but the circumstances surrounding the dropping of this appellation on yours truly are a bit out of the ordinary. Without going into details, let's just establish the fact that my mother was not always discriminatory when it came to the men in her life. Mom is a wonderful person, would give a friend the shirt off her back, and in fact has done just that on many occasions. Unfortunately, there were times when she should have kept it on. Apparently I was conceived during one of those times, so I guess there is one instance I cannot complain about. At the time of my birth, mom was living in Brooklyn. There are stories about Brooklyn, and there are stories about Brooklyn. Most of them are true. There are stories about bartenders, cops, crooks, politicians, hot dog vendors, and all sorts of people. Those already from Brooklyn know these to be entirely true. There are so many wild, improbable true stories from there, that there is absolutely no reason to make any others up.

Anyway, nine months later, mom was in labor, and she had to go to the hospital in Brooklyn. Mom made the mistake of reliving some of her exploits to the charge nurse. The nurse was not impressed and when the time came to name mom's creation, the same nurse was there, paper and pen in hand. She asked mom what to name me, mom thought about it awhile then said, "I think I'll name him after his father. I believe his father was Bob, I'll name him after Bob." The nurse wrote 'After Bob Coffman' on the report, using Mom's last name for mine. Mom signed it without paying attention to it and that's how I got the name. Of course, over the years, I tried to talk mom into getting it changed, but she thought it was clever and funny. She told me it would add to my character. Maybe it did. At any rate, I never got around to changing the name, and now I have gotten used to it and the effect it has on people.

I managed to get through high school with the usual mental trauma associated with that age group, plus the broken nose and several bruised egos. All in all, it was a worthwhile experience. I spent some of my graduation money losing my virginity in a sleazy motel room with a lady of the night. She was missing several front teeth, had too much deodorant and perfume on, charged me twenty dollars, and had me out of there in 5 minutes or so. It was a relief, both to have the virginity thing dealt with, and to get out of the room. One other girl finally legitimized my masculinity after a drunken party on a pontoon boat during my first semester in college. She was drunk and so was I. I remember that we went out on a raft together, but that's about it. My fellow drunks told me about it the next morning, so let me first admit that neither of us was discreet, and somewhere there are Polaroid pictures to prove it. The girl was so embarrassed that she immediately left school, and none of us ever heard from her again. I suspect she entered a nunnery. So, even though I don't remember the experience, there is proof out there somewhere. That's it for my sexual history.

I was majoring in criminal justice, and that is where I first learned that only criminals get justice. Certainly, the victims rarely do. I graduated, tried for the Police Academy, failed the physical, and somehow earned the scorn of the rest of the incoming cop class when I began extolling some of my views on police brutality in Brooklyn, my anti-war views in general, and the fact that I thought that cigarettes ought to be outlawed. I was 22 years old, no job, a degree that meant I could do almost nothing, and mom was gone to some far away island with her latest beau, so I did what I had to do. I left Brooklyn for the big, wide, wonderful world.

I did odd jobs here and there. I was a night watchman at a

department store, I was a valet at a high-class restaurant and I tended bar. I was going nowhere until one day while tending bar, I met a Private Investigator. He regaled me with story after story about his job, and I developed an interest in his line of work. One night at the bar, two of the faithful decided to take each other's heads off, and while trying to break up the fight, I managed to get my nose broken for a second time. After leaving the hospital, I learned that I had been fired from my bar job, as much from not being a very good mixologist as from not stopping the fight. Upon returning to my rented room, I got out a map, closed my eyes and stuck a pin randomly into it. The first pin went into the Atlantic Ocean, and I seriously thought about it, but then decided to try it again. The second pin went into a little Midwest town called Hustle. That name had just enough promise to lure me here via Greyhound, and upon alighting from the diesel monster, I immediately went to City Hall to see what it would take to become a licensed P. I. Ten dollars later, I was licensed.

I had been staying at a cheap motel, but money was rapidly running out. I scanned the newspaper ads for a residence, found Mother Teresa's ad and applied for her cheapest room. She took pity on me and said I could have one of the 3rd floor rooms, use of the telephone for local calls, and 2 square meals a day, if I was on time for them. I was on my own for lunch. She charged me one hundred a month up front, and I thought this was an excellent deal. When I asked how she could afford this, she just smiled and told me that everything was O.K., and that I could make it up to her in future if I felt the need to do so. I then met my fellow roomies. Paul Grease is a brand new reporter, fresh out of college, has coke bottle glasses that he constantly loses, and he is so easily distracted that he ends up in my room as often as he does his. It matters little whether I am in the room or not, and it took a while to get used to him barging in at any time, only to see him become disoriented when realizing where he had ended up. He is a good guy, I have respect for his writing ability, and so do his bosses. He has graduated from Classified Ads to Obituaries in record time, so the sky is the limit for him. Someday, he may make enough money to buy a new pair of glasses.

Then there is my other 3rd floor housemate....Soot. Soot is a large black cat, going to gray around the muzzle. Soot hates the world, and me most of all, it appears. Mother says he likes me better than the last tenant, but I don't see how this is possible. Soot will find a perch near the top of the stairs, hide there and just wait. If

Paul or I come up the stairs, and not pay enough attention, Soot will jump from his perch, land on our shoulders, dig in his claws and generally hang on for the wild ride to follow while we try to remove him. On two occasions, this has resulted in injury. Paul fell down the stairs, breaking his collarbone, I fell down the stairs breaking my nose. I had just recovered from this third break when I got my first real P. I. job, the case I am currently trying to describe. Soot took pity on Paul for some unfathomable feline reason, and has left him alone recently, but that has left him time to redouble his attacks on me.

I had been spending most of my days trying to find a cheap, but clean office area. I had arranged some interviews with several people who had the odd corner to rent out. One was particularly promising, it was the back room of a building primarily used by a team of lawyers. I thought that this would be a good way to get clients, so I spent an extra long time and more effort than usual to look my best. If I really work at it, my best is passable. I put on my best trousers, spent the money to get my blazer dry cleaned, polished my shoes, got a haircut and was ready to go meet my prospective landlords. I decided to take one last look in the bathroom mirror, and exited the bathroom. It was that particular day that I was fallen upon by Soot. It was a particularly brutal attack, and resulted in a ripped blazer, the broken nose, bruises on my knees and screams that woke up the rest of the inhabitants of Mother Teresa's. Mother herself was not much help, she picked up Soot, checked the little hellion over for damage, then with him purring contentedly in her arms, she began to lecture me on how to be kind to animals. She also took the time to berate me for dripping blood on her carpet, and tsk tsked about the condition of my clothes. "Really, Mr. Coffman, if you expect to have a respectable law firm rent space to you, you should try to look your best for them. First impressions are so important."

After a quick trip to the hospital, where my nose was encased in the now familiar plastic guard and bandages, I did my best to clean up, and then went to my belated meeting with the lawyers. They were kind, too kind, smiling and offering me coffee. They asked if I wanted to sue the perpetrator that had obviously been much larger, quicker and stronger than I, then they ushered me out of there as fast as they could, while promising to call if they decided I would become their tenant of choice. The next day, I walked by and saw that they had rented the place to someone else. There was a man working on the windows, trying to make the place shipshape. I sauntered over, attempting to look nonchalant, and asked the gentleman if he was the new renter. He said that he was, and that it was the funniest thing, the law firm had previously turned him down, but the night before, he received a call stating that he could have the place for twenty dollars a month less, if he would take possession the next day. He readily agreed, and was told that morning that the decreased rent was to keep an undesirable person out. I grimaced, but asked him what he did, and he replied that he was a Taxidermist. The lawyers had originally thought that his line of work was too far removed from theirs, but an incident the day before had changed their minds. I asked him how much he charged to stuff a cat, and rolled away without receiving an answer.

Stopping off at the local hardware store, I picked up a small water pistol, filled it at the fountain at City Hall and limped back to my digs. I was ready for the little devil, but pretended to not be expecting him. He fell for it and leapt at me from the top of the stairwell. I attacked in kind, dousing him liberally with the water gun, ruffling his feathers and soaking his mealy tail. He escaped down the stairs, my laughter echoing in his laid back ears. I didn't see him for 2 days. However, one night Paul rambled into my room by mistake, excused himself absent-mindedly and went on about his business. The next morning I awoke soaked in cat urine, the papers on my dresser had been carefully ripped to shreds and the garbage can had been overturned, with the unfinished contents of a soda bottle overturned and sticky upon the remaining contents.

I went to the bathroom to clean up, stuffed my bedclothes into the hamper, and went in search of the little monster. Of course he was on his mistress' lap, sleeping contentedly, so he was able to salvage one of his nine lives at that point. There would be other times, I was sure. Since then, we have had minor skirmishes, but nothing amounting to anything much until this morning's incident with the shredded coverlet. This put me in a foul mood once again, as I descended the stairs for my meeting with Jocko.

One other thing that you should know, I did finally get an office. It was about two weeks later, and I was just taking a morning walk, trying to figure how I got into the mess I was in, and how to get out of it again. I noticed a flea market near the older part of town. It was nothing much to look at, old white paint over a stucco surface with green and white striped canvas awnings over the windows. There was a sign that might be 10 years, or 50 years old proclaiming the establishment as 'Roy Mack's 2nd Hand Shoppe and Flea Market'. I opened the door, as much out of curiosity as to why the proprietor placed a 'pe' at the end of Shop, as I was interested in looking at the goods inside. I even had a crazy idea that there might be real fleas for sale inside, and that I could get some for Soot. Unfortunately, I was basically broke, and if it weren't for the two squares a day that Mother was feeding me, I would already be in dire shape.

Bells tinkled gently as I entered the musty interior, and I stood there momentarily waiting for my eyes to adjust to the darkness within. I could hear the bustling of a body moving about somewhere inside, and when my eyes finally adjusted, I saw Santa Claus, or a very merry brother of his behind the counter. I walked up to him, smiling, as his was the friendliest face I'd seen in Hustle.

"Good morning!" I said cheerily, walking up toward the counter.

A face full of character smiled back at me. Roy, if indeed this was Roy, had the white hair and bushy white eyebrows to go with Santa's, but his beard was truly spectacular and easily had his more famous twin's eclipsed in length, width and thickness. It was truly luxuriant. He had the round wire framed glasses, the rosy cheeks and a briar pipe clenched between his teeth. A fruity aroma exuded from the pipe, almost making me rescind my attitude about smoking, and smokers in general. "How are you, young man?" he replied, taking in my nose, mismatched ears and general feeling of deflated worth all in one moment. His smile was generous and warm.

"I've had better days," I said.

"Nothing's happening here at this particular instant, why don't you tell me about it."

I couldn't believe it, I spilled my guts, even telling him about the Polaroids. He listened attentively, and hummed and tsked in the appropriate places.

"Sounds as if you need a break," he said after my soliloquy. "I may just be able to be of service to you."

"Really?" I jumped forwards, nearly crashing into the counter. "What do you have in mind?" I cried excitedly.

"Well, I recently lost my evening employee, he worked from 6:00 till close at 10:00. Some nonsense about getting married or such." He looked at me quizzically, "You aren't planning on getting married anytime soon?"

Before I could assure him that this was far from an event that was likely to happen, he continued without interruption. "I think we could both help each other out here, I have a small room in the back that you could clean up, and make into an office, and in return, maybe you could take the evening shift off my hands. I'll pay you a little and throw the room in free until you get on your feet. You'll need to clean it up and maybe spell me for lunch a time or two."

Neither the famous Mother Teresa, nor my landlady had anything on this guy. I couldn't believe it, but decided to take the offer on the spot. "My only problem is that I may have to do my own work some evenings," I worriedly stated, fearing the worst.

"I expect you'll be fairly busy soon enough, but then you can pay me rent, and we'll find another employee." This guy probably took in strays all of his life, and wasn't afraid of getting bitten. He obviously hadn't met Soot.

"I'll take it, do I start tonight?"

"That would be wonderful....umm, er..."

"After," I volunteered.

"After what?" his concerned look shamed me a bit.

"My name," I stammered, "my name is After. I was born in Brooklyn." Again, this simple explanation seemed to satisfy him, as it did most everybody. "And I'll be glad to start right now cleaning the room if you show me where it is, ummm, Mr. Mack!"

He smiled and led me to the back saying, "You can call me Roy, that's what everyone calls me." He showed me the room, gave me a skeleton key off a rack next to the door, and worked it into the lock. The door opened with a protesting squeal, but the space inside was perfect.

The room had a grimy window near the ceiling, a bare bulb hanging from the ceiling and plenty of room for a desk, file cabinets, some chairs and a phone. It was dirty though, so I looked about for the best place to begin.

"I doubt if there is much of value in here," Roy said, "but if you have any doubts, just come ask me." There was a small dumpster out back, rags and cleaning solutions in the bathroom, and after a few hours work, I had managed to cart out all but a few interesting old salt and pepper shakers, an old brass lamp and some boxes full of old comic books. I had swept and mopped the floor, and once I cleaned the window, I was surprised to see the sun working its light in from the southern exposure the room allowed.

I approached Roy, "Some of these old comic books may be worth something, you may want to keep them." He grinned and said I had a future in antiquities. He also came back a bit later with a small desk, a chair and a nice glass fixture for the ceiling light. The place was almost cheerful; all it needed was a client.

I went home for supper at 4:00, promising to be back by 6:00 to finish the night out for him. I had a bounce in my step that I hadn't had for a long, long time. Mother even noticed the change, and remarked upon it. "You certainly look like you had a good day!"

"Yes, old Roy Mack rented me an office and gave me employment today. I begin at 6:00 tonight!"

Her mood darkened slightly, and turning, she began to walk away, but thought better of it. "I am happy for you," she began carefully, "but don't take any unnecessary chances with him."

I was going to ask her what she meant by that, but she walked away saying, "Go clean up, I'll make you an early supper."

Walking up the stairs, I didn't notice Soot in attack mode till the last second, but I was able to adjust just in time, and he went sailing past me, landing 5 steps down from the landing. I snickered at him; he pasted his ears back and sauntered down the rest of the flight. I took this as a good omen, boy was I wrong.

Back to the story at hand.......

I tried to appear casual, nonchalant and in total control as I entered Mother Teresa's dining room. I felt that Jocko probably took little notice of the fact that I tripped over the carpet runner and held onto a chair in order to not hit the floor in an unceremonious fashion. We had three other house occupants as guests; one was an old fossilized friend of Mother Teresa's, who had lived in the house longer than Mother had owned it. Mother just didn't have the heart to throw her out. The lady was nearing 100, couldn't hear a word I said, and probably didn't know I was alive. Her name was Beulah, or Providence, or Emma, something like that. Another tablemate was a second floor dweller name Hal, who worked as a consultant for the city, and was only planning on living there long enough to fix the sewer system in town, maybe a year at most. The third was a young college student named James. He went everywhere on bicycle and generally found other places to spend the night.

"Afternoon all!" I greeted everyone. Everyone but the fossil looked and smiled, and man, did they have something to smile about. Mother had piled cold cuts, home made fries, wheat bread, rye bread, pumpernickel and white bread all over the table, slices of several types of cheese, as well as sun tea, milk, sodas, and fruit of most descriptions. Hot steaming corn on the cob was coming through the door in a large bowl carried by a beaming Mother Teresa. I resolved to invite Jocko over at least once a week. There was no need for talk; we all entered the fray with gusto, eating as if we had been on a deserted island, or eating hospital food for months. I outdid myself, and even Beulah/Providence/Emma had a hearty meal. You knew she meant business when she put her dentures in.

"How have you been Carol?" Jocko asked the fossil. I knew her name was something like that! Trust Jocko to remember her name, but then he knew her when she was younger.

Carol smiled and said, "Fine, just fine, especially since you are here, as no one else even knows that I am alive." She gave Hal and me a slight frown, causing Jocko to give a start as he looked in a hard manner at both of us.

Hal kept eating, and I tried to look contrite as I said, "Please pass the corn."

"Carol here is the Grande Dame of Hustle, she is a member of the D.A.R., initiated many of the clubs in Hustle, used to run the town in the old days, and is the grandmother of our Mayor," Jocko volunteered.

"Here's to the old days," I said, "pass the watermelon please." I hadn't eaten this well since one of mom's boyfriends owned a restaurant. I was doing well that day too, until they tried to make me eat spinach greens, and I got sick all over the place. I don't know if that broke them up, or if mom just moved on naturally. I understand where the first President Bush was coming from on the broccoli thing.

Lunch went on like this for a bit, and Mother even joined us for a little of it, accompanied on her entrance by a plate full of fresh baked chocolate chip cookies.

After the appropriate sighs, grunts of approval, and stretching, Jocko excused himself and went to the living room, with a backward glance at me that was meant to convey... 'You're next.' I decided to help Mother clean up the table first, hoping that the food and some relaxation would make Jocko mellow. I was able to kill 5 minutes or so with this, when Mother shooed me out of the kitchen, and I found myself walking into the living room where I saw a sight that almost made my heart stop. Soot was sitting on Jocko's lap, rubbing his head appreciatively and adoringly under Jocko's hands and up across Jocko's jaws. I could hear him purring from here. It was disgusting and I think Soot knew it was too, for when he noticed me, he decided it would be more seemly to curl up on Jocko's lap instead, where he immediately faked going to sleep.

"OK," Jocko started, "tell me a few things".

"Just ask, I'll follow," I replied as I sat in a chair facing him.

"How long have you been a P.I.?"

"Got my license a few weeks ago, but got my office two days ago."

"Why a P.I.?"

"I'm not cut out for police work, but I like the business."

"Not much call for P.I. work here in Hustle."

"Maybe not, but I am working on something."

"What might that be?"

"Have you ever heard of Felix Jeffries?"

This got a response; Jocko straightened up, jostling the fake sleeper a bit. Soot opened an eye, looked at me, yawned so that I could see that he still had plenty of teeth, and curled up again. "How do you know Felix?" he asked me.

"I don't actually, but two evenings ago, at my first night on the job…did I mention that I work part time for Roy Mack?" Jocko raised an eyebrow, said nothing then waved his hand in an effort to prod me along.

"Anyway, two nights ago, Felix's mother, Felicia came to me while I was at Roy's, asked me if I was really a P.I. and asked if I could do a small job for her."

"Felicia is dead, didn't she run in front of a bus two days ago?"

"That's correct, but she paid me $100.00 up front, and I used it to pay Mother's rent for the next month, so I thought I'd earn a bit of it."

"O.K., can you tell me what she asked you to do?"

"Sure, she asked me to find Felix, or at least a clue as to where he is. She had just found out I was in the business, and so she wasn't prepared. She went home to get a key to his apartment, so that I could have a look around, after paying me the retainer. She never got back, thanks to her accident."

Jocko shifted again, careful not to waken the faker on his lap. "Do you think this may not have been an accident?"

"I don't know, do you?"

"Homicide is looking at it, but there were no witnesses, it was dark, and the bus driver wasn't paying a lot of attention when she stepped in front of him. By then it was too late for her."

I tried to look a little upset and sorry.

"Is that why you were flying through the air at Felix's apartment complex when I first met you?" Jocko asked.

"Yes, the gorilla in charge didn't like me snooping in the dumpster."

"Care to tell me what you found there?"

I decided that Jocko need not know about the illegal foray into the apartment itself, as only one other person knew that, and they probably weren't talking either. I said, "Well, there were a lot of old papers, and flyers, broken stuff, but no food. It had been a while since it was used...except..."

"Yes?"

"Well, there was one recent newspaper dated the 4th, as well as a flyer announcing the opening of 'The Green Frog' for the night of the 4th."

"What do you make of that?"

I couldn't tell him about the paper scrap I had illegally found, so I shrugged, "Nothing maybe, but I thought I might go to the Green Frog in the next evening or so. Felicia's funeral is tomorrow morning, so I thought I would go there too, just to see who shows."

"She wasn't exactly well liked here in town, a bit of a nuisance really," Jocko stated, starting to rise, Soot jumping to safety. "You keep me informed if something else comes to mind?"

"You betcha," I replied.

"I think maybe the boys in Homicide need to know about this, maybe get a warrant to search Felicia's and Felix's places."

I nodded my agreement.

"Anything else?" he asked again, looking me straight in the eye.

"That's about it," I lied, looking him right back.

"O.K. then, I'll be moving on."

"See ya later, Jocko, thanks for the lift home."

"No problem," then as he was closing the door, he smiled and continued, "better be careful, nasty lump on your head," and he closed the door.

I went to my favorite chair in the living room, and decided to go over the events of the past few days, while trying to plan something for the next few as well.

Two nights ago had been my first day of work at Roy's. I walked into the building at 5:30, already happy with the ambiance and happily comfortable with the look and feel of the old place. Roy greeted me as I walked in.

"How's it going, After?"

"Fine, just dandy!" I said, meaning it.

"Let's get started then," he said. He walked me through the store, showing me the appropriate places where his various goods were placed. At first there seemed to be no pattern to the random mish-mosh of items strewn around, but eventually things started to sink in. I found that glassware was away from the window, items of clothing were kept away from light as well. Metal things were near the window, and heavier items were near the door, as lighter items might take it in their heads to walk out more easily. The more expensive things were locked in several cabinets behind the counter where Roy spent the better part of his day.

"Where do you get all this stuff?" I asked, as Roy was preparing to depart.

"I pick it up here and there, I go to garage sales, estate auctions and other stores like mine, where the owner may have some items that I have a clientele for, but doesn't seem to be able to move in his store. I usually trade my stuff to him straight up. We move things better that way."

I had a lot to learn and must have looked worried, because he laughed at me and said, "That's my problem, you just sell the stuff. Actually it won't be too busy this time of evening. Let the people dicker with you, but don't go down more than 30% from what I have listed. Something unusual comes up, have them come back tomorrow and see me. The keys are in the money drawer, and here's an extra front door key for you, just lock it all up when you leave, and take a twenty dollar bill home with you every night as your pay, OK?"

I grinned and told him I was just as happy as could be. No one showed for the first hour, so I spent some time dusting some of the more derelict pieces, and cleaning the windows. I also spent a little time in my office, trying to plan how I would place things. I noticed that Roy had pulled in an old wooden file cabinet with drawers that actually worked. I also noticed that the hinges to my door were well oiled and that it no longer squeaked. I could see that I couldn't spend too much time there while working, as it was out of the line of sight of the front door and counter, and I dared not miss anyone. I closed the door with a sigh, thinking of the better days sure to be ahead.

My first customers came in around 7:00, they were a young preppie looking college couple. At first they seemed standoffish and a bit snobby, so I left them to their critiquing and minded my own business, but tried to keep a sharp eye out nonetheless. The girl was dressed in a very form fitting beige sweater, tan slacks that showed her body to its best effect and had her hair done in that casual way that only comes with expensive hairdressers and a lot more time spent than they would have you think. No wedding ring, but lots of jewelry anyway. Daddy's girl. The young man was similarly dressed. Polo shirt, pressed light jeans, tasseled loafers, and a sweater tied around his waist…a very white sweater, and somehow he was keeping it clean. Two clean cut rich kids from the big city looking for bargains.

Finally, they ambled up to me, looking at me like I was their last chance at finding anything worthwhile at all. I smiled and asked them if they had found anything to suit them at all. They looked troubled and said, "No, and we aren't really looking for anything for us, or we might have picked up a thing or two. We are actually looking for something a bit unusual for her daddy," the young man declared.

"How unusual?" I asked.

"It's hard to say actually," the troubled youth continued, "he is sort of a free spirit, collects old bar signs, movie posters and that sort of thing, restores them, or frames them, whatever…. and places them in his office at work. Then every year he gives them away as presents to his staff, depending on who seems to like what!"

I had an idea, "What about old comic books?" I went to my office and brought out the box. "I have no idea what these are worth, maybe nothing, maybe a little bit anyway."

They were delighted, and spent the next ten minutes looking through the box. There were 25 books in there, and they decided on ten of them. "These are perfect!" the girl gushed, "What do we owe you?"

"I truly have no idea, first night here."

The young man pondered, then said, "I have heard that some books are worth more than others, how about $100.00 for these ten, and if we find that one of us is way off, the other will make up the difference."

"Sounds good to me," I took one of Roy's business cards and wrote my name on the back. The young man handed me one of his cards as well. I took it, and placed it on the counter without paying much attention to it. I took their money, placed it in the register and walked them to the door.

"You've been very helpful," the girl said, and smiled as she tripped lightly to the late model BMW parked at the door. The young man shook my hand and got in the passenger side, they drove off gaily. They were the last people that I saw until 9:45 P.M.

I was about to close up without further incident, when the door bells tinkled lightly, and I looked up to see a rail thin lady with thinning, straggly blondish gray hair step in quietly. She had large, nervous eyes, and moved in a jerky motion, as if she had a faulty transmission, or a sticky clutch. She stood in the doorway a bit, as if to adjust her eyes, but as it was nearly 10:00 P.M., that shouldn't have been the problem. I wondered if she might have been confused because Roy wasn't there.

"Roy is off tonight," I offered. "I am here evenings now."

"Oh, I just saw Roy a bit ago, I came here to talk with you, he said you might be able to help me."

Oh that Roy, my guardian angel! Already soliciting business, looking for the rent on my office room no doubt. That was O.K. though, as I was looking for the same thing.

"Come on in, I am about to close, we can talk." I took the keys, locked everything up and then locked the front door behind us, noting that she appeared even more uneasy. I moved away from her, to give her more space. She had a thin cotton dress on, some sort of floral print, no makeup, sandals, and no bra, not that she had ever needed one, I thought.

All of her movements were furtive and mouse-like. She made me nervous just watching her, but I owed people money, and Roy had sent her, so I was in.

"What do you charge? Are you really a P.I.?"

I had thought about this and had decided to start low, and hope that quantity might help a bit. "Fifty a day plus expenses."

She found a previously invisible pocket on her dress, and pulled out five twenty-dollar bills, handing them to me and saying, "I think this will be a quick job, but let me know if you need more."

"O.K., fair enough, what do you have in mind?"

She started to tear up, "My son," she faltered, then collected herself. "He's been missing for about one week now. I want you to try to find him for me."

"Wouldn't that be a job for the police?"

"I really don't th-think he'd appreciate that, no...not at all."

"I see," I said, and thought I did. Maybe sonny boy had had a brush or two with the local gendarmes and maybe he was hiding from them as well. "I'll do my best; where do you suggest I begin?"

"He, he lives at Boulevard Estates, on the north side of town. His name is Felix Jeffries, and I am Felicia Jeffries." She fidgeted and looked around. "Lately he's been somewhat secretive, he usually c-calls once a day to ch-check on me, but not f-for a week now." She started crying, dabbing at her eyes with her sleeve.

"O.K., I'll run by the place tomorrow," I began, "what apartment is he in?"

"That's just it, he isn't in, I went by a week ago, and it's cleaned out, but someone had been there, it was too clean." She whispered, bringing her head close to mine, "I had a key made when he moved in." She paused, added as an afterthought, "Apartment B-23."

"Great! Just let me have the key, and I'll run by first thing in the morning."

"Oh thank you, I appreciate this, maybe you can find something. He usually keeps notes here and there, sometimes under his pillow, sometimes in the medicine cabinet. I haven't always known what they meant, but he was secretive about something. I will run home and get the key and bring it right back for you." She got up to leave.

"No, don't do that, just meet me here at 7:00 tomorrow morning, and I'll go right over."

She seemed unsure, but nodded anyway, then moved toward the door.

I opened it for her, and she stuck her head out cautiously, looking both ways.

"Forgive me for asking," I asked, "but are you in trouble?"

She started as if shot, but recovered, not looking me in the eye, but rather at my ears, "No, but with the company he keeps, it's always best to be careful."

"Again; forgive me for asking, but the reason you know about his notes, is it because you go to his apartment regularly?"

I finally got a smile out of her. "Of course I do, I AM his mother! Thanks again, see you tomorrow."

"Be careful." I admonished, but apparently she wasn't because the next time I heard her name was on the radio the next morning, as the announcer stated that she had died as a result of being hit by a tour bus.

Back to the story at hand. I lay back in my chair, thinking about what I had been through. Two nights ago, I had met Felicia Jeffries, and had taken her money for a case. Later that night she was dead, and I had a problem, should I continue without a key and any proof, or not? I spent that day chewing on that problem like a piece of stale gum; the only thing I did was work at Roy's that night. Nothing much, sold a few pieces to people that didn't really know what they wanted. You may have done some similar shopping yourself at times.

The next morning, I woke up ready to give her her hundred dollars worth, and that's how I found myself flipping a quarter outside apartment B-23. Now, as I had the Homicide department working on the case, and they would eventually find Felix for me, I thought I was free and clear there. I did think I could do one more thing for her though, I could try to find out if there was a connection between Felix and 'The Green Frog'. I pondered several ways of doing this, given what I knew.

I was feeling somewhat sleepy after my big morning and satisfying lunch, and I must have been dreaming, for I saw myself at Felicia's funeral, looking over the sparse crowd, looking for suspicious faces, but all of the faces were blank and out of focus. I peered into the distance through the surrounding trees lining the perimeter of the cemetery, seeing nothing unusual. A warm rain started falling. My clothes were getting wet! With a start, I awoke; finding my pants wet and myself sitting in a chair that stunk like…cat urine! I got up, incensed, and thought about looking for a dull knife to skin the now invisible Soot.

three

I waltzed into Roy's at ten till six, still wondering if I had entirely removed Soot's unsolicited present. Roy greeted me, but was busy with two groups of people. I let him have the better-dressed couple, and took the other couple. We did a little dealing, and both couples left happy. I told Roy about the comic books and he grinned. "I saw the business card on the counter yesterday morning, and I was wondering why the Governor's son would leave a card here."

"The Governor's son?" I exclaimed. "Wow, maybe I helped him out after all. But, they were buying the present for the girl's dad."

"Ahhh, then, that would be Senator Andrews," he replied with a twinkle. "If you read the grocery store rags at all, you'd know they are a couple."

"Well, it may pay to have comic books in high places," I opted.

He looked at me slyly and said with a mocking grin, "It just might, it just might."

He grabbed his coat and hat, and headed for the door. "By the way, you haven't taken any money for yourself yet, I think you have sixty dollars coming after tonight. It's Friday, I'll see you Monday, but feel free to come on in and use the office, if you need to."

"Thanks Roy, I may need to, have a good weekend."

He waved and went out the door.

OK, it was time for me to earn the rest of my retainer. I had a slight plan on how to proceed, and the first part was the easiest. I planned on contacting Paul at the 'Hustle Herald'. I looked the number up in the phone book and called it, figuring that Paul never got home till nearly midnight, so he would probably be putting final touches on the obits. The gal answered the phone with a desultory, "Hello, Hustle Herald front desk, can I hep ya?"

"I hope so, I need to speak to Paul, ummm…" I stalled here, as I didn't remember Paul's last name.

She asked, "Who? I don't know a Paul."

"He works in obituaries, has thick glasses, walks into things."

"I'll go look," she said unenthusiastically.

I waited for about 10 minutes before she returned, saying, "Sorry, had to use the john, but I found him."

"Good, can I speak to him please?"

"Oh, yeah, I'll get him."

I figured that unless she had a bladder infection, it would just be a few minutes before she returned, but it was almost 10 minutes before she returned again.

"He wants to know who this is."

I sighed, "Tell him it is After Coffman."

"After what?"

"Just tell him I am the other guy on the 3rd floor of the rooming house."

"Why don't ya just tell him in the morning, I'm busy here, it's Friday night and I gotta do my nails."

"One more try, please?"

"O.K." she replied grudgingly.

This time I got a much quicker response. Paul was on the phone. "Who is this again?"

"Paul, this is After, the guy whose room you keep wandering into."

"Oh, Hi After. What do you need?"

"I need a favor that only a newspaper person can help me with."

He seemed impressed. "Is this for one of your cases?" he asked, some excitement in his voice.

"Yes, for my only case actually."

"What can I do for you? Will I get in trouble?"

"You won't get in trouble, Paul, I just need some quick information."

"Oh, O.K." He sounded vaguely disappointed.

"Does your paper ever print flyers that go out with the paper?"

"Sure, it brings in an extra buck or two."

"Can you check to see if you guys printed a flyer around the 4th of the month, dealing with the opening of a nightclub called The Green Frog?"

"Sure, I can do that."

"Also, if it isn't too much trouble, see how many days it was in the paper, and who ordered the print job, if possible."

"O.K. boss, that should be O.K., I am well liked here, and I can probably get a lot of help on it."

"Fat chance" I thought, not if the receptionist is any example. "Just do your best. Paul.... I appreciate it."

"No problem, do you want me to tell you tonight?"

"Only if you happen to wander into the wrong room, and feel that you need to talk."

That was kind of fun, having a co-conspirator, and having him calling me boss. I had to grin. What a combination, a sleuth that had pudding for a nose, and a near sighted reporter. It would have to do. It was all I had.

As there were no customers in the Shoppe, I decided to tackle the phone calls. I had been trying to figure out how best to present myself. I figured that if there was a connection between 'The Green Frog' and Felix Jeffries, that the said connection would not necessarily be very forthcoming on the phone, so I thought that the devious route might work best. I would just call and invite the person on the other end of the phone line to meet me there tomorrow night at 1:30, as the scrap of paper had noted.

Picking up the phone, I dialed the six digits that I already knew, and added a zero. I got a recording telling me that the number had been disconnected, and was no longer in service. The same held true when I substituted the one and the two. I got a bit lucky with the three.

"Hello," a man's voice on the other end.

"Hello, meet me tomorrow night at 1:30 at 'The Green Frog', I'll wear a polka dot tie."

"Is this Ed McMahon?" he asked.

"No," I answered, somewhat confused.

"I don't talk to no solicitors, unless it's Ed," and he hung up.

That could have gone a lot better, but at least I had 4 potential numbers out of the way. Substituting a four got me the recording again. Who said private investigation was boring? I was having a great time listening to dial tones and recorded messages. I also knew that most jobs are routine; mainly drudgery, punctuated by short moments of thrills and accomplishment. Private investigative work is often just going through records, talking to a few people and maybe following a person, just to see how they spend their day. It is mostly working on little things, as murder and large thefts are generally handled exclusively by the police. You may have heard that most P.I. work is domestic, I think that is probably true.

Substituting a five for the last digit, I dialed again. A female answered, "Hellooooo." Like that. I paused for a beat, then went into my spiel anyway.

"Meet me at 'The Green Frog' tomorrow night, I'll be wearing a polka dot tie."

A pause, then, "Kewl, but you'll have to buy, I'm not working."

I asked then, a bit belatedly, "Ummm, would there be anyone else there that I may need to talk with?"

"Nope," she answered cheerily enough, "I live here alone."

"Do you always just show up at a place when someone you don't know calls you up? What if I am not your cup of tea?"

"If I don't like you, I won't stop, but if you wear a polka dot tie, chances are I'll like ya!"

"Oh."

"Byeeee."

Hmm, I was no closer to the person on the scrap of paper, but apparently, I had a date for tomorrow night.

After taking a breath, I plunged in again. The only other number in service seemed to be the one that I was looking for. I dialed the nine, and a man answered. "Yes?"

"Meet me at 'The Green Frog', tomorrow at 1:30, I'll wear a polka dot tie."

Silence, then, "Is this some sort of joke?"

"No sir."

"We'll just see about that." He slammed the phone down. At least I imagined him slamming it down. He didn't sound all that nervous, but then, he hadn't seen my tie.

Perfect timing, I was done with the calls, made a few notes about which numbers were working, placed them in the top drawer of my little desk, and went out to the main room, just as the door bells jingled. I spent the rest of my working time selling painted saw blades to a couple of collectors.

Tomorrow was going to be a busy day, I mused as I gathered up my sixty dollars, leaving Roy a note to inform him that I had done so. I had to dress for a funeral, and then find something to go with my yellow tie with various sized polka dots on it. I also had to decide whether or not to inform Jocko about my date with destiny tomorrow night. Ah well, some things to sleep on.

I walked home, it was a lovely night, and I was impressed with the town as a rule. Even though I walked through the older part of town, past a few liquor stores and taverns, the roads were well lit and there was just a minimum of trash and broken bottles lying about. I went to my room, but the door had not been opened, it was apparently Soot proof for the time being. I went to Paul's door and knocked softly, but got no response. I wondered if he would be home before midnight. I doubted he would come up with anything this soon, but I couldn't help but hope.

I went down to the living room, Hal was there watching an old movie on the television set, so I grabbed a soda and sat down to watch with him. I started to ask him how things were going, but he shushed me.

"This is a classic, wait till the commercials." Groucho was doing his Captain Spaulding dance, and Chico was playing the piano. I was about to leave, when the door opened and Paul barged in, knocking over the hat stand and excusing himself to it.

I wandered over to him, while he was apologizing to the stand, and told him, "Paul, that isn't a person, just the hat stand."

"Oh," he said, obviously relieved, "the coat on it confused me there, for just a second."

"Of course," I agreed, "happens all the time. Did you find out anything on the flyer?"

"Yes!" he whispered, "but don't you think we ought to go somewhere sound proof?"

"No, not at all," I rejoindered, "but maybe someplace Groucho proof." This earned us a glare from Hal. We walked into the dining room, and sat down at the table.

"OK, Paul, I really appreciate this," I offered.

"It was fun," he said excitedly, then lowered his voice. "It wasn't really that difficult."

I smiled, not knowing if he could even see me, but encouraged him, "Go on....."

"Well, we did print the flyers, but they didn't go out with the paper, they were independently distributed. The man who had them printed is named Harold Gibbons, but they were picked up by a fellow named Fred Jacobs, or something like that."

"How did you know who picked them up?" I asked.

"I Xeroxed the order sheet and the bill, which was signed by the person who picked them up."

"You are fantastic." I praised him. "Well done, do you have the copy with you?"

"Oh sure, here it is." He fished it out of his pocket.

I brushed the lint off the paper and read...not Fred Jacobs, but Felix Jeffries!

"It's Felix Jeffries that signed for it!" I gasped.

"Yeah, I knew it was something like that."

This would probably be information that Jocko would want to know, and since he worked the night beat, I thought I'd give him a call.

"Thanks Paul, you've been a great help."

"Let me know if I can bail you out of any other messes."

I wasn't aware that I was in a mess, but he must have been prescient, because I was deeper in than even you may be suspecting right now. "Sure Paul, you can count on it."

I heard him go up the stairs and say, "Good kitty." A moment later I heard him enter and close a door, then the door opened again, then very shortly after that, another door opened....oh boy, he was lost again. I raced up the stairs, never saw Soot, ran through the open door to my room, looked everywhere for the varmint, and satisfied that the room was still Soot proof, made my way to the bathroom, cleaned up and went back downstairs to call Jocko.

I got to the telephone, and called the Police department, asking if there was a way to reach Jocko.

"Patrolman O'Reilly is home tonight, he has Friday and Saturday nights off."

The O'Reilly explained the red hair and freckles, anyway. I thanked the lady and hung up, deciding that midnight was too late to bother a new daddy, and that it could wait until tomorrow. I wandered up the stairs and back into my room, wondering if Soot had found a new home to haunt, as his lack of presence was almost as noticeable as his attacks.

The next morning was gray and somewhat blustery. I saw the shadows of the trees dance across the room, from the dank light of a lazy sun. A perfect day for a funeral. I had decided to go conservative, but not in mourning, after all, I wasn't family. I wore khaki slacks, a dark polo shirt, brown loafers that didn't look too scuffed, and sunglasses. I wanted to see people's eyes without them seeing mine.

Mother had breakfast ready for me, and I hungrily devoured my eggs, toast and orange juice. I even managed to say "Good morning Priscilla," to the fossil. She must have been in a grumpy mood, as she didn't even acknowledge me. I rose from the table, taking my dishes to the kitchen.

As I walked past the table, the old fossil said enigmatically, "Carol."

I smiled, and said, "Of course," having no idea what she meant, but trying to humor the old biddy.

I went to the tortured hat rack, which doubled as a coat rack, and retrieved my raincoat, for there was a feeling in the air, as if it might rain. I took off down the street to where I knew the cemetery was, from previous strolls around the neighborhood.

I knew the graveside service was for 8:00 A.M., and I was about thirty minutes early. I saw where the backhoe had done its work. There was a tent placed near the open pit, and the casket was on plastic turf cleverly designed to look like plastic grass. No one was in sight, so I sat on one of the folding chairs and waited.

At 8:00 sharp, a dark Ford Contour drove up and a slightly built man got out. He walked up to the site, placing glasses on his overlong nose. Of course, next to my nose, all appear to be overlong. He peered at me, not unlike a hawk looking at a mouse from a long distance away, then asked if I was family.

"No," I replied, "just an acquaintance."

"I am Pastor James," he stated, holding out his hand.

"After Coffman," I volunteered.

"Ah yes, the new investigator in town."

"Have we met?"

"No, but Felicia was worried about Felix, and I told her to get some help. She wanted to wait a bit before contacting the police, and then Roy Mack suggested that she come see you. You work in his shop, I understand." I wasn't sure if shop and shoppe were pronounced he same way, but admitted that I did work there.

"Yes, we all meet with several other seniors on Wednesday nights. It is interdenominational, and last Wednesday was my night. You are welcome at any time."

I bristled at being included with seniors, but decided to let it pass, as he was presiding over a funeral and probably had the salvation of a soul weighing heavily on his mind.

"We may as well begin," he sighed, "as the son is apparently gone for good, and her daughter hasn't been home for over ten years."

"You mean that it is only us?"

"Probably."

We did have one other arrival though, as Roy showed up a moment later. I asked Pastor James if there was anything I could send to the church for Felicia.

"Flowers are always nice, just don't send petunias, as I recall, the entire family is deathly allergic to them."

That was interesting; irrelevant, but interesting. I made a mental note to send lilies. I always remember lilies at churches, probably because I usually only went to church on Easter and Christmas, and it was the wrong time of year for poinsettias. Come to think of it, August wasn't a good time for lilies either.

"What church?" I asked.

"Our Holy Mother of the True Rock." Pastor James beamed back at me. "The only one like it in the area."

I pretended astonishment, then sat down, as it was obviously show time.

Pastor James did the routine service, but I also felt that he meant what he said. There just wasn't much need to elaborate. Roy and I sat appreciatively, and bowed our heads when instructed, and generally managed to live through the service. As the Pastor wound down, we rose and I caught a movement out of the side of my eye. An old silver Volkswagen bug was driving by slowly. I couldn't see who was in it, so I turned slightly. At my movement, the bug sped up and got out of the area as quickly as possible. I thought that a large male drove it, with a smaller, possibly female passenger. It had out of state license plates, but that was all I could see in the short look I had. There were probably not many silver bugs in town, I would relay this information to Jocko when I saw him next.

I stood around, exchanging pleasantries with Roy and the Pastor, mostly to see who else might show up. They were ready to leave in a few minutes though, so I said my good-byes and turned to walk away. The Pastor offered Roy a lift home, which he accepted, so I continued on with a wave in their direction. I wandered away, but circled back after they left, finding a tree a short distance away. I took up sentinel there, waiting to see if there would be any other visitors. No one showed for two hours, and I finally made my way reluctantly out of the cemetery. I thought that it was definitely time to contact Jocko, so I found my way to a pay phone and was lucky enough to discover a phone book actually attached to the chain.

Good old Hustle, a pretty safe, clean town, unless you count the crack I received on my head, the death of Felicia Jeffries, and the disappearance of her son. There seemed to be an unseen undercurrent of mystery and a potential for violence that I was ready to plumb, maybe with the help of Jocko.

I dialed his number, and a lady answered. To my untrained ear, she didn't sound young enough to be a young man's wife, but I went ahead anyway.

"Mrs. O'Reilly?"

"No, this is his mother-in-law."

That explained it. "Is Jocko home today?"

"No honey, he and Bitsy went to the city to go shopping, I am baby-sitting today. Could I help you?"

I was still recovering from the Bitsy bomb, but managed to say, "I would appreciate it if you would tell him to call After when he gets home." I couldn't help but wonder what they had named their poor child.

"That's bad English." She remarked primly. "You should not use 'After when' together."

I sighed, and explained, "After is my name, please ask him to call, or drop by, he knows the address."

"Certainly young man, but I don't expect them till late," she replied, but without the warmth. I suspect she thought I was trying to get out of a grammar lesson with a lame excuse.

There was nothing to do except walk home, so that is what I did. Upon my arrival, Mother greeted me with some news. "Several men from Homicide were here to see you, they said to wait here, and that they would be right back."

That was fine, as I was going nowhere else until late tonight. I went into the living room, hoping for a good movie. The fossil was having friends over. The room smelled of old ladies, and was not a place for me. I smiled and turned, then went up the stairs to my room. Suddenly tired, I took off my shoes and lay down for a nap.

A few minutes later, there was a knock on my door. Getting up to answer it, I realized that I must have dozed off for quite a while, and that I hadn't even removed my overcoat. I am sure that I appeared somewhat disheveled when I opened the door, but the two men on the other side seemed to take it in stride. I figured that they were used to dealing with corpses, so a live person in any shape would have to be an unknown diversion, and perhaps I was no more unusual than the next.

"Hello," said the taller of the two. "I am Lieutenant Howard, and this is Detective Moore. We are with Homicide." He made a gesture toward his companion.

"Pleased to meet you."

"Perhaps we could take a walk, as the house seems fairly well occupied at present."

"That would be fine, I think the fresh air would be a good idea."

I put my shoes on and followed them down the stairs and into the late afternoon sun.

I looked the two of them over. The Lieutenant was a tall, black man, well groomed, and with a definite air of authority. I felt like a student in 3rd grade looking at the Principal. The Detective reminded me of a fireplug. He was short and swarthy, with an apparently perpetual five o'clock shadow on his face. He walked bow legged like a character out of an old western.

Lieutenant Howard said, "Jocko said you may have an idea or two to help us on a missing person's case."

"I'd be glad to help, but since when did Homicide work on missing persons?"

"As the missing person was associated with the recent death of his mother, we thought it best to explore the possibilities."

The Lieutenant seemed to be the designated speaker, and the Detective was along for the ride, so I directed myself to the Lieutenant.

"Jocko said you were going to search both of their places, is there anything you can tell me about that?" I ventured.

"No, nothing that we can share, except that we are still on the case."

"OK."

"Now, we need to know a few things. One, how did you get on the case; two, what do you know about Felix Jeffries; and three, what are your plans?"

"Let's see, Felicia Jeffries asked me to investigate her son's disappearance, but she died before she got me the key to his apartment."

"Was she killed on the way home, or on the way back to see you?"

That was a good question, one that hadn't occurred to me. "I don't know, which way was she walking when she was killed, toward her home, or toward Roy Mack's place?"

"From what we gathered, she was walking back to Roy's, but she only had the key to her house on her."

"Hmmm," I mused, "Well, that begs the question of whether you found Felix's key at her place."

"All I can say to that is that someone was at her place before we were, and that we found no key there either." He looked at me, a bit of an edge to him. "You wouldn't have just wandered by there would you, perhaps looked in her trash?" This brought a smirk from the Detective. I decided to continue to ignore him for the rest of the interview, just for that. So Jocko had related the dumpster story, well, no surprise.

"Lieutenant, I have no idea where she lived."

"O.K. then, what do you know about Felix Jeffries?"

"I know that he is Felicia's son, that he has a long gone sister, that he is missing, and that he has some sort of association with a new nightclub, 'The Green Frog'." This elicited a response. They would never admit that they didn't know this, but they covered well.

"How did you come by this knowledge?" the Detective asked.

I spoke to the Lieutenant. "Oh, I was rummaging through Felix's trash, you ought to try it sometime." I was perturbed by the garbage insinuation, as if that was all I was qualified to do. Unfortunately, that was all I had really done...that I could talk about anyway.

Both cops glared at me, then the Lieutenant smiled at me. It was not a pretty sight, he looked big, mean and menacing. "O.K. smart guy, what did you find in Felix's garbage?"

"First of all, I wasn't sure if it was Felix's, but a flyer for 'The Green Frog' was under his window, and I made a few calls, and discovered that Felix was the man who picked up the flyers from the printers. As you undoubtedly know who the printer was, I figure you already know all of this."

They didn't, and it was obvious, but now they were going to have to find out this information for themselves, if they wished to save face. I felt a moment of superiority, even though I knew I was outclassed.

"O.K., third question, what are you going to do about the case?"

"The last thing I was going to do was go by 'The Green Frog' tonight and ask around. I have a date!" I announced proudly.

"I guess that's all right," the Lieutenant allowed. "But that's all you should be doing. Leave the rest of this up to us. Stay out of trouble, and if something turns up, call us first...got it?"

"Loud and clear," I lied.

We were back at the rooming house, and apparently they thought that this was the time to leave, which they did, without another word. I let it pass, dealing with stiffs all day probably meant never having to say 'Good-bye'.

Now, that that was behind me, I had two important items on my agenda. Make sure I was on time for Mother's supper, and then to try and figure out what would go well with my polka dot tie.

I went upstairs, still no sign of Soot. Now I really was worried, what if he had found a place to die, what if that place was in my room, and what if I would be blamed for it? I could lose my room here, and the meals, and ....well, that was all, but that was enough. I went to Paul's room and knocked on the door. He muttered something that I took to be 'Come in,' so I did.

"Paul," I asked, "have you seen Soot lately?"

"No, I didn't even know we had a fireplace here. Help me find my glasses, I have misplaced them."

I decided to let the fireplace thing slide by, Paul probably didn't even know we had a roof on the building. We searched the room for a bit, to no avail. While we were looking, I tried another tack. "Have you seen the old black cat that lives here?"

"Not since last night, when I wondered into your room by mistake, he was on your dresser."

"He was? And he didn't trash anything?" I was shocked. Had a truce been declared?

"Not that I could see, but then I couldn't see too much having removed my glasses."

I did a quick detective job, right on the spot. "Paul, if you had removed your glasses, after wandering into my room, perhaps that is where we'll find them."

Paul positively glowed. "You really are a great detective! Let's go see."

"Ummm, Paul, a Detective is a policeman, I am a Private Investigator."

"Oh yeah, well, whatever."

We got into my room, and looked around. I finally found Paul's glasses on the floor, under my dresser, along with my scrap of paper from Felix's apartment, and two of my socks that had been missing for some time. What had that cat been up to?

"Here they are, Paul," I said, handing him his glasses, relieved that they were found, and also strangely relieved that Soot was still among the living, though wary as to his most recent motives.

"Cracked that case yet? Did my information help?"

"Still working on the case, but your information has led to a meeting tonight that might help."

He seemed gratified. "Mother said the cops were here today."

"Better get used to it, I will be dealing with them from time to time."

"They looked around in your room for a bit, but then I wandered in, looking for you, and they left."

"What?" They didn't have a warrant, and they hadn't mentioned anything about that! I guess I owed Soot, as they obviously hadn't seen my note on the floor amongst the socks. That might have been hard to explain.

"They seemed like nice guys, but they sure left in a hurry."

"I'll bet they did, and I'll bet they looked in my garbage too." I couldn't help sneering.

We went down to supper. It was great; meat loaf, mashed potatoes and gravy, fresh green beans, some sort of wiggly Jell-O dish with fruit cocktail, and lots of tea and coffee. I was satisfied that I was fortified enough for whatever tonight might bring.

Back in my room, I went through my sad assortment of clothes. What would go with my polka dot tie? Nothing actually. I had picked the tie because it was distinctive, but it really matched nothing in my repertoire.

The tie was yellow with blue dots, of various sizes, kind of unusual anyway. I had never seen anyone else wear one like it. I had no blue shirts, nor yellow shirts, and figuring that yellow and blue make green, I settled on a green short sleeved shirt with most of its buttons remaining. The top button was gone, but I thought that the knot in the tie would hide it, and if anyone noticed, I was sure that it would just be assumed that I was looking cool, with the top button undone. That settled, I chose some gray and red checked slacks, mainly because they were the only clean and pressed pair I had left, and I wanted to look my best. My slightly scuffed loafers would have to do, and I still had some clean, dark socks, so I was ready to go.

I showered and shaved, applied a liberal amount of after shave, dressed and decided to case the joint early, it being about 9:00 in the evening. I also thought that I could ask around, maybe find out who Harold Gibbons was, and if Felix had more than a passing association with the ownership of 'The Green Frog'.

I found the place without problem, one can walk nearly anywhere in Hustle without spending an undo amount of time in arriving, so I was still fresh when I walked into the new nightclub. I have no idea what nightclubs are supposed to look like. I guess I'd seen too many old black and white movies, but I sort of imagined a smoky room, with a bar, semi-clad women hovering over small, round tables.

'The Green Frog' was bright, airy, well lit, with a loud, rock rhythm blasting out of a jukebox. I assumed that Bill Kirby and His Sound Makers weren't making sounds till later in the night, if they were indeed the band de jour.

I had sixty dollars in my pocket as I entered the anteroom where coats and hats were checked, but the bouncer informed me that I had to part with ten of them on weekend nights to pay for the talent. I asked if Bill Kirby was still playing, and he assured me that they would begin at 11:00. I paid him, entered and took in the clientele. It was early for a nightclub, and there were maybe twenty people there, including the help. The place was large enough to hold ten times that many, so I hoped for more people as the night went on, to help me with my anonymity. I walked to the bar, sat on a stool and asked the barkeep for a scotch and soda. I hadn't had a drink in ages, but it was a Saturday, I was dressed up, and by gosh, it was the last thing I was going to do on this case. I was determined to do it in style. The bartender raised his eyebrows at my tie and remarked, "We don't get many like that in here."

"You mean there is someone else with this type of tie?"

"You're right," he admitted, "we don't get any like that in here."

He seemed willing to talk, so I asked a few opening questions about him, how long the club had been open, and if more people would show later.

"Oh yes, the place will be hopping by midnight, people are still eating supper, going to the movies, that sort of thing. Most won't start to show till 10 or later."

"I see, I am new in town, just been here a few weeks, and saw the flyer. Finally got around to getting down here."

"Glad you could make it," he grunted, and went off to serve another customer.

I looked around. The early evening crowd was mostly singles; the waitresses were not on full point yet, so I assumed that most of the customers must be regulars. The pace was languid at best, so I was gratified when my new friend returned. I took the opportunity to observe him as he worked. I thought it a good idea to observe, quantify and store information on people whenever possible. I had convinced myself that it keep my mind honed to a razor sharp edge. He was quite tall, thin, but not reedy. He had a face full of character. He had a high forehead, dark eyes, and a nose that went in more directions than Harrison Ford's or mine. He had acne scars, but somehow these made him look more manly. He was well dressed and was one heck of a good barkeep.

"Name's After," I volunteered, offering to shake his hand. He took it and smiled.

"Had a friend named 'Squint' once….had one eye. My name is Joe."

Of course it was. I asked 'Joe' for another drink, gave him a five-dollar tip, and now had his attention. "Know anyone by the name of Harold Gibbons?"

"Sure, he owns the place, ought to be in later."

"Will you point him out to me when he shows?"

He laughed, "You can't miss him, but yeah, I'll make sure you meet him."

I smiled my thanks and went back to looking the place over. Various tunes played on the jukebox, several more customers filed in, some in pairs now. A few couples began to show, but mostly there were groups of unaccompanied guys and gals looking for an acceptable partner for the evening. I wondered if my girl was going to show.

As 10:00 o'clock was approaching, I did notice that the place was filling quickly. I ordered one more drink, and decided to find a table with a view of the band's stage as well as the front door. Finding an acceptable perch, I alighted, and was immediately accosted by a red head with too much cleavage to be natural, too much make-up to be pretty, and too much hair to be comfortable. "Hi there honey," she purred, "I'll be waiting on you tonight, I am Pearl." She winked, nearly losing a false eyelash, and I nodded, now determined to begin nursing my drinks. If she began to look good, it would be my warning signal that I had had too much to drink.

The hours went by, I had another scotch and soda, before switching to soda pop. I had just begun to know every face in the room, when at midnight sharp, a man in a full white tuxedo waltzed into the room, flanked by two guys that were obviously his bodyguards and at least half a dozen cheerleader/bimbo types. I don't mean to infer that cheerleaders are bimbos, they aren't. However, these girls had probably never been cheerleaders, they were professionals all the way, but trying to act like cheerleaders. They fooled no one. I glanced at Joe, and he nodded. I waited until my quarry had a seat, looked fairly relaxed and had had a few drinks, then I slowly made my way over there, trying not to look too threatening. I didn't want to have to hurt a bodyguard if I could help it. It wasn't a problem, the two goons barely even looked at my imposing 5' 9", 160 pound body as I approached the man himself. I waited while he flirted with one of the bimbo/cheerleaders, then when he actually looked at me, I managed to clear my throat and approach a bit.

"Hello, Mr. Gibbons?" I managed to put a question mark in my voice.

"Yes, what can I do for you?" he asked. He was a big man, red, husky face, beady blue eyes, with nice caps on his teeth. Big and tubby looking, but still just enough muscle left that you wouldn't want to fight him, even without the bodyguards. He looked like a pro wrestler gone to seed. He was at least 6' 4" and totally commanded the space he was in.

"First of all, I'd like to compliment you on the nice place you have here," I said, meaning it.

"Thanks," he mumbled, looking bored and about to lose interest.

"Second, I was looking for a friend of a friend, and thought you might know something about him."

"Sure, I know lotsa people."

"This guy may not ring a bell, but he's been missing a while and his mother has been looking for him."

"Poor little boy got lost from mommy?" he said, not unkindly, but still not too interested.

"He may have worked for you, or at least for someone with the nightclub, his name is Felix Jeffries."

That got quick results, his eyes narrowed, the bodyguards instantly noted my existence and the room temperature went down 30 degrees immediately. Even so, my body decided to break out in a sweat, without my permission.

"Maybe you should leave now," he said.

The two goons came forward and stood on each side of me, beginning to squeeze. I didn't know quite what to do, but I knew I didn't want to leave just yet.

"Maybe you don't know him," I gulped, "I'll just tell his mom he's probably run off with some girl, or maybe a guy. Heck, I don't know, maybe a girl and a guy, maybe two guys." To me it sounded like I was rambling. It probably did to him to, as he got a glazed look on his eyes and waived to his goons, who withdrew to his side.

"Have a good time here tonight, since you're here, you may as well stay for the show, but this is the last time you come here, got it?"

I nodded, grateful for the reprieve, as I still hadn't met my phone buddy, and that was the reason for coming anyway.

"I'll just go back to my seat and sit down, watch the show, maybe have a drink," I murmured as I backed off.

He nodded in dismissal, then called after me, "Order the Chivas."

I sighed, sat down and Red came over for my order. I asked if she had heard the boss, and she nodded, "Chivas double coming up!"

I was in now, so I nodded, and awaited my fate.

I saw the opening set from Bill Kirby's group, and it wasn't half-bad. I was beginning to get semi-sloshed and Red was even beginning to look sort of halfway not too bad, when I noticed someone looking at me oddly.

There was a young woman, brown hair, large brown eyes, somewhat stringy hair and the most awful polka dot dress on I had ever seen. She was just staring at me. I grinned up at her lopsidedly and asked if she would care to sit down. She looked around, as if maybe embarrassed to be seen with me, then decided to go ahead. I placed her about 25 years old, maybe 5' 5", 100 pounds. Her dress was knee length, showing thin legs with pretty good muscle tone. The legs of a dancer, I thought.

Red came by, and didn't seem disappointed at all that I had a companion. Red asked her what she wanted. She ordered a double Chivas as well, so I pulled out my last twenty, and hoped it would hold out for the night.

The girl peered at me, I could see that she was slightly cross-eyed, so I couldn't really tell whether she was actually looking at me or not. I tried to focus on her eyes, found this to be difficult, so I looked at her thin, straight nose instead. She placed her hands together under her chin, and gave me a most careful going over. I felt dissected. She said, "Your left ear is higher than your right ear."

I laughed, and barely slurring my words commented that people generally thought that my right ear was lower than the left. She took this in carefully, continued to look, then said, "No, your left ear is definitely higher than the right ear."

Well, if it was definite, then that was that. Case closed, discussion over.

"Listen," I began, trying to get out of this gracefully, "I am expecting someone tonight, so I won't be able to finish this delightful little chat we're having."

She looked confused, then hurt. "I thought you were expecting me!" she cried. "You said Green Frog, polka dot tie, 1:30, I know I'm a bit early, but…" and she got up to leave.

Ooops! This was my date, I had forgotten about her, totally forgotten. How was I to get out of this?

"Sorry, I am so sorry," I said, rising out of my chair. "I was expecting a man."

"Oh? I didn't take you for that type."

This wasn't going well, and now she was leaving, dabbing at her eyes with a handkerchief that had mysteriously appeared. I stumbled after her, losing ground. My feet seemed to be tangling up in other people's legs, while she stepped lightly over all obstacles.

"STOP!" I shouted, hoping to get her attention. I did better than that, the entire room went quiet, the band stopped playing. Mr. Gibbons sent a knife sharp glance my way, the goons awakening from their stupor, the scent of fresh meat in their noses.

She stopped. I looked at her and implored, "I don't like guys, I like girls." This brought snickers from all those around me, Bill Kirby started the band up again, and the goons sat down. I wasn't worth their trouble.

The girl stopped, and allowed me to catch her. "Are you sure?" she asked.

"I'm sure," I said forcibly, "I have never dated a guy."

She smiled. "No, are you sure you want to meet me?"

"Oh yes," I exclaimed, not sure if it was the booze talking, or just me. "I just lost track of the time, I wasn't expecting you yet!"

This seemed to satisfy her. She thought about it for a moment and asked, "Care to dance?"

"I can't dance," I admitted.

"Neither can I." She laughed.

"Someone could get hurt," I admonished.

"I know some first aid."

We did pretty well; people took notice of us, and stayed away. We basically clung to each other, and swayed back and forth. It felt different to be holding a girl, and it felt good too. From the way she was holding me, it had been awhile since she had experienced something similar. We made it through several dances in this way, when

I remembered that she wasn't the one I was going to meet. I glanced at my watch, and saw that it was 1:45, past the time I had said to meet my mysterious man on the phone.

"We need to sit down a bit," I said.

She smiled and said that she needed to use the lady's room. I wandered back to our table, only to see two men there. One was a monument to steroids, he had muscles to move his muscles, and both sets were big. The guy with him looked like the Fonz with bad teeth, acne and a hygiene problem. The slicked back hair couldn't have been greasier. I took a look at the table, I couldn't remember if my date had had a purse or not.

"Whatcha looking at creep?" Steroids asked.

"My date and I were sitting here, I thought she might have left her purse."

"No purse here."

I looked anyway, and Steroids was getting steamed. "Get lost, punk," he growled.

I thought about getting lost, then in what sounded like someone else's voice, said, "No sir, I think that YOU should get lost, this is my table."

He looked shocked, then looked at Greaseball, then back at me, and then he unexpectedly laughed. He laughed hard and long, then, wiping the tears from his eyes, said, "You can't be serious."

I looked back at him and admitted, "I guess I wasn't."

"Look," he said, "we were here looking for you anyway. You're the guy in the polka dot tie that told me to meet you here tonight, right?"

"Oh, yeah, I mean, I guess so. I didn't really know who I was speaking to."

Steroids and Greaseball got up, and Steroids said, "Let's take this outside. He had me by the arm, and could have taken me down right then, and no one would have cared, I knew I had no fans in the room.

I went peacefully, and as we neared the door, remembered the girl. "Maybe I should leave a note for my date."

Steroids just shook his head no, and escorted me out the door. The night was fresh and clear. Steroids looked at me strangely, then without warning slammed me hard in the stomach with a massive fist. I doubled over and fell to the ground, wondering where all the oxygen on the planet had disappeared to. He picked me up, pulled me to his face and said, "One warning only, mind your own business." He dropped me.

Rolling around on the gravel parking lot, I managed to get a breath of air in, then another, and finally, got enough in to be able to speak. "Now that you have my interest," I gasped, "It's not likely that I'll be able to do that."

Big mistake; Greaseball came up to me and kicked me in the head, I started blacking out, then saw the foot coming back at me again. That did it, I blacked out.

I woke some time later, lying on the parking lot, several people looking on, but only one face that I recognized. Jocko.

"Do you want a ride home, After?" he asked.

I spat out some blood, and said, "Yes, that would be a good idea."

He helped me to the car, opened the door, got me in somehow, and strapped the seat belt on me. Boy Scout!

We drove away. He said, "It's a good thing you left a message for me, or you may not have survived that. I thought you might need some help tonight."

"Thanks," I muttered.

"No problem, but I'll want a report tomorrow."

I nodded, fell asleep, and vaguely remembered being led up the stairs, Jocko and Mother undressing me and putting me to bed. The last thing I saw before I fell asleep were two large green eyes staring unblinkingly into my own.

four

*T*hinking back on that night, I assume I got to bed somewhere near 3:00 A. M. I am sure it took a little bit for the house to settle down, for Jocko to go home and for Mother to get back to bed. I wouldn't know, as I was fast asleep. I do remember being in a half awake state at times as my body was aching from the beating I had incurred. It was later in the night, probably just before morning's first light when I finally decided to work my way to the bathroom to get some aspirin for my headache. It was probably a slight concussion, but I was going to have to treat it with something if I was going to get any rest. I had every intention of forgetting everything about the case, and planned on telling Jocko about how I got the scrap of paper, and how it had caused the most recent troubles. I felt that I had done my hundred dollar's worth of work for Felicia.

Anyway, I rolled over slowly, got my knees on the floor by the bed, and groaning with every move, I managed to get myself to a standing position. My head was throbbing, but I wasn't dizzy, just unbelievably sore and creaky feeling. I walked slowly to the door, which was slightly ajar, and walked slowly and quietly to the bathroom. Leaving the light off, I poured my water, and took two aspirin and then I noticed a shadow slip by the bathroom door sliding along towards my bedroom door.

I crept out of the bathroom, thinking Paul must have worked

late and wandered to my room again, and I did not want to startle him. I walked carefully to my room, but just as I got there, I heard spitting sounds. I had shot enough guns when I was trying for the Police Academy to recognize the smell of cordite, and I had heard a muffled gun shoot before. It took a second or two to sink in, but someone was shooting up my room. I turned to go back down the hallway, but it was too late. The shadow came to the door, and it was the Greaseball from the nightclub, gun still in hand. He looked momentarily startled, but then a wicked smile came over those acne-ridden features. Using his gun as a baton, he pointed me to the head of the stairs. I went, trying to figure how I was going to get out of this. He began to give me a push, when somewhere from the blackness, a silent dark missile hurled through the air, attaching itself to the Greaseball's face and began raking away at it. With a bellow of pain, the Greaseball tried to unleash his assailant, but Soot had found a new mark and was clawing him up for all he was worth. Greaseball and Soot fell down the stairs together, rolling, cussing and clawing at each other. They didn't stop at the second floor either; they flew down the next flight and ended up on the landing where Mother Teresa magically appeared with a broom. Out the door they all went, the Greaseball with Soot on his head, and Mother Teresa beating the Greaseball liberally with the broom. They disappeared into the night, Soot snarling and the Greaseball screaming, the steady thwack, thwack of Mother's broom on his backside.

I went to the phone and amazingly dialed Jocko's number from memory. A sleepy Jocko answered the phone. "Yeath?"

"Jocko, this is After, there's been a break-in at Mother's, some shots were fired, but they hit no one, and Soot and Mother are chasing the assailant down the street!"

"I'll be right there." It always amazed me how fast cops could wake up. I was pretty sure he already had his pants on, and that his shirt would be going on as he went out the door.

I limped down the stairs; by now the other four roomers were awake and congregating near the foyer. Paul was wondering around with Hal. The fossil was on the first floor, with her robe and slippers on, and the final roomer, James, who was on the second floor, was on his way down the final flight of stairs as well. I was surprised to see that he was not at his girlfriend's house, as we rarely saw him at Mother's.

"What's going on?" Hal demanded.

"Someone broke in and tried to shoot me," I replied, the implications of that just sinking in.

"You look terrible," Hal said, "are you sure he didn't shoot you?"

"He did hit me, earlier in the evening, along with a friend of his, but not with a bullet."

"Well, it's almost morning, might as well see if we can rustle up some grub." Hal took off for the kitchen, followed by the college kid and the fossil.

"I'm going to look for Mother," I told Paul. "Wait here for Jocko, and tell him what happened."

"O.K."

I grabbed my raincoat, and stumbled out into the street barefoot and began to walk in the direction that I had last seen them go. I was rewarded with the sight of Mother stalking down the sidewalk in my direction. I neared her, and cried, "Are you alright?"

She nodded, and continued on past me, back to the house. I turned to follow her, and we entered the foyer just as Jocko pulled up in his car. He hit the ground running and got to Mother as fast as he could.

"What's going on?" he asked me, as he hugged Mother.

"Come on in." I sighed. "I think the excitement's over for the time being."

The fossil and Hal were making coffee and toast. James, the college kid, was setting the table and Mother went to the kitchen, still having not said a word. Jocko waved at me to sit down, so I joined him at the table.

"O.K., what happened?"

I told him about waking up; the shadows in the hall, Soot to the rescue and the parade out the front door.

"Looks like you didn't make any friends at 'The Green Frog' last night."

"No, I didn't, but I don't think these guys are involved with Harold Gibbons, at least not where I am concerned. Those two bodyguards of Mr. Gibbons could have escorted me out of there any time they chose to."

"That's true," he agreed, "they aren't shy about kicking people out. Tell me about last night."

I told him about talking with Joe, about the quick meeting with Harold Gibbons, and how he reacted to Felix's name. I had to backtrack to tell Jocko about Felix having signed for the flyers. I then told him how I met the girl, and how the two creeps were waiting for me at the table when we returned from dancing.

"Why did they pick on you, and who turned them onto you?"

I admitted that I had put the word out that I would be there that night looking for clues as to Felix Jeffries' whereabouts, but I told him that I wasn't sure if Joe, Gibbons, or someone else had pointed me out. I don't know why I didn't tell him about the phone number on the scrap of paper. I had been planning to, but something just kept holding me back.

"Mind if I take a quick look upstairs?"

"Be my guest, I don't feel like accompanying you just yet."

"I'll be right back."

He left, but the others came in, and amazingly, the table started to fill with food. Toast, juice, scrambled eggs, jellies, coffee, and breakfast rolls were everywhere. Mother entered, surveyed the scene and asked, "Where's Jocko?"

"He's looking my room over, searching for clues."

Jocko bounced in about then, holding a plastic baggy with two bullets in it. "I'll have these analyzed, see if we can come up with something. This is turning out to be a bit more complicated than I thought. Kind of makes me think Felicia was helped in front of that bus."

I nodded, "Me too, and I don't have high hopes for ever meeting Felix either."

The rest of the roomers were following this discussion open mouthed.

Mother looked at all of us, then issued orders. "Everyone eat up, then Hal and James clean up, while After and I go looking for Soot."

I forgot, Soot was last seen masquerading as the Greaseball's hat as he fled down the street. I felt responsible for that and gobbled my food down as fast as possible. Excusing myself, I limped back up the stairs, but all in all, I was feeling better. The aspirin must be working, and that, along with the food and the excitement had me ready to go, maybe at half speed, but forward nonetheless.

I got into some shorts, a tee shirt, some sneakers, and went back downstairs. I grabbed my coat. Mother was waiting at the door. "Let's go," she said grimly.

We went up the street for a bit. There was quite a bit of blood to follow, I could only hope it wasn't Soot's. About one block away, I saw the gun. The sun had peeked above the horizon, and it was easy to see. I grabbed a twig lying nearby and used it to pick the gun up, placing it in my coat's pocket. The silencer was still attached. We followed the blood trail to a corner, where it abruptly disappeared. I was worried, as I did not know the difference between people blood and cat blood. Jocko drove by at that moment, and got out of his car. I gave him the gun.

"This looks like the end of the trail," he said with a worried look, "Someone picked him up in a car, I'd wager. Can I give you two a lift home?"

"You two go, I'll keep looking for Soot."

Mother actually smiled at me then, and got into the car with Jocko.

I knew the neighborhood fairly well, and I went up and down all the streets in the area, as well as alleys. I called his name softly, knowing that he wouldn't come running, but figuring I might at least get a growl. There was absolutely no response. I saw several cats, lots of dogs, and a sleepy raccoon, but no Soot.

I looked hard for two hours, then decided I should check back in. I trudged up the stairs to the house, and taking my overcoat off, went in to tell Mother the bad news.

She was in the kitchen, cooking up something that smelled delicious. I told her about my journey and she took it pretty good.

She said, "He's a smart cat, but has never been an outdoor cat, we'll just keep looking and hope for the best. He's so old though." A tear came to her eye, and she turned away.

"I am going to try and clean up, even the dogs are afraid of the way I look right now." Tiredness had finally caught up with me, and I needed a long, hot shower, and clean clothes.

Jocko said he'd be back later, along with a fingerprint and blood lab crew. He asked me to keep from touching surfaces in my room. I told him that the shooter never got in, that he had just stood by the door. We both agreed that the crime scene was fairly hopeless by now. I changed the bedclothes anyway, noting the two holes near my pillow.

The shower was great; I just put boxers on and went back to my room. I would shave and finish making myself presentable after my nap. It was only 8:30 A.M., and so I set my alarm for 10:00, fell into bed and lost contact with the world.

The rest of the morning went without incident. I got up, feeling just about as creaky as I had earlier. I shaved, forcing myself to work on the tender areas as well. I had a black right eye, and it looked to be a whopper. Otherwise, just a few more cuts and scrapes to go along with the ones Soot had previously given me. I went downstairs, where all the usual suspects were loitering. The only one to go to church today was the fossil, so she was gone, but Mother, Hal, Paul and James were taking it easy in the living room.

"Thanks for the early breakfast, Mother," I said.

"That was no problem, After," she replied. "I need to ask you something."

"Yes?"

"I am used to things happening in my house, as I have been boarding people for a long time, in fact, your friend Roy Mack was one of my first. However, I have never had a gun fired in my house, and never been involved with murder cases. Is this likely to continue?"

"Probably," I admitted. "It goes with my line of work." I sighed, "I'll start looking for a new place tomorrow."

"Oh no!" she cried, "I haven't had this much fun in years, but I think we need better locks."

I was amazed.

Paul was grinning, "I have been helping After too," he offered to anyone willing to listen.

Hal said, "If there's anything I can do, let me know."

James grinned at us, "I have some friends that play football, if you need some muscle."

I was touched. "Mother, I'll go by the hardware store tomorrow morning, and get some better dead bolts."

"That will be just fine...after you take another walk around the neighborhood for Soot."

"Of course," I assured her.

There was a knock on the door; it was Jocko, with two other gentlemen.

"Hi all," he greeted us as he entered on his own. Looking at me, "You certainly look better."

"I feel a bit better," I allowed, "but now I am confused. I was going to let this case slide away, but it seems that it is now looking for me."

Jocko nodded his head in agreement. "You'd best be careful, you're in it up to your neck now, for whatever reason." He nodded to the two men, who went around looking for blood samples, and whatever else they could find. They were there for about five minutes, then left quietly, with a nod to Jocko.

During a lull in the conversation, I asked, "Does anyone have any idea where I can buy some flowers on a Sunday? I promised Pastor James that I'd bring some down to the church in memory of Felicia."

"Yes," Jocko offered, " I work at the local supermarket on weekends, and am actually on my way there now. Want me to take you there?"

"Thanks." I walked out to the now familiar car, and got in. "I hope I didn't get any blood on your seat last night."

"Not that you'd notice." Jocko grinned. The car was immaculate; I had the feeling that he had had to clean it up after last night. "Put on your seat belt." I did as I was ordered.

"Listen," he began, "I don't know everything that is going on, but is there something that I should know?"

"I think I've told you everything pertinent, but there may be a small detail I have missed." That was mostly the truth.

"Sometimes, it's the small details that do you in."

"I know that, and I am trying to figure out how that guy even found out where I live."

"Probably followed us home last night. May have wanted to know how the law got to you so fast."

"That must be it," I mused, "but why those two, and what do they have to do with 'The Green Frog', and Felix Jeffries?"

"Those are the questions, all right." We arrived at the supermarket, and alighted.

"Just go back beyond dairy, they have cut flowers there, you ought to be able to find something."

"Thanks, Jocko, I appreciate everything."

"No problem, glad you called me last night."

"Me too."

I followed his directions, there were no lilies. I found a nice bunch of mixed flowers, no petunias, for about five dollars and I bought them. I had enough money left for a soda pop, so I bought one for the road. I looked around for Jocko, but didn't see him, so I headed out for the 'Our Holy Mother of the True Rock' church, which was within short walking distance.

Services were over by the time I got there, but the main door was still open, and Pastor James was just inside. I apologized for not having the flowers there in time for services, and he laughed. "That was just the morning service, they'll all be back for afternoon Sunday School, and then services tonight. The flowers ought to last through Wednesday night service as well."

That was some committed congregation. I asked, "Was Felicia a steady churchgoer?"

"No, she would show once or twice a month, and leave quietly. She just started coming to Seniors a few weeks ago."

"Thanks Pastor."

"Have a good day After."

I walked back home, wondering what was going to happen next. The house appeared normal, and quiet, and I sat in my favorite chair, preparing to relax, and maybe clear my brain out a bit. Priscilla came by and offered me a glass of ice cold lemonade, which I gratefully accepted. "Thanks, Priscilla," I said, meaning it. She looked at me and grinned, no dentures in, and walked away.

Things were finally calming down. I finished the drink, and thought about going out to look for Soot again, when the phone rang. I heard Mother answer it, then she came into the room, with eyes sparkling, and said that I had a lady calling me.

"Girl friend? Or a case?" she asked.

"Given those two options, it has to be a case, but more than likely, I owe someone money."

I rose, I had gotten too relaxed and the body was stiff again, so I took my time getting to the phone. "Hello."

"Hi there!" a cheery voice chirped on the other end. "I missed you when I got out of the lady's room last night, then I heard that you had to be driven home after a fight. How exciting!"

My date, of course, I had forgotten her again. "Yup, just another day in the life of After Coffman."

"Is that your name? That's a really nifty name."

Nifty? "Oh, ummm, thanks, I blame my mother for it."

"Oh, I like it, so what happened?"

"I tried to reclaim our table last night, but two goons had other ideas, and escorted me out. Did you have a purse?"

"Yes, I kept it with me all evening, I had it while we were dancing, didn't you feel it?"

"No, I was concentrating on not killing both of us."

She laughed, again somewhat chirpily. "Are you O.K.? I mean, did you get hurt?"

"Not that you'd notice," I replied, "just got kicked in the head a few times."

"Poor baby, I'll be right over." She hung up.

I found Mother. "I guess I'll be having some company for awhile, and apparently it isn't a new case."

"Good, I'll bake some cookies, and we still have some ice cream."

So that was Jocko's secret, he probably didn't get the ice cream treatment until Bitsy came along. Ahh, Mother the matchmaker.

I went upstairs to insure that I looked presentable. I didn't, but it was the best I could do on short notice, and there was no hope for my nose and ears anyway. Anyway, my mystery woman had already seen them. I figured that it was time to find out her name.

I got all of my dirty clothes; meaning all of my clothes, into a pile and then tossed them into plastic bags, ready for a trip to the Laundromat. As soon as mystery girl was gone, I had some cleaning to do. I went back downstairs to wait, then decided that I could wait out on the porch just as easily. Maybe keep an eye out for Soot.

As I walked out the door, I caught a glimpse of a silver Volkswagen just turning the corner. Coincidence? I thought not. I walked as fast as I could around the side of the house, through the back yard and cut through the alley. There was nothing terminally wrong with my legs, and the kick to my stomach didn't hurt my breathing, so I was able to make pretty good time, but I never did see the Volkswagen again. It did serve as a reminder to keep an alert eye peeled for anything, anybody, anytime.

I went back into the house, my appetite for fresh air momentarily vanquished. I wandered into the dining room and slumped into a chair. I was wishing it were Monday, so that I could look forward to working at Roy's. Here I was, working a case, or being worked by a case, with no future, no money, and the possibility of pain around every corner. Hercule Poirot would've solved this one by now, and may not have even left his room. Of course, Hercule didn't have Soot, Paul and Mr. Steroids to deal with.

A few more minutes went by while I felt sorry for myself. The phone rang, and it was for me again. I went to it, expecting my date to announce that she had better things to do, but it was Lieutenant Howard instead.

"Mr. Coffman," he began, "we would like to see you down at the station tomorrow morning. We seem to have found a body connected with your case."

Shocked, I asked, "Mr. Jeffries? Felix Jeffries?"

"No such luck, I'm afraid, this is a totally new character to me, but I believe you may know him as Charlie Underhill."

"I've never heard of him, Lieutenant."

"From the description Jocko gave us, he was last seen leaving your house around 5:30 this morning or so, with a cat on his head, and Mother beating the tar out of him."

The Greaseball was dead? "Oh my gosh, I didn't think he was beat up that badly, Mother was hitting him with a broom, and Soot isn't strong enough to do much more than scratch him badly."

"It wasn't the cat, unless he put two bullets into Underhill's head."

"Wow," I managed to say, "this case is weirder than ever."

"Be here tomorrow, try to make it by 11:00, and don't leave town."

I was a suspect, I could tell. They never tell you not to leave town unless you're a suspect. What was I going to do, get a bus with the $3.25 I had left? Was I going to walk out of town? I guess that's why they didn't come pick me up on the spot. Suddenly, I was depressed.

A small, green sedan, with peeling paint and missing a front fender pulled up in front of the house. I went out on the porch to meet my friend. Yes, that was she, wearing a more sensible pink dress and nice shoes for this visit. I walked down to greet her.

"Do you know, I haven't even gotten your name," I greeted her.

"That's right," she giggled, "it's Felicity."

"Felicity," I repeated, "kind of an old fashioned name, isn't it?"

"Yes, but maybe I am too."

"Maybe." She sure couldn't dance any better than I could, so maybe she was kind of backward. She looked pretty good this morning. Her crossed eyes were large and pretty, her face was free of makeup, but had a healthy glow, and there was an athleticism about her that spoke of long walks and exercise.

"My landlord made us fresh cookies, and ice cream," I stated.

"That sounds wonderful," she said, as she reached up to lightly touch my eye. "I guess that's from last night, looks like it hurts terribly."

Her hand was cool and didn't hurt the eye at all. "Right now, it feels wonderful." I grinned.

She grinned back, then ran toward the door, beating me there and opened it, then walked in like she owned the place. Mother was beaming when I entered, and said, "She looks like a nice girl."

I grinned back, "Yes, I think so too."

Felicity had entered the dining room, taking in the wallpaper, lights and candles; all of the things that I paid no attention to. She remarked on how lovely everything was. Mother beamed again, and told her to sit down for a treat.

"No, I want to see the kitchen," Felicity said, and waltzed right in ahead of the widely smiling Mother Teresa.

"I'll be eating cake and ice cream for weeks." I thought cheerily, as I expected the Jocko treatment to follow in toto.

Mother and Felicity returned in a few minutes with the cookies, ice cream and a pitcher of milk.

"After, would you see if anyone else wants a snack?" Mother asked.

Who was I to deny her anything? I looked in the living room. No one was present. I went to the fossil's door and knocked. No response. I went upstairs, James' door was open, the room was a shambles, and he was not there. I knocked on Hal's door. "Who is it?" he called.

"Cookies, ice cream and milk downstairs."

"I'll be right down!"

I went up to my floor, and knocked on Paul's door. "Cookies and ice cream in the dining room!"

Paul appeared at the door in record time. "That sounds great! Let's go." He actually went down the stairs without running into anything at all.

All was fine for our repast. Mother enjoyed having a young lady there, Paul cleaned his glasses to have a better look, then grinned stupidly every time Felicity opened her mouth. Hal was on his best behavior, but I noticed that he managed to sit the closest to her. I didn't mind as I sat across from her and studied her closely. Yes, her healthy looks were beginning to appeal to me, I felt myself being reeled in. As for her, all of her conversation was a little on the ditsy side, but delightful. She charmed everyone in the house.

Mother was cleaning up after us, and said to me, "If you want to spend some time with her, I'll take the clothes to the Laundromat."

Felicity jumped right on this. "Oh no you won't. I have my car here, we'll just go together."

Hal said, "I have some dirty clothes, I'll just come along."

I must have finally made a face, for Felicity looked at me, then smiled at Hal. "I think we can handle it ourselves, Hal. Why don't you just bring your clothes here, and we'll do them for you."

Hal looked at me, decided against it, and said, "No, that's alright, I'll get caught up later."

I grinned, ran up to my room, amazed at how good I was feeling, got the two bags of laundry, and flew back downstairs. Felicity opened the door for us, and Hal mouthed the words "Lucky guy," to me. I was feeling much younger and very much healthier right at that moment.

Felicity got us to the Laundromat, and in no time, we were sorting darks from whites and making sense out of my wardrobe.

"You need some new clothes, After," she remarked.

"I know that, and I'll work on it. Listen Felicity, I am just now starting to work, I can't afford things like movies and dinner out, and all of that."

"I gathered that, so I guess we'll watch a lot of TV, and Mother already invited me over for supper tomorrow night, while you were up getting your clothes."

That was great! Mother, what a woman she was!

We had four loads going, and Felicity sat in a chair to wait with me. I sat next to her, and sort of leaned back into the seat.

"What do you do, After?" she asked, placing a tiny hand in mine.

" I am a Private Investigator," I replied, "I work out of Roy Mack's 2nd hand store right now."

"Do you have a case?"

"Right now, I think a case has me."

"Tell me about it," she whispered.

I started to give her the bare details, but about two minutes into my recitation, I found myself telling her everything, even about the scrap of paper that I had withheld from everybody else. Anything to keep her hand in mine. When I was done, she kept her hand right there, and was quiet for a moment or two.

She turned to look at me. "Sounds like you might need some help."

I startled. "I might need help, but I don't want you involved."

"Well, maybe you could just discuss the case with me each evening, and I can learn, and you can throw ideas off of me."

"I would like that, very much," I said, looking at her.

The washing machines were finished so I reluctantly gave up her hand, and we went to the dryers, filling two up with the newly fresh smelling items I generally wore. She took a fierce interest in making sure everything was just right. As the clothes came out of the dryers, they were neatly folded, and organized. They had never looked better. I decided then and there to buy a few new clothes each week to try and upgrade a little…beginning with underwear.

We drove home, I was feeling on top of the clouds, and she was chattering happily about how nice the town was, that she had just been here a day or two, and that the phone call from me must have been Providence.

I said nothing, just enjoying the happy sounds, and we got out of the car. She insisted on seeing my room, and I led her up the stairs, worried about the squalor. Mother had gotten there ahead of us, the windows were open, a fresh breeze blew in, the curtains were blowing in the wind, and the bed was made, the dresser dusted. It looked passable after all. She reorganized my dresser, rearranged my closet, and sat down on the bed when we were finished.

"Thanks for calling me, After," she said.

"Thanks for showing up last night," I replied, "and today too."

She kissed me lightly on the cheek, and suddenly embarrassed, took off out the door, racing down the stairs.

I ran to the stairs. "Wait!" I shouted.

She turned, blew me a kiss, and said, "I'll see you tomorrow at supper." Out the front door she went.

I floated for the rest of the evening, and slept like a baby that night.

five

I awoke the next morning, which was a Monday, ready to tackle the world. I jumped up out of bed, only to be reminded of the sorry state of my body, which had grown stiff and sore overnight. No headache, however, so that was a plus. I wandered into the bathroom, spent some time trying to make myself presentable, then ran back to my newly reorganized and clean bedroom, determined to keep it that way. Feeling better the more I moved, I went downstairs for breakfast. It was exceptional; bacon, eggs, oatmeal, several types of juices and pancakes with blueberry syrup. Everyone enjoyed themselves. I thanked Mother and she asked how I felt. I told her I was a bit sore, but in a great mood. She smiled.

I said, "I think I'll take a walk, and see if I can scare up Soot."

"That would be very nice, After."

"I think the old boy can take care of himself, but he may not know that!"

She laughed, and agreed, but still had a worried look on her face. "What shall I make for supper? Does your lady friend have any preferences?"

"I honestly do not know, but I am sure she will be happy with anything you dream up, plus she looks like she hasn't eaten a solid meal in months."

With that, I wandered out the door and began retracing my

path from the previous day. It was nearer mid morning this time, and there were no raccoons and quite a few less dogs and cats as well. There were children out however, and one or two even trusted me enough to talk to me. None seemed to have seen a cat that matched Soot's description. I wandered throughout the neighborhood for an hour, thinking that I ought to do this every morning until the rascal showed up, or was found. It was good exercise and I was able to think a bit as well. I was trying to piece together why I was being singled out for extinction. There were two possibilities; one, that someone thought I had some evidence that might be harmful to them…that could be the person that whacked me in Felix's apartment, two; it could be Steroids and the continuing aftereffects of my anonymous phone call to 'The Green Frog'. Either way, I must be getting someone worried that I might be getting near to figuring out about the disappearance of Felix Jeffries. I was interested in what might have happened to Charlie Underhill, a.k.a. the Greaseball, and was actually looking forward to my visit downtown. Any information gathered might help me with my own case, if it could still be called a case, with no client, a missing person that may have just left on his own, one witness apparently dead, and another that appeared to be a pale version of the Hulk. Like it or not, Steroids was my only lead, and I was going to have to deal with him. At least I knew his phone number.

As I walked, I looked around for Soot. I realized the little twerp liked heights, so I kept an eye on the tops of fences, ledges near windows and low tree limbs. The neighborhood was one of those old time neighborhoods, where there were wide sidewalks, well away from the street, houses neatly kept, also well away from the street. There were verdant lawns where children and their pets and friends played. The old, large front porches had swings that were actually used on summer evenings. Driveways with older cars parked in them, very rarely a garage. It reminded me of a 'Leave It To Beaver' show, and it made me feel safe. It was a far cry from the various neighborhoods of my youth, where one had to dodge bottles thrown by drunks, speeding taxis, or pedestrians made out of steel that could walk right over you. There had been no lawns, just wide areas of concrete bordering rocky, littered patches of dirt. Billboards with women in various stages of undress were everywhere. Delis, bakeries and open trash cans competed for the attention of your nose.

None of the houses I had lived in looked like any of these either. Most that I had been familiar with were second or third story flats with broken front doors, lending them to use by the homeless or other lost souls that inhabited the streets. I got used to dodging the bottles, the drunks and the others, but was never comfortable with them. I was happy with my third floor room at Mother's. It was the way life should have been with my own mother. She never seemed to catch a break. She couldn't hold a job, couldn't keep a man, and never stayed at one place for more than a year, at best. I managed to attend several different schools, sometimes finding myself back at one I had left a few years before. My senior year, I was in two separate schools, probably explaining the lack of a social life, and self esteem.

Anyway, I had been at it for an hour, when I found myself outside the hardware store where I had bought the water gun that I shot Soot with. I went inside and asked the girl at the counter if I could establish a credit line with the store.

"Sure," she smacked, her mouth working furiously at a large wad of gum. "What's your name?"

"After Coffman, I live at Mother Teresa's," I told her.

"K," she said and wrote my name on a piece of paper. "Pay on the first or we charge ya interest."

"Good deal," I exclaimed. Try to get that sort of trust in Brooklyn.

I wandered about a little, until I came to the door area. They had all sorts of doors, and the associated hardware that goes with them. I finally found two dead bolts that I thought would work on Mother's doors, and took them up to the check out girl. "I need to put this purchase on my account," I said.

"What's yer name?" she asked.

"I just got done talking to you, and gave you my name just a few minutes ago," I said, somewhat amused and taken aback at the same time.

"Doesn't mean I remember it."

"After Coffman." I sighed, wondering if she was related to the girl that had answered the phone at the newspaper.

"Don't get many Coffmans in here."

"Do you get many Afters?"

"After what?"

"Never mind. Can I take this now?"

"Just sign here," she said, handing me a receipt.

I gathered up my purchase before she could forget anything else and scurried out of there. I walked home, trying to look for Soot, however realizing that he was probably not to be found in the manner I was searching.

I got home, checked the bolts to see if they would fit the front and rear doors, then went looking for Mother. I found her in the kitchen, cooking, as usual.

"I got new dead bolts for the doors. I was wondering if you have a drill and screwdrivers, that sort of thing?"

"No, but someone generally does, I never seem to have the need for tools. Usually someone living here is handy enough or knows someone with tools."

I figured that Roy Mack would have something I could use, so I said, "I'll try to round something up, and fix them tomorrow."

"That would be wonderful," she said with a smile, "now run along, and leave me to my cooking."

"Yes, ma'am."

I went to my room, determined to find some clothes that would make me look at least somewhat dignified for my visit to the Homicide Department. The problem that I was having was that none of my socks truly matched. I know that I hadn't bought them as mismatched sets, and I usually had the same number come out of the laundry process that went in, so all I could really ascertain was that the dryer gods occasionally asked for a sock sacrifice, and somehow gave back to me other people's socks that didn't make the final godly cut. Anyway, I found two dark socks, one with lines, one with a pattern, but basically the same colors, got my best dress shirt, a pale blue one with good buttons, and managed to locate my best khaki slacks. I had time to add a bit of polish to my loafers, so I felt somewhat ready to meet Lieutenant Howard and Detective Moore.

Tossing off a cheery wave to the fossil as I went out the door, I felt ready to face whatever they had for me. I turned up the street and began my walk to the station. I thought I saw a glint of silver, and thought about the Volkswagen, but never got a real good look as the block had lots of trees and bushes, not to mention kamikaze kids and dogs that one had to dodge constantly. I passed it off as paranoia, and continued my walk. It was going to be a hot day, and I took my time so that I would be as fresh as possible when I got there. Nevertheless, I had a light sheen of sweat on my face, and my shirt was clinging to my back when I entered the air-conditioned Police house.

I went to the front desk, and asked for the Lieutenant. The desk officer told me to have a seat, and did absolutely nothing else. I waited, saw him give two other people the similar treatment, and decided that things must get done somehow, and decided to be patient.

Sure enough, a few minutes later, Lieutenant Howard breezed through the door and motioned me to him with a wave of his hand. I got up and followed. We went through a warren of halls, past cubicles and doors with frosted glass windows lining them, until we reached some stairs. We ascended a floor, and came into a large open room, totally crammed full of desks, filing cabinets and trash cans which were overflowing with the paperwork that seems to be endlessly generated by the government. Each desk had an overworked ashtray, and the room had that off brown hue that rooms get when subjected to heavy smoke on a steady basis. It was livable today though, as the room was relatively devoid of people. I followed the Lieutenant to the far side of the room, and we neared the only area in the office that was immaculate. The desk was tidy and recently polished, no ashtray, and the bulletin board on the wall next to the desk was neat and orderly. The desk gleamed softly under the unforgiving florescent bulb overhead. I saw no pictures of family, or anything to indicate a home life on or near his desk. The totally organized professional. It made me feel better somehow.

He motioned me to the chair alongside his desk, and I sat. I noticed that his chair was the same, no rollers, and no cushion. "They treat you well around here, don't they?" I offered.

"My choice," he grunted, "if I get too comfortable around here, I tend to stay at my desk, instead of working the cases."

I nodded in understanding, as if I had a similar viewpoint. Come to think of it, there were no papers or ashtray in my little office either, and I had just recently cleaned it, so I felt on an equal basis with him. I did notice that his socks matched.

"Anyway," he stated without preamble, "I need to know what you did from the time you chased Underhill out of the house till about 7:00 that morning."

I told him everything, the call to Jocko preceding the chase, the chase itself, the subsequent visit from Jocko, the search for Soot and the discovery of the gun.

"Just so you'll know, the gun that you found was not the murder weapon, the gun you found was .38 caliber and the one that killed him was a .22."

"Good, I'm relieved, I thought maybe I'd shot him for a minute there," I joked.

The Lieutenant wasn't smiling. "I thought so too," he said, "until Jocko vouched for you."

I gulped. " I was just kidding, Lieutenant. I haven't held a gun since I was at the shooting range while trying for the Police Academy."

He stared at me for a moment more, then decided to let me off the hook. "Police Academy huh? Let's go get some coffee."

I hopped up, happy to oblige. I was aware that the room had managed to fill up with cops, cigarette smoke and high energy foods, such as doughnuts, bagels and granola bars. I was glad to leave, the smoke had already gotten to me, and I wouldn't be able to wear these clothes again until I had aired them out. I figured a night or two hanging outside my window ought to do it, they weren't dirty enough to wash yet, for goodness sake.

We walked out of the building and across the street to a little dive that was probably the safest place in the city to eat, as there seemed to be no one there but cops, or people associated with them, such as secretaries and lawyers. In fact, there were several members of the law firm that occupied the building that I had tried to rent earlier. I felt like going over there to thank them for allowing me to find Roy.

We sat down, and the Lieutenant asked me what I'd have. I declined, but he said it was on his expense account, so I opted for a glazed and a cup of orange juice. He sat and looked me over carefully, then said, "There seems to be something you aren't telling me, you know....it could be important. You are now loosely associated with two murders. In fact, you may be the last person besides the murderers that saw these two."

"Are you now considering Felicia's death a homicide?"

"I am, the department doesn't see it my way though."

"Hmmmm," I mused, "I don't have a clue why anyone would want to kill her. She just recently joined a church group; they met on Wednesday nights with Pastor James. Other than that, I don't know whom she saw, how much she knew about Felix, or anything else about her. I haven't even seen where she lived."

"There was nothing suspicious at her house either," the Lieutenant said. "We didn't find a key to her son's apartment, that's for sure." He looked at me quizzically.

"I never got it, either in person, by mail or from anyone else."

He seemed satisfied with this, but was clearly struggling with something. Maybe he didn't even know what it was. Our snack arrived and we talked around the food, general stuff, about my past, mostly.

"I do have one item to offer," I said, after finishing my dough-nut, "but it probably amounts to nothing."

"What's that?"

"Well, just recently, I have become aware of a silver Volkswagen showing up where I happen to be. It is always too far away for me to see the driver, but I have the feeling it is keeping tabs on me, for some reason or other."

"Is that so? Could you recognize it if we find it? There can't be many Volkswagens still around, and silver makes it even easier to find."

"I'm sure that I could," I said, "the way it looks, it's sort of like someone spraypainted it, or the color has faded drastically, almost looks like shiny primer, but as I've said, it's never been all that close to me. I wouldn't be totally surprised to find that the guy who was with Underhill at 'The Green Frog' is the driver."

"Makes sense to me, I'll put the word out and maybe have a patrolman in your neighborhood in the early hours, see if you might be wrong, and find that they just head out to work early each morning."

"Like I said, it may amount to nothing." The lieutanant was done eating and waiting for me to finsish. A thought came to me and I asked, "How does a town the size of Hustle manage to support a Homicide Department? Is that a true necessity?"

He smiled and explained that Hustle was the only town of any size in the county, so the police department actually covered the entire county. This allowed for a greater tax base, better equipment, pay and manpower. Everyone was happy and the situation worked out well for all.

I finished my drink and he got up, "I guess that's it for today. Let me know if anything else turns up."

"OK, thanks for the snack, the next one's on me."

"See if you can wrangle me an invitation to Mother's for a meal one night, that'd do just fine."

I laughed and said I'd work on it. The Lieutenant didn't seem so intimidating at the moment and we left on good terms.

I took my time walking home, enjoying the late summer day, but realizing that the time was nearing for worsening weather, and the holiday season. I dreaded the holidays. It generally meant that I had to find where mom lived, figure out a way to go visit her, and what to get her. That was not a huge problem anymore, but the seasonal festivities still did nothing to improve my life, my mood or my pocketbook. Oh well, still months away, it was only August after all. Also, I had a dinner date with Felicity tonight, even though it would be Mother doing all the work. I decided to get on home and see if I could help. I took the long way, going through the alleyways and looking at the tops of fences and trees, seeing if the kooky cat was perched on any of them. No luck, and it was almost 1:00 by the time I arrived.

I was pleasantly assaulted by the smells emanating from the kitchen as I entered the door. I strolled in there, and told Mother how good everything smelled. She smiled, gave me some cookies and milk and told me to get lost. I was to disappear until 4:00, when Felicity was to arrive. We were eating a bit early, as I had to be at work that evening. I appreciated the extra effort as well as the cookies and milk. I took them into the front room where the fossil was asleep watching some old romance movie. I sat down quietly, munching away and feeling sorry for older people. They fell asleep so easily, they seemed to accept that life need not run at 100 miles an hour, and were glad to be off the treadmill. I felt somewhat superior to this lifestyle and was glad to be in the fast lane. Those were my last coherent thoughts before I fell asleep as well.

Hal came in a bit later and woke me up. He sat next to me, and I noticed he was crunching on my last cookie. I glared at him, then laughed at myself for falling asleep. I excused myself with the thought that it must have been the old movie. I asked Hal how the day had gone, and why he was home so soon.

"It's not that early, nearly 3:30, and there are days when I am simply not needed," he said.

"That late?" I was astounded; I had slept the afternoon away and needed to clean up a bit for Felicity. "Sorry Hal, I need to go clean up a bit!"

"Don't worry," he leered, "I'll keep her company for you."

"Right," I said, as I hopped up. "You took the last cookie, you get to take in the empty glass!"

He grinned and assured me that he would. I ran upstairs, peeling my clothes off and setting them on the windowsill to air out, closing the window on them to insure they wouldn't blow away in a wind. I ran to the bathroom, performing the obligatory quickie cleanup and went back to my room to look for suitable attire.

Paul was in there, in boxers and tee shirt, looking around.

"What's going on Paul?"

"I was trying to figure out whose room this is, do you know?"

"It's my room," I said.

"Can't be, it's too clean."

"Mother cleaned it up for me, must have gotten tired of it looking like it did."

"She never does that for me," he complained.

"You need to start dating then, I'll bet Jocko didn't get the good treatment till he met Bitsy."

"Ah, so you noticed he got the royal treatment too."

"Yes, I did," I admitted. "Now, run along, I need to get dressed, and so do you, if you're going to eat with us."

Paul got out of the room safely, and I continued my deliberations, finally settling on a decent golf shirt and a nice pair of blue jeans. I decided against mismatched socks and just wore the loafers. I splashed on some cologne and declared myself fit for humanity.

I closed the door out of habit, mostly because of Soot encounters, but thinking about it, I reopened the door, thinking that the room was doing well during its airing out procedure, and Soot wasn't around to despoil things anyway.

I walked down the stairs, to see Felicity being entertained by Hal, James, Paul and the fossil. Mother had the table set beautifully and I salivated at the smells coming through the doorway, fresh bread being the most prominent.

Felicity was laughing at something that Hal had whispered to her, causing her to blush a bit. Hal was standing entirely too close to suit me, but didn't give an inch as I approached.

"Hi Felicity," I croaked, as I neared the group. "How was your day?"

"Hi After," she chirped, "I didn't do too much today, just loafed mostly. I managed to pick up a few things for the apartment, and I had a faucet problem that Hal said he could fix for me."

Why women pull this stuff, I'll never know. All of a sudden, I hated Hal, had no use for Felicity, and lost my appetite. She just had to know that men don't like these things, but then, as I was only one of several in the area, she had every reason to play the field.

She must have seen my depression building, because she took pity, and said, "Of course, he'll probably need help, so maybe he can come over with you sometime and the two of you can fix it."

Hal looked a bit stricken, but recovered well, saying that would be fine, then he sauntered off to the dining room, followed by the fossil. All of a sudden I had my appetite back. Felicity grinned at me and winked, rolling her eyes in Hal's wake. James was lounging in a chair, legs over the side. He yawned and said to call him when dinner was ready, he wanted to watch Roadrunner beat up on Wile E. Coyote some more. Paul just sort of stood there, hemming and hawing. He finally got up some nerve.

"Um, Felicity..." he stammered. "Y-you w-wouldn't have a sister, or a f-friend that could stand a g-good time do you?"

Felicity smiled. "No Paul, I just got ba... ummm... here in town, and I know no one. The only relative I have is a brother, and we don't get along at all. I'll keep an eye out though. Aren't there girls at the newspaper?"

"The only one that likes me is the switchboard operator, and she always forgets my name, in fact, she asked me if I wanted an application last week."

"She must like you then," I ventured, "if she thinks enough of you to want you to work there." It was lame, but the best I could do. It seemed to work.

"Yeah, that must be it, I think I'll ask her out tonight!"

"You do that," I urged, trying not to smile too much.

Felicity grabbed my arm, saying, "Come on, I haven't eaten all day, and I am starving!"

I followed easily, letting her keep my arm, I had an extra leg and all of my hair to loan her if she wanted it. She was right too, the smell was overpowering.

Mother had outdone herself. There was fried chicken, cole slaw, potatoes as well, the little small ones, with the green flecks of something or other on them. Fresh rolls, marmalade and that fabulous honey butter. Corn on the cob, several things to drink, and a big, fat triple layered chocolate cake smack dab in the middle of the table. Cloth napkins that had the good silver wrapped within, the plates were her best, sitting on hand made lace place mats. There were two candles, unlighted, as it was daytime, but the effect was wonderful. There was hardly a word spoken as we settled in to graze, except for the occasional "pass this, pass that, please".

I forgot to tell you how wonderful Felicity looked, as first Hal, then Paul, and then dinner had preoccupied me. I looked up long enough to notice that James had joined us. Hal asked if Roadrunner had been eaten, and James told him no, grinning all the while. Anyway, Felicity was in a red summer dress, with white polka dots, just the hint of makeup, and had her hair in some sort of ponytail, but with a fancy thing holding it back. She wore little gold heart earrings, and sandals, so the effect was casual, but arresting. She smelled great too.

I whispered to her, "How do you do it? You look and smell great, and I'll bet you didn't think twice about it."

She grinned and said, "I must have tried a hundred things until I settled on this, you look good yourself." Then she turned her head away.

I felt great, and didn't mind grinning at Hal across the table, to let him know that compliments had been exchanged. The cad just grinned back at me, then winked at Felicity. I was wishing for Soot to come back, I wanted to put him in Hal's room and close the door while he was gone to work one day soon.

Supper was super, and I had two pieces of cake, an extra glass of milk and when everyone was suitably gorged, most of us went into the living room to digest it all. Mother had already put out a full coffeepot and mugs, so it gave everyone but James a chance to relax after the repast. James, of course, went up to his room, returned a few minutes later in shorts and a tee shirt and went jogging. What a waste of good fatty foods.

I felt that I was suitably dressed for work, so I got up at about fifteen till six and announced that I was walking to work. Felicity would have nothing of it and said she'd drive me. That was that, everyone got up, stretched, said their good-byes and went to do their own particular thing. It looked as if it might rain, so I grabbed my raincoat, then held the door for Felicity and walked to the car with her. She turned around and waved, I looked back and saw Mother waving at us. I waved too, got a smile and then Felicity and I got into her car. It was old and worn, but spotless, and somehow I knew it would run like a top. It did.

"Sorry about this car," Felicity said, "but I haven't had work in some time and it was all I could afford."

"What sort of work do you do?" I asked.

"I try to paint, but it isn't always how good you are, sometimes, it comes down to who you know. I've been told I have talent, so I keep plugging away. I generally do housecleaning to earn money."

"Where did you live before coming here?"

She gave me an odd look, thought about it and said, sighing, "I'm not truly sure that I live here, it is just a side road to me. There is no way to sell my work here, and I haven't been inspired to paint at all. That's one of the reasons I came here, was to get a change of venue, maybe discover another side of myself, and see if I could get started again."

I settled back somewhat grumpily, realizing that if she hadn't been inspired, that I hadn't had much of an effect on her. Anyway, who knows what inspires artists, maybe near death experiences or a lost butterfly in a hailstorm. Who knew?

Before I could get too upset about it, we were at Roy's. She pulled over, and I asked if she'd like to come in.

"No, not just yet. I may run a few errands, then I might drop by later!"

That was good enough for me. I thanked her, and she smiled, but didn't lean in for a kiss, so I got out as graciously as I could.

"Tell Mother I had a great time, and that the food was the best I've had in years."

"I will." Somehow this sounded like goodbye to me. "Thanks for the lift."

"You're welcome," she said. Then without meeting my eyes, she smiled in my general direction and drove off.

I didn't think I'd done anything wrong. I truly could not think of a thing I had said. Going over the conversation, I realized that it was something that she had said, that could have gotten her upset. She may have realized that there was nothing here to inspire her, and she was thinking that it was time to go. I had to let it go at that for now.

I entered the building. Roy was hard at work selling something small, dark and metallic to a couple that seemed excited about their find. I smiled and went into my office, where I sat down to think. Before long, I heard the door bells tinkling and the door to the street closed behind the pair.

I went in to see Roy. "How'd the day go?"

"Pretty good, I got some new things over the weekend, spent some time bringing them in, and then the people kept coming. I've been busy and made some money." He pointed over to a pile of quilts on the floor near my office. "Do you think you could shake those out and place them on the benches by the back door wall?"

"Be glad to," I said.

"OK, then I'll leave it to you."

"Have a nice evening!" I said to him as he pulled his jacket on. I almost forgot. "Do you mind if I take a few tools back with me, I need to do some repair work on Mother's front door."

"Sure, help yourself," he replied. Then he too, stopped and

turned just as he reached the door. "By the way, I wouldn't get too chummy with Jocko, if I were you."

I was shocked. What could Jocko possibly have done to elicit that comment. "Why not?"

"Well, he was a bit of a hellion when he was younger, got mixed up in some things as a young man, had some big city friends that used to come down here, spent time with him. Occasionally he would go up to the city as well, then come back with money, sometimes a flashy girl. People talked. He may have grown out of it, but it didn't look good to me then, and I still worry about it now. Most of those guys were sent to prison on drug charges. No one ever came here to talk to Jocko, not that I know anyway. He met Bitsy, settled down, his uncle got him a job on the force, and he's been good as gold since then. You just never know when your past will come back to haunt you, and there may be a reason that he is still only a beat cop, making the minimum salary."

This was something to ponder, and I nodded farewell to Roy as he went out the door.

Still shaking my head over that news, I went to the quilts, picked a few up and took them out back to shake them. I know very little about quilts, but even I could see that these were fairly nice. Not many rough or worn spots, if any. The stitches were very small, and just irregular enough that I could see that they were done by hand. I resolved to find a nice one, and place it aside, perhaps as a Christmas present for Mother Teresa. Now I was worrying about the holidays again.

The doorbells rang and a stringy looking, tall gent in a cowboy hat, and a cloud of cigarette smoke walked in. He looked at me, then asked in a very loud voice, "Hey pardner, where's Roy?"

"Gone for the evening, I'm the new night help."

"Pleased ta meet ya!" He came over, grasped my hand and broke every bone in it with the strongest grip I'd ever felt. "I'm called Grits, real name Jim, don't ever call me that."

"Pleased to meet you, Grits," I said, trying to see if the Jell-O at the end of my right arm would ever be worth anything again.

"You don't get out much, do ya?"

"No, not much." I wasn't even going to argue. The man could break me like a twig, I'd had my nose broken by a girl, and been terrorized by a cat. This was no time to act macho.

"Listen, I'm an over the road driver, and I need a new piece."

"Piece of what?" I asked, feeling the fool, and knowing it would come to pass that I was, indeed, a fool.

"A piece, you know, a gun."

"Oh sure, well, I don't think we have any."

"How long have you worked here?" he asked.

"My second week, all Roy has intrusted me with is comic books and quilts."

Grits laughed, blew some smoke in my face and said, "Look in the big box behind the counter."

I hustled over to the box and tried to open it, but it was locked.

"Key's under the cash register, on a piece of twine."

I looked, and sure enough, there it was. I took it to the box, opened it up, and found a dozen pistols with the numbers removed through what appeared to be filing or rasping. I was shocked, and it must have showed.

"Don't worry, Roy's been doing this for years, surprised he hadn't told ya yet."

"Ummm, yeah, well, ummm."

"OK, let me take a look, I need something with stopping power, never know who you're gonna see on the road these days, and my German Shepherd is a little too immature to do much more than keep me company."

"You need a dog AND a gun?" I gasped.

"You need to take a run with me sometime, I think you'd be surprised. I'll take the .45."

"I don't know what to charge you for it."

"Just tell Roy I took it, he knows I'll make it up to him."

"Do you mind if I ask you something?"

"Sure, be my guest, but I hope you don't mind if I don't answer it, 'cause I may not!"

"OK," I said, "is there anything else that I should know about Roy?"

Grits smirked, then said, "Probably."

He went to the door, turned and said, "Better lock up the gun chest, Roy may not like them out in the open like that."

"Yeah, sure....thanks."

"Oh," he stopped again, "don't worry, your hand'll feel better soon." He laughed then, and with a wave, went out the door.

My hand hurt.

After locking up the box, I picked up another quilt with my good hand and went out back to shake it. Grits was correct, by the time I got done shaking out the quilt, my hand felt pretty good, and I felt I might live through the evening. Going back in to place the quilt on a clean bench area, I stooped to pick up a few more, when the bells tinkled again. I stood up, and saw Felicity walk into the room. She had changed to blue jeans, a flannel shirt, and boots, but the hair and the earrings were still the same.

"Hi After," she said merrily as she neared me.

"Well...hi!" I said, amazed that she'd show up, it was nearly 8:00 and I hadn't even begun to dream that she would return. "What have you been up to?"

"I had a few things I needed to clean up, a few errands to run, and I'm just about done, so I thought I'd come by and check out your office. I brought some sodas."

"I'm so glad you showed."

She sat down near the door, popped a top and began to drink. She motioned me over, and I sat beside her. She offered me a can of root beer and I accepted it. I was sort of awkward about everything. As I've said before, I have very little experience with the opposite sex, and I wasn't sure what she was looking for. We sat there, sipping our sodas, and making small talk.

After a few minutes, she grabbed my arm, and asked to see my office. I was glad to accommodate her, and we strolled over to the office. I turned on the light and she walked in, turning around, taking everything in. She was biting on her lower lip, thinking hard.

"It needs work, but it's doable. Maybe a few of the quilts, a watercolor on the wall, a bit better light and a radio for music. Yes, that would help a lot."

"I'll see what Roy can spare," I said, delighted at the ideas, and the fact that she was willing to participate.

She smiled and began to leave.

"Can I see you tomorrow?" I asked, somewhat panicky.

"We'll see how the rest of my errands go tonight," she said with an enigmatic smile. "You can keep the rest of the drinks, one is all I allow myself, and after that dinner tonight, I've really overdone it."

She left, and I was no closer to figuring her out than I had been the first night at 'The Green Frog'. Oh well, now my mind was as messed up as the rest of my life.

I spent the remainder of the evening shaking quilts. No one else came in. I took a few quilts to my office, placed them randomly, but where traffic would not dirty them, and prepared to leave for the evening. I went to the cash drawer to get my twenty, seeing as I was broke again. Upon opening it, I gasped. It was totally full of hundred dollar bills. I did a quick count and realized that there was well over thirty thousand dollars there. I made sure it was well locked up, and with shaking, if no longer numb hands, went to put on my overcoat. The rain was just beginning to fall, as I could hear the drops peppering the windows of Roy's place. I was about to leave when I remembered that I needed some tools for the door repair job at Mother's.

I rummaged around in the back room, found a few screwdrivers, a small crowbar, a hammer, a rasp, a sharp knife and a tape measure. My hands were full, so I stuck the crowbar and the screwdrivers in the large pockets of my overcoat, and carried the rest with me. I got outside, then turned to lock the door, trying to keep my head down to avoid the rain, which was picking up pace and intensity. As I completed the job, a shadow reached out from beyond my peripheral vision, coming up to my nose with a rag. A strong smell assaulted me, and I felt myself losing consciousness.

six

*T*hump! Thump! Thump!

What was that noise? My head was aching, I had no idea what was going on. Thump!

Why couldn't I see? That was not entirely accurate, I could see, of sorts, but what it was I was seeing was definitely unclear. I saw a red glow from time to time. It was variable in its brightness, as if it were blinking irregularly. Thump!

I tried to move, but found that my body was not responding, my eyes were smarting and the smell of...something, was still in my nose. My arms seemed....Thump!.... to be wedged to my sides, so I tried to roll over....KaWhump! Thump! That question was answered anyway, it was my head hitting the floor of whatever I was in. I realized right then, that I was IN something. The red glows were some sort of hint. I panicked and tried to shout, but couldn't quite catch my breath. I couldn't move, I was paralyzed, as much by fear as by having inadequate space to move IN. I knew where I was now, I was in a car's trunk. The red glows were taillights, the variations in intensity were when brake lights came on. The road ...Thump! was bumpy, so I was on a gravel or unfinished road with lots of potholes and bumps. I figured that it wouldn't be long before my chauffeur would have me at my destination, so I tried to breathe again. No better. I tried struggling, pushing anywhere with all my might. Nothing happened, metal and locks are stronger than yours truly.

I was in a real tight spot, literally, and if the driver was who I thought it was, he would have no trouble finishing me off, not with the muscles that Steroids had shown me at 'The Green Frog'. I figured I was being taken out to the country to become worm food, and imminently too.

I tried again to breathe normally; it was just impossible, as I couldn't even get my head positioned comfortably. It was twisted over my right shoulder and I was looking at the rear of the trunk. It was a good thing that my head wasn't facing the other way, or I may have taken longer to figure out where I was, and time was clearly of the essence.

The car slowed, and I thought that this would be it. I was sweating and gasping for air. I did realize that I may gain a slight element of surprise by feigning unconsciousness when the trunk was finally opened, but it would do me no good, as I was sure that I would be killed the instant the trunk was raised, conscious or not.

I needed something; a good idea would be nice, then the car apparently turned a corner sharply and my body shifted, placing my left hand over my coat pocket. It was the pocket with the crowbar, but I hadn't figured that out yet. The car sped up again. Fighting my panic and newfound claustrophobia, I tried to calm myself. I let out a wail. At least I was breathing again. I took quick shallow breaths and tried to count to 10. I got to 4 before I opened my eyes again and panicked. I wasn't going to get out of this, not alive anyway. I wondered if Jocko and Lieutenant Howard would solve my case. I wished now that I had told them about my break in at the apartment. I tried to move again, but the only thing I could move was my left hand. I felt the crowbar! I recognized it for what it was! I felt a glimmer of hope. I tried to remove it from my coat pocket. I couldn't find the edge of the pocket. I tried bunching the fabric with my fingers. That helped a little. I worked the fabric down to the edge of the pocket and felt the metal of the crowbar.

Thump! Thump!...the car had hit a new stretch of thumps! I had no idea what that meant, but that last thump had caused me to lose my grip on the crowbar.

I started over again, a bit quicker this time, until I regained the edge of the pocket. I held the fabric tightly, determined not to let the crowbar fall out of my grasp again. I took my time, and looped my index finger around the crowbar, and slowly pulled it free. I made sure that I got my other fingers around it this time before I loosened my thumb from the fabric.

I got it to a good position on my side, then tried to move it to where I thought the locking mechanism should be, somewhere between the red glows. I couldn't move my arm, I needed leverage room. There was only one thing to do, try to get on my stomach and get the left hand closer to the lock. I tried twisting, but there was no room to twist. I tried again, no luck. I tried to make myself small, I blew out all my air, and twisted as hard as I could. THUMP! A big bump, and my upper torso moved to the right. I had my hand near the lock, I knew it, but I was so uncomfortable, that I couldn't breathe. I was going to lose consciousness again, and my back had shooting fireworks going up the spine. I jabbed with the crowbar, and hit solid wall. I could not see where I was hitting, so I slid the bar around until I felt a groove. It had to be the junction between trunk and body. I pushed with what might I had left, and felt the tip of the crowbar engage. I pumped up and down on the bar. I felt something give, and then I blacked out.

I woke again fairly quickly. I had some room to move, the space was bigger. I had managed to pop the trunk, but it had not opened all of the way. I grabbed the edge of the door and opened it a bit, not wanting the driver to have a clue as to what I was up to. I had room to maneuver, and maneuver I did. I got myself turned around, I could see the road falling away behind me as we sped along, and I was able to breathe real air! I drew in as many breaths as I could, then realized that I'd better be rolling along out of there. Without thinking too much about it, I grabbed the crowbar, opened the trunk and rolled out onto the road. I was probably saved from a fatal beating by the fact that this was truly a country lane, and the car was probably only doing thirty. Nevertheless, I rolled approximately thirteen thousand times before stopping in the middle of the road. I just barely saw the car turning a corner ahead of me. It looked to be an old green car, with a fender missing, the trunk flapping wildly in the rear. It seemed familiar, as well it should. It was Felicity's car.

I saw the glow of the brake lights as the car disappeared, and I knew they had discovered my escape. To this day, I don't know how I got on my feet, but I found myself at the edge of the road, looking over a hill that sloped down to running water. I tried walking down, hanging onto trees and bushes, but lost my grip and fell/rolled all the rest of the way. I splashed into the water, which was icy cold, and it felt wonderful. It certainly woke me up. I sort of dragged myself and swam out to the center of the water and let it pull me downstream. I also had the presence of mind to look back to see if I was being pursued. I was not surprised to see a dark figure upstream, but that was all that I saw, as the water began rolling me over and over. My clothes were becoming a hindrance now, and suddenly the water didn't feel so refreshing. I managed to balance myself, and began to work my way towards the opposite shore. I heard a shot ring out, then another, and all was quiet. I knew I was far out of range of anything short of a powerful rifle, so I took my time and secured myself among the brush I found at the other bank.

When I felt some strength return, I pulled myself on shore, and managed to get my coat and shirt off. I was shivering mightily, but I was able to wring them out, I then put my shirt on between shivers, lay down and pulling my coat over me, passed out.

I dozed in and out, sometimes clearly awake, and sometimes drowsy. I couldn't tell if it was the aftereffects of the chemical that zonked me, or the bumping my head had received in the car and on the road. I was also trying to figure out what I had been doing in Felicity's trunk. Had she been abducted, or hurt by my kidnapper? Was she somehow involved? I didn't seriously consider the latter, but if she wasn't involved, her car sure was. It was up to me to get back to town to get some help for her, if I wasn't too late already. I was about to start moving when I heard a rustle not too far away. Someone was moving above me. The glow of a flashlight was making itself known to my left. I froze, and under the early morning conditions, it was almost a literal freeze. The light was moving away from me, going downstream. My pursuer thought me further down stream than I actually was. I was a sitting duck though, if I remained here, so I tried rubbing my hands together to get some circulation back. I watched the light recede as I continued to rub. After a decent interval, I groaned myself into a sitting position, and then onto my knees. I stayed there for a minute, hoping everything still worked. I would surely be paying for this tomorrow. Actually, it was probably already tomorrow, though it was still black out. The water picked up faint gleams from the thin moon and the stars, and I was able to get oriented. I crawled up the bank, and soon found the road, about twenty yards away. I decided to walk to the area where I had seen the flashlight. If I could at least get a glimpse, I would have most of my questions answered, if not all of them. I had to be careful though, my opponent was potentially armed and certainly dangerous. I was actually starting to warm up, and was beginning to walk fairly well. Luckily, it was just a cool morning in August and not later in the year. My feet were the last to warm up, and by the time I got to where I thought the car ought to be, I was doing OK. There was a curve in the road, and as I neared it, I heard a door slam, and a car start. It roared away before I could reach the curve, so I missed the driver. I thought it was a small man, but I couldn't be sure, having not gotten a clear look.

I stumbled along the road, seeing no other sign of human life. A few animals watched me warily from the trees that bordered the road. It wasn't too long before I came across blacktop. There was a sign ahead, stating that it was 24 miles to Hustle. That was good to know. I figured that someone would be along soon, and I could hitch a ride. Then, I realized that it could be my abductor that came along, so it might be best to travel on foot until I could get to a phone and see if Jocko could bail me out again.

I traveled along in this manner for about an hour, before I saw headlights. I scurried to the trees like a rat in the big city, and waited till the vehicle passed. It was just a stranger in a small truck. It was too late to flag them down, so I continued my walk. Over the next two hours, this event repeated itself three more times, never allowing me a chance to get relief. The next sign said 18 miles, so I had covered one fourth of the distance. My feet were hurting, so I sat down and took off my shoes. My sockless feet were becoming badly blistered, and I knew my walk was over. I sat by the side of the road, determined to take my chances on the next vehicle. A car soon appeared, I raised my hands, trying to wave it down. A young girl looked at me, opened her mouth in terror, and drove on. I supposed I looked pretty bad and somewhat derelict, but I had no choice. The sun had started to cause its own light, lending a grayish cast to the surroundings when a pick up truck drove by. I had enough strength to wave my arms weakly, and he pulled over.

"What's wrong with you?" the driver asked.

"Had an accident and fell in the river," I replied wearily.

"Well, you're too messy for my cab, but you can hop on the bed if you wanna."

"I wanna," I replied, and limped to the truck, climbed on back, and fell onto the softest gunnysacks ever made by man.

"Ya goin' to Hustle?"

"Yes, please."

Without another word, he drove off. Compared to my ride out, it should have been wonderful, but it was cold, cold, cold, and windy.

I guess I am hard to please. It probably only took 20 minutes to reach town, but I was totally exhausted when I got there. He dropped me off outside a doughnut shop that had its lights on, and I stumbled down off the truck. I smiled my thanks to the driver, an older fellow, with a kind face, and he waved and drove off.

I put my shoes back on and went into the shop. The girl behind the counter looked me over, and said, "Looks like you fell way off the wagon last night."

"Worse than that," I croaked, "where's the restroom."

She pointed the way, and I spent the next ten minutes running my hands under warm water, rinsing my face off and trying to get the mud from the hillside off of my clothes. At least I was warming up when I limped back into the brightly lit eating area.

"Could I have a half dozen warm doughnuts, a cup of coffee and some orange juice, please?"

"Nothing personal, but I'd better see some money first," she wisely requested.

I fumbled around in my pockets, coming up with my twenty of the night before, and I handed the soggy mess to her. She took it gingerly, and placed it on a part of the counter where it could dry and die in peace. She got my order together, and handed it to me, along with my change.

Those were the best doughnuts ever baked, or cooked, or fried, or however they make them. I savored every crunchy mouthful, and enjoyed the cold versus hot sensations as I drank the hot coffee and the cold orange juice. I was in control of my own body again, such as it was. It was time to get on with solving the case. It was now crystal clear that I was in for keeps, and that an active role was now required. I needed to make some phone calls, get home and get my wits together, then get back to work.

I looked at my watch, it was nearly 7:00 A.M., and I found a few lonely coins in my pocket. I went to the pay phone on the wall by the door and pulled up the phone book, looking up the number of the Police Department. I dialed the number, and asked the man who answered the phone if there was a way to reach Jocko.

"Who is this?" he asked.

"Just a friend of his, who had a little trouble, I was hoping he could give me a lift home."

"He didn't show for work last night, better call him at home." He hung up.

I called the number I had memorized. This time a younger female voice answered. "Hello?"

"Is this Bitsy?"

"Yeeeees." Hesitantly.

"Hi, this is After Coffman, I met Jocko a few days ago."

"Hi After, I've heard of you." She laughed. I wondered why she was laughing.

"I wanted to speak with Jocko, please."

"Oh, well he's not due home until 8:00, I'll tell him you called."

"Is he working the beat now, or the grocery store?"

"Oh, he's on the beat, he works nights, you know."

"Yes," I answered, troubled. "I know. Thanks for giving him the message."

"No problem, drop by sometime."

I resolved to drop by, if only to wring his neck. What was he doing last night, fooling around? Or was he finding some quality time with his friends from the big city, whatever big city that might be.

I was troubled, but decided to try and walk home, blisters and all. I hobbled to the door, passing the counter, when the girl behind the counter stopped me. "Couldn't get a ride?"

"No," I said morosely. "My friend wasn't home."

"I'm off as soon as my help gets here, I'll give you a lift. You don't look as creepy with the color back in your face."

"It's good to know I don't look creepy." I laughed, and she joined in.

I sat down, and in a few minutes two new people attired in the shop's outfits came in to relieve her.

She bounced up front and walked to the door with me. We went to a nice, new Lincoln Town Car parked in front. I must have looked astonished, for she explained, "My parent's car."

She handed me a towel that she must have taken from the shop. "Better sit on this."

I took it, spread it out on the passenger seat and sat on it.

"Someday, you're going to have to tell me how you got into this mess."

"It's a long story, but I'll do it some night when I have insomnia and need doughnuts."

She laughed, "Better call me first, the store doesn't open till 6:00, but I go in at midnight to cook the doughnuts. Just call the number in the book and let it ring. I'm not there on weekends. My name is Gloria." She was talking non-stop, but held out her hand without taking her eyes off the road. I shook it.

"I'm After Coffman."

"Neat name."

"You can thank my mom."

"Of course," she giggled, "where do you live?"

"Mother Teresa's on the other side of town." I gave her directions and we were there fairly soon. I got out, stretched and turned to walk to the door, my bed and more food!

"Thanks Gloria," I said. "You're a life saver."

She grinned, showing perfectly white teeth, and a great smile, hit the accelerator and peeled rubber in her parent's sedate Town Car.

I shook my head and hobbled to the door. Mother was waiting inside, about to serve breakfast. "What has happened to you?"

"I was kidnapped, and had to swim through a river, and walk, and hitch a ride to get home."

"Are you hungry?"

Amazingly enough, I was. "Yes, ma'am."

"Go get some dry clothes on, clean up, and I'll have hot cereal for you when you get down."

That sounded wonderful, so putting Steroids, Jocko, Felicity, Felix and Felicia out of my head, I trudged up the stairs, slowly but surely, got out of my clothes, and found my terrycloth bathrobe, went to the bathroom, did a quick clean up job, and went back downstairs.

There was hot oatmeal, with a bowl of crumbly brown sugar, and a small pitcher of milk at my seat. Hot, buttered raisin bread toast, some fresh bananas and oranges, and a cup of hot tea soon followed this.

"This is wonderful," I gasped. "Where is everyone else?"

"Either at work, or up to something else, they all ate a while ago. Paul didn't show up last night though. He didn't call, and I am a bit worried. Could you try and find him today?"

I assured her that I would, but really figured that with all the deaths, he was overworked at the Obituary desk.

"Now, tell me all about it," Mother insisted.

I did tell her all about it, except for the part about not reaching Jocko, I didn't want her to worry about that until I knew more. I was going to call him after a shower and a nap anyway, so I'd be on top of that situation soon enough.

She was interested in the kidnapping, but also very interested in everything Felicity had done. "Shouldn't you call the police?"

"Oh my gosh!" I jumped up, "I was so worried about myself, that I forgot that she could be in trouble."

"Do it!" Mother ordered.

I called the Police Department again, and asked for Lieutenant Howard. This time I had better luck as he answered the phone right away.

"Lieutenant Howard? This is After Coffman. I had an interesting night last night, and I'll tell you all about it, but first I need to know if a friend of mine had any problems last night?"

"Who is you friend?"

"Her name is Felicity." I didn't know her last name, I just realized. "This is embarrassing, but I don't know her last name, or where she lives…BUT, I do have her phone number," I quickly appended.

"OK, no one had problems that we know of last night, but give me the number, and I'll look it up."

"Thanks Lieutenant."

"OK, want to tell me the long version, or the short one."

"I'll tell you the short one, then I'm taking a shower and a nap." I told him the skeletal outlines, and when he heard about the shots by the bank, he whistled. I told him everything, again leaving out the details about Jocko.

"OK," he muttered. "You sleep till noon, and I'm picking you up for lunch."

"Sounds fair to me. And… thanks Lieutenant."

"It's my job, and you're making me earn every penny." He hung up.

I went back upstairs, took what was definitely the best shower ever enjoyed by man, then shaved, brushed my hair and fairly flew into my bedroom. I noticed that my clothes were still out on the windowsill, obviously soaked from the rain, and so I decided that they might as well dry out there too. As bad as the weather was last night, the day was looking beautiful. I was glad to be around to enjoy it, but decided that the thrill could wait until after my nap. I fell into the softest bed ever made by man, and promptly fell asleep.

I didn't waken until I heard someone knocking at my door. I got up, every joint creaking and every bone hurting, and went to the door. I opened it, and saw Lieutenant Howard standing there. I got flustered and looked at my watch. It was about half past noon.

"Get some clothes on, we have a lot to talk about."

"How's Felicity?" I asked first, standing my ground.

"My guess is that she made it through the night just fine, but she's nowhere to be found."

"OK." I found some jeans and a tee shirt, and some socks, my feet hurt too much not to. My loafers were still soaked, probably ruined, so I put on some old sneakers. I looked out the window, and my other clothes were still damp, so they would get to dry some more today.

The Lieutenant had been waiting outside my door, and we went downstairs together. It looked nice out still, so without any other delays, we were out the door and got into his unmarked police car.

He took us to a little bar and grill at the city limits where it was fairly quiet, and we could get some talking done. I ordered a burger with the works, some fries and an iced tea. He ordered a salad, no dressing and water. I shrugged, that was his call; as for me, it appeared that several people wished me dead, so I was going to indulge in cholesterol, whether it killed me or not.

The waitress brought the food quickly, and grinned at Lieutenant Howard. He grinned back, then started into his food. My food still needed catsup and salt, so I got busy adding them. About halfway through the meal, he started with the questions.

"OK After, you said someone was shooting at you from the bank of the river about 24 miles out of town." My mouth was full, so I just nodded yes.

"You saw Felicity's car drive down the road after you escaped?" I nodded again.

"The last time you saw Felicity was a bit before you closed Roy's place for the night."

Nod.

"Here's some information you may find interesting. You were not the one being shot at. We found a body on the bank this morning; it appears to be the big man you met at 'The Green Frog'." I looked up at this, surprised.

"You mean Steroids?"

"Whatever. We're running prints on him to get an identification, and we'll check him out when we get a hit, through all the files that are available to us. That brings me to the cars. We found the silver Volkswagen last night, parked at a motel south of town. We found Felicity's car this morning. We ran a check on the license plate, and found it registered to Rebecca Riggins. I guess your friend uses an alias. We will run all prints on both cars. Did you ride in it at any time, I mean in the seat?" he amended with an apologetic grin.

"Yes, several times," I responded.

"Then, we'll need you for prints as well."

"Mine are on file, both at the Police Academy in New York as well as down at your place. I had to give prints for my Private Investigator's license."

"You know that the license is only good in Hustle, you have to take a state test and show proficiency to practice elsewhere in the state."

"I didn't know that." Now I was dejected. Things were not going well. "Anything else, Lieutenant?"

"That about wraps it up. We traced Felicity's phone number, she had it disconnected yesterday. She lived in a small apartment over a real estate office down next to the supermarket. Ever been there?"

"Jocko took me to the supermarket where he works, if that's the one you mean. I already told you that I didn't know where she lived."

"By the way," he asked, a bit too casually, "did you see Jocko last night?"

"Nooooo," I said, trying not to look too interested. Changing the subject. "Was the man on the bank shot with a .22?"

"Yes, he was killed in the same style as the man who tried to take you out in your room."

"Same person doing both shootings," I mused.

"Probably."

"Same gun?"

"Most assuredly."

"Hmmm," I muttered. "Seems to be easy enough. I wonder why no one shouts to me that they are the person behind all of this."

"Doesn't anyone come to mind?" the Lieutenant asked gently.

"You don't mean Felicity?" I gasped. "She's surely got nothing to do with this. She happened to leave before I did, and the creep must have stolen her car."

"Why didn't your kidnapper use his own car?"

"Even I know that there is not anywhere near enough room in a Volkswagen's trunk for a body."

"You may have a point," Lieutenant Howard conceded, "but I will be very interested in the fingerprint results when they come in."

"So will I."

"By the way," he continued, "the press is getting a hold of this. Your part has been kept fairly well under wraps, just that you were a witness. Best just to give them a 'no comment', if they should try to speak with you."

"No problem, Lieutenant," I said.

That seemed to be all of it, as Lieutenant Howard called for the check, paid it and we went back outside.

"Can I give you a lift home?" he asked.

"No thanks, I think it's probably safe for me to walk, and I want to walk, maybe clear my head. It helps me to relax too."

"O.K., but take it easy, and let me know if anything else happens. I'll get in touch with you tomorrow, with the fingerprint results. Oh, by the way, the motel room that your assailant was at, was registered to Charlie Underhill, the man who tried to shoot you."

" I remember." I shuddered.

I stumbled on home, not in the shape I had hoped to be in. Even so, it did manage to help me work some of the sore spots a bit. I worried about Felicity the entire time. I kept thinking that it was time for me to take some action, but the action kept taking me. I was worried about Jocko as well. He didn't seem the type to get into trouble, no matter what Roy said. I found myself wandering a bit, and happened to notice that I was near Roy's Shoppe. I got there quickly and entered the door. Roy looked up with a smile, but it left his face quickly. I must have looked pretty grim, as he asked, "What's the problem, After?"

"I guess I owe you for some tools," I said, then proceeded to tell him everything, except the part about Jocko. That Boy Scout had some explaining to do. I also mentioned Grits and his 'purchase', managing to convey a bit of disapproval. Roy had the grace to look a little uncomfortable, then shrugged. He looked at me again, then admitted, "I was going to tell you about the gun thing, just never seemed to be a good time. We all do what we have to do."

"Let's just forget about it, and as I didn't actually take any money, I can honestly tell the cops that I've never sold a gun here...not that they would ever ask me." I gulped.

"We'll leave it at that, but please, let me know if you get into a pickle and it causes a problem. Give me a chance to clean the place up."

"I owe you that, and I will if I can."

"Good enough, and don't worry about the tools, they are so

cheap at the garage sales, that I generally don't even mess with them. There are lots more in the shed out back, if you still need some."

I did need some, and went back to the shed, finding all that I needed for the job at Mother's. Feeling like the morning wasn't a total loss, I went back through the Shoppe, waved at Roy, and finished the walk home on sore, but dry feet.

There was still plenty of time left, so I got to work on the front door, and had a new dead bolt in before supper. I went upstairs to change clothes, and I discovered that Mother had taken the clothes out from the window, and laid them on my bed, window closed, room neat. For some reason, the clean clothes reminded me of Felicity, and I fell onto my bed, staring at the ceiling, trying to determine how she fit into this mess, and whether she was an active participant, or an innocent bystander.

I got up for dinner, going down the stairs without any real appetite for food or life. The food was great, I remember, but I don't recall what it was. I finished it, and walked back to Roy's, where I spent an uneventful evening selling old chains and some glasses to a man and his wife. She told him what to do, when to do it, and how he was ruining everything he touched. It didn't help my mood any, and I was glad there were no other customers. I grabbed my twenty from the drawer, locked up, and remembering my incident at last night's closing, slunk out the back door and crept home like a criminal.

I fell into a deep sleep, and awakened only after I slept through a long, stormy set of dreams, bed soaked with sweat, and feeling that I had somehow let Felicity down.

seven

Something ought to be done about the sun. It's never around when you need it, and then it decides to ruin whatever rest you get by poking itself into your PRIVATE bedroom, and announcing quite cheerily that you are a deadbeat if you stay in bed one second longer. Wednesday morning was worse than usual. Some silly bird was outside my window chirping merrily at nothing, no doubt, and between it and the sun, was making my much needed sleep-in a total disaster.

I rolled over and tried to reclaim my unconsciousness, but after realizing that sleep hadn't been all that good either, I tried to justify getting up. The last thing I had thought about was Felicity, so I got up guiltily, realizing that she might be in trouble and that I'd better get cracking, if I was to be of any assistance. There was also the Paul question. Where in the heck was he, or had he come home last night sometime? There was also the Jocko question. What in the world was he up to? Too many missing persons and too many dead ones.

I stumbled into the bathroom, and tried to clear my mind during my shower. Paul ought to be easy, if he wasn't in his room, then I'd call the newspaper and try to get past the numbskull at the switchboard. Then, I could run down to Police Headquarters, try to find news on Jocko, and see what the Lieutenant had found through the fingerprint results and other work he may have ferreted out.

Wrapped up in my robe, I shaved, and saw that my black eye was now green and yellow, with the white of the eye somewhat bloodshot. So, at least that was something, but still called for sunglasses. I took a look in Paul's room and saw no sign of life, and assumed he hadn't shown up yet.

I found some clean clothes, basically a pullover shirt and some passable jeans, still folded nicely from when Felicity had helped with the laundry. I began to feel a sense of urgency and decided to put things into high gear. I finished dressing, got downstairs and found the phone book in the living room. Looking up the Hustle Herald, I dialed the number and got someone that spoke in some unintelligible language to answer the phone. I plunged forward bravely, asking for Paul. Of course, they had no idea who I was talking about, so then I asked for Obituaries. The goof on the other end had no clue, so I finally asked testily for dead people….surprisingly, that got me through.

"Obits," I heard Paul announce into his mouthpiece.

"Where have you been Paul?" I asked. "Mother has been worried."

"Who is this?" he asked.

"This is After, you nincompoop, and you haven't been at the house lately."

"Oh, hi After! I took your advice and asked the switchboard girl out, and I guess I haven't made it home yet."

"What? You asked her out and it's been going that well?" I was impressed and let it show.

"Yep, I told her I was working with a Private Investigator, and that I had helped on the case, and she wanted to talk more about it, so we went out for coffee, and one thing sort of led to another." I could hear him gloating from here.

"I should have called yesterday, I guess. Mother needn't have worried," I said grumpily.

"You wouldn't have found me, I took the day off. Never got out of bed, well…except for showers and pizza." Definitely gloating now.

"I guess you'll be home for a change of clothes then?" I growled.

"Sure, but tell Mother not to wait supper on me, I can't guarantee I'll be there."

"Sure, Paul, sure. I'll tell her."

"Great!" He chortled, then he sunk to a conspiratorial whisper,

"She's an animal!"

"I'll bet," I growled again. I just couldn't help myself.

"She's so smart too, says I need laser surgery."

"What?"

"Laser surgery for my eyes, says I look like Pee Wee Herman with my glasses on, but like Brad Pitt with them off."

I felt nauseous, but refrained from asking if she needed glasses as well. Instead I congratulated him, and told him to bring her over, as Mother might need a new girl to cook for. I didn't tell him that Felicity was gone, and I don't believe it would have computed with him at this time anyway.

I went in to the kitchen to tell Mother, and she was relieved. She said, "I hope he brings her for supper soon, I have a new lasagna dish I've been dying to try out." She was back to her naturally bubbly self, and I felt a bit better that I had actually deduced something for a change.

Now for the police station, and Lieutenant Howard. I was hoping for some good news, like maybe that the case was solved, but I wasn't going to hold my breath. I approached the station, and wasn't paying any particular attention, when I received a bit of a jolt. There was the Volkswagen, right in front of me, and Felicity's car right next to it. Hustle isn't big enough for an impoundment yard, most of the work is done right in front of the Police Station, so I shouldn't have been surprised. Even so, it jolted me back to reality, and my concern for Felicity made me increase my pace, such that I was fairly running, and breathless when I entered the building.

By now, the desk sergeant was becoming accustomed to my increasingly frequent arrivals, and he actually paid attention when I asked him if Jocko had been on duty last night. He thought about not answering for just a beat or two, then shrugged his shoulders and said that Jocko had put in a full shift last night, but was probably at home by now. I then asked if I could see Lieutenant Howard, and he waved me on through. I went up the stairs, and into the large room that he shared. Looking around, I spotted him at his desk, so I walked over, half anticipating some good news and half dreading the potential bad news. I was just glad something might be getting done.

I stopped just short of his desk, as someone was dropping off some important looking documents, but he saw me and motioned me to sit in the chair across from him. He looked the documents over and added them to a pile of papers that had appeared since my last visit there.

"OK, After," he began. "First for the good news. Felicity hasn't shown up, her fingerprints were on her car, but nothing showed on the steering wheel. The bad news is, we don't know where she is. More bad news," and he paused. He paused again, looking at me. I felt my stomach doing flip-flops, and I tried using whatever part of my brain that was responsible to get it to calm down. Either my brain wasn't tuned in, or my stomach had a mind of its own, because the flip-flopping continued.

"OK, here it is… The fingerprints we lifted from other parts of the car match the ones the city has on file for you, no surprise there. Another set matches the corpse that you knew as Steroids, whose real name is Patrick Bacon. He was a small time hood, never brought up on any big-time charges, just mainly muscle for hire. It doesn't seem that he was the type to kill someone, but his greasy accomplice was. The man you knew as Charles Underhill, who is now resting by Mr. Bacon in the morgue. The third set of prints is the most interesting. We found a match right here in our own files. The third set belongs to a Ms. Felicity Jeffries, sister of Felix, daughter of Felicia. She was booked, but never brought to trial on prostitution charges about 10 years ago. Here's the mug shot." He slid a photo over to me, and there was no doubt that it was a younger version of my Felicity.

I sat in silence, somewhat at a loss for words. It just goes to show that you can't judge people, even if trained for it…not that I was actually trained anyway. Lieutenant Howard was watching me, and what he saw was apparently enough to make him say, "Don't worry, she was never charged, it was his word against hers, and the officer wasn't too sure of what was going on anyway. The man involved was pretty much in trouble all of the time, and was trying to plea bargain, after being caught with billfolds that weren't his. She was supposedly in on a pickpocket scam with him, and when he was caught, he told us about the alleged prostitution."

I was a bit mollified, but I was upset that I hadn't seen the connection between her and Felicia. They had the same body build; Felicity, Felix, Felicia were all similar names. Then there was the brief history that she had told me when we were discussing her, she had mentioned a brother, and leaving her home, I should have put it all together.

"Anyway," Lieutenant Howard continued, "her last known address was in Chicago at this site, does it ring a bell?" He slid an address across to me, but having no clue as to Felicity's past where-abouts, I was only able to nod dumbly in the negative.

"Now, remember, you aren't to leave town, so don't get any strange ideas."

"Am I still a suspect?"

"Let's just say that you are the only person still alive, or in town at this point that has anything to do with this case, and I want to know where you are. I have shared more information with you than I should, but I hope this will satisfy you for the present. As you may gather from what is going on here, this is now officially a double homicide case, perhaps a triple, and we are pulling everyone avail-able into it. Got it?"

"Got it," I sighed. "Can I go home now and digest this?"

"Sure, get lost. Check in tomorrow."

"OK, and thanks for the information."

I got up and found my way out of there, and walking home, I didn't know whether to be sore, happy, really mad, or just confused. I reverted to form, and opted for confused, at least I was consistent that way. Things were going to take some sorting out, and I decided to grab some food at Mother's, then go talk to the local gun smug-gler …Roy, and see if he knew more than he was letting on.

Lunch was on me, I was able to go to the kitchen and rustle up some leftovers. I found some cold cuts, bread and those fancy deli chips that Mother preferred. Finishing things off with a cold glass of skim milk, I retired to the dining room. While I was eating, I heard some strange noises, sort of like scratching sounds. I couldn't determine where they were coming from. I rose and went into the living room, but found no one. The noise seemed most noticeable by the front door anyway, so I went over to it, and cautiously opened it. Given what had happened at Roy's door the other night, I was prepared for almost anything. I wasn't prepared for this, however. I looked at eye level and saw nothing at all, but I did feel something brush past my leg. That something was a somewhat thinned down version of Soot, the irascible one had finally returned. I wasn't sure whether to be relieved or worried. I decided that any cat who would leave the house on the head of a greaseball deserved a hearty wel-come, so I said, "Stay out of my room, and we'll get along fine." He ignored me, and looked back toward the door. I started to close it, but wasn't quick enough. A bundle of fur swooshed past me and into the house, taking up its place next to the old boy. A small, somewhat thin calico cat was taking its stand by him, and showed no intention of leaving. As I reached down to pick it up, I received a hiss from the new arrival, and Soot bit my shoe.

This called for a higher authority, so I went off in search of Mother. I was working the entire house, but could not find her anywhere, when I heard a squeal of delight from the front room. Mother had found her baby, and was letting everyone know. The fossil bolted out of her room, as quickly as molasses on a sub-zero day. James wandered down the stairs, took a look and slunk back up. I marched in, and started to apologize for the uninvited newcomer, but saw Mother holding both cats and smiling as if her entire life had found meaning. "After, look, our friend is back, with a girlfriend as well."

I did the hardest thing I had ever remembered doing, and smiled.

"What are we going to name you?" She cooed as she carried them into the kitchen for a huge repast, no doubt. I got a good look at the two scalawag's faces as they turned back and deigned to glance at me. Soot's eyes were half shut in bliss, but the little hussy's were wide open with a promise of retribution for even thinking of trying to evict her from her new digs.

Oh well, at least I didn't have to feel guilty about Soot anymore, I just had to retrench and go back into my paranoia mode. Not that it would be too difficult to do that. I was pretty sure that someone still wanted me dead, and now that Soot was back, I could count on a few good maulings as well.

I went back to the dining room and finished my meal. I had a plan forming in the back of what was once my brain, and I wasn't entirely sure when I would be sitting here eating a square meal again. I really needed to talk with Roy, and I also had a few other errands to run. I bolted down the remainder of my food, and took the dishes into the kitchen, where a definitely mellow Soot was eating last night's leftovers and sharing his meal with the new hussy. At least Mother was happy. If Mother was happy, everyone would eat well.

"I was thinking of calling the new kitty 'Sugar', what do you think, After?" Mother asked through her smile.

"Doesn't really go with Soot too well, does it? What about 'Mud'?" Mother must have thought I was joking, and she laughingly shushed me out of the kitchen, saying that she would do my dishes. I gladly complied, looking back to see the old boy eating away, but the latest female in my life just showed me her pearly, pointed teeth.

I went upstairs, found a plastic bag in one of my drawers, threw in a few tee shirts, some underwear, a few pairs of socks and another pair of jeans. I went to the bathroom, got my toothbrush, my razor, a washcloth, and an almost new bar of soap and tossed them into the bag as well. I felt a little like the boy who was leaving home with the bag on the end of a stick, but I had to find Felicity. If I was going to be in trouble with Lieutenant Howard, I wanted to be sure that I had a good head start on him in any case. I needed to talk with Roy about some transportation to Chicago, and maybe borrow one of his guns as well. I was sure I'd be in a big pile of the smelly stuff when I returned, but I had decided that Felicity might just have some answers for me. I wondered why she had conveniently turned up just as her brother was going invisible, and her mother was going dead. I didn't suspect her of much more than being an innocent bystander that might know too much to be healthy for her, but as I was in somewhat the same boat, I thought we should ride this thing out together.

It was getting later in the day, and I decided to walk to Roy's a bit early, maybe take the long way and enjoy the walk, perhaps working some of the kinks out of my still sore muscles. It was a nice day, with a touch of the harvest in the air. You could tell that the seasons were about to change, a not unpleasant time of year. I like pumpkin pie, Halloween and pretty leaves, so this prospect was not unpleasing to me. The kids were out of school, presenting their usual roadblocks, and I spent some time sidestepping bikes and skateboards, as well as the peripheral junk that accompanies these items. Empty water bottles, crushed boxes of Jell-O, candy wrappers and comic books. The occasional condom lying around.

I was pleasantly tired when I got to Roy's, and I went straight to my office to relax a bit. Upon entering the room, I was met by about 100 pounds of teeth and snarls attached to a very lean, mean looking German Shepherd. I got out as fast as I could, shaking and not quite sure what was going on. I was greeted by laughs from Roy and another man, who was hard to see through the gloom of the early evening light.

"Don't you remember me, After?" came a familiar drawl. I forgot to tell you that I put my dog in your office so that she wouldn't eat my cab up while I was in here with Roy." It was Grits.

"What did you need a gun for?" I squeaked.

Grits laughed, "I really needed it to protect me from her!"

"I can believe it," I admitted. "Why are you back so soon?"

"Time is money, my man, and Roy has another shipment on its

way to Madison tonight, that I need to get loaded as soon as it is dark."

I didn't need to ask what the shipment was, but I was interested in how he managed to hide guns among whatever else he was hauling. So I asked, "What is the regular cargo that you haul?"

"Industrial waste, maybe even nuclear waste...it's all the same to me." He smiled, looking suddenly like a barracuda.

"Ewww, doesn't that stuff get into the g-g-...the other stuff that Roy has you haul?"

Roy laughed, "We're among friends here After, you can say guns in front of Grits. Besides, why should these people care how they're shipped? They'll mostly all die an early death anyway." I couldn't help it, he still looked like Santa Claus to me, so I decided to probe a bit further.

"Who do you sell these guns to anyway, Roy?" I asked.

"The Irish Republican Army, at least this trip. Maybe someone else next time." Depends on what I get my hands on, and who pays the most. It also depends on where they pick them up, Grits only runs in the Midwest."

"Oh, I see, and Grits is going to Madison tonight?"

"Yup," Grits offered.

"Guys," I began. "I could use a favor, and this seems to be a great opportunity to ask."

"Sure After," Grits spoke, "What do you need?"

"I need a ride to Chicago, I could be there a few days. I hope that won't put you out too much Roy."

Roy shrugged. "We all have our reasons for doing things, I can cover for you here, or just close early. What's happening in Chicago?"

"Maybe nothing," I admitted, then I told them the entire story, including that I might be in trouble with the Lieutenant upon my return.

"That's nothing. I'll be clean by then," Grits said offhandedly. "You're welcome to tag along, but you'd better get square with my dog first...give her some raw meat and if she lets you live, try to pat her head. If not, you'll have to find another ride."

"I don't suppose you have any raw meat around?"

"Just fixin' to feed her myself," Grits said, then tossed me a bag of scraps. I trundled over to the door, and opened it slowly. The dog just sat back and looked at me.

"Nice doggy," I offered. "Do you want something to eat?"

No response, so I left the door open for a quick retreat, then opened the bag and spilled its contents onto the floor for her. She looked at me, decided correctly that I was harmless, and came over to eat. I slowly put my hand out and patted her on the head. Amazingly, her tail wagged.

I heard a laugh behind me, and Grits stood there with a big smile. "I guess you'll do, she's never let anyone but me do that to her."

"What's her name?"

"Never named her, only had her a half a year or so, I'll get around to it sometime."

I didn't understand Grits at all, but I was very glad he was on my side, and I was grateful for the unexpected lift to Chicago.

Roy came up and said, "After, go ahead and put in a regular night, as we need to get this stuff loaded. Then, as you are now an official member of this group, take a few hundred for expenses. You might need it, as I don't think this girl will be easy to find."

I was so grateful, and it must have shown, for Roy just smiled and walked away.

Grits laughed, "He isn't being benevolent sonny, he's covering his butt too. Now that you are being paid, you're committing a felony. You're one of us now."

"Just tonight, then I'm forgetting any of this ever happened."

Grits roared out another hearty laugh, and followed Roy out, shaking his head.

"Well girl," I said to my new friend, "if you can behave yourself, you are welcome to join me at the counter." The dog got up and followed me to my usual chair, curled up and went to sleep.

I wasn't concentrating too much that evening. I was trying to figure out where all of this was going to lead. If I could find Felicity, I was going to have to figure out a way to get her to come clean with me. If she was holding out before, what was to keep her from holding out, or running away again? I was hoping to find her quickly, and catch her by surprise. She must have been planning on leaving Hustle before the day she actually left, as she had had her phone disconnected. That means she wasn't spooked the night of the kidnapping, even though that could explain why she left so abruptly. I was sort of upset that she left without telling me goodbye, or even leaving me a note. I realized that I didn't mean too much to her, but then, why had she spent so much time with me? Maybe she knew nothing about her brother and was trying to see what I knew, then, when Steroids and the Greaseball started putting pressure on me, she realized that she should leave as well. Why didn't she take her own car then? Why wasn't any trace of her found if Steroids had taken the car from her forcibly that night? Who shot Steroids? Had Steroids gotten rid of Felicity earlier, and come back for me? I had no idea how long I'd been unconscious, they could have had time to kill her, then come back for me. All of these questions, and I was getting ready to get into big time trouble with a very large Homicide Lieutenant by leaving town against his orders. I was only hoping that I could appease him with a few answers when I got busted.

The night went slowly, no one showed. It was 10:00, and I was cleaning the place up. I went out back with the dog, so that she wouldn't get uncomfortable while travelling, and locked the door behind me when I re-entered. I was beginning to wonder what the timetable was when I smelt cigar smoke coming from the main room of the Shoppe. The dog wagged her tail, and I guessed that Grits and Roy were back. I was only half-right; Grits was waiting alone for me.

"Are you ready pardner?" he asked. "Thanks for taking the pooch outside."

"As ready as I'll ever be. Where's Roy?"

"Probably home in bed, I have my own key. Well, I guess we'd better light her up and get out of here. It's an all night drive to Chicago."

I grabbed my plastic bag, and followed him out, remembering my money, and quickly darting back in to get the two hundred dollars that Roy had offered, plus this night's twenty.

I clambered up into the cab of Grits' semi, and sat on the surprisingly nice seat he had. Also, there was a bed, a TV, a small refrigerator and a mat for the dog behind the seat. It was pretty cozy.

"Looks like you do OK on the road," I ventured.

"When you live out here on the road, it pays to be as comfortable as you can, although I don't like too much stuff in here. That way no one will relieve me of anything. Even with the dog and gun, there are some rough people out there." He didn't look too worried by it all, so I decided to look cool about it as well.

We were on the road in short order. Grits smoked one cigar after another, but as he was my host, I said nothing and tried to breathe my air from the right side of the cab. The miles passed by, and Grits turned out to be a good conversationalist, regaling me with stories of adventures he'd had, or heard about while on the road. I started nodding off after midnight, and he asked me if I'd mind if he put on some tunes. I nodded that it would be OK, and was about to fall asleep, when I was shocked by what I was hearing. He was playing Mozart on a CD. I looked at him quizzically, then said, "I figured you for George Strait at night and Rush Limbaugh in the daytime."

He snorted, "Give me a break, do I look that stupid?"

I laughed, and prepared to sleep to the classics.

I awoke at several times, and heard Beethoven, Hayden and some opera that I couldn't place. Grits seemed to drive, eat, smoke and drink simultaneously, and I assumed I was in good hands. I looked him over a bit more carefully. He was a raw boned man with perpetual stubble on his face. Over six feet tall, he always smelled of tobacco. He had bright blue eyes that stood out from the darkness of the rest of him. Longish black hair that needed washing, a dark tan and of course, the cowboy garb. His voice was low and husky, due to his smoking, no doubt. Some time during the night I must have crawled into the bed in back, as I woke one time under a blanket and the dog piled unceremoniously atop me.

The rest of the night was uneventful, and I was still slumbering peacefully when Grits yelled back at me, "Wake up After, the next stop is yours!"

I got up, not disturbing the dog, rubbed my eyes and crawled back up front. "Grits, I really appreciate this!"

"No problem After, I hope you find what you're looking for."

He pulled into a truck stop, and let me out. As I was leaving, I shook his hand carefully, as I might need its use later in the day. He said, "I'll be here on my way back tonight around 10:00 P.M., if it so happens that you want a return trip. I'll have room for you, and your lady friend, if necessary. I'll wait till 10:30."

"Thanks again, Grits. I really appreciate it!"

Here it was, Thursday morning already. Had I really been on this case for 8 days? A lot had happened in that time. All for a lousy hundred dollars. I should have told Roy I'd rather run guns at two hundred a pop. I supposed you could get killed doing that as well. I expect that I was just not the criminal type. I always heard that you have to think like a criminal to catch one, and I wasn't doing well there either. I wasn't sure if Felicity was a criminal. I only knew that she was a girl, and I resolved not to think like a girl, if I could help it.

Grits had stopped right next to a Chicago Transit Authority

station, so it was just a matter of minutes before I was on my way into inner city Chicago, which was where Felicity had last worked. I was going to start there to see if they had any clues as to where she had lived. My guess was that she was still living here, and had just come to Hustle as part of the Felix problem. Nothing else made any sense to me. The question was, how did Steroids and the Greaseball fit in? Were they working separately, or were they following Felicity for some reason?

I got off at my stop, looked around and found a liquor store that had a newsstand associated with it. I went in and purchased a map of the city of Chicago. I was only a few blocks from my destination and I walked along the streets and marveled at how Chicago managed to be cold, even in August. Maybe it was due to the skyscrapers not letting the sun warm the streets. Maybe it was cool air coming off the Lake. Maybe it was the extra pollution blocking gamma rays or something. Anyway, I needed a jacket, and I hadn't packed one.

I arrived at the address, just before my core temperature dropped to coma level, and gratefully stepped into the foyer. The place was a small brownstone that had been converted to more apartments than it was built for. I looked at the names on the mail slots. Only half of them had names, some were yellowed with age, others simply had none at all. I decided that I was going to have to look up the manager, so I headed for the nearest door and knocked. A small, dark haired woman with a moustache to kill for answered the door with a grumpy, "Wha choo wan?"

"I am looking for a tall thin lady with brown hair named Felicity. Her last address was here."

I received a blank look in reply.

"Do you have a girl looks like that, or one that lived here recently?"

"No, on'y men live here."

"Really? There couldn't be a mistake?"

"No, there is one man has a cleanin' lady come in once't a while."

"Which one is his place?"

"Numba foah, at the top o' the stairs."

"Thanks, I guess that's better than nothing."

I was hoping this man might at least remember a girl that looked like Felicity. I went up the stairs, mindful that they were falling apart, and trying to find solid wood. I was just as glad that Felicity didn't live here, it was a definite downer.

I found a door, the number was long gone, but a lighter colored area remained, showing where a 4 had once resided. I knocked, and waited for some sign of life. I heard some rustling from the other side, followed by a few grunts and a sleepy, "Who is it?"

"I am sorry to bother you, but I was hoping you could help me find a friend of mine."

"Why would you be hunting for a friend? Friends are easy to find, 'less they're hiding from you."

"She's not hiding, but this is the only address I have for her."

"Must be a mistake, no female lives here."

"The lady downstairs said that you have a girl come in and clean every now and then."

The door opened and a small, beer-bellied man of about forty peered out at me. He looked me over, then correctly deciding that I was no threat, gestured me inside. The building might be a mess, but his apartment was very well taken care of. A small jewel among charred ashes.

"Nice place," I said, meaning it.

He looked at me some more, then asked, "Who was you looking for?"

"Her name is Felicity Jeffries, but she may go by another name. She is tall, thin, has brown hair, she is also an artist."

"Hmmmm," he mused, seeming to concentrate. "I dunno...."

Pulling out a twenty, I laid it on a small desk by the door. "Perhaps you can help me."

"Did'ja say she was blonde?"

Pulling out another twenty, I said, "No, she's got brown hair, shoulder length."

"Yes, she comes in here from time to time, straightens things up for me. Place needs a woman's touch now and then."

"Great!" I cried. "I have come from quite a distance to give her some news on her family. How do I get a hold of her? Does she have a phone number?"

"I dunno if she has a phone number, I just leave word next door at the Laundromat, there's a bulletin board there, and she checks it. Didn't answer my last message though. Maybe she's moved on. Too bad, she cleaned the place just as I like it."

I thanked him again and went downstairs to the door, exited and found the Laundromat to the right. I entered and found the lady in charge where she was napping behind the counter, a dead cigarette drooping from her mouth.

"Do you mind if I look at the bulletin board?" I asked. The lady, if that was what she was, slumped up to the counter, stubbing out the cigarette, then tossing it to the floor.

"Help yourself, handsome," the toothless beauty murmered back. "If there's anything else I can do for you, let me know." She then gave what she thought passed for a provocative wink, and went back to her seat, sitting astride it, and showing much more thigh than was necessary. She was probably thirty, but looked fifty. I felt sorry for her, but there was nothing I could do, or was willing to do. Life is tough in the big city.

I looked around for the bulletin board and found it between two of the noisiest, clattering washing machines ever built by man. I scanned the few items that were posted on it, but didn't find anything from a cleaning lady, or cleaning service at all. I did see the card from the man I had just left. It said: 'F....please come to #4 when you can.'

I looked again, then decided that there just wasn't anything there. Dejected, I looked around for another board, but was only able to find cracked walls, peeling paint and stains of indeterminate age and origin. I decided to try sleeping beauty again. I wandered over to her counter and stood there for a minute until her eyes could focus on me. She finally zeroed in and asked, "Did you find what you were looking for?"

"No, I didn't," I replied. Then more out of mercy than need, I pulled out a twenty and laid it on the counter. "I am looking for a tall, thin brunette that checks the board for cleaning jobs periodically."

"You just missed her, she was in here 10 minutes ago, and took her sign down."

"What! I was that close?" I felt like running out the door, screaming up and down the street. This meant two things. One, she was safe and alive, but two....she wasn't coming back. I looked and felt utterly dejected. So close, yet so far.

I just sort of stood there, empty of mind and spirit. The girl just stared back at me, we were obviously kindred spirits. I turned to go, not really thinking much at all, when she asked, "Don't you want to know where she lives?"

My heart leapt, and I turned back quickly, saying, "Oh yes, yes, can you help me with that?"

"Sure, she's just around the corner, go down two buildings on your right, turn the corner, #11, 2nd floor, apartment 'C'."

"How do you know this?" I asked, relief in my voice.

"I live across the hall from her."

I waved my thanks, and raced for the door.

She called, "Hey, you didn't stay for your twenty dollars worth!"

I stopped, then realizing what she was saying, said "I got a lot more than twenty dollars worth, thanks a lot."

I saw her smirk as I raced out the door.

eight

I walked the short distance to Felicity's building, and decided that I ought to slow down a bit and check the scene out. Something didn't seem just right. She had a call girl type neighbor across her hall, she cleaned houses, but may have had only one client, and that was only from time to time. The more I thought about it, the more I wanted to know. It was beyond being personal, I was now trying to figure out some apparent inconsistencies in how the facts were presented to me, and what I was actually observing.

There was a little coffee shop across the street, and it had lots of windows, so I decided to go in there, get some breakfast and watch the building for a bit. I was hungry, it had been a long time since yesterday's sandwich at Mother Teresa's and my feet were tired. I strolled over and entered the coffee shop.

It was a relic from the 50's; gleaming Formica counters, stainless steel chairs, black and white tiled floor. The character behind the counter actually wore a white chef's hat. The hat was spotless, starched and looked appropriate somehow. The entire facility was spotless. I relaxed, this seemed to be a good omen.

I found a table by a window where I could watch the place across the street, and sat down, my arches feeling immediate relief. It wasn't long before an aproned waitress came over with water and a menu. She smiled and said she'd be right back for my order, would

I care for coffee? I smiled my thanks and said that I would, black please.

I took a look at the edifice across the street. It was another brownstone, and looked to be in much better repair than the first building I had visited earlier. In fact, it seemed to be the only reputable looking place in the area, other than this coffee shop. I glanced at the menu, where every type of wholesome breakfast appeared, and I settled on pancakes, sausage, hash browns and orange juice. I had no idea when I'd eat again, so I decided to make the best of it, and find something that would stay with me for a bit. The waitress brought my coffee, took my order and waltzed away.

I saw no one enter or leave Felicity's building while I waited, and the street was generally devoid of significant activity. No panhandlers or street people nearby. The occasional customer to the coffee shop seemed to be the bright young business type, both male and female. I gathered that the neighborhood catered to people getting a start in life, and maybe the toothless girl at the Laundromat was the exception. It seemed more reasonable that a struggling artist, as Felicity claimed she was, might pick a place like this to live.

My breakfast arrived and it was as good as I had hoped. I savored it, and had a few more cups of coffee, which I rarely drink, as I usually get an upset stomach from it. I tipped the waitress, went to the restroom, and decided I was ready to visit Felicity. I was still carrying my plastic trash bag full of clothes with me, but otherwise I looked presentable. I left the shop and traveled the short distance to the front door. The wood was solid, the frame and windows in good repair. I wondered if her name would be on the mailbox, but then I remembered that I had already been told her apartment number, 2nd floor, apartment C.

I tried the door. It was locked, and that was no surprise. I rang the bell, and a male voice asked what I wanted and who I was. I replied that I was Mr. Coffman here to see Felicity.

"Who?"

"Felicity, tall brunette in Apartment C."

"Who is this again?"

"My name is Mr. Coffman.

"I don't know who you're talking about, but I'll tell the lady that lives in 'C'"

"I'd appreciate it."

All I got was a grunt. I stood there for quite a while, figuring that Felicity might not even be there, then wondering if she was, and might be ignoring me. No matter what, I determined to only wait ten minutes until I tried the doorbell again. Of course, this side of the street was chilly, and in shadow, so the coffee shop was starting to look good again, and I was beginning to resign myself to a day of waiting there. It was a nice place, so I wasn't sure how the management would respond to me hanging out there all day. Shifting my weight from foot to foot, I waited my ten minutes and rang the bell again.

"Who is it?" the same voice asked.

"This is Mr. Coffman, I was waiting to hear from Felicity."

"You're still here? No one answered her door."

"Can I come in and leave her a note, so she'll know how to get in touch?"

"No."

Just then, the door opened, and a very huge man came out. I smiled at him, but his face had no smile lines. He made Steroids look small. He looked me over and said, "Beat it." It was the voice I had heard on the intercom.

I said, "Listen, this isn't difficult, I just need to leave her a message, then maybe find a place to sleep tonight. I know she'll want to talk to me."

"You left your message...with me, now scram, before I have to get, you know, physical with you."

He didn't seem like a hood, just an overbuilt, overprotective house guard type. I had no idea how he fit into the picture. There was nothing else to do. I could leave under my own power, or be jet propelled someplace else. I nodded, and walked back across the street with as much dignity as possible.

I turned back to see if he was watching me, and he was, so I continued on past the coffee shop and turned the corner, out of sight. I found a doorway to stand in, out of the chilly breeze, and waited about ten more minutes, then went back to the corner and took a quick look. The large man was gone. I hustled into the coffee shop, took up my post by the window, and told the waitress that I was waiting for a friend, and if she could just keep the soft drinks coming. She smiled and tripped off to the urn, returning with a nice icy cola. I sat there, trying to figure what to do. The street still had no measurable activity, and it was still not quite lunchtime, so I figured it would be a long, slow morning.

I was correct, I saw the big man leave the building and go down the block. I was tempted to run over there and try the doorbell again, but I wasn't pleased about the prospects for my survival should he return abruptly. For once, my instincts served me well, as he returned almost immediately. Nothing else happened there until the lunch hour arrived. I had drunk so much liquids while waiting, that I had to go back to the bathroom, and because of that, I almost missed my opportunity. As I returned from the bathroom, I saw the toothless wonder coming home from the Laundromat. I threw caution out the window, and ran out the door of the coffee shop and called out to her just as she was about to enter her building. She turned, kind of squinted at me, then smiled and waved me over. I shook my head no and gestured at the coffee shop, and then called to her. "How about lunch?"

She thought for a moment, then shrugged, and yelled back at me, "Let me do a few things and I'll be right over. Order the special, whatever it is."

I went back inside, and ordered two specials. My waitress looked at me strangely, and I assume she saw what I was up to. I smiled back innocently, and she went on her perky way.

I sat there hoping that the big guy hadn't seen or heard anything. I guess everything was cool, as the Laundromat girl came out again in a few minutes, a nicer coat on, another cigarette in her mouth, and as she walked across the street, I could see that she had even changed into a nice pair of jeans. I hoped I wasn't getting in too deep here, and I determined to let her know my predicament up front. She entered the shop, came and sat down, put her cigarette out and smiled at me again. I noticed that she had dentures in, and she looked considerably younger. "Did you order?" she asked. "I only get 45 minutes for lunch, so I need to eat fast."

I assured her that I had, and it was only a short wait until we were served. "So, what did you want?" she asked directly. I knew that whatever she had to offer was on the table, it was probably just a matter of money.

I decided to play the gentleman. "Let's just eat first, my matter won't take long. Enjoy yourself."

She seemed a bit taken aback, but then decided to relax, and she did indeed enjoy herself, making small talk about the weather, her day job, and asking me what the weather and city was like where I came from. She was doing all of this while wolfing her food down. I called the waitress over and ordered my friend a large blueberry pie alamode and received another warm smile. I was in, if I didn't find a way to screw it up.

She was about done with her pie, when I cleared my throat, catching her attention. "Um, I do have a favor to ask of you," I began, "I need to get a hold of Felicity, but the guy at the door won't even acknowledge that she lives there."

"Oh, she lives there all right. She was there when I changed clothes a minute ago."

"She was?"

"Sure, she showed up yesterday, been gone for a week or two."

"That's right, that's when I met her. She was back in her home town of Hustle."

"Sounds right," she mused, then stuck out her hand, "I'm Sugar."

I shook her hand, "I'm After."

I got the usual look, and I shrugged and smiled. She grinned back saying, "Really, my name is Sugar. A lot of girls that work like I do use stage names, but mine is real. I dance at a club around the corner four nights a week."

"My real name is After, no reason to make up something like that!"

She smiled again. "Well, After, you've given me twenty bucks and a great meal, the least I can do for you is hook you up with Spice."

"Who is Spice?" I asked.

"That's Felicity's stage name, we used to do a dance act together, you know, 'Sugar and Spice'?"

"Oh, yeah, sure." I said, totally taken aback. "She told me she was an artist, I assumed she painted, or drew, or something. She even told me she needed to be inspired more."

"I don't doubt that at all, she does paint, and she's pretty good. She gave up the dancing a year or so ago, and cleans houses now."

I was relieved now, it appeared that she hadn't been lying at all. I ventured forth, "Well, how do you plan on getting me to see her?"

"I work till 5:00, meet me here, and I'll take you up to my room. Then, we'll try to find her from there."

"I don't think the big guy at the door will go for that."

"He'd better, that's his job. He doesn't let people in unless they are with one of us girls, then he'd better or he's out the door."

"Won't he think it odd that I was asking for Felicity, then show up with you?"

"Naw, he'll just think you're kinky. Now, I have to get back to work, and I'll be back here at 5:00. Be here, OK?"

"OK, and thanks Sugar."

"No problem, thanks for the chow." She got up to leave, and my only problem was trying to decide how to keep myself occupied for the next 4 hours.

Luckily, I was in one of the biggest cities in the world, and if you can't find something to do in Chicago, then you have no imagination at all. The only problem was that I was in a mostly residential area, and there was no way to get somewhere else except by public transportation, cabs being out of my price range. I decided to see if I could find a newspaper and a park, so I tipped my waitress and asked her where I could accommodate myself. She gave me directions to both, and told me it was only a 10-minute walk, so off I went. I found everything just fine, and spent a nice quiet time reading in a very nice neighborhood park. Detective work requires patience, and a high tolerance for inactivity at times. I was an expert at inactivity, having practiced it since puberty.

It was a quarter to five when I found a waste can for the newspaper, and began the walk back to the coffee shop. People were out more, the weather had gotten considerably balmier, and my spirits were rising. I was about to confront Felicity, and discover the answers to quite a few questions, or so I hoped. It would have been much nicer if she had just told me she was Felix's sister, but that explanation would have to wait until I talked with her.

I got to the shop just before five, and saw Sugar walking toward her house. She noticed me and waved me over, so I crossed the street and caught up with her at the door. She used her key, and sure enough, the big fellow was standing guard. He recognized me right away, and held up a meaty hand to halt our progress.

"What do you think you're doing Thomas?" she asked.

"This guy was here earlier, asking about Spice," he answered.

"So?" she retorted, "He's with me now." Sugar grabbed my hand and pulled me along. I decided not to look back, and followed her up the stairs. She was Apartment 'D', across the landing from 'C'. We went into her apartment first. It was simple and neat. She said, "This is where I live, I have another place where I work."

I nodded, trying to appear worldly, but totally out of my depth. She was bustling around, setting things just so, then went into the kitchen, returning shortly with a couple of bottles of beer. I smiled my thanks, and took a long draw from my bottle. She asked to be excused, and took her bottle into what must have been her bedroom. She returned a few minutes later, with too much make-up on, a skimpy outfit and high heel shoes in her hand.

"Getting ready for my dancing tonight. Most of my costumes are at the club, but you have to keep up appearances when you enter and leave. Do I look OK?"

I told her she looked fine, and she said, "Thanks, 'cause, you know, people always say that, but you don't really know if they mean it."

I replied, somewhat guiltily, "I guess you do run into some shallow people in your business."

She said, "Yeah, but then, everyone has to look after themselves, and I don't hold it against them. Finish your beer and we'll go across the hall."

I gulped down the remainder and stood up. I wanted to find some way of thanking her, and began to pull out another twenty. She placed her hand on mine and said, "This one is between friends, OK?"

I smiled, put the money back in my pocket, and followed her out the door, to the apartment across the landing. She knocked on the door a few times, and after what seemed an eternity, the door opened. Felicity looked out and saw Sugar first, started to smile, and then saw me. She turned pale, and began to close the door. I said quickly, "Felicity, I'm not here to cause problems, but I need some answers."

I thought she was going to finish closing the door, when Sugar said, "C'mon girl, this guy's been waiting to talk to you all day. I think he's nice, give him a few....OK?"

The door stopped just short of closing all the way, then opened slowly. "All right After, but five minutes is all you're going to get."

"That ought to do it," I replied. Sugar smiled, gave me a peck on the cheek and said it was nice to meet me, but it was time to go to work. I gave her a hug and ventured into Felicity's apartment.

It was a very charming, light, and airy room that she led me into. There were watercolor paintings in nice frames on the walls. Mostly outdoor scenes, like trees, waterfalls, lakes and mountains. I remarked on how nice they were, and she said, "Thanks, they're mine."

"I thought so," I replied, trying to find a comfort level that might not be possible. Then, a combination of relief, anger and fear caused me to blurt out, against any self-control I may have had, "Felicity, why did you leave, I was so worried, and Mother is worried, what were you thinking, how did you get away from that big guy on Monday night? Did you know I was almost killed?" I ran down, she didn't move, just stared at me.

"I take it back, After," she said. "Let's go out and get a bite to eat, I think this may take awhile. Let me change clothes."

I sat down, very relieved to finally have an opportunity to get somewhere on this thing. She was only gone five minutes, but she managed to do that simple, yet stunning look again. She flashed me a great smile, and I told her, "I'm underdressed. I have a change of clothes, maybe I could spruce up some?"

She pointed to the door, "The bedroom, go there and change, I need a drink."

I went into her room, and started through my plastic bag. I found my clean jeans, and a tee shirt. I hadn't planned on dressing up, I thought I'd be the next thing to a fugitive myself. I found my razor, and decided to use the bathroom off of the bedroom to shave quickly. I tried to keep my eyes averted. This was her private place and I wasn't going to betray her trust in sharing it with me by snooping. I made quick work of the shave, and came back into her room, feeling better. I grabbed my plastic bag and headed back into the front room. Felicity noted my bag, and said, "You can leave that here, no sense in dragging it all over town."

I smiled my thanks and walked to the door. She turned on a few lights, and followed me out. I was happy to see her again, and it appeared that she was going to talk to me, and allow me to go back home with some answers after all.

I hailed a cab, and asked her to pick the restaurant. She told the cabby the name of an Italian sounding place and we were off on our little adventure for the evening. She looked me over and remarked that my eye looked better, and wondered if I had stayed out of trouble. I told her about Paul's date, and that Soot had returned. We stayed in this cautious mode all the way to the restaurant. It turned out to be a cozy place with checkered tablecloths, real linen, and the obligatory wine bottle with the candle in it. I have always been a sucker for those, and my mood kept getting better. The menu posted outside the door was within my price range, and I would still have enough money to get a bus home, if I were to miss my rendezvous with Grits tonight.

We sat at a table, I ordered a bottle of Lumbrusco, and salads with the house dressing, and then I decided it was time to talk seriously.

"I won't get into too much detail, but did you hear about the attempt on my life, and the subsequent death of my kidnapper?"

"Yes, I did, and that's why I left town. I have a bit of a checkered past there, and I figured I'd better get going or I'd be hauled in as a suspect."

"I don't believe you are a suspect, any more than I am, but the Lieutenant wants some answers. There are too many bodies, and with your brother missing...."

She had the courtesy to blush at this, and said, "After, I am so sorry I didn't tell you everything, but believe me, I have my reasons. I think I can tell you most of what you need to know now."

"OK, that's fair enough, why don't you talk, and I'll listen."

The waiter arrived with the wine and the salads, and she talked while we ate.

"I left Hustle about ten years ago after I was suspected of prostitution." I raised my eyebrows, and she said, "Guilty, but the jerk that got me into trouble was a bad guy, and they didn't believe him. There was nothing to do but leave town and try again. I hit several towns before landing here. I worked the streets, but kept my eyes open for other opportunities. I also found that I had some talent in painting. I decided to quit the business and paint. There was no money coming in but I didn't want to work the streets again, so I landed a job at a club....dancing. That's where I met Sugar, and we came up with our act. It was lousy, but we got paid well. Then, all of a sudden, I was selling some paintings, and about one-year ago, I decided to quit the dancing and paint full time. I just wasn't selling enough, so I began to clean houses."

At this point, the waiter came back for our orders. We both ordered spaghetti with meatballs, and garlic bread. Her story rang true to this point, so I suggested we eat now, and finish later. She sighed heavily, said there wasn't much more, but that sounded good. Maybe we could finish back at her place when I got my bag. That decided, we sat back, and enjoyed our meal. I kept looking at her, wondering how she got into this mess. I guess she read my mind, as all she said was, "Like mother, like daughter."

I nodded, that was enough for me at this point. She kept looking at me, and then a tear rolled down a cheek. "Do you despise me now, After?"

"Not at all," I replied, and I meant it. I wasn't to judge her, I was no raving success story myself. She smiled, took my hand, gave it a squeeze, and held it for a bit. I returned the squeeze, then we finished up without any more conversation, but I took the time to look into her eyes, and I thought I saw hurt there, as well as a promise of, what? Friendship after all? I was probably deluding myself, but we were still here, and I thought the worst was over.

I paid the bill, and we went outside. I was looking for a cab, but she took my hand and said she wanted to walk a bit. That was fine with me, so we went by stores whose lights were just now coming on as dusk was settling. As we walked, she asked me where I was staying. I told her that I had made no plans, but now it looked as if I could return home tonight with a ride I had arranged. She was quiet for awhile, and we continued, hand in hand. It was much better weather than it had been during the day. There was no wind, and it seemed warmer. Maybe it was the wine, maybe the girl, but I was happy and content.

After a bit, she asked, "When is your ride?"

I replied, "I have to be at a truck stop by 10:00 tonight. I can get there via CTA."

"That's good then, perhaps we should get back to my place and finish this up?"

"That sounds good to me."

I hailed a cab, and we returned. I met no resistance from the man at her front door this time. I was beginning to wonder if he ever did anything else. We walked up the steps and entered her cheery abode. She fussed a bit, setting things the way she wanted, then asked me if I wanted anything to drink. I told her that water would be fine, I still had a nice glow from dinner, and didn't want to upset it any. She returned, gave me a nice tall glass with ice and water, then sat down in a chair next to me.

"OK, what else do you need to know?" she asked.

"Mainly, whatever you can tell me about your brother," I said.

"Felix," she sighed, "I never was too close to him He was five years older and truly wild. When I left home, I never expected to see him again, and did not keep in touch. Then, about 4 weeks ago, he shows up here. He'd made friends with Thomas downstairs some-how, and talked his way in. He never told me how he found me here."

Felix went up a few notches in my estimation, as I would have figured Thomas to be immovable. I sat back, convinced that I was about to hear the salient facts at last. I didn't expect any bombshells, but was about to receive one amidships.

She began, "Felix got up here, as I said. He told me that I was the only one he could trust. He said he'd found where I was a bit ago, and did a little 'research' as he put it to me. He thought I would be his ally. It seems that an acquaintance of his, the guy who owns the 'Green Frog' is into drugs, from the importing of them all the way through street distribution. Felix had been transporting some from the place where the stuff is packaged to whatever town the shipment was to go. He was never supposed to handle any money. Anyway, apparently, one of the people he delivered the drugs to claims he gave Felix $2,000,000.00 in cash. Harold Gibbons asked Felix for the money, and Felix had no idea what was going on, or so he said to me. Gibbons told him he had two hours to bring it to him, or he would die, as would his family members. Felix got out of town fast. He found me after a short search and that's when he came to visit me. I said we needed to go back to the guy who stiffed him for the two mill, and he agreed. He got the two guys that gave you a rough time, you know…Steroids and the Greaseball, and the four of us went to see the guy. After all sorts of problems, we got the money, but the Greaseball; Charlie Underhill, killed one of the man's bodyguards. We went into hiding, but Felix thought it was time to try to square things with Harold Gibbons, so he went back to Hustle. I guess that mom found out about some of it, and Felix set up a meeting with Harold, told mom he left some things in his apartment, and that she would be cared for, should anything happen to him. The most important thing was a key to a box he owns somewhere."

She continued after a sip of water and a deep breath. "Mom says he never came back from that meeting, so she went to his apartment, found it ransacked and didn't know what to do. She waited a few days, then went in, removed all that she could, cleaned it really well, and took everything she found apart, piece by piece, but whoever got there first, knew what they were looking for, and took it."

I sat up straighter, "This is where I come in, and where your mother suddenly becomes a liability. I have no idea if you are safe, but apparently Steroids had nothing against you, it is Harold Gibbons' goons that are eliminating people."

She nodded, "That's the way I see it, and now that they are gone, I really need to become scarce, at least until I find out if the two million dollars is still around somewhere."

"OK, so we think that Harold Gibbons is eliminating anyone associated with Felix until Felix comes clean, or Harold gets his revenge. There's a possibility that Felix is still alive."

"Maybe, but I doubt it." She started to cry. "We were never close, he wasn't a good person, but now I have no family."

I walked over to her, and stood near her. I said "The only questions I still have is why Steroids was kidnapping me, and who killed him?"

"I can't help you there, we weren't friends, and he was doing his own thing anyway. We had stopped talking. I think he showed at the 'Green Frog' to intimidate me as much as you."

That was about it, so I went to pick up my bag and started for the door. I turned to say goodbye to her, and saw that she had followed me. She reached up and touched my cheek. "After....what time were you going to meet your ride?"

"I should be going now, the schedule is a bit tight."

"What were you going to do if you didn't find me?"

"Find a motel room, keep looking and take a bus back."

"So, your ride isn't expecting you?"

"Not really."

"Do me a favor, sit back down and wait a minute, there is still one thing I need to do."

"Sure." I sat, a bit mystified, and expecting nothing much. Maybe she would offer a note from Felix, or names and addresses of the other participants in this mess. I wasn't prepared for what happened though. Felicity had been gone for about 5 minutes when I heard the door open to her bedroom. I turned and saw her standing there, wearing nothing but a terry cloth robe and a smile.

"Maybe you'd like a good, hot bath and a nice bed to sleep in, before you catch your bus tomorrow," she purred.

My bowels turned to water, my mouth went dry as a result. My pulse quickened, and I froze. She giggled and said, "I'll run the tub." Then she dropped the towel, turned around slowly and disappeared.

Well, damn....Grits was just going to have to get back to Hustle without me!

I know that you want details, but you aren't going to get many. Let's just say that we had a long, hot bath, went to bed with another bottle of wine, and didn't talk a lot. We did manage to hug and kiss a lot, and I went to sleep for a while. About 1:00 there was nothing to do but see if I had anything else to learn about her body, one thing led to another, and we ended up getting ready to shower again.

She left the bed and told me to wait a bit, then follow her in. I thought that sounded reasonable, so I rolled over to the nightstand and fumbled for my watch, to get a better idea of the time. I had drunk too much wine, and as a result, I dropped my watch into the partially opened drawer. I found the light switch on the lamp atop the stand, turned it on, and then opened the drawer a bit further. I reached down, and couldn't feel my watch, just a bunch of envelopes, pictures, trinkets and such. I got out of bed, pulled the drawer open, and saw my watch, I pulled it on, and noticed it was almost 2:00 AM. As I began to close the drawer, I noticed something else in it that froze my blood. I believe I even stopped breathing, the find was such a shock to my system. I grabbed the object, just to be sure, but I knew what it was. My long lost billfold, the one I last had the day I was searching Felix's apartment. The implications were immense. Felicity had conked me on the head, or knew someone who had. I was in the web of a black widow spider, and I was about to be wrapped up and disposed of. That wasn't the only explanation, of course, but in my addled condition all I wanted to do was get out of there...and fast!

I grabbed some underwear, got into my jeans, found my shirt and shoes and ran for the front door, stuffing my reacquired billfold in the other hip pocket of my jeans. I managed to get into my shoes, and was pulling the shirt on as I stepped into the hall. It was funny, I noticed that the light was on under Sugar's door as I careened down the steps and out into the now, very chilly air. I guess the big doorman did sleep at times, as there was no resistance as I fled into the abyss that passed for Chicago at night.

I got a few blocks before the panic left, and I hailed a taxi. I was torn between confronting her and forgetting her. I decided that the best thing to do was get back to Hustle and have a long talk with the Lieutenant, telling him what I had learned, and letting him decide which was fiction and which was fact. That meant telling him I broke into Felix's apartment and withheld information from the police too. I had time to ponder all of that, as the cabby took me to the Greyhound station. There was a bus leaving fairly soon to the large town near Hustle, and I figured I could find my way back to Hustle in the light of day. One thing at a time.

The bus was already there, and they allowed me on early, so I got as comfortable as I could, and fell asleep. I dreamt of being chased by a spider in a terry cloth robe.

nine

The large bus trundled through the night. I had started the night in a warm, soft bed, and was now perched sideways on a hard padded plastic seat, trying not to bang my head against the window too many times. There were five other people on board at first, but the number would vary as the bus stopped at every jerkwater town on its route. I was always being wakened by the hiss of air brakes, and the stops and starts associated with this type of transportation. Some of the people were quiet, some weren't. Everyone was trying to get some sort of sleep, with varying degrees of success.

I finally gave up on sleeping and remembering my reclaimed billfold, decided to have a look at it. There was no money in it. The few items that it retained were in disorder, but all accounted for. It was good to know that I need not reapply for my driver's license. Even without a vehicle to my name, it was nice to know that I could rent a car, or borrow one should the need arise. Checking the contents of my other pocket, I still had about fifty dollars left. I resolved to give this back to Roy as well as the rest of the two hundred he had so generously shared with me to buy my silence. I wasn't planning on turning him over to anyone, but I didn't want to 'owe' him anything either. The rest of the trip was spent with me sitting miserably by the window, waiting for the sun to appear. When it finally showed, I wondered why I had wished for it, as I was tired and it promised to be a long day ahead.

We got into the larger town near Hustle around 11:30 AM, and I still had to navigate my way back home. Hustle is an older town, no industry to speak of, and was now basically a bedroom community to the larger towns in this part of the state. People left town by 6:30 in the morning and returned by 6:30 at night.

I was about 20 miles away, and I decided that I could walk until someone took pity on me. The first few miles weren't bad, a few semis tried to blow by me and send me to oblivion, but after a while, that wasn't a problem. I got used to it, and besides, my feet were killing me. I had left Felicity's place without socks and my feet were chafed at this point. By concentrating on them and trying to hobble along on the gravel shoulder, I was barely aware of the trucks going by. I was about to give up when a large car pulled in front of me, stopping rather abruptly and causing a slight panic to well up in me. If some bad guys were still after me, I was dead meat, as I sure couldn't run, and fighting was never an option. The car looked familiar, and a blonde angel alit from the driver's side. "Hi After!" the angel said.

I recognized the girl from the doughnut shop…what was her name? Oh yes! "Hi Gloria." She beamed at me, no doubt for my startlingly good memory. I didn't become a Private Investigator for nothing. I generally remembered cute girls' names. I was even getting a handle on the old fossil's name, and knew I'd have it down pat in the next month or so.

Placing her hands on her shapely hips, Gloria asked in a mockingly stern tone, "Where are you coming from this time? The river's the other direction."

"Almost as bad," I replied, "I just got off the bus from Chicago."

"Do you need a lift?"

"I'll say, that would be terrific. Do you remember where I live?"

"Oh sure, in fact I drove by there yesterday evening, they said you were at work though, nothing about Chicago. I guess they try to cover for you, huh?"

"Nothing like that, they didn't know I'd left. It was sort of a surprise to me too." I got into the other front seat.

"Wow! P. I. Work must really be a thrill!" She grinned as she spun daddy's good tires in the soft shoulder and fishtailed into the traffic."

"There are other things more thrilling." I said as I tried to fasten my seat belt while retaining some equilibrium. She was a maniac, but no one seemed to mind as she weaved her car in and out of the paths of the various other cars and trucks. She'd wave gaily at the other drivers. The guys would wave back while the women would stare in astonishment that one of their own kind was so reckless. I was beginning to think that the Lieutenant would be the least of my problems, and wondered if Pastor James would be eloquent at my funeral.

We came back to earth just outside Hustle, and she slowed to sub-light speed. We managed to end up in front of Mother's, by some miracle, and I opened the door with all that was left of my strength, then managed a weak thanks as I fell out of the metal monster.

"Don't mention it....but...there is a price for my services." She waited, mouth parted, looking stunning.

"Sure, whatever, I'll pay it." I grinned, feeling better now that the ground I was on was no longer moving.

"I'll be by tonight at quarter to seven, you're taking me to the movies." She squealed off before I could respond. I was supposed to work, I had no way to get a hold of her and I knew that bad things were going to come of this.

I went up the stairs, and entered the house. It was generally quiet near noon, and today was no exception. My feet hurt on every step to my room, sending needles up both legs as I wearily advanced. I approached my bedroom door, and found a note taped to it. It read; 'After, Please call Lieutenant Howard when you get in. He needs to speak with you. Mother'. I dreaded the walk back down the stairs, but had to do it. I got to the phone, slumped into a chair and dialed the station. I asked for the Lieutenant, but he wasn't in. I left a message and somehow negotiated the stairs up again. I took a detour and went straight to the bathtub, poured some nice hot water, and got my shoes off, placing my feet in the water for a good soaking. Not as good as the last bathtub I was involved with, but definitely safer. In a few minutes, the ache had subsided, so I poured more water in, and removing the remainder of my soiled clothes, cautiously lowered myself in.

I soaked for 15 minutes, then got out, dried off and wrapped a towel around myself. I limped into my room, and fell into bed. I figured someone would awaken me when the Lieutenant arrived, or until the next disaster happened. I slept for about an hour, when there was a knock on the door. Mother asked if I was in, and I made some sort of noise that she must have taken for a 'Yes' as she said that the Lieutenant wanted me downtown in an hour. I mumbled something else that must have passed for an affirmative answer, as she left with a cheery laugh.

I managed to find a thick pair of socks with only a few holes in the toes, but I figured the cushioning effect would ease the pain of walking. I had left my other good jeans in Chicago, so I found my tan slacks, as well as a blue shirt with all of its buttons, and walked down the treacherous steps again, to find the feline contingent at the base of the stairs.

I warned Soot, "Don't try anything today smart aleck. Just remember, if it weren't for me, you wouldn't have found the little princess here." Soot was his usual unimpressed self, and proved it by yawning in my general direction, then walking off in a stiff-legged fashion. His admirer followed suit, and I gave them no further mind and began to think about my immediate future in jail.

I went through the now familiar routine, and ended up at Lieutenant Howard's desk, this time as a penitent. I was forced to stand nearby while he pointedly ignored me. He read several pages of typewritten copy, then giving me the briefest of stares, indicated that I should sit down. I did so, relief flooding the soles of my feet. He didn't glance at me again for several minutes, and seemed intent on intimidating me. It worked too, I was intimidated, though I had no idea how much he knew.

Finally, he sat up, took me in and said, "We need to go downstairs, to the interrogation room."

"Why?" I asked. "I'm cooperative."

"Because, I am going to book you, as a material witness."

That got my attention, but I wasn't surprised. I offered though, "Isn't there a better way to do this?"

"I could take you out back and work you over, but that wouldn't be professional, now would it? I trusted you, and you let me down. Let's go." Then he rose, and started walking without looking back, so I got up and followed, like the whipped puppy I was.

We went through the maze of halls, cubicles and desks, finally ending up in a little room off the main entrance to the headquarters building. We entered the room, the Lieutenant turning on an overhead light and having me sit on one side of a large library desk, while he sat on the other side. He opened a drawer on his side, pulled out a tape recorder, checked to see if it was working and spoke into it, describing the particulars of our situation, explaining again that I was being booked as a material witness, and that I was considered a risk to flee.

After the preliminaries, he looked at me, had me state my name, then read me my rights, asking if I understood the charges and if I wanted a lawyer. I said I did, and didn't.

"OK, After, where were you last night?"

"Chicago."

"Why were you there?"

"I was trying to locate a friend of mine."

"Did you remember that I asked you not to leave town."

"Yes."

"Why didn't you inform me that you were leaving?"

"The situation arose quickly, and I just left, that's all."

"You do realize that we have two murders, another person dead and two people missing, don't you?"

"I found one of the people," I offered.

He raised an eyebrow. "Who did you find?"

"Felicity Jeffries."

"Where is she now?"

"I have no idea, I left her after I found her, and whether she intends to get in touch again, I have no idea."

"Is there anything else I need to know?"

"Probably, but if you don't mind, this is probably a good time for me to consult an attorney." We were getting near the point where I was going to have to come clean about the break in at Felix's, and once I started down that road, there would be no turning back.

"OK", he stated into the recorder. "The interview with After Coffman is terminated pending his acquiring an attorney." He shut the machine off.

"Would you like to hear some things off the record?" I asked.

"Love to," he grunted, "but I think we'll go by the book. You can make your phone call now."

I was torn between calling Roy or Mother Teresa, and decided on the latter, as Roy may not be whom I wished to be associated with criminally. I got to the phone, told Mother I was booked and if she could find an attorney willing to work with me, I'd appreciate it. She clucked and said that she'd see what she could do, and hung up.

The Lieutenant led me to another officer, and told him I was about to become a guest there. The officer took me to a small room, took the mug shots, redid my fingerprints and was about to give me some state issue clothing, when he was interrupted by a phone call. He answered, got a bit offended by what he was hearing, glared at me a few times, then said, "I guess you know someone important, you are apparently free to go. Don't go out of the city unless you check with the Lieutenant first."

"Does the Lieutenant know about this?" I asked.

"That was him on the phone, guess you have friends in high places."

I looked confused, and it must have shown, as he finally gave a quick grin, and showed me the door. I walked out, went to the front desk and asked, "Do you know when I am to be in court?"

The officer looked at me and said, "There are no charges anymore, so no court either."

I got out of there before he could change his mind. I was walking back to Mother's when I decided that it was time I treated myself. I went into the local clothing store and bought myself six pairs of socks, the good ones, with the gold toes. They were all one color, in case I needed to appease the washing machine gods again. I was learning the ways of the world; women, washing machines and cats were slowly coming into focus. I felt that an offering or two to all of them might make life easier for me.

I got home without further incident, and as it was only mid-afternoon, I decided to fix the dead bolt on the back door. I had already fixed the front door, and I wanted to return Roy's tools tonight.

Mother came back to see what I was doing, and I told her that I had found a mysterious benefactor. She smiled at me, and said that she knew.

"Was it you?" I gushed.

"No, it was Carol, she is the Mayor's grandmother, you know, and she vouched for you."

"Who is Carol?" I asked.

She looked shocked and stated, "The nice lady that lives on the bottom floor here. You break bread with her every day."

"Oh…that Carol," I stammered, red faced. Mother just looked at me, shook her head and prepared to leave. Then she turned around as if to ask me something, thought better of it, and stopped.

"What is it, Mother?" I asked her.

"I was worried about Felicity, is she what all the commotion is about?"

"She's involved, but it isn't the entire story," I said.

"Will we see her here again?"

"I doubt it," I replied.

She shook her head again, then walked back to her kitchen. I finished the dead bolt, got the tools together and went back to the front of the house, looking to thank Prunella.

I didn't find her anywhere, but I would surely thank her when I got the chance. I decided to watch a little television and rest my feet for a bit. Things were very quiet, and I found myself sliding in and out of sleep, my head falling to my chest from time to time. I had just decided to get up and take a breath of fresh air when I heard a knock at the door. Mother bustled to it and I heard her give a gasp, then talk excitedly to our visitor. She came in with the newcomer in tow. I couldn't have been more surprised, as it was Felicity!

I got up quickly, but Felicity motioned for me to sit. Mother smiled and backed out of the room.

Felicity asked, "May I sit down?"

"Sure," I managed to croak. "What are you doing here? How did you get here? Why did you come back?"

"Last question answered first," she said. "I came back to take care of whatever business I have to, whether it is the cops, or my brother. I don't really want to confront Mr. Gibbons. I was hoping you'd be able to help me with that."

"I just got out of jail, I don't think I'll be much help to you." When she gave me a questioning look, I continued, "The Lieutenant didn't like me skipping town."

She nodded, then said softly, "I guess you want to know about the billfold in my drawer?"

I guessed that she was correct, and nodded my head.

"Well, it's like this, I was going to my brother's apartment, and I saw the door open a bit. I heard someone in there, so I took off my shoes and sneaked in as quietly as possible. I saw you snooping around, and all of a sudden, you seemed aware of my presence. I did the first thing that came to mind and hit you with a shoe. I'm so sorry, I didn't know who you were or why you were there. I thought you might be one of Mr. Gibbons' men. I took your billfold and got out of there. I didn't know what I was going to do about you, whoever you were. Imagine my surprise when I saw you at 'The Green Frog', and associated you with my phone call and the apartment. I had to get to know you before I'd admit to hitting you. Once I knew you, things were going so well, I just kept putting it off. After, I am so sorry. I wouldn't hurt you," she pleaded, with wide-open eyes.

I was elated, the explanation made sense. I was relieved and happy. I could relax around her again, but I had to ask, "Is there anything else I need to know? Any more surprises?"

"I honestly don't think so," she said, looking straight at me. "If I think of something, I won't make the same mistake, and I'll tell you....OK?"

"Sounds good to me!" I allowed myself a smile. The smile was returned, and things got even better, as Mother came in with cookies and milk. What a woman! Felicity and I both thanked her, and she smiled back, informing Felicity that she was welcome for dinner. Felicity looked at me, and I nodded yes. Mother bustled out of there, saying that she needed to go to the store and for us to just relax and get 'caught up'.

"How did you get here?" I ventured.

" I rode the bus to town. I don't see how you got here though, that's the only one that comes here all the way from Chicago."

"I took an earlier bus, and hitched the rest of the way in."

"Do you think we can start all over again?" she asked, giving me the big eye treatment again.

I melted, "Of course, and the first business are these cookies!"

We dove in, then relaxed and watched some television, just making small talk. I told her I bought some socks. She laughed and said that we might go back to the Laundromat again tomorrow. She got up, went to the front door and returned with my plastic bag full of clothes.

She smiled and handed them to me, saying, "Honestly, it took me awhile to figure out why you left. I went looking for you, and even asked Thomas if he'd done something to you. He said 'No', and when I went back upstairs, I saw the drawer open, saw what was missing, and figured it out. I told Sugar that I was leaving for good, and I'd get back to her as to where to send my things. I don't think I'll ever go back there. My next stop is the police station, maybe they'll give me my car back, do you think?"

" I doubt it, not right away, it's associated with a murder. Let me call the Lieutenant, and see if I can smooth things over."

"Thanks, After," she said and took my hand. We were getting close to kissing, when the front door opened and Hal barged in.

"Hi guys," he waved as he strode up the stairs. We waved back, but the mood was broken. I walked to the phone and dialed up the Lieutenant.

"What do you want, Coffman?" Lieutenant Howard growled.

"Would you be interested in speaking with Felicity Jeffries?" I asked triumphantly.

"You bet, just name when and where."

"She's here at Mother's, and wants to speak with you."

"Put her on, After!" he cried. We were back on a first name basis again; I could sleep better now.

Felicity went to the phone, talked for a few minutes, then came back in. "I have to see him tomorrow, and he'll see what he can do about getting my car back then!"

"Sounds great!" I gushed. "Looks like things may work out after all."

"Maybe," she replied evenly. "I am going back to my rented room, as I paid through the month anyway. I'll go do that now, and see you for dinner!"

"Great!" I exclaimed, as I showed her to the door.

I was relieved that things were OK with the Lieutenant, and that Felicity was back in the picture. It had been worth the trip to Chicago to get all those loose ends tied up. My feet didn't hurt at all as I danced up the steps to my room, carrying the bag full of my clothes and bathroom supplies. I made short work of returning things to their proper places, and had time to clean up and shave. I was determined to let the Lieutenant handle the rest of the case, as Mr. Gibbons was a bit out of my league anyway.

I heard the phone ring, and Hal came to my room a few minutes later, saying that there was a crying woman calling me. I wondered what could have befallen Felicity, and raced to the phone to see what it was all about. To my surprise, it was not Felicity.

"After?" the lady sobbed.

"Yes," I answered, mystified by the unfamiliar voice.

This is Bitsy, Jocko's wife, do you know who I am?" Her voice was unrecognizable through the tears and shaking.

"Sure, is something wrong with Jocko?"

"I'm not sure, and I don't know who else to call," she wailed.

"OK, calm down if you can, and tell me about it." I tried to sound professional and reassuring.

"Well," she began, "I called for him last night, and his watch commander said he didn't show for work...again. I asked what he meant by that, and he stated that Jocko had missed quite a few nights lately. Jocko didn't come home this morning, hasn't called and his supervisor claims that it is an 'Internal' problem, and that they are working on it."

I didn't know what to say, so I just asked, "What would you like me to do?"

"I really don't know," she sobbed, "but you need to do SOME-THING."

I told her I would get on it, ask around, and for her to call me if anything came up. I decided to go into work early and get Roy caught up with developments, and ask his advice about Jocko.

I told Mother that I was going to be leaving early, and she said she'd fix me a sandwich to go. I sat at the table and tried to figure out just where I was. I figured I had paid Felicia back, and the Lieutenant knew all he needed to know anyway, except for Gibbons' potential role. I planned on asking Felicity to tell him about all of that, and I didn't care if she told him about finding me in the apartment. I felt that perhaps I had heard the last of the case after all, and could concentrate on Jocko. I remembered what Roy had told me about Jocko's start in life, and his more recent past before Bitsy came into his life, and I was sort of worrying that he might show up in a crack house somewhere.

Mother came out with a large brown bag and a thermos. I got up and hugged her and told her thanks. She grinned, then said, "You know, I think we will name the new kitty 'Mudsy', it does sort of go with Soot, don't you think?"

"It sounds fine to me," I said, not really caring. I was sure I'd have new names for both, even though they had behaved themselves so far. I was ready to go, and was actually out of the door, when I thought of one thing, that led directly to another. I retraced my footsteps and went back to the kitchen.

"Mother," I began, "I forgot that Felicity was to show up for dinner. She has no phone and I can't reach her anywhere. When she shows, could you tell her I went to Roy's early to work on a new case?"

"A new case?" she beamed, then looked concerned, "I hope it's less dangerous than the last one." I didn't have the heart to tell her it concerned her precious Jocko, so I shrugged and said it may amount to nothing, just a temporarily missing husband.

She grimaced, then smiled and said, "I had already thought about Missy Felicity, and I was going to tell her that you were at Roy's. I packed a double meal for you two."

What a saint! I hugged her again, then got to topic number two. "Uh, Mother, that little blonde girl that dropped me off this morning wanted to return tonight, and I don't know how to reach her either. I will try her work, but if that fails, please give her my regrets and get her phone number."

She looked at me, smiled and said, "You and Paul, with your girlfriend problems."

I replied, with a question in my voice, "Paul has a problem? I haven't even seen him for days. I thought things were going well."

"His girl wanted him to get his eyes fixed, then a nose job, then yesterday she said to perm and change the color of his hair. Today she suggested elevator shoes to make him taller."

"Has he done any of this?" I gasped.

"He can't, not on his salary," she said. "I think it will be over soon, and she hasn't even been over to eat."

What a cad that Paul was, to deprive Mother of a new female to feed! Mother said that she'd tell Gloria that I was on a case, and tender my regrets. I thanked her again, and headed to Roy's, planning on stopping by the doughnut shop on the way.

It was a nice night, and I felt pretty good about everything but Jocko. I hoped that it was something he had to do, and that there would be a good explanation for it, but I had my doubts. I was going through things in my mind as I approached the doughnut shop and I almost missed it. I came to my senses when the smell assaulted me, and entered the door. There was a man behind the counter, looking bored. I went up to him and asked, "Is Gloria here?"

"You her father?" he asked.

I bristled at that, as I was maybe 5 years older than her, tops! "No," I replied, "just a friend, but I need to get a hold of her."

"She's probably home, why don't you call her there?"

"I don't have her number."

He squinted at me, and asked suspiciously, "If you are her friend, why don't you have her number?"

I shrugged and replied that we hadn't gotten around to it yet. He glared at me, and decided that might get rid of me. It didn't.

"I'd appreciate the number, as we were to meet this evening, and I won't be able to manage it."

He said, "I would never give out a number without her permission, all I can say is that you're on your own and unless you want to buy something, I'd prefer that you leave."

I turned and went to the door, unable to block the sound of his laughing at some private joke he must have thought up. I left with as much dignity as I could. Her father! Indeed!

I got to Roy's about 5:00, and I heard him bustling about in the back, so I went to my office and sat down to think. He came by a moment later, and peeked in. "I was hoping that was you. I heard the bells over the door, and thought I'd check though. Everything turn out OK in Chicago?"

"I found my friend, and she's back in town. You may get to meet her this evening, and I have a few things to run by you."

He was preparing to come in and chat when I heard the bells tinkle over the door again, and he shrugged and went out to service his visitors.

Things got quiet for a bit, and I was thinking that I might be able to use Felicity's car tomorrow if she got it back. I was intending to ask Roy about Jocko's old friends and where I might find them. Some were out of town, I remembered, and I thought a set of wheels might come in handy.

I began to hear raised voices and there was some sort of argument going on, then all sound stopped. I got up and went out the door of my office, and looked around the corner. As I've stated before, my office door is somewhat hidden from the main counter, so I was able to observe what was going on. There were two men with their backs to me, and they seemed to have guns pointed at Roy, who was staring calmly back at them. If Roy saw me, he gave no notice. I had no idea what was going on, but I owed Roy, and we'd figure out what this was about later. I grabbed a lamp stand by my door, and walked quietly behind one of the goons. Roy surely saw me now, so I figured he was on his own with one of them. I raised my weapon and conked the guy on his head with what I hoped was enough force to put him out of commission, but not permanently. Roy ducked down, and the other guy shot at the spot Roy had just been. He turned to look at what had happened to his partner, saw me, raised an eyebrow, drew the gun on me, and I thought it was over, when Roy's voice said, "I've got a bigger gun than you have."

The goon glanced at Roy, and looked into a 10-gauge shotgun leveled at his pointy head. Discretion being the better part of his limited valor, he wisely dropped the gun.

Roy glared at him, then said, "You tell your boss that if he wants to see me, he comes here himself, without his friends, talks nice and polite, and we'll get something worked out....got it?" I swear, he still looked like Santa Claus, but with an attitude. The now cowed man nodded yes.

Roy said, "Thanks for the two new guns, I appreciate them, now take this trash out of here." Roy pointed at the unconscious man, who twitched slightly, and let out a groan. Good, I hadn't killed him. The man picked up his partner by the shoulders, and dragged him out. Roy looked at me and winked. I fainted.

When I came to, Roy was over me, with a concerned look. "After, are you OK, buddy?"

"I think so, what happened?" I groaned.

"I believe you may have gotten carried away in the excitement."

"What was that all about?" I asked, sitting up gingerly.

"Just the cost of doing business." He handed me one of the guns he had just acquired. It was a .45, and it looked large enough to blow down a tree. "He won't be needing this anymore, but you might consider packing it. I notice that it is unmarked. Some one, probably a criminal, filed the numbers off." He winked at me again.

"Criminals..." I muttered. "Where would we be without them?" I took the gun, hefted it, and resolved to get out in the country soon, practice shooting it, and see if the recoil would break my wrist.

"That's the spirit!" Roy said, slapping me on the back.

"Roy, there are a few things we need to discuss," I started. "First, I don't want to be involved with you and Grits, so I'm paying the two hundred dollars back, and I don't want to know anymore about it."

"Fair enough," Roy said. "Let's just say that you paid your debt off tonight, I think that's more than fair."

"OK." We shook hands. "I need to find out more about Jocko too. He's missing and Bitsy is worried."

Roy looked concerned, and sat down. "You'd better fill me in."

I began by telling of the trip to Chicago, leaving out a bit or three. Then, I told him about Bitsy's call. He looked concerned, and said, "I really thought he might be able to put his past behind him. I was rooting for the kid." He sighed, got up and followed with, "I'll ask a few people to keep their ears open, maybe we can find out something by morning. Come back here and check in then, OK?" I think things will be quiet the rest of the night, if you want to go home."

"No, Felicity is coming in to eat supper, Mother packed us a few things."

"That's great, I can't wait to meet her. I sort of remember her as a skinny little girl, before she ran away from home. Hope she turned out OK."

"She's had some rough times," I said. "I think she's working on it though."

Roy cleaned up a few things, hid the other gun and replaced the shotgun under the counter, then left with a cheery wave, calling out, "Don't worry, we're even now After. Thanks again for bailing me out!"

I felt better. I was off the hook for the guns, and I could look Grits in the eyes and act naturally around him, not having to take any orders from that quarter either.

I was looking forward to a nice quiet evening with Felicity. As usual, I was about to discover that things rarely go that easily.

ten

I sat at the counter and waited. It was 6:30 P.M. when the door opened and Felicity waltzed in. She'd done whatever it was that she would do and looked elegant again. I couldn't see exactly what it was precisely, but she was able to manage it. No one else had come in and I was sure our two visitors would not return, so I felt comfortable with spreading the repast out on the counter for us to eat. Mother had packed turkey sandwiches, heaping with onions, lettuce and tomato, plus that fancy gray mustard. There were homemade chips, steamed vegetables that were still a bit warm, and the thermos was filled with tea. For the finale, there were two large slices of chocolate cake. How she ever packed all of that into that sack, I'll never know. I would have to find another bag just to pack the trash out. There were also napkins and plasticware to supplement. She even had two of those little wet cloths to wash our hands with when we were through.

"Wow!" I gushed, when it was all laid out.

"That's not all," Felicity said with a grin. She had a bag with her, and she pulled out a chilled bottle of Zinfandel and two plastic glasses. This was going to be a treat indeed.

We were well into it, and basically just had the cake to eat, when she opened the bottle and poured us both a drink. We raised our glasses for a toast, when the bell tinkled over the door. I smiled apologetically, and she smiled with understanding. I looked to see who entered and was shocked to see Gloria there. She had her hair all piled up on her head, beautiful make-up, a short pink miniskirt that showed five miles of great legs, and a neat tube top that showed off the rest of her body and her tan. I was sure I had stopped breathing. She was carrying a bag with her.

"After, I stopped by the house, and Mother said you had to work. I guess you didn't have time to tell me before I raced off." She smiled, and I felt dizzy. What a knockout!

Then, Gloria's eyes seemed to become accustomed to the darker room, and she noticed the situation, and took it all in at one glance. The air turned 50 degrees colder as she said frostily, "I didn't realize you had company." Barbie doll had turned into the Abominable Snowwoman just that quickly.

"Gloria, meet my friend, Felicity," I offered. After all, this wasn't my fault; I was an innocent bystander, but was afraid I would be the only real casualty. It certainly looked that way. I turned to meet Felicity's eyes, looking for a friendly smile. I saw Godzilla's eyes. They could also have been the eyes of a large cat just before it devoured its prey. I couldn't tell if I was the prey or if Gloria was.

"How do you do?" Gloria asked in a quavery voice.

"I do very well, thank you," Felicity said, the edge in her voice very plain.

"Gloria," I said, "I was never going to be able to go tonight, and I had no way to contact you."

"I understand, After," she replied, and then it looked like all of the air went out of her, and she placed the bag down, turned and walked out the door.

I turned again, to see Felicity gathering things up. "What are you doing?" I asked.

"I can see that I am not welcome here," she stated.

"Oh Felicity," I started. "She picked me up the morning after I was kidnapped, and again this morning as I was hitching back into town."

"How convenient," she almost whispered. "Both times you had just gotten rid of me. I'll bet you were simply crushed."

"Now wait a minute," I said, but that's all I got out because she floated to the door, opened it, stood there in silhouette and slammed it behind her as she left. I waited until the vibrations and quakes in the building stopped, and until the temperature of the place went up a few degrees, then I took a look at the food, and the bag that

Gloria had left forlornly by the door. Our wine was still untouched as I went to pick up the bag, which I intended to return it to Gloria. I soon discovered that it wouldn't be necessary, as she had brought food as well. It was Chinese, with another bottle, this time of champagne.

There were days that I was so hungry I would have almost eaten out of trashcans. There were days I had met beautiful women that I would love to spend some time with. So, how did I end up with two gorgeous girls and two great meals at one time, and then....to be suddenly bereft of both.

I raised my plastic wineglass to the door and saluted, "To lousy timing," I said. I drank the entire bottle, but didn't enjoy it at all. I didn't enjoy the entire bottle of champagne either. The walk home was interesting, and I must have heard something funny in my head, as I giggled all the way there, occasionally breaking into a loud chuckle. I noticed that the other people who were still abroad at 10:00 that night gave me a wide berth. I navigated the steps to Mother's, placing the empty bottles in the trash, and the two pieces of cake on the counter. I put the uneaten Chinese in the refrigerator and trudged to the stairway. I was halfway to my room when I accidentally stepped on Mudsy's tail, causing her to emit a loud screech. She literally ran up my leg, using her claws to dig into my flesh, and then jumped off out into space, landing with a thud in the living room below. Soot came out of nowhere and gazed at me with a promise in his eyes. Hal, James, and the fossil came out of their rooms to see what had happened. I looked at all of them, then shook my head and dragged my injured leg the rest of the way to my room.

I took off my clothes and was preparing to fall into bed when Paul barged in. "After, something must have happened. Mother and the rest of the folks are all downstairs. Something about an accident and Chinese food, and wine bottles. Do you think a truck overturned in the street and killed a Chinese person?"

"Worse." I moaned and rolled over, falling asleep instantly.

The next morning, I awoke to hammering noises. I went slowly to my door, looking to see where it was coming from. It wasn't in the hallway. It seemed to be behind me. I turned quickly, and the room was revolving in a strange manner. I fell to the ground and realized the hammering was the pulse inside my swollen brain. I crawled back to bed, found my trash can and threw up in it. I felt a bit better then. I took inventory to survey the damage. My leg was swollen around the claw marks left by Mudsy. My heart was swollen from Gloria's and Felicity's claw marks. My head hurt and I was in foul temper. Now the room stank as well. I tried to stand again, it was OK if I didn't move too fast. I gathered up the trashcan, took it into the bathroom, flushed the contents down the toilet, rinsed it in the bathtub and ran that mess down the toilet as well. I found some aspirin and iodine in the medicine cabinet. I dabbed some of the iodine on my leg, thought about drinking some, but decided to stop feeling sorry for myself. I took a few aspirin, and managed to get back into the bedroom, where I fell asleep again.

Late that morning, Mother knocked on the door and came in. I told her what had happened, and she sighed.

"I guess I wasn't meant to have nice friends and nice food, at least not at the same time," I said softly. She had somehow known that I was hung over as she had come prepared with tomato juice and something else mixed up together. She urged me to drink it, then told me to come down for lunch in about one half an hour. She said I'd feel better soon, and I said that I couldn't feel worse.

Amazingly, the stuff seemed to work. I belched a few times, and got up at the prescribed time, put some loose jeans on, pulled on a tee shirt, and went downstairs. I looked terrible, I knew, but I had lost my pride. I sat down to vegetable soup and tea. There were crackers too. After a bit, the old fossil joined me and asked how I was. I told her that I was feeling a bit better, and that I decided to live a bit longer.

I remembered her act of kindness on the previous day. "I really want to thank you for yesterday," I said. "I had no idea how I was going to get out of that situation."

She patted my hand and said, "You remind me of my son at your age. Don't worry, he turned out just fine, and I expect you will too, eventually."

I took it as a compliment, and smiled. She ate her soup and left quietly. I went upstairs to change and noticed that the cats had rearranged my dresser top contents, knocked over the trash can and messed all of my new socks up. I got down to retrieve them, and only counted nine. I had apparently just made a sacrifice to the cat god, and I hoped it was sufficient.

I gathered up two of the socks, some clean underwear and trundled off to the bathroom for a shave and shower. Those went well, and except for a slight headache and the sores on my leg, I felt I might survive.

I wasn't quite sure what I was going to do next, when there was a knock on my door. I went to it, and Felicity danced past me into the room, sitting on my bed.

" I came to apologize," she began, "I was wrong last night. You had no commitment to me, and when that bimbo…I mean…young lady showed up, I just sort of lost it. I hope that you'll forgive me."

"There's nothing to forgive, and I was as surprised as you were when she showed."

"Mother told me about it, she had no idea that the girl would follow you there. What is she, twelve years old?"

"I think more like twenty, but it doesn't matter."

"Let's go to the Laundromat, you need some clean clothes," she offered.

This was getting back on familiar ground, so I acquiesced easily and we gathered up my slim pickings, and worked our way downstairs. Reaching the bottom of the stairs, we were met by the cats, who wrapped themselves through Felicity's legs and generally made asses of themselves. She bent to pet them and they closed their eyes, purred and fell on their backs to have their stomachs scratched. I was not convinced, but decided to scratch Mudsy in apology for stepping on her tail last night. She was doing fine until I actually touched her, then she growled at me in warning. Standing up as fast as my wounded leg would allow, I granted her her personal space back. The spell was broken, however, and the two sulked away.

Felicity laughed at them, then at me, saying, "After, you sure have a way with females, don't you?"

"I don't think females should be legal," I growled.

"Oh, we have our uses," she purred, and taking me by the elbow, led me to the clothes, and we walked out to her car.

"You got your car back!" I shouted, feeling idiotically happy. That had to be a good sign, apparently the Lieutenant wasn't too upset with her. The car looked good, I did notice that there was some baling wire holding the trunk closed.

"Yes, I talked to the Lieutenant about my brother, and he said that I was to stay in town, not do anything rash, and tell him anything else I might remember. I didn't tell him about meeting you in Felix's apartment, and I didn't tell him much about those two jerks I had dealt with. Charlie and Patrick. I expect he'll want to follow up on all of that. He was mainly interested in Felix's whereabouts, and I told him that I was too, even though we were no longer close."

"Did you tell him about Harold Gibbons' men, and his possible involvement?" I asked.

"You bet I did."

"Well, he ought to be able to finish things up then," I said hopefully.

"Are you off the case?" she asked.

"If the Lieutenant has anything to do with it, I am. Frankly, I think your mother got her hundred dollar's worth."

"I think so too," she said, as she squeezed my arm. "However, we may still have to deal with Gibbons, he may not let this slide."

"I doubt he'll do much with us," I opined, but not terribly sure of myself.

"We're the only links that he has though."

We entered the Laundromat, and spent the next ten minutes sorting clothes and loading washers. I got change and soap, and we got three machines going. We sat down together, and I rested my head on her shoulder. She smelt good, and I was tired, but all in all, things were OK. I had to get back with Roy and see what he found out about Jocko, and a phone call to Bitsy was in order as well. I was thinking these things and must have fallen asleep, for I woke in a bit finding my head propped on a pair of my folded jeans, and I saw Felicity folding the rest of my freshly laundered clothes. I didn't let her know I was awake, as she had her back to me, and she was wearing gloriously tight jeans. So, I sat back, relaxed and admired the view.

In a bit she noticed I was awake, as she turned to me, and gave me a knowing look. I must have blushed, for she laughed, came over and with a peck on my cheek, asked, "See anything you like?"

"You bet, and I'd like to take it out to a movie tonight."

"That would be super!" She glowed.

"I have to do a few things, and run by Roy's, but I ought to be able to shake free by five," I said.

"Great, we'll get you home, I'll go clean up, and then I'll come back for you then. I'll drive, you treat at the show."

"It's a deal," I said laughing, "but you sure don't need to freshen up, you look great!"

"Shows what you know." She sniffed good-naturedly.

With that, we gathered all the clothes, piled them into the car, and got back to Mother's, chatting and laughing about nothing important at all.

We got up to my room, got the clothes put away, she helped me make the bed, then she sat down on the side, patting for me to sit next to her. I complied and was greeted with an earth-shattering kiss that went on for a long time. She hugged me, and I hugged her. I was just about to go exploring when she got up, and said, "That's my apology for last night. There's another apology you've got coming for me hitting your head at Felix's. I think you'll like that one better. Do you think Mother will mind if I spend the night?"

"I don't know, that's uncharted waters around here. Paul doesn't bring his gal here, and I've never seen Hal with anyone. James is hardly ever here, and as far as I know, Mother and the dear old lady on the first floor don't have sleepovers. At least not in the past forty years!"

"I guess we'll just have to see how she responds in the morning then, I have a new little nothing I've been dying to wear." Then, she smiled that great smile, and walked out the door, and I think she may have added a bit more sway to her hips.

I sat there for a bit, savoring the moment, but soon felt guilty about Jocko, so I went downstairs and called his number. It rang and rang, and just as I was about to give up, it was answered. It wasn't Bitsy, I thought it was the mother.

"Hello," I started, "This is After Coffman. Is Bitsy or Jocko there?"

"This is Bitsy's mother. She went to the store. She said that if you called, she hasn't heard a thing. She's terribly worried. What can we do?"

"I'm working on something," I replied, "and I'm leaving to get started on it right now."

"Thank you, young man," she said, sounding a little relieved and hung up.

I got my shoes on, put my billfold in my pocket, as it had somehow fallen onto the bedspread during the gropefest, and headed out the door.

I was walking along, minding my own business, when all of the sudden, I was flanked by two men, and a rather large car pulled alongside us. The man on my right stuck what appeared to be a gun into my ribs and suggested with his eyes, that I might want to get into the car. I thought about struggling, but realized that there was no use in it. These two had picked their spot well; they obviously knew my routine and had planned it all too carefully. Running would only get me shot.

I got into the car, and the two guys slid in on either side of me. I was frisked right on the spot, but as I was clean, there were no problems. The driver didn't even turn around. None of them talked to me, and I was in no mood to speak with them. We drove on, and presently entered the parking lot of 'The Green Frog'. This was when I opened up, saying, "Guys, I think there's been a mistake. Mr. Gibbons told me never to come back here again."

That didn't get a rise, or even a glance. They were obviously not ready for light repartee. We drove right up to the door, they got out, and I followed. We went in, and the first one in turned and sucker punched me as I entered the door. "No more smart talk," he said with cold eyes boring into me. I gasped, trying to stand, but I gave up and sat on the floor. The other guy picked me up, and half dragged, half carried me into the large room where I had first been introduced to Mr. Gibbons. I noticed that we walked past Joe, the bartender, who was drying glassware. He gave me a quick, sad look, then went on with his drying.

The two creeps who had picked me up were the two body-guards from that earlier, fateful night. The only major difference was that one wore a green shirt, and the other one, the one that punched me, wore a blue shirt. Both had greased back hair, and the kind of bodies and looks that would have made them Chippendale material, had they been a bit younger.

Mr. Gibbons was at his table, and rose when he saw me stagger in. He looked at his hired help and tried to look aggrieved, "I told you he wasn't to be injured."

The blue shirt said, "He slipped coming in the door, musta been the light."

Mr. Gibbons looked at me, and I stood my ground, staring back, not saying a word. These tough guy tactics were intended to intimidate, but I was OK, as long as I kept my wits about me. I knew that this was a planned session, and that they were in no hurry.

"Sit down, sit down, Mr. Coffman," Mr. Gibbons offered. "We like our guests to feel comfortable. What was it, double Chivas on the rocks?" He tilted his head and green shirt went to the bar. Not a word was spoken until he returned with two drinks. He placed one in front of his boss, and one in front of me."

Mr. Gibbons raised his glass in salute, and when I didn't follow suit, drank from his with a shrug. He looked at me again and said, "I understand you are looking for a former employee of mine, a Mr. Felix Jeffries?"

I was a bit taken aback, I wasn't surprised that he knew this, but why would he care? He shouldn't, if he had dusted Felix, as Felicity had suggested.

I nodded, saying, "I was hired to find him, yes...but I've had very little luck. He was gone well before I was on the scene."

"Yes." Mr. Gibbons nodded. "He seems to have disappeared into thin air. Perhaps you assumed I had something to do with that?"

"The thought had crossed my mind."

"Well, I haven't. Do I look like a magician, someone who can make people disappear?" He smiled, then looked at his boys, who both laughed half-heartedly at his sense of humor.

I waited, not sure what to make of this.

Mr. Gibbons took another drink, then motioned me to do the same. "Come on, Mr. Coffman, that's good stuff, don't let the ice melt."

I took a small sip, then sat back and waited again.

"So, you say you haven't found him yet?" Mr. Gibbons asked. "I understand you have been doing a little work with my old friend Roy Mack."

I nodded warily.

"He doesn't pay too well, does he?"

I shrugged, "It gets me by."

Mr. Gibbons laughed. "You come in here with buttons missing, old shoes, you live at Mother Teresa's, and walk everywhere. Really, Mr. Coffman, that is not getting by. That is not even existing." He stopped, tried on a smile, saw that it didn't fit his face, gave up on the smile, then continued. "In spite of the unusual circumstances involving your trip to see me, I mean you no harm. I understand that you are working with Lieutenant Howard on this situation. He's a fine man, and not one I'd care to cross, and I am sure that you feel the same way."

I nodded.

"I do have a proposition for you though, and as you are already on the job, so to speak, it should only come as a small inconvenience to you."

I waited.

He continued, "All that I am asking, is should you find Mr. Jeffries first, that you tell me one hour before you tell the Lieutenant. We are all happy that way, are we not?"

I didn't move, as I waited for the punch line.

It was not long in coming, "In return for this small favor to me, you will have my undying gratitude; not a small compensation in these trying times. Also, there will be a slight bonus of five thousand tax free dollars finding there way into your wallet that same day."

I still didn't move, I sat and waited.

He finished up, "Think about it, Mr. Coffman." He got up and started away. "Show Mr. Coffman to the door, and try to make sure he gets out of here without further injury."

The two jerks got me up, and green shirt made a show of brushing off my clothes, and they escorted me to the door. I waved at Joe as we passed. He just looked at me as we left the building.

The car was still there. Blue shirt opened the door and indicated I was to enter. I shook my head and began walking, figuring they would leave me alone. As I reached the end of the parking lot, I turned back. The two bodyguards and the driver hadn't moved. I guessed that they were making sure I didn't take anything off the property.

I was thinking that the situation had just gotten interesting again. Just when I had things all wrapped in a tidy little ribbon, Mr. Gibbons tosses a wrench into the plans. I wondered how he knew so much about me. I wondered if Roy was talking and playing both sides, or if there was a snitch on the police force. Mr. Gibbons knew entirely too much to suit me though.

I got to Roy's and was gratified to see that he was there. He had mentioned that weekends were hit and miss, there were times he'd be at a sale, and not open up. I was happy to see that this was not one of those days. I walked in as he was placing some antiques into a small box for a happy couple.

"These ought to suit you just fine," he said to them.

"Oh yes, Mr. Mack, these are just great. I can't believe that you've been around the corner all this time and we had no idea of all of the marvelous things you have here." The middle aged couple left in a bustle of bags, boxes and smiles.

"I'm glad to see you, After," Roy said.

"I'm glad to see you as well," I answered. I wanted to see if he knew that Mr. Gibbons was on my tail, so I told him what happened. He didn't seem too surprised, but didn't look guilty either.

"I'd stay away from that snake, if I were you," he said, after I had completed my tale.

"I'd come to that conclusion too, but he sort of got the jump on me."

"Watch your back, and I'll keep my ears open. Speaking of which, that's exactly what I've been doing. I may have news about Jocko."

I got interested and sat at the counter, like a puppy about to receive a treat.

"Now, this may or may not amount to anything," Roy said, "but apparently one of Jocko's boyhood friends got out of prison a few weeks ago, and has been seen in the area. A friend of mine says that he and some other bad people are holed up north of town on Route H, a gravel road that dead ends in a forest. Word has it that there are people there with guns and that actions of a questionable nature occur after dark. I thought that maybe you, me and Grits could pay it a visit tonight, once it's dark."

"I think that's in order," I agreed. "I had a date with Felicity tonight, but she'll understand."

"OK," he said, "I'll be here with Grits at eight sharp. That will give us time to go over things, but it will be dark soon after. Wear the darkest clothes you own."

"Gotcha," I said, and got out of there. I supposed I was getting good at breaking dates with girls, so I was hoping that Felicity wouldn't have a huge problem with me canceling this one. After all, it was for a friend of mine, and he had been there for me. I was hoping that the situation wouldn't call for Jocko going to jail. I was also hoping that the situation wouldn't call for me going to dead.

I got home by six, only to find that Felicity was in the kitchen, helping Mother with dinner. I went in and gave both of them hugs, then motioned for Felicity to follow me out for a minute. Mother shooed us out, and told Felicity to take her time.

I told Felicity about my visit with Gibbons, leaving out the part where I was offered money, just saying that it was a feeling out sort of meeting. She grimaced, and asked how I felt about it. I suggested that I was still on the case, like it or not. I then told her that I needed to help a friend out tonight, that there could be danger, and outlined the problem, but not telling her who the friend was.

She gave me a funny look, not what I expected, then said, "Of course you must go. There is one small condition though."

I waited for the other shoe to drop. It didn't take long to drop, as she then looked me straight in the eye and said, "I'm going too."

My jaw dropped, and I protested, "You are NOT!"

She stood her ground and said, "I won't go to the house, but I can handle a gun, I have street smarts, and I can drive the car. If something goes really wrong, I can come get help."

I tried various arguments, but she wouldn't budge, so I compromised, telling her she could go with me to Roy's and let him decide what to do. That suited her, and I could almost sense her strengthening her eye-batting muscles. We went into the dining room where the usual characters were assembled and had a nice supper of chicken, fresh tossed salad, baked potatoes and strawberry pie for dessert. Everyone was happy to see Felicity, and she seemed in great spirits. Once supper was over, she helped Mother with the dishes, then she told me to go up and change my clothes for the evening. She waited downstairs while I put on black jeans, a black tee shirt and black socks with my loafers. I didn't feel all that equipped, but it would have to do.

Going back downstairs, I met Felicity at the foot of the stairs and we went out to her car. We got in and drove to her little apartment by the supermarket. We entered, and I saw that there was not much there at all. There was a small entry room, with doors leading to a small kitchen and another to a bedroom. The bedroom had a bath off of it. There was only a dilapidated bed with a sheet on it, and no other furniture. No closet that I could see either. "Nice place," I lied.

She shrugged. "I've lived in worse, at least it is quiet."

"You weren't planning on staying here long, were you?" I asked.

"No," she said, " I was hoping to move in with mom, but that never happened."

"Why don't you move to her place now? You might even get some answers about Felix if you look hard enough."

"That's a great idea, After!" She cried, throwing her arms around me in a hug.

I was hoping for another great idea, but must have reached my limit, as my brain went as blank as it usually did around her.

"I need to sell her house, sell the furniture and get things settled, it would be best for me to move there while I do that, then I can do as you suggested, and look around a bit. Plus..." she winked, "it will take care of the sleepover problem at Mother's"

Obviously, one good idea had led to another, and I was very satisfied. She went into the other little room of her tiny apartment, and came out with similar garb to mine.

"We still have about a half hour, do you want to smooch a bit?" She asked.

It didn't take a half-hour, but was close to that by the time we got our clothes back on and she ran a brush through her hair. We got out to the car, both still a little sweaty from our exertions, and she managed to navigate our way to Roy's.

We entered at 8:00 sharp, as directed. Roy and Grits were sitting near the counter. They both nodded at me, then stared at Felicity. Roy stood up, beaming, and said, "My gosh girl, I'd have recognized you anywhere." He went to hug her.

"Hi Roy." She smiled as she hugged him back. "It's been a long time."

"It has, at that, but you look great!"

Grits made a noise, and we introduced the two of them. Grits was impressed, and made no effort at hiding it, calling her 'Gorgeous' and 'Miss Sexy' and other terms whenever he could. Felicity took it all in stride, and didn't budge when Roy thanked her for dropping me off, but suggested that we had other items on the agenda tonight.

"I'm going," she stated flatly and firmly.

"What?" Grits yelled. Roy stood by and laughed.

"I'm going, and that's final. I'll bet I can outshoot either of you, and you need a lookout, as well as a babysitter."

Roy laughed again and said that it was all right with him. Grits looked at me, and I smiled back. "She's OK, Grits," I said.

There was nothing else for him to do, so he agreed grumpily and we waited around until dark fell, about nine o'clock. We got into two cars, agreeing that Felicity would stay down the road a bit, while we took Roy's car nearer to the property. Felicity and I got in her car and trailed them to a dark spot in the road, where Roy pulled over. He got out of his car, came back to us, and handed me my .45, saying, "I thought you might need this tonight."

I got out, gave Felicity a hug, and started off with the other two.

Roy said, "If we don't return in 40 minutes, get out of here, and you might as well get help too, 'cause I'd guess all of us won't be coming back."

Felicity swallowed hard, and nodded her head 'Yes', and we got into Roy's car for the final part of our journey.

It was very dark, no moon to speak of, and the little gravel road was no more than a tiny, unlit lane by this point. Roy stopped the car, and we all got out.

"The rest of the way is on foot," he whispered. "Don't show any light."

We crept along, letting Roy lead the way until we approached a small, dilapidated looking shack at the edge of the woods.

"This is it!" Roy whispered again. "Grits, you sneak up front, I'll take the side windows, and After, you get to the back door. Just

have a look, see what you can, and meet back here." We both nodded and separated. I got as low to the ground as I could and used
some brush as cover. There were a few old cars behind the house,
and I got to them without incident. I waited there a minute, then
looking for the best route to the back door, made my way cautiously to it. There was no window on it, but it was ajar, and I could
hear voices from within.

None of the voices were familiar, but there seemed to be an
argument going on, when someone yelled, "What's that? There's an
old man out by the side window!" The game was up. I heard bodies
moving and people rushing out the front door. I heard Grits' voice
saying, "I wouldn't be in such a hurry if I was you." Then all hell
broke loose. A man came running out the back door, taking me by
surprise, and then an explosion rocked the house, shooting flames
out the door behind him. He fell to the ground, and I raced over to
him, tackling him and holding him down. We rolled around, trying to get grips on each other for leverage. The small house was
going up in flames quickly, and I was losing my slight initial advan-
tage over him. He rolled over on top of me and started to hit me,
when he stiffened slightly. "I've been shot!" he gasped.

There was so much commotion that I hadn't heard anything,
but the man was holding his side. He stiffened again, and this time
I heard the report of the gun, a vague 'pop'. Whoever was shooting
wasn't too careful; either of us could have been hit. I pulled his face
to mine and shouted, "Where's Jocko, I have to save him, then I'll
come back to help you."

He thought about it for a second or so, then gasped again, "He's
in the storm cellar under the house."

I threw him off me, and rolling to the side, tore to the house,
tossing my gun aside. I took my shirt off as my hands were going to
need insulation against the heat. I opened the door to a blast of heat
and entered the inferno.

eleven

I battled my way through the door; heat was every-where, but no flames were in the general vicinity. I couldn't breathe, and remembering that one was supposed to stay low in fires, I got on my stomach and crawled in. My face was very hot, but I did manage to get to a little breathable air lower to the floor. As I pro-gressed, I saw the fire coming at me from the right, so there was no hope there. I turned left and soon came to a wall. I touched it, and it wasn't too hot yet. I followed the wall into the house and soon came to a door. The fire was behind me now, and there was only one way to go with any chance of finding Jocko. I reached up, but couldn't get high enough to find the doorknob. I took a deep breath, closed my eyes, wrapping the tee shirt around my hand, and stood up. The heat was very strong here, but I found the knob, turned it and fell through the door. I landed hard and started to roll down a flight of stairs.

There was no light, and the smoke would have made it impos-sible to see anything anyway. It was a short flight of maybe ten steps....I never went back to count. I was on a dirt floor that felt cool after the heat above, but I knew the smoke would kill us soon. I tried to call for Jocko, but couldn't get any sound out of my mouth. I groped around, and came to a leg! I pulled myself to it, and found that its owner was in a chair. I tried to pull the person to me, but they didn't budge. I realized that they must be tied to it. I felt for knots, and finally found the rope and duct tape holding the person prisoner. I started to rip and tear, having no knife. The person started to struggle as well, and we got an arm loose. Then we made some real progress. It was just a matter of seconds before they were free, and I started to pull them toward the stairs.

I figured that they couldn't walk well if they had been tied for too long, but there seemed to be more resistance then I would have thought. The person grabbed me and pulled my hand to their face. The mouth was covered with duct tape. I pulled hard and it loosened. I started to tug again when a raspy voice said, "There's one more down here!" I started to grope again. Luckily the cellar was probably only 10 feet by 10 feet, and the other person was easy to find, and with two of us working, we got them free in short order. I began to pull this one to the door as well, but they were not helping. I felt for the mouth and it was covered with duct tape as well. I ripped it off to ease their breathing. The smoke was heavier, and it was difficult to breathe. This second victim was not helping at all, and I had lost contact with the first victim. I hoped the first victim could find their way out, because I was going to have to carry this one myself.

Have I mentioned that I am not the biggest guy in the world? If I haven't, I'll do it now. I was weak and couldn't see, but I dragged the person to the stairs by dead reckoning, and started to pull them up. The smoke made everything black, and about halfway up, there was no air to breathe. I was getting faint, so I left my person halfway up the stairs, and went back to the cellar. I lay on my stomach and pulled in as many breaths as I could. It was now or never, as this low room under the fire was beginning to fill with smoke.

I got a deep breath in and stumbled back to the stairs. I grabbed my charge and dragged him the rest of the way up the stairs. I wanted to pick him up and carry him out, but the fire was right there. I pulled and tugged as hard as I could and headed for where I thought the door was. It seemed to take forever, it was so hot. I held on for dear life and half dragged him, and half fell out the door into the night air.

I fell down gasping, and noticed that I hadn't gotten my person totally out of the house, so I dragged him the rest of the way, and got him to safety. I turned him over, but couldn't tell who it was as his face was blackened and pieces of duct tape were randomly scattered all over it. I couldn't see well anyway, as my eyes were streaming tears and everything was blurry. I put my ear to his mouth, but could hear no breathing and no air was touching me. I started mouth to mouth, and in no time, was gratified to hear him cough. I turned him over and he began to retch. Things started to move in slow motion for me then. I began to wonder about the man I had fought with, about the shooter, and whether they were still out there, and also about Roy and Grits. My man was starting to breathe better, so I went in search of the man I had fought. He was where I had left him, on his stomach. I turned him over. I didn't recognize him at all, and would never get to know him, as there was a bullet hole placed neatly between his eyes.

I got up and went back for my gun, as Roy and Grits might be in trouble, but all of the exertion must have gotten to me, as I suddenly got weak and fell to the ground, losing consciousness bit by bit.

I became aware of flashing lights and sirens blaring, and somewhat later there was someone talking to me, and trying to get me to respond. I tried to talk, but gave up; my throat was too sore. Soon, another person was helping me, and they half carried, half dragged me to an ambulance. They placed me inside and made me lie down on a gurney. A paramedic placed a mask over my nose and fed me oxygen. Things cleared up immediately. I got glimpses of other people, and finally saw Grits walk by. He looked at me and gave me thumbs up. I relaxed and lay down on the gurney. There were many cars and trucks moving about, though I was sure the little house was a total loss.

It wasn't long before we were on the road back to Hustle, and an entire procession of vehicles was pulling into the hospital entrance. I was in the back of an ambulance with a character I didn't recognize. We were escorted into the emergency room, which had filled with doctors, nurses and police. I was taken to my own cubicle, and seen immediately by a doctor. He checked me over, had a nurse place salve on my face and arms, and told me I might have some burns, trouble breathing and maybe internal injuries. I was to be their guest for the night. He would check in from time to time. They took me to a room, gave me some liquids, some pills, started an IV, and I soon fell into a nice, deep sleep.

I woke a few times during the night. I felt feverish and sore, but my breathing was fine. I had worried that I might have fried my lungs, but I guess I lucked out. I could smell the stench of smoke, the burning and all, but I was in a hospital gown and apparently not too badly off. One time when a nurse came in, I asked if Jocko was OK. She said she didn't know him, but would ask for me. She came back later, and told me he was in worse shape than I was, but alive. I fell asleep again.

The next morning seemed to arrive quickly, and I awoke to find five people sitting in my room, just waiting on me to wake up. Roy, Grits, Felicity, Lieutenant Howard and a young lady were all there. I sat up and let all know I was awake. Roy and Grits smiled broadly, Felicity and the other girl jumped up and kissed me. It hurt, as my face was sore, but I really didn't mind at all. The Lieutenant just looked at me, tried to look stern, then laughed, stuck his hand out and shook mine.

He said, "In case you are wondering who this young lady is, it's Bitsy O'Reilly."

I took a look, she was cute and apparently happy, so I felt good about last night's escapade. She hugged me more, then started to cry. I just let her do it, I felt a bit like crying myself.

I could have put up with this for another hour or so, but I needed some air, and some answers. I pushed her away gently, and smiled. She smiled back, saying, ""Jocko will be in the hospital for a little while, you gave him mouth to mouth and saved his life! I want you over for as many dinners as you can eat, once he gets home!" She hugged me again, then got up.

"I'm going to see him now. He was worried about you," she continued.

"Tell him I'm fine, and that I'll be by later," I said.

She left with a smile for all, and then Roy and Grits got up as well. Roy shook my hand and Grits smiled. They left the room together. The Lieutenant looked at me, then at Felicity, and asked her if he could have a moment of my time. She said sure and left the room, blowing me a kiss.

The Lieutenant pulled his chair close to my bed and said, "I don't know what you found out, how you found out, or what you had to do with all of this, but I want you to know that you are OK in my book. I'll do what I can to fill you in on your case and help you any way I can. Jocko's a good man, and even though I only know a little about what is going on, he's going to be all right and you are the reason. Come see me when you feel up to it."

"Lieutenant," I began, "I have no idea what that was all about, but I got word that he might be there, and my friends and I went for it. I didn't know what he was up to either, and I'm sorry I didn't call you."

"We'll discuss it later, but don't worry, you did more good than harm. I'm back to work; we have another Homicide to deal with. You wouldn't know anything about that, would you? There was a dead man outside the back door of that shack."

"All I can say was that we were struggling, he was shot, but he told me where Jocko was, and he was still alive when I left him."

"Yes, he was shot three times, but the third shot was at close range, and it's the one that finished him."

"Wow!" I exclaimed. "It was touch and go there for a bit, and it's all pretty confusing."

"Come see me when you can, I'll tell your girl to come back in. I do believe you'll be released today."

"I sure hope so," I said.

"One more thing," he continued quickly, "there were several guns at the scene, as if they had been tossed aside at the last moment. There was a .45 by the back door as well."

I gulped, I had forgotten about the guns. I couldn't say anything to him.

He looked at me, then said, "I placed them in evidence bags and turned them in, but it appears that someone cleaned all of the fingerprints off of them. We have no idea who they belong to. The numbers were filed off as well. I guess it's just one of those unsolved mysteries that we run into from time to time."

I smiled at him, and he smiled back. He left, and Felicity came right in and sat with me as I tried to decide what to do next. I asked her for a mirror, and she gave me one reluctantly. I looked and saw that my eyebrows were singed off and most of my hair was gone. My face was red, my lips cracked. I grimaced and she laughed.

"None of that is permanent," she said. "The doctor says that you'll be as good as new in a few days, and your hair will just be shorter for a week or so."

"I want to take a shower and clean up," I grumbled.

"Let me go see if that's permitted," Felicity offered.

She left and returned a few minutes later with a short, redheaded nurse. The nurse was bubbly and cheerful, and I felt better just looking at her open and friendly visage. The nurse assured me that it was OK to bathe, and got me some soap and towels.

"Can I wear my own clothes?" I asked.

"Your clothes are ruined," Felicity said. "I'll tell you what, I'll drive over to the house, get you some clothes and come back with them. You may get to go home later, but just in case, I'll bring some for tomorrow too. Do you have any more shoes? Your loafers are ruined."

"Just some tennis shoes in the closet."

"I'll bring them as well." Then she was gone.

The nurse assisted me to the bathroom. I was pretty sore and stiff, but declined her offer of assistance. I took my time, and washed my hair several times, trying to rid myself of the burnt smell. I felt human again when I got out, and I put on a clean hospital gown, and returned to my bed. It had been freshly made, and I was feeling a bit of energy return, so I opted for the chair instead and decided to watch some television.

Felicity returned with some comfortable clothes and helped me get dressed. She went to the drawer of the built-in dresser and got my billfold for me.

"I wanted you to realize that I didn't abscond with it again." She laughed.

I laughed back and felt pretty good, now that I was dressed. I asked her, "Can you fill me in on all the details that I missed?"

She sat down and began to talk. "Well, you guys drove away, and I got out of my car and sort of walked around. You were gone about twenty minutes when I heard a big explosion and saw flames. I got into my car and drove to where I saw Roy's car. I could see people in the distance and saw all sorts of pandemonium. I couldn't make out anybody, and I was uncertain of what to do, so I waited in case one of you came back to Roy's car. Then, I heard what I thought were gunshots, and I got into my car and drove to a house we had gone by. I had noticed it as we drove in. I went up to the door, and asked the lady who answered it to call the police and fire departments. She said she would, and I went back to my original spot. It wasn't too long before I heard the sirens, and then saw all the vehicles streaming by. I got into my car and followed. By the time I got there, the police had several people in cuffs, including Roy and Grits. The firemen were working on the house, and ambulances were arriving. I tried to look for you, but they kept me away."

She paused, got us both a drink of water and sat back down again. "After a while, the ambulances pulled away, and all I did was follow. Once I got to the hospital, some things had been ironed out, as Grits and Roy were already out of the cuffs and talking to several officers. I saw Lieutenant Howard come through, and asked him about you. He said he had just arrived, knew nothing and asked me to wait in the cafeteria for him. He came by a half-hour later and told me that one man was dead of a gunshot wound. Two were in custody. You, Jocko and another man were being treated for smoke inhalation and burns, and then he said he wanted to ask me about what was going on. I saw no reason to lie, so I told him everything up to that point, and he told me that I might as well wait here with him. Bitsy showed up a bit later, and we all started our vigil."

I nodded, and said that caught me up. I knew that it was near noon the following day, so I assumed they had given me something to help me sleep.

We were quiet for a bit, and the nurse came back in. She took my temperature and other vital signs, then told me the doctor would be in shortly. Felicity and I watched 'The Flintstones' for a bit, and were rewarded with a rather quick entry by the physician in charge of my case.

"Well, hello Mr. Coffman," the doctor smiled as he entered, busily flipping through my chart. "It would seem that you are in fairly good shape, considering your ordeal. I want to look you over one more time, and I think we can let you go home."

That sounded good, so I let him poke and prod, and was gratified to hear him pronounce me fit. He gave me some cream for my face and hands, then suggesting that I pay attention, he did the first treatment himself. He then told me to take it easy and call him if I had trouble breathing or sleeping. I said I would, and he signed me out.

Felicity and I gathered up my clothes and medicine, then she escorted me out to her car. I was about to enter when I thought about Jocko. I insisted that we go back in, so that I could see how he was doing. She led me back in, and we went to the desk to find Jocko's room.

We got there, it wasn't far from my room, and he had the same nurse I had had, so there was no problem getting in. Upon entering, I saw Bitsy, and a person I took to be her mother. They sure looked like mother and daughter. Introductions confirmed this to be the case. Jocko was asleep, some bandages around his face and hands, plus he seemed to be suffering hair loss as well. That same, cloying burnt smell hung in the room. Bitsy said that he was mostly sleeping, but that he would be OK in a day or so, and that I might as well go home. I told her that I'd return tomorrow and to tell him I was glad he was OK.

She said, "After, I can never repay you, and I did find out that he was working undercover. I know he'll tell you all about it when he's able to. Don't worry, we will all be all right." She and her mother both gave me hugs, and Bitsy hugged Felicity as well, inviting us both to dinner when Jocko got home. We agreed to come soon, then left. I felt a lot better and was ready to get back to life.

We got into Felicity's car, and she asked if I felt up to a detour. I said sure, and we drove up to Pastor James' church. The sign proudly proclaimed 'Our Holy Mother of the True Rock', and had the up-coming services listed. I looked questioningly at Felicity, and she motioned for me to get out and follow her. I got out and we went in.

"Pastor James has the keys to mom's house. I called him this morning and asked if he thought it was OK if I moved in for a bit. He said that there was no will, but that it ought to be all right until the lawyers got involved. So, we're here to get the keys."

"Great!" I said. "I'd much rather you were there than that little apartment."

She took me by the arm and we found Pastor James' office. He rose from behind his desk as we entered and beamed at us.

"I see the hero of the hour is up and about." He smiled, shaking my hand.

"I don't feel like a hero, but I am glad to be on the mend," I said.

He chatted a bit about the house and its general condition. He said that church members had cleaned it up a bit, and thrown away most of the perishable items, but that the power and water were still on. He also said he'd be by in the next day or so, and that a lawyer for the church would come by and offer Felicity some advice on her next moves.

Felicity said, "The house means nothing to me, I barely knew mom, but I'll try to do right by her. Maybe the church can get the house and sell it, or something."

Pastor James said, "That would be wonderful, and we'll work towards that, but your brother has a claim as well."

None of us had anything else to say about that point, so we said our good-byes and went on our way.

We drove up to a smallish, but clean house, nestled between two very similar homes, a tribute to tract housing. It was wood frame, one story, but had a chimney. It was better than I had thought it would be.

We used the key and entered. It was clean, the furniture old, but well cared for. There were bright curtains on the windows and throw rugs of all colors throughout. The kitchen was fairly modern, but the bathroom wasn't. Felicity remarked that the kitchen had been upgraded since she had lived here. There were two bedrooms. Felicity had shared one with her mother and Felix had used the other one. I entered Felix's room, and saw that there was only a bed and a dresser there. It hadn't been used for much since he left home. I opened a dresser drawer and found a few photos and some handkerchiefs in it. The other drawers were empty. I went back to the first drawer and took everything out and gave everything a quick look. Felicity came in and watched. I told her that I had found nothing so far. I pulled the drawer out and looked at the bottom of it. Nothing to find there. Felicity followed suit, and we hit pay dirt on the third drawer. There was a key taped to the bottom of it. The tape was clean and clear, not yet yellowed and cracked with age. The key had 3 numbers on it, and the words 'Baltimore Station #2'. I smiled and told Felicity that we might have something here. We would have to see if the Lieutenant would let us out of town in the next day or so.

A quick tour of the rest of the house turned nothing up. We found an old photo album and looked at a few pictures of Felicity and Felix as they grew up. Felicity disappeared from the album after a bit, but I was able to get a good idea of what Felix now looked like. I asked Felicity for a particularly clear picture of him, and she pulled it out and gave it to me. I thought that we might need it on our probable trip to Baltimore.

We made sure that all of the utilities were properly turned on in the house, and then Felicity said that we ought to get me back home. Mother had told her to come for supper when she went to get my clothes, and she knew that Mother would be glad to see me again and know that I was safe.

We locked up the house and drove back to Mother's. It was about an hour before supper, so we waved at Mother as we entered, receiving a smile in return. We went up to my room, where Felicity put more salve on my burns, then she busied herself rearranging my room while I just plopped down on my bed and took a quick nap. I awoke to find no one in the room. I went to the door and heard voices downstairs. There were at least three female voices, and they were laughing, so I assumed none of them belonged to Gloria. I went to the bathroom, made myself as presentable as I could and went downstairs.

The now regular throng were entrenched at Mother's large dining room table. Hal, James and Beulah were in their usual spots, and I nodded at all of them. Paul was sitting with a smug look on his face, but Mother and Felicity weren't in the room. I heard them laughing and talking in the kitchen, so I knew they'd be in shortly. I sat down, and fielded a few questions about my adventure the night before. Paul wanted to know if he could interview me later, as he was going to see if the paper would let him do a story or two. I said that would be fine, not expecting any sort of follow through.

The ladies appeared about then, bringing in the dishes. Mother was first, followed by Felicity, and finally by a dark haired beauty that I took to be a relative of Mother's, as she had the same coloring. There was no other reason for her to be here that I could see. She was tall, maybe 5' 10", long brown hair, dark eyes, and the kind of body you see on swimsuit calendars. I was impressed, and she must have noticed, as she paused to take me in. I tried to close my obviously open mouth, and I tried to take my eyes off of her. She could only be 19 or 20 years old, but wow!

I received a light rap to the back of my head, and turned to see Felicity glaring at me, but then she broke into a smile. "Isn't Niki gorgeous? She has that effect on everybody."

I nodded, then determined that I would no longer even glance at her, as I knew there would be hell to pay if I did. I looked at Niki, and asked, "Where are you from, are you visiting Mother?"

"No," she replied in a girlish giggle. "I am here because Paul and I are dating, he thought I should meet all of you."

"You're the switchboard girl?" I asked, astounded.

"Yes," she replied and began filing one of her very long fingernails. She then sat down next to the smug looking Paul, and proceeded to wrap her arm in his, forgetting instantly that I ever existed.

I determined right then and there, not to look at her again. Felicity sat next to me, and put her mouth next to my ear, whispering, "She's a man killer, watch out for Paul."

I stole another look at Niki, and she caught it, winking at me. My bowels turned to water, as I determined not to look at her again. The food was great! Meatballs in red sauce, obviously steeped in wine. There were fresh peas and corn on the cob. Tossed salad with lots of new stuff in it. I knew that there were bamboo shoots and maybe some other Chinese things, but I tried it anyway, and found it to be delicious. There were Mother's homemade noodles, as well as potato soup. I didn't look at Niki for the next five minutes, well OK, maybe every 30 seconds or so, but I didn't linger, well, not more than a few times. She obviously had Paul under her spell, and for once, Hal wasn't hanging on every word Felicity was saying. James was the only male that seemed immune. He ate seconds, excused himself and declined Mother's invitation for dessert. That was a mistake for him, but my gain. He raced up to his room, reappearing in seconds with his bike riding gear on, and tore out the door. Moments later, he could be seen pedaling up the street on his ten speed.

Talk at the table centered on what Paul and Niki were up to, which appeared to be nothing more than watching videos at her house. Poor guy, how was he going to stimulate his mind? Dessert was fantabulous. It was butterscotch meringue pie, and I did not hesitate to take James' piece as well. I had been working hard saving the world, and I felt entitled. Mother just grinned at me. I looked at Felicity a bit more as I was beginning to realize what an absolute airhead Niki was. All she could talk about were her nails, her hair and vague references to rock groups that all sounded like cuss words. Paul was in too deep; he'd never surface. I figured the nose job for next week, and the eyes next month at the latest.

Niki even suggested that I do something about my hair, but was cut short by Felicity, who said that I was fine just as I was. I determined to not look at Niki again.

After supper, Hal and Beulah went their separate ways, while Felicity and Niki helped clear the table. Niki leaned over me and picked up my plates, brushing me with her breasts, and overpowering me with her perfume. She lingered just a bit, and I was beginning to get a little faint. Felicity came to the rescue, and took my elbow, guiding me out the front door, onto the porch.

"You looked like you needed some fresh air," she said.

"No, I just needed to breathe, I'd forgotten how to there for a minute."

She gave me a mock glower, then laughed, "You'd be a terrible poker player."

"As a matter of fact, I am a great poker player," I avowed.

"Let's go back to mom's then, and I'll take you on in strip poker," she offered.

I had to sit down on the porch swing, as my knees were weak. Felicity laughed and sat next to me and we spent an hour or so just swinging and relaxing, not saying much at all. A bit later, Paul and

Niki strolled out of the house, hand in hand, and went up the street. I looked questioningly at Felicity, and she told me that Niki lived a few blocks away.

"Poor Paul," I muttered as I watched Niki's hips sway away up the sidewalk.

"I am sure he is suffering," Felicity purred.

A few minutes later, Mother joined us with lemonade, and she and Felicity started talking girl talk. I listened for a bit, but realized that I was getting sleepier and sleepier. Felicity noted this after a bit, and suggested that I go to bed, as I had been a busy boy and needed to get caught up on my rest. I hugged her and Mother, then excused myself and went upstairs to my room, where I removed my clothes, put a bit of salve on my face, and sank into a deep, quiet sleep, not even awakened by the sun and the cheerful birds in the morning.

I finally woke about 8:30, and decided to try and make things right with Gloria. Poor kid, it wasn't her fault that Felicity had shown up at Roy's on Saturday night. I grabbed some jeans and a tee shirt, and went down to the phone. I looked up the number of the dough-nut shop and called it. A man answered the phone, and I asked if Gloria was working. He said 'Yes' and asked if I wished to speak with her. I told him that I'd be right down. I raced up to my room, put on socks and shoes and went out the door, up the street and on my way to the doughnut shop.

I arrived a few minutes later, and walked up to the counter. Gloria turned to wait on me, then noticed who I was. She turned red and started to walk away, then did a double take and noticed my burns and lack of hair.

She ran out from behind the counter and asked me, "What happened to you?" She led me to a seat, and squirmed in beside me.

I told her the short version and she was an enraptured audience. I then apologized for Saturday night, telling her that I was sorry we didn't do the movie, and that I was also sorry that Felicity had shown up so unexpectedly. I hadn't meant any harm or anything. I also told her that I'd tried to call her. She was appeased and apologized for assuming too much. We were smiling and laughing again. I took the plunge and asked if she'd like to see a movie this following week-end, and she said she'd think about it. She wrote her phone number on a napkin and gave it to me, telling me to call her on Friday. I said I would, and followed her back to the counter, where I got a glazed doughnut and small orange juice to go. She waved as I left and I felt a lot better.

My next stop was the hospital, where I was planning on getting the story from Jocko, if he was able to talk. I entered the front door, where a nurse met me. She took one look at me and told me that Admitting was around the corner. I bristled at the suggestion that I might look bad enough to be admitted, but smiled at her in spite of my attitude, and said that I was actually here to see how my friend was doing. I made my way around her, and she let me by, not entirely sure that I was telling the truth. I found my way to the elevator and went up to the second floor, where Jocko's room was. I walked down the hallway, where I met my friendly nurse. She asked how I was doing, and I told her I was much better. She gave me a sunny smile and pointed to Jocko's room.

"He's a lot better today," she offered, "I think he'll go home tomorrow."

That was good news, and I waved at her as I entered his room. There were flowers everywhere. Bitsy and her mother were nowhere to be found, but Jocko was propped up in bed, watching the television. He didn't seem to notice me, so I rapped lightly on his door, and he turned to me. He grinned when he saw me, and motioned me in.

"Hi After!" he said. "I sure don't have any idea how to thank you, but I want you to know how much I appreciate you returning me to my family!"

I sat down next to his bed. He looked the worse for wear. His eyes were dark and sunken. There were patches of his hair missing, and his entire skin had an unhealthy yellowish glow to it.

"You look pretty good," I lied.

He just turned to me and grinned. "I know what I look like, but I have to tell you, I am so happy right now, just to be alive and able to carry on."

"I know, and I sure am glad I found you. Now, what the heck was going on out there, and where have you been all those nights you've missed work?"

"Well, the secret's out anyway. I was promoted to Detective about a month ago, but it was kept a secret as I was assigned to an undercover job. I was to infiltrate a known drug ring out of town. I had some boyhood friends who had gotten into trouble, but as a condition of parole, one of them was released early and was to assist me in trying to break into this drug ring. He moved back here and was living in the house you pulled me out of. He was going from here to Buffalo, and working that angle, trying to get in good with the big shots. Drugs are being smuggled into Canada, and Buffalo is one of the storage areas before the deals are finished. Anyway, he was introducing me to some of the runners, and other middle men involved, and I was going to move on up into the inner circle and try to make some drug buys."

He paused, took a drink of water and continued, "About five days ago, one of the guys came down from Buffalo, and recognized my pal, whose name is Greg, and started talking about old times. I happened to arrive at the house at that time, and he must have recognized me as well. A few nights later, I was entering the house, when I was ambushed. I was bound and gagged, then tossed into the basement. They let me stew there for at least a day, then they pulled me out, gave me some water, then beat the holy crap out of me. Greg was tied up as well, in fact, you apparently untied him before you got to me."

I nodded, and asked, "Where is he now?"

He stuck his hand out and pointed toward the door, "Just down the hall, you'll see a uniformed cop outside his door. Remember, he was on parole, and isn't really in trouble with the law, but the Chief doesn't want to take any chances." He took another sip of water, then continued, "After those creeps got done beating me, they untied me and told me I could walk, if I told them what was going on. I only have a few names in the organization, and I figured they were just going to see what I knew before they killed me. I decided to play as if I was more hurt by the beating than I actually was, so I pretended to faint. They brought me around, gave me a little food, and started to question me again. They were threatening to hurt Bitsy and Edward, my son, but I was hoping that I could hold out another day before trying to lie my way out of this. They questioned me about a suspected gun running scam from this area as well. I told them I knew nothing about it, but I've filed it away as a bonus."

I tried not to show my concern, so I grabbed for a cup and drank some of his water. It was flat and warm, but I was able to choke it down to avoid further comments about the guns.

"That's about it," Jocko finished up, "they left three guys in charge of us, and we were in the basement. They booby trapped the house and were about to come finish us off when all hell broke loose. I guess that you fought one of the guys, while Roy and Grits took the other two down. The guy you fought is dead, but the other two are in custody. Those two are just goons, but the guy you took was the middle man from Buffalo, as well as him being the guy who wanted to know about the guns."

I tried to look innocent and serene, but probably just looked like I had gas. It didn't matter; Jocko was winding down and was ready to rest.

"Thanks again, After," he said. "I think I'd better get some sleep now."

I shook his hand and told him I'd try to get beck in the next day or so, but that I had heard he might be released soon.

"Come by here, or the house. Either one will be fine," Jocko said quietly.

I left him to his television and rest, then wandered down the hall to where I saw the policeman sitting outside another room.

I went up to him, and said, "Hi, I'm After Coffman, and I was wondering if I could have a few words with Greg?"

"Nope, not unless it's cleared by Lieutenant Howard, or the Chief."

I understood that and decided that it was time to go anyway. I needed some lunch, then I thought I'd go see what the erstwhile Lieutenant Howard had discovered and what he might wish to share with me. I walked out of the world of antiseptic hallways and bedpans into the clean, crisp air of Hustle, and made my way back to Mother's for a snack.

twelve

*I*t was quiet at Mother's. She must have gone to the store, and not one of the others was around either, so I figured that she took the old fossil with her. Maybe it was to time to get more blue in her hair. Lately it had been a nice shade of gray, and very soft looking. I liked it, but blue seemed to be in. When I was younger, my hair was longer, and all the old ladies with blue hair in tight curls would tell me how unnatural it was to have long hair. I held my temper, but it was difficult at times. Now, with my receding hairline and thin hair, it isn't a problem and the old ladies love me. I personally think it's unnatural to lose hair, but I can't appeal to a higher court, and I live with it. I have even noticed that some of the older ladies have got a decidedly pink look to their hair now. Maybe they are getting hip after all.

I tossed a sandwich together out of cold cuts, mustard and lettuce, threw some potato chips on a plate, grabbed a can of soda pop and sat down to eat. I was trying to piece the entire case together, and I had just about decided that Harold Gibbons was throwing me a red herring. He must know what had happened to Felix, and was covering his steps along the way by pretending to hire me. The last thing he needed was an investigation into his business, so by intimidating me and having me off on a wild goose chase, some of the pressure might go elsewhere. I had no illusions that he thought

I was capable of solving the case, I figured that he knew I was talking to Lieutenant Howard and Jocko, so perhaps I would unintentionally throw them on the wrong scent.

The sandwich was finished. My feet hurt, so I thought I'd stop by the department store and get a new pair of shoes while I was on my way to see the Lieutenant. I cleaned up my mess and walked out the door. It was another great late August day. Fall was approaching, but the humidity was near zero, there was a light breeze and autumn's colors were shouting at me. The kids in the neighborhood had worn down for the summer, and were about to go back to school, so the streets were relatively empty except for an occasional bike rider. I loved walking, it reminded me of the days of my youth when you knew what grass smelled like, and which gutters would have the water stopped up deep enough to wade in after a good rain. One knew where the good worms were, which neighbors had rhubarb growing in the back yard, where all the good cherry and apple trees were and when to harvest their fruit. Anyway, I was thinking all of these mellow thoughts as I entered the department store. I was greeted by a chirpy young salesgirl, and was informed that I was in the middle of the 'Back To School' sale. I ended up with a nice pair of loafers, some new tennis shoes, and I still had a few dollars left in my pocket.

I wore my new leather loafers, placing the old tennis shoes in the bag with my new ones and headed out to the police station, hoping to find the Lieutenant. I felt as though I was walking on air, the shoes were that wonderful.

I arrived at the police station in good shape and in record time. I was in luck, the cop at the door waved me back and I was soon in the crowded upper room, nearing the only neat desk in the area.

"Hi Lieutenant," I offered as I neared him.

He looked me over and said, "After, for all you've been through, you don't look that much worse than the first time I met you." He laughed.

I remember what I looked like the first time he met me, so this was no compliment. I sat down without comment, and waited for any new developments.

"We have Jocko's jailers in custody, but they were only following orders from the man you fought. I need to ask again, was he alive when you went in after Jocko?"

I nodded yes, and he sat back to digest this. I said, "He had been shot, maybe more than once. I could have been as well, but was just lucky, I guess. Anyway, I was looking right at him when he told me where Jocko was, and he was hurting at that moment, but not dying. I didn't see what happened after I left him."

"Well," the Lieutenant said, "He was shot in the side, and a leg, then in the middle of the forehead. I'll bet you can guess the type of bullet."

I must have opened my mouth in amazement, but was unable to speak for a second, and then I managed to squeak, "A .22?"

He nodded, and said, "The ballistics check out, it was the same gun used to kill Charlie Underhill and Patrick Bacon. Your shooter was in the area."

I had just figured that out as well. I was trying to make the connection. Someone was involved with saving me from my kidnapper as well as the man I was fighting with Saturday night. Who could it have been? I instantly thought of Roy, but he would have had to have foreknowledge of the kidnapping in order to be on that gravel road. I couldn't see him involved to that extent. The only solution was that one of Harold Gibbons' men was more involved than I had previously thought. I determined to factor this in for any future dealings. I also wondered why they would wish to keep me alive. I must be more useful to them this way, as they had had ample opportunity to take me out. The Lieutenant could see me pondering all of this, and he let me work through it.

"Lieutenant," I began, "I think someone is keeping me in the picture to throw you off the real track."

He nodded, saying, "I think so too, but what IS the real track? Is it Harold Gibbons' underworld dealings, or is it just the disappearance of Felix Jeffries? I have a feeling that we don't know the entire motive in the case."

I agreed with a nod of my head. "Is there anything else you can share with me?" I asked.

"Actually, I think you are as up to date as I am," he said.

I got up to leave, grabbing my bag. He got up with me and walked me to the door. He stopped as I was about to leave, then said, "Be sure to look around more, watch your back, re-evaluate your friends, your enemies and your situation. I think we are nearing a crisis point here. Basically, take care of yourself."

He seemed a bit embarrassed by this, and I was too. A little bit anyway. I needed to get some things done though. I also needed to go to Baltimore, so I said, "There are a few things I need, maybe you can help."

He looked at me, saying nothing.

"One," I began, "I need to talk with Jocko's friend, Greg, if possible, but you need to tell the officer at the door that it's OK."

"I'll do it right away," he assured me.

"Now, I also need to know if it's OK for me to leave town for a day or two. Felicity and I wanted to go to Baltimore. I won't lie to you, it may have something to do with the case, and it may not. I want to be able to go though, will it be alright?"

"You can come and go as you please, After. You are obviously no longer a suspect, and after what you did for Jocko, you are a bit of a hero around here. I would be laughed out of the department if I treated you as a suspect now."

"Thanks," I said, as I shook his hand. He gripped mine and said to be careful again, and that it might not hurt to let him know when I left and when I returned. I told him I would do so, and left the building, on my way back to the now familiar hospital.

I made my way to the elevator, and walked down the hallway, taking a peek into Jocko's room. It was empty, I hoped he had been sent home, as there were no flowers, or anything else to indicate he had been there. The alternative was that he'd been transferred. It wasn't a big enough hospital to move people around that much, so I felt sure he was home with his family. I proceeded to the officer in front of Greg's room. He nodded, and I told him who I was. He got up, and shook my hand, and told me the Lieutenant said that I could have 30 minutes of Greg's time. I told him thanks, and that it would probably be far less than that.

I entered the room and met Greg formally for the first time. He was in his 30s, a well built, dark haired man. He had a few tattoos on his arms, but otherwise he seemed to pass as your normal neighborly type. I introduced myself and he grinned. "I was hoping you'd stop by, I owe you my life and want to repay you, however I can," he said.

"All I require is information," I responded.

"Did Jocko tell you about me? Did he tell you we've been friends for 20 years, but that I made some mistakes and landed in prison?"

"Yes," I replied. "He did. He also said that you were helping him on a case, but that your cover was compromised somehow."

"I was living at the Boulevard Estates, and Jocko would come by and check on me. I think someone there blew my cover. Not the best clientele live there, you know."

"I know," I said. "That's where I met Jocko for the first time. I always wondered what he was doing in the neighborhood that morning."

"Looking after me, I suppose." He winced a bit, then said, "Say, could you pull that cord closer to me, I need to call the nurse for more medication. Got some bad burns on my chest and legs. I need something for the pain."

I pulled the call cord to him, and pushed the call button. He then laid back and gathered himself. The nurse entered quickly and took his order cheerfully. She bustled out again, saying she'd be right back.

I asked Greg, "So, what do you think tipped them off?"

"Well, this cat from Buffalo recognized me, and he put two and two together and came up with our plan. He was already paranoid, and this threw him totally over the edge. It was torture."

At this point the nurse returned, and gave him a shot. She said that he'd probably get dozy fairly quickly. I nodded and thanked her, as did Greg.

"Anyway, I thought we were goners until you showed up. I am sorry I ran out on you there, but I just panicked, after being tied up for two days, and feeling terrible, then the explosion and the smoke. I thought you might even be one of them, trying to kill me."

"No problem," I said, "I understand totally. Have you ever heard of Harold Gibbons?"

"That's a bad man," Greg said, "however, I don't believe I'd heard of him until they started to question me. I don't know how he is involved here, except that he might be a rival of my captors, because of his own drug deals."

"How about Felix Jeffries?" I asked.

"Oh, I've known Felix all my life," Greg responded. "Not the brightest bulb in the box, but a decent guy. His name never came up in this incident. Why, is he involved in this too?"

"I'm not sure. He's been missing, and it may have something to do with Mr. Gibbons."

He shook his head, and I noticed that he was getting slower to respond. I decided that I had all I was going to get. I stood up to leave. He looked at me and smiled, saying, "Come on back anytime, After. Thanks again, and let me know if anything comes up."

"I will, Greg," I said. "You get better, and we'll get caught up some other time."

He was asleep as I left the room. I went back down the hall, down the elevator and out into the sunny afternoon sky. There was time for a quick walk past Felicia's old house and then home for supper, before I went to work at Roy's.

I enjoyed the walk immensely, and really liked my new shoes. I wanted to show them to Felicity. I got to Felicia's house, but there was no old green car there. I knocked on the door, but there was no answer. I waited for a few minutes, then gave up and made it back to Mother's.

I entered my room, and noticed that Hurricane Soot, or Typhoon Mudsy had been at it again. My trash was dumped, all the contents from my dresser top were on the floor and the bedcovers had been totally disheveled. I sniffed to see if either had urinated in the room, but it seemed fresh. I considered myself lucky, and cleaned up the mess before I went downstairs for supper.

There were no extra females there, and James was off to wherever it was he went, so Hal, Paul, Estrella, Mother and I were the contingent for supper. Also, since there were no female guests, the food was bland, by Mother's standards. Cold ham, baked potato and leftover vegetables, along with assorted beverages was the fare for the evening. Nevertheless, it filled me up, and I considered the day to have been a success.

Estrella got my attention near the end of the meal and said, "After, your young lady called this afternoon, but I had no idea where you were. She said she'd drop by work tonight."

I said thanks and told her she looked particularly nice this evening. Her hair wasn't blue after all, but had received a perm. Mother beamed at me, as did Estrella. Hal snorted and asked me if two women weren't enough. This earned him reproachful glares from Mother and Estrella, and I gave him a quick wink, which he disregarded. I did notice that I got the largest slice of pie for dessert, and this fact was not wasted on Hal, as I saw him doing the mental math, conceding me the larger arc of pie; or was it pi? I took my dishes into the kitchen and headed out the door, on my way to work.

I arrived shortly before six, to find Roy sitting at ease behind the counter. He greeted me with that Santa Claus dimply smile and said, "It's good to have you still alive and kicking."

"I feel the same way, and thanks for all of your help and assistance that night."

"It won't do me any harm to have a friend on the police force," he retorted. "Besides, I've always had a soft spot for Jocko, known him since he was a baby."

"Speaking of Jocko," I warmed to the subject, "he told me that the man that was killed was asking about a gun running operation that was supposedly running out of Hustle."

Roy was surprised at this, and mused, "I guess all good things must come to an end. I was closing it down anyway, but now I should get it done tonight. Better call Grits." He rose and went to the phone, dialing a number from memory. He spoke with Grits, asking him how he was and suggesting that Grits come over to his house tonight as they had things to discuss.

I was very relieved, knowing that I would not have to lie to Jocko, or anyone else about illegal doings at Roy's Shoppe. I figured that Roy was probably up to other things as well, but so far I was unaware of any other nefarious goings on.

Roy busied himself for a few more minutes, took some items out of the drawer and said his good-byes. I didn't ask about taking time off to go to Baltimore yet, as I wasn't exactly sure when Felicity would want to leave. I busied myself, sold a few items and generally goofed off until 9:00 o'clock when the bells over the door tinkled and Felicity entered. She was in jeans and a tee shirt, somewhat dusty and dirty looking.

"Hi After!" She called out as she entered. "Excuse my appearance, but I've been all over mom's house looking for more clues on Felix. She's got some old stuff in the attic, and basement, but nothing we can use. I think she was pretty organized. I didn't see anything of mine, except those photos we saw earlier." This last phrase was said somewhat sadly.

"Well, I guess that's what we'll have to deal with then," I said. "We have the key and a destination. When would you like to go to Baltimore?"

"How about Wednesday morning?" she asked. "I could stand to do a bit more cleaning, then I thought I'd turn the place over to Pastor James and mom's church. They could sell it or use it in some manner, don't you think?"

"That's a wonderful idea," I exclaimed, sincerely impressed. "I think you should consider all the implications though. You could use the money, and Felix may show up to claim some of it."

"He could, but I doubt he'll care too much, it isn't worth all that much, and the church could really use it. If Felix is alive and two million dollars richer, he won't want the house, and he won't want to come back to see Mr. Gibbons anyway. I just want to find him, and see what he's really up to."

That was about all there was to it. We rummaged through Roy's desk, and discovered an old road map and discerned that it would be about a ten-hour trip to Baltimore. I took my money out of the cash drawer, and gave her a few dollars, telling her to get her car looked over, and maybe change the oil. She asked me to come by the next day and help her move a few things. I told her I'd be happy to. She then looked me over, told me I wasn't using my medicine and to shape up. I saluted and told her I would. She left Roy's with a cheery wave, blowing me a kiss and wiggling her hips as she walked out the door. I decided that it was time to invest in a deck of cards for the strip poker match.

I closed up the place, and, as the Lieutenant had suggested, was being extra cautious about locking the place, making sure doors were secured, and insuring that the coast was clear before I headed out the door. In case I was being followed, I took a different route to Mother's. There were no surprises, and I got home by fifteen after ten. Hal was watching the news, and I sat down to join him. He glanced at me, and asked if I wanted some tea or lemonade, stating that there were fresh pitchers of both in the refrigerator. I told him that was a good idea, got myself some lemonade, and grabbed a handful of cookies, as well. I offered him some, and he accepted, so we snacked our way through weather and sports, and made our separate ways back to our rooms. I folded my clothes and got into bed, where I had an uneventful night's sleep.

I awoke the next morning, feeling pretty good. I went into the bathroom, found Paul's glasses in the sink and took them to him. He was blundering through his room, apparently looking for them. He thanked me, and I asked him how Niki was.

"She's wonderful, After!" Paul exclaimed. "Tonight we are painting her apartment, then I am buying her a few new pieces of furniture for it. She really can't afford anything at this time, so I'm helping her out."

"Did you come home last night?" I asked casually, not really caring either way.

"Yes, her cousin was in town and they decided to visit, so she was unavailable last night," he said.

"Oh, is she pretty too?" I asked innocently.

"Is who pretty?"

"Her cousin."

"Her cousin is a guy, she hasn't seen him in months, and he was staying at her place last night. He's going back home today."

It didn't sound all that great to me, but it was none of my business, so I let it slide, wished him a good day, and went back to the bathroom, where I shaved, showered and put on my medicine. I am generally a fast healer, and lately that's turned out to be a godsend, so I was feeling better than I had in quite some time when I went downstairs in my best shirt, clean jeans, a new pair of gold toed socks, and my new shoes.

Breakfast was pancakes, eggs, and fruit, so I was in good shape after eating. Mother asked me what the plans were for today, and I told her that as far as I knew, just helping Felicity clean up her mother's house. She thought that was nice and said I needed a day off just to clear out my mind.

I had to ask, "Mother, would you happen to have a deck of cards I could borrow?"

She raised an eyebrow, then said that there ought to be a few decks in the hutch next to the television in the front room. I wandered in there after clearing off my dishes and found several newer looking decks, as well as one older set. I grabbed one of the newer sets, and counted the cards. They were all there, so I put them in my pocket and sauntered out the door, again, after looking in all directions to insure that it was safe to venture forth.

Just as I was leaving, Paul came running out the door, asking me to stop. I stopped, turned to ask him why, and he smiled shyly, reminding me that I had promised him an interview.

"I thought you were going to paint Niki's apartment," I said.

"Oh, I am, but this shouldn't take too long, come back in, I'm all ready to go."

I couldn't refuse him, so I trudged back in, and went with him up to his room where he had a pad of paper and several pencils of varying lengths at the ready. He sat on the edge of his bed and looked at me expectantly.

I looked back at him. He looked at me. I felt that this could go on indefinitely, so I decided to break the ice. "What do you want to know?" I asked.

"I don't know," he admitted. "This is the first interview I've done."

"It's my first one as well," I told him.

"OK," he said, "let's start with your name."

I looked at him in astonishment, "Paul, you know my name!"

"Oh yeah, I guess we can skip that part, and where you live too, and even what you do, I guess I can fill all that in later."

"Good," I said. "Maybe I'll just tell you what happened, at least the part I can share without breaching any confidentiality."

"Maybe I should call you an unnamed source. They like unnamed sources, more mysterious!"

"Sure, do whatever you like." I then proceeded to tell him about getting information about a local policeman being held prisoner in a little house outside the city. I told him that three friends went along. I told him about the fight, the fire and the rescue. I told him about the hospital and that things should work out OK for the cop and his friend. He asked me who the other three were. I told him Roy and Grits, and let it go at that.

Paul was satisfied, and went back over a few points, as he didn't write especially quickly, and his pencils kept breaking. "This will get me out of obituaries for sure," he gushed.

I was more than happy to get him out of obituaries, and I hoped it would help him gain esteem in the eyes of Niki, to the point where he might not need as much cosmetic surgery.

I went downstairs, grabbed a few pieces of toast and some orange juice and strolled out the door, feeling pretty good. I made my way to Felicia's house, knocked on the door, and hearing a cheery "Come in," decided to do just that!

The place was looking better. The windows were open, and were freshly cleaned. Felicity had been polishing the woodwork and the house had that lemony smell, mixed in with that fresh outdoor scent. The curtains had been washed and re-hung. It was amazing how much it had improved in looks and smell.

"The place is really looking good," I remarked.

Felicity came up, threw her arms around me and gave me a dusty kiss, as her face was somewhat streaked with the removed grime and dirt. "Thanks, After. Would you care for a drink? I have tea, lemonade or water."

"Lemonade sounds very good," I said, and she promptly went to the refrigerator and took out a big glass pitcher of the stuff, poured me a glass, tossed in some ice cubes and gave it to me. It tasted wonderful.

"I haven't cleaned the refrigerator or the stove yet, been concentrating on the walls and floors."

"Let me do those two then, and you keep doing what you are doing."

She handed me some gloves, some scouring powder and a bucket of water, and I went to work. The two appliances weren't in bad shape and it didn't take me long to get both gleaming and clean. I then went to work on the cabinets, removing all the remaining food and tossing whatever looked hopeless. There were a few bugs and mice droppings, so I figured the cleaning was overdue. Through all of this work, Felicity and I took extra care to keep an eye out for any clues or information that Felix or Felicia may have left behind. We found nothing new. By noon, we were a bit back weary, so I suggested we go out for lunch. She agreed, and went to her room to freshen up. It just took a few minutes, but she managed to transform herself again, and suddenly I was going out with a pretty sexy number. I felt inadequate and told her so, but she assured me that all I needed to do was wash my face. I went into the bathroom, and determined that it would be the next room to clean. The tub was old, there were stains by the drain, and the tile was falling apart in places. I knew that we weren't spending a lot of money, just to turn the house over to the church, but I thought a little expenditure might be worthwhile. I cleaned up and we left the house, walking up the street to a fast food hamburger joint. We walked hand in hand and I thought that I might actually get used to this before long.

I told her that I wanted to pick up some grout at the hardware store after we ate, and she thought it was a marvelous idea. We ate lunch, and she surprised me by pulling out a hundred dollars, and saying that she had found a stash of her mother's money while cleaning the house. She insisted that lunch was on her mother, as was the grout, so I accepted and thanked Felicia silently.

We went to the hardware store and bought the grout, some tiles, and a hammer that she thought she needed. We then proceeded to the grocery store where we bought a few necessities, and Felicity bought a nice bottle of wine. She suggested that I come over to drink it after I finished work for the night. I pulled out the deck of cards, and she had the courtesy to blush. We both grinned, and I said I'd be over.

We returned to the house and I busied myself in the bathroom, replacing the bad tiles and using the new grout. The job wasn't difficult, the old grout was crumbly and I had the job done by 4 o'clock.

Felicity came in after a bit and kept me company. She asked me again when I thought we should head out to Baltimore, and I told her I'd ask Roy that night if he could spare me for a few days. Felicity also thought I should get a phone for my office and get the number listed. She had found an old answering machine in her mother's bedroom, and gave it to me. I promised her that I would make the phone a priority, and that was about it.

I needed to go to Mother's, get cleaned up and eat supper before going in to work. I gave Felicity a hug and a quick kiss, and she led me to the door. She thanked me a few more times, and I told her I hadn't had that much of a good time in quite a while. I left her at the door, and returned along the route to Mother's, thinking about how nicely my life was going for a change. Things stayed upbeat until I turned the last corner, and as I approached Mother's house, I ran right into Harold Gibbons' goons.

"Hello, Mr. Coffman, would you have a few minutes for Mr. Gibbons?" one of the guys asked politely. He was not the one who had sucker punched me, so I thought about it for a moment, trying to conjure up an excuse. Thinking of none, I decided to go along. They seemed friendly today, and I truly had nothing new to tell Mr. Gibbons. We got into their car and headed back to 'The Green Frog'.

thirteen

We drove in silence to 'The Green Frog'. The guys didn't seem upset or worried about the situation or me, and I had no idea what was going down. I wished that I had had a chance to tell someone where I was going, as it would probably be pretty easy for me to disappear without a trace. We arrived and entered the front door. Joe was at his station, with a few early customers. He looked at me without acknowledging me in any way. I nodded anyway. One of the goons relieved me of my new answering machine, but he walked along with us, and I kept him in sight.

Harold was at his usual table, sitting with two floozies. He snapped his fingers and they got up, scurrying away and leaving through a door behind him. He smiled and asked me to sit down. I did so.

"Well, Mr. Coffman, I see you've been a busy little soldier." He was not unfriendly, but he was playing his cards close to the vest.

"Just had to help out one of my friends," I replied.

"You may not know it, but you did me a big favor as well. Those guys were trying to move in on some of my territory. Legitimate stuff, of course," he added, with a wink.

I tried to look non-committal, but still had some trouble swallowing.

"Get us a few drinks," he told one of the goons. Then Harold leaned back in his chair, closed his eyes and appeared for all the world to be taking a nap. I just sat there, waiting for the drink.

It came shortly, a Chivas double on the rocks. I was impressed that they still remembered me.

Harold roused himself as his drink was given to him. The goon stood patiently by his boss as Harold took a sip. He seemed startled when Harold looked at him and ordered him to get lost, but he walked about 30 feet away and took up his new station reluctantly. I tried not to look too dangerous as I asked, "Why did you want to see me again?"

"Well, after your heroics Saturday night, I thought I'd just have another talk with you, and see if there were any new developments in the Felix Jeffries case."

"Nothing new," I said, "as far as I know, the two cases have nothing to do with each other." I thought I was telling the truth, for even though Felicity was at the scene of the fire, she was basically along for the ride. There was nothing to indicate this drug group was involved with Felix. I began to rethink that idea though, as it might have been a coincidence that two drug groups were working the same area, and it might not be such a stretch at all. Maybe Felix was double dealing Harold and working with the other group. Maybe Harold was thinking the same thing. Either way, I wasn't going to let him know I had gotten myself up to speed on this aspect of the case(s).

I sat back and waited for whatever it was he needed to tell me. I didn't wait long. He leaned back again, fixed his gaze on me, then asked, "Are you sure there are no new developments in the case? You have been talking to the Lieutenant quite a bit, and I don't like you being so friendly with this Irish cop either."

I must have finally gotten a look on my face, as I felt myself redden and begin to get angry. How dare he tell me who to be with and not to be with? I got up to go, and the goon started toward me. Harold put up a hand, stopping both of us. He motioned lazily for me to sit down again. I thought about it, then decided to sit one more time.

Harold's mood shifted, he tried to smile, and did a passable job of it. He said, "I see that you can't be bullied, and I admire that in you. Actually, I was feeling badly that I had hired you on a contingency basis. You ought to be paid for what you are doing for me."

I wasn't aware that I had actually been working for Mr. Gibbons, but I decided to hear him out. I sat there quietly, saying nothing.

He examined me a minute or so more, then reached into his shirt pocket, pulling out a wad of bills. He tossed them onto the table, and I watched them land in front of me. He said, "There is a thousand dollars there, maybe it will help you in your search for Felix. You still get the five grand if you tell me where he is before you tell anyone else."

It sounded like a fair deal to me, but I didn't want to work for him. I gently pushed the money back at him and said, "Sorry, I'll do what I can, but I am not working for you."

He stood up, picked up the money and started to walk to the door, motioning for me to follow. I did so, and watched as the goons fell in behind us. I prepared myself for another blow to the belly, but it never came. Instead, Mr. Gibbons placed his arm over my shoulder, and watched patiently as one of the goony boys opened the door. He then shoved the money into my hands, and said, "Take it." The other bodyguard returned my answering machine to me and the meeting was over.

Harold pushed me out and the door closed behind me. There was no one outside with me, so I assumed I was to walk home. I didn't know what to do with the money. I knew I'd been had, but wasn't really sure how. Harold wanted a hold on me, but he could have had that by continually beating me up. Maybe he decided he needed a friend. I considered just leaving the money there, but it would have disappeared and I would have never been able to prove that I had done so. I decided to put the money in a safe place, and forget about it until I could return it to him, preferably, with witnesses. Having assuaged my conscience, I walked back to Mother's, making it to the door without further incident. I took my machine up to my room and placed it on my dresser.

There was enough time for me to clean up and get downstairs for supper, but I was pushing it a bit. As usual, James was not there, but the others were. As there still were no female guests tonight, the fare was a bit more mundane. Bacon, lettuce and tomato sandwiches on toasted rye, with Mother's home made fries and tall glasses of milk. I had seconds and topped it off with a helping of chocolate pudding with cherries mixed in. I've always loved that dessert. Paul looked at me, and told me that he was almost done with his story, I smiled back encouragingly and went on eating my pudding. I felt that it was nice of him to take an interest, but I had no hope that he'd succeed in selling that story to his boss.

I carried my dishes in, and told Mother I'd be working late at Felicity's house, and not to worry if I didn't come straight home. She smiled and said nothing. I went upstairs, found one of my un-matched socks, stuffed the thousand dollars in it as best as I could, then hid it under the other socks in my drawer. I put on clean clothes and checked myself over, as I was hoping to pass for clean and natty when I got to Felicity's later that night.

I made sure the room was in good shape, and that there were no cats in it, then closed the door and tripped lightly down the stairs, waving to everybody as I went off to work.

Roy was in his usual jovial mood, and Grits was there as well, along with his dog. She came up to me, tail wagging and I petted her as I made my greetings.

"How ya doing, Grits?" I asked.

"Fine, just fine After," he said. "How are the burns?"

"To tell you the truth, I keep forgetting to put my medicine on them, and they don't seem to be bothering me too much anyway."

I then asked Roy if he could spare me for a few days, and he said that he could. Grits popped up again and asked if he could work my nights while I was gone, as he had no road trips coming up, and could use the cash. Roy looked at me, and I said that it was fine by me. That was settled and I was glad, as I had imposed on Roy quite a bit lately.

I also told Roy that I had an answering machine now, and was thinking of getting a phone installed. He agreed that this would be a great idea, and said to do it anytime. With that, the two friends left me to run the shop, Roy again reminding me to watch out for myself, that it might not be safe out there just yet.

I had a fairly busy night, selling quite a few pieces, and ringing up several hundred dollars for the cause. I took my earnings that I had obtained, including the night's work, and felt ready for a quick trip to Baltimore. Felicity's car didn't look all that great, but it actu-ally drove well, and seemed solid from the inside. I felt that we could make good time, now that I had reacquired my driver's li-cense and could help with the driving. The evening went quickly and I closed up shop right at 10 o'clock. I called Mother and told her I was going out of town for a few days, and might make a quick trip home for clothes. She thanked me, and told me to please be careful. I made sure that the coast was clear, but couldn't really think about whom might be after me, as Mr. Gibbons was my primary suspect and he seemed to be with me at the moment.

All was quiet as I exited, and made my way to Felicia's house. Once I got there, I spent a few minutes outside, looking around the house, to see if there was anything suspicious. There was nothing, it was a nice fall night, with some cicadas chirping and an occasional dog barking. The moon was bright, and I felt like a million bucks as I went to the front door. I knocked, and Felicity answered. She smiled and let me in. I looked around, and she had rearranged a few things, and it looked more like her place somehow. It was very comfortable, and still smelled of a fresh cleaning. Felicity ushered me into the kitchen where there was a plate of cut vegetables, and some fruit, as well as cheese and crackers. The wine was chilling in a bucket of ice and I allowed myself to totally relax and prepared to enjoy a fantastic evening, the type I had dreamt about all of my post puberty life.

"It looks wonderful!" I exclaimed, meaning it. I sat down and sampled some of the treats. Felicity sat across from me, wearing a patterned sundress, sandals and a barrette. Again, minimal make-up and it suited her.

We talked about the house a bit, and she told me she was just about done with the cleaning. I told her it was looking superb, and she gleamed with delight. She asked me about Baltimore, and I told her I was basically ready to go, and we could leave whenever she liked. She thought about it and said, "Well, you might as well sleep here, we can eat breakfast and get going as soon as we wish. I think that it's only about 8 hours to Baltimore if the traffic isn't too bad." I had thought it was a longer trip, but I wasn't going to argue about ANY of her plans.

We opened the wine, had a few glasses, then feeling pretty comfortable, we took the bottle into the front room, along with some cheese and crackers, and settled down onto the couch. The kissing began somehow, became a bit more intense, and just about the time my hands decided to do some exploring, she sat back, grinned at me and asked, "Did you remember the cards?"

I laughed and fumbled around, half-tipsy and half feeling silly. I discovered them in a hip pocket and handed them over to her. She riffled the deck like a pro, cut them with one hand and dealt out five cards very quickly. Being a Private Investigator, I am highly trained in watching people, as you know. It was obvious from the beginning that she had dealt cards before. I was determined not to let her deal every hand. I looked at my hand; I had a pair of 4s, a ten, a jack and a queen. I asked for three cards and was gratified to see my third 4 appear. She took one card, and we prepared to lay them on the table. She had a full house, kings high, so I was beaten.

She looked at me, grinned and said, "Shirt." I took my shirt off. She won the next three hands, so I had lost my shoes, socks and pants before she lost her first hand.

I said, "Dress," and she took her dress off. That's all she was wearing besides her sandals, so I felt I'd won 3 hands. I couldn't take my eyes off of her, and she was feeling no pain or embarrassment either.

I kept looking, and she did too. Then, she just got up and walked to the lamp, turning it off. She took the food into the kitchen and placed it in the refrigerator. Languidly, he took her shoes off, flung them to the wall, and proceeded to remove the last bit of my clothing. I picked her up and we went to her bedroom, where we proceeded to spend the next hour getting close before we both fell off to sleep.

I awoke alone in bed the next morning, feeling pretty good. I heard water running in the bathtub, and wandered into the bathroom. She was just standing there, hand on her hip, waiting for me.

"I heard you get up, and thought I'd wait to see if you wanted to join me for a bath." She grinned up at me.

We got in and spent an enjoyable time in the tub, washing each other, laughing and planning our trip.

Once that was over, as well as a few other interesting tidbits that you need not know about, we got dressed. I shaved, using one of her razors, and we went to the car. She drove me to Mother's, and I raced up the stairs, got a bag and tossed in a few shirts, another pair of jeans, and some socks. I was ready to go. I glanced at my watch and it read 8:30, so I thought we'd done rather well. Actually, I thought we'd done fantastically well.

We got into the car, went to the gas station, filled up the car's tank and got on the road. We drove for about 6 hours, got out, stretched our legs at a scenic overview, and sat on a bench, where we just sort of relaxed for a half hour. It was my turn to drive when we got going again, and she did well with navigating as we neared the city and its increased traffic. It was just around 5:30 PM when we actually got to town. The traffic was as bad as one might think, given that it was rush hour. I never know why they call it rush hour, as no one was moving at all most of the time. There was an old man pushing a grocery cart with all of his belongings on the shoulder of the road and he passed us by, disappearing over the horizon. We never did catch up to him. I wanted to eat, so we diverted to a mall, and found a café court, where she had pasta and I ate Chinese. We decided to go to the restroom/telephone area and try to find the place where Felix's key might have come from.

After a search for a phone book proved fruitless, I was finally able to cajole the cashier out of a book of yellow pages. I looked up and dialed many numbers. I tried the bus depot, and all of the post offices, but none of them knew what Station #2 was. I was feeling stymied, when Felicity suggested we try looking under 'Mailboxes'. Bingo, there they were. Stations #1, #2, and #3. I got the address for Station #2 and we got back to the car and drove to a gas station where we purchased a map of the city. Felicity continued to navigate while we drove around the city, trying to decipher our way through the one-way streets and dead ends that just didn't seem to show on the map.

We finally arrived at our destination, and got out of the car. We were in an older, but carefully preserved area near the waterfront. The houses were all of the elegant brownstone variety, rarely more than two stories high. The streets were clean and well kept. The houses had small lawns that were neatly trimmed and devoid of any plastic deer or tiny coachmen holding lanterns. No wooden cut outs of overweight women bending over to pluck flowers or any sounds of Country or Rap coming from the windows, so we felt pretty safe about our surroundings. I wasn't sure what scared me most, the plastic figurines on people's lawns or the fact that some people actually thought Country passed for real music. I guess the latter scared me most, as maybe one might think plastic deer were real from a very far distance, but how anyone ever thought the 'Dixie Chicks' or Garth could pass for anything musical was beyond me. You go, Dr. Dre!

Anyway, we found our target nestled between two staid old houses, it was a reclaimed version of its neighbors. It had a nice gray door, with a simple gold colored sign affixed to it reading 'Mailbox #2'. We entered together, hoping they weren't closed. An older man was behind the counter, and when we expressed our relief that he was still open, he merely said that they were open twenty-four hours a day, seven days a week. I held out the key we had recovered from the bottom of Felix's dresser drawer and asked if we could go to its box. He asked me to sign in, and I deferred to Felicity, saying that she was his sister. He balked at this, saying that these were very much like safety deposit boxes and that we had to be an authorized user. We told him that the box's owner might be permanently missing and that we thought a clue as to his whereabouts might be in it. He didn't budge. I pulled out the picture of Felix that Felicity had given me from the family photo album and asked if he looked familiar. The old man started in recognition, paled a bit, but managed to stammer that he'd never seen the man in the photograph before.

I could see that we were getting nowhere, and Felicity seemed to agree, as she looked at me and arched an eyebrow. I told the man thanks, and that we would try to get some sort of release to look at the box. He agreed that we should do exactly that, and he ushered us out the door, watching us as we went to Felicity's car and obviously not trusting us to drive away.

We drove for a few blocks, and I found a parking lot to drive into. I turned to Felicity and asked her what she thought we ought to do.

"I don't know, After. I'm worn out and I didn't expect this. Maybe we should get a room somewhere and sleep on it, then try something tomorrow morning."

I was tired too, so we drove around and found an older, but clean motel and got ourselves a room. It wasn't all that late by the time we checked in, but having been up most of the previous night, and having driven all day, we were just disappointed upon our arrival. I was tired and ready for bed.

Felicity soon amended the situation when she appeared in the bathroom doorway with nothing on but a smile, and asked if I would care to join her in the bathtub.

I hopped to it, suddenly rejuvenated, and we spent an hour splashing and playing in the tub, then dried off and spent the rest of the evening in bed, watching MTV and finally dropping off to sleep around midnight.

I woke at just after 7 o'clock, and realized that Felicity was gone. The room was empty, and her purse was nowhere to be seen. I got some clothes on and went to the door. The car was gone as well. There was no note, and nothing to do except wait. I turned the TV on and watched the news. Felicity opened the door a few minutes later and bustled in with her arms full of packages. One bag had hot bagels and muffins, another had two coffees. The third and largest, was from Wal-Mart.

"Thank goodness Wal-Mart is open all night," she panted as she unburdened herself. She gave me a quick hug and went to the bathroom with her Wal-Mart bag.

I settled down to a bagel with cream cheese and a cup of decent coffee. As a younger man, I didn't drink coffee. It used to make me sweat and gave me a burning in the stomach, but I had apparently developed a tolerance for the stuff. Mother brews great coffee, by anyone's standards, so I was spoiled. Anyway, I needed fortification, and I wasn't going to be picky. Felicity appeared in a few minutes wearing a killer low cut dress, with hose and heels. She had done her make-up and looked somewhere between sexy, alluring, and trashy. She was wonderful and I told her so.

"Well, I thought I'd see if I could influence the guy who works the day shift," she murmured while attaching some spangled ear-rings. I thought that it was a great idea, she would have influenced me for sure.

"What if it's a female working behind the counter?" I asked.

She grinned and said she'd do basically the same thing, just change the words. I would have given anything to know what the magic words were, but wasn't going to get the chance, as she told me that I was staying in the car, while she was going in to retrieve whatever was in the box.

We finished up the food, got our stuff together, took a last quick look around the place and left, tossing our clothes and bags into the trunk of the car. We found the old brownstones again. I gave Felicity the key to the box and she got out of the car and waltzed her way into the building as if she owned the place. I sat in the car patiently and still wondered what she was saying to the person behind the counter. I was also wondering if she was going to return empty handed or with up to 2 million dollars in tow.

One of those extra large pick up trucks pulled in behind me. It was on raised wheels and had all sorts of chrome on it. Lights on a rack on top of the cab, decals stating the driver was a 'Bad Ass' and that sort of thing. It pulled up right behind me and idled. The fact that no one got out of it bothered me a bit, but I figured Felicity would be right along, so I started her car and let it idle as well.

I tried to get a glimpse of how many were in the truck. With trucks, you never know. I've seen trucks with entire nuclear families squashed in them, from grandparents all the way down to babies and dogs. I never could figure out why eight or more people had to squish into a cab. Maybe it was so they could all hear Reba at once. I couldn't see a thing however, as the windshield was one of those black types that police hate, hiding any and all occupants.

Anyway, I didn't have to wait long. Felicity came racing out of the building, pulling a shoe on as she came, sort of hopping and running at the same time. She jumped into the car and gushed breathlessly, "Get out of here!"

I didn't wait; I peeled out, looking in the rearview mirror as I did so. I saw a man run from the truck into the building. I had to stop behind a large delivery van for just a second, and I stole another peek in the rearview mirror. The man was running out of the building, back to the truck, and it was pulling quickly out into the street as he clambered back inside it.

I hoped that no one was coming the other way, and I pulled out around the van and sped by him. No one was coming, which was good for us, but bad as well, as the large truck behind us had no qualms, and was racing down the road after us. I turned right and sped down the new street, knowing that I couldn't out race the truck, but hoping I could outmaneuver it. It was gaining on me when I spied a narrow alley to my right. I turned hard into it and was gratified to see that it went clear through to another street. I drove quickly, and saw that the alley was quite narrow, with dumpsters and other trash receptacles scattered along its path. I managed to avoid the obstacles, but I noticed that the truck was gaining on us and slamming into the dumpsters, bins and cans, tossing them aside as if they were cardboard.

"Someone doesn't like us," I managed to gasp as I struggled with the steering.

"Maybe it was something we said?" Felicity retorted.

"Or something Felix did," which was all I could manage to say, as I swerved and merged into the traffic on the other side of the block. I tried to insinuate myself between two larger vehicles, but that was a mistake as they were slower than those in the lane next to us were. It wasn't long before the large pick up was to my left, looking a bit under the weather for having scrabbled its way through the alley. I still couldn't see the occupants, black windows being the norm on this vehicle. All of the sudden, the passenger window rolled down and the end of a shotgun poked out.

I yelled "DUCK!" just as it blasted at us. I was getting as low as I could and I turned the wheel blindly to the right and put on the brakes. The truck behind us rammed the back of our car, and it spun us in a near circle, such that I was now sideways in the lane, my side of the car facing the oncoming truck. The driver was apparently trying to slow down, but he broadsided me anyway sending us off toward the shoulder again. We slued into the soft, loose gravel, where we continued on into a somewhat controlled slide down a slope. We stopped and I poked my head up and looked around. The front windshield was missing, and the dashboard was peppered with holes. Felicity was pale, but sitting up alongside me. "Are you OK?" I asked.

She nodded, and then pointed. The large truck had pulled onto the shoulder ahead of us and was racing at us in reverse.

"We'd better get out and run!" Felicity screamed.

I tried to open my door, but it had been damaged, either by the truck hitting us, or the shotgun, so I motioned that we needed to get out her side. It was going to be too late anyway, as the large truck was on us. Deliverance came in the form of a patrol car, which screeched to a point between our vehicles. The patrolman got out and was advancing toward us, when I saw the gunman jump out of the truck and follow the patrolman as he neared us.

I cried, "Look out!" just as the gunman raised his shotgun. The patrolman stopped, spun and pulled out his gun in one fluid motion. He hit the dirt rolling to one side and shot the shotgun wielding creep twice, hitting him in the chest both times. The man fell to the ground and the truck sped off. The patrolman got up, yelled at me to stay put and got into his car, turning on his light and siren, then racing off in pursuit.

I had no intention of staying put, so I put the car into gear and tried to get back up the incline. The ground was too soft and the car couldn't navigate it. There was nothing to do but drive through the grassy lawn we were near, in front of some sort of office building. The car tried to stall out a few times, and we were almost stuck in the softer areas, but we did get to a parking lot, and drove directly over the cement wheel stop, and onto solid ground.

I stopped long enough to see if the truck or the cop had returned, but the only thing I saw was a crowd gathering around the body of the gunman. I drove to the end of the parking lot and continued out the exit on the other side. I felt that we needed some room between us and all of the commotion, so I drove carefully through an older part of town, where a car with a missing windshield would not necessarily be unheard of. We managed to drive on in this manner for some time, and I finally spied a car wash that looked somewhat enclosed and safe. I pulled into it, and Felicity and I spent some time removing the glass and debris from the car, and cleaned it up as best we could. We then took it to the vacuum machine, and cleaned the interior. There was nothing else to do except attempt to return to Hustle as quickly as we could.

I found my way to the highway, and we got oriented back onto the westbound lane. I had to squint to see against the wind, but was saved when Felicity gave me a pair of sunglasses. They were a bit small for my face, but served as an effective windshield for my eyes as I drove. Felicity got into the back of the car, where she had a bit of respite from the wind.

I tried to talk with her as we drove, but it was pretty noisy, so I gave up. We'd been on the road for three hours, when I spied a truck stop and pulled off. I was hungry, tired and confused, and I needed to get caught up.

Felicity must have felt the same way as she got out of the car with me, groaning and complaining about being stiff. She wanted to get into the trunk of the car, and get a change of clothes, the red dress and heels being too conspicuous. While she was rummaging through the trunk, I asked her, "Did you ever get into the box?"

She nodded and grimly handed me an envelope. I opened it, noticing that she had already ripped it earlier. Inside was a sheet of paper with about 20 numbers and letters on it. The first thing I thought of was some sort of bank account, but it would take further study. I wanted to ask Felicity what had happened inside the building, but decided to wait until we were sitting and eating. She grabbed some clothes and marched into the restaurant, going straight to the Ladies room. I decided to stay outside and stand guard.

She was out in no time, and handed me her fancy clothes. She asked if I would take them back to the car and place them in the trunk while she found a table. I did exactly that; hitting the Men's room on the way back, and finding her more composed and relaxed at a table with a clear view of the parking lot. We wouldn't be surprised again.

We ordered burgers, fries and soft drinks and sat back to wait for our order. I started to ask her about the morning several times, but she quieted me with sharp looks. She just wasn't ready to relive it at the moment. Our food arrived and we ate in silence. As I was polishing it up, I had a disquieting thought. "What if those guys trace us by the license plates?"

She actually grinned at this and said, "I never buy plates, I took those off another car in Chicago. I can always claim they were swapped with mine, if I get caught."

That made sense for a moment, and I remembered that Lieutenant Howard had thought she used an alias. Then I had two other thoughts. "What if they go after innocent people?"

She shrugged, unconcerned, "There are no innocent people."

"What if you were pulled over and they bought your story about the license plates, but then asked you what your original plates were?"

"Hmmmm, I hadn't thought of that. I guess I'd better get some plates then, huh?" Still fairly unconcerned, but I could see that she was bothered by the fact that she hadn't thought this one out clearly.

"OK," I began, "it's time to find out what happened in there."

"Well, I went in and there was a young man behind the counter. He was friendly and even flirted a little. I told him I needed to get into the box and he asked me to sign in. I signed Felix Jeffries, and he didn't buy it. I said that my name is Felicity, but that everyone calls me Felix. He still didn't buy it, and he asked me to wait. He went into a back room and I heard him dialing a phone. I snuck in behind him and heard him tell someone 'They're back'. I took off my shoe and conked him on the head."

I must have grimaced, as she stopped, gave me a concerned look and then had to laugh. I laughed then as well.

She continued, "I figured that our goose was pretty well cooked, so I looked around, found the box, unlocked it and found only the envelope. I got out of there, trying to put my shoe on and all. I saw the truck behind you, and knew we were had. You know the rest."

"It was too close for me," I sighed.

"Me too," she agreed.

We sat back and relaxed, enjoying the respite. I just sort of let thoughts float in and out of my head. We had traveled for about three hours, and I figured we'd make Hustle by evening. We could try to get the car repaired tomorrow, and then maybe try and make some sense of the code on the piece of paper in the envelope. I was beginning to get disgusted with Felix. Did the guy have to write everything down all the time? Was there no end to the trail of cryptic scraps of paper, and keys, and questions he was raising? I needed to have a serious talk with the lad, if I ever got to meet him. I was pretty sure he was buried in the ground somewhere, or had become fish food, or maybe had been fed to some hogs at a farm far away. If these characters were willing to kill us in broad daylight, they would have gotten to Felix by now, I was sure.

We got up from the table, paid for our meal, and bought another pair of sunglasses for me at the counter. We left our haven and got back into the car, pulling on our glasses, and ready for the adventure to end. We drove into the afternoon, fairly quiet at this time, as it was still difficult to talk against the wind. I was getting tired, so we pulled over around 4 o'clock and she took over for the last leg into Hustle.

The sun was directly in our faces as we crested the last hill and saw the town sprawled out ahead of us. We got into town and drove to Felicity's, where she pulled the car as far into the driveway as she could. We got out and unpacked, entering the house and collapsing on her couch.

I must have fallen asleep for a bit, as I was startled by a noise, only to find that Felicity was scrounging up some food for us. It was getting dark outside and I figured it was time for me to go home.

I walked into the kitchen and said, "I'd like a snack, then I think I'll walk home."

She turned to face me and said, "I think that would be a good idea, I'll have something ready in a moment.

I walked back to the front room, found the envelope and took out the piece of paper, studying it. I tore the flap off the envelope and copied the code onto it, then folded my scrap of paper and placed it in my billfold. I returned the original to the envelope.

Felicity entered with some leftovers from two nights before, as well as some bread and cold cuts. They tasted wonderful. We munched away in silence, and then both stretched and sighed at the same time. I got up, went to her, gave her a hug and told her I'd check in on her in the morning. She nodded, picked up the dishes and smiled at me. It was time to go. I went out the door, locking it behind me and began my walk back to Mother's.

fourteen

There was definitely something going on at Mother's. There were a half dozen people sort of sitting on her lawn. There was a van out at the street curb and lawn chairs set up at various places. I was concerned, as there were no police cars or ambulances, but also, no reason that I could see for the mass of people. As I got nearer, I noticed that the van had an antenna protruding from its roof, a powerful looking one at that!

I increased my pace and got within a few yards of the place when one of the men noticed me, jumped up, looked at me and shouted, "There he is!"

Everyone started running towards me. I thought that they were the bad boys from Baltimore, and I began to run back the way I had come. They began to outflank me, some were quite young and in pretty good shape. One young blond stud seemed to gain on me effortlessly and drew up next to me. I stopped and got ready to fight to the death, but I couldn't catch my breath, so I just stood there, awaiting my doom. It presented itself in the form of a microphone. The young man said, "Really, Mr. Coffman, we just want a word or two with you."

I sat down, still gasping for air. What would a person with a microphone want with me? He waited solicitously while I searched for a combination of oxygen, nitrogen and trace elements that would allow me to continue my existence, and by the time I got back to near normal, the rest of the group had caught me. I stood up, brushed myself off and tried to look presentable.

The blond man and a cameraman come forward, they did a few things, and I was finally able to ask, "What in the world are you doing, and why are you doing it with me?"

The blond man grinned and stated, "You are now a celebrity Mr. Coffman. We have interviewed Jocko O'Reilly, Roy Mack, several cops, and we've all just been waiting for you. Have you been out of town working on a case? Would you care to discuss that case as well?"

It was all too much for me. My mouth must have been hanging open, as I knew that my tongue was getting dry, and it was suddenly difficult to swallow. This was my big break, and I was acting the fool. I excused myself, turned my back to all of them, and counted to ten, while attempting to put my thoughts in some sort of order.

I got a bit calmer, and turned to them, with what I hoped was my best smile. A lady came forward, brushed the reporter's hair, straightened his tie and jacket, and looked doubtfully at me. I grinned, and she came forward and did the best she could with me as well. I had lost hair, nothing was cut evenly, I still had remnants from my burns, my eyebrows were singed, but I assumed it would add color to their story.

The young man did a sound check then turned to me, the cameraman at his side. "We are talking to Mr. After Coffman, a recent hero here in the small town of Hustle. Last Saturday night; he went into a burning house to rescue an undercover cop and another man, both victims of kidnappers. He also single handedly took down a known drug runner, who is unfortunately dead, and can't help us with the details of this story." He turned to me, "Mr. Coffman, would you care to tell us what happened this past Saturday night?"

"I didn't do that much," I began uncomfortably. "In fact, if others hadn't been along and shown up to help, it would have gone very badly. I owe a lot to the police in Hustle."

"Yes, but you are the one who went into the burning house, after dispatching a hardened criminal and rescued the two men trapped inside, is that not so?"

"Yes, but I had lots of support."

"Granted. Granted." He paused, looked at the camera, and continued. "Our unlikely hero is a new Private Investigator in Hustle and has been working out of an office in a 2nd hand store. I assume you'll be getting a more upscale office now?" He grinned as if we were in on an inside joke. All of a sudden, I didn't like him.

"I have no plans on moving to any scale office, I am happy at Roy's, and that's where I can be found in case there are future interviews."

Pretty boy made a motion to cut, and the camera went off.

"I guess that's it, we'll wrap it up elsewhere." The group left without a thank you or further looks at me. That suited me just fine. The next time I rescued someone, I would remember their attitudes. Big city snobs.

I went back to Mother's, unmolested by the news crew, even though they were all still milling around the yard, cleaning up their detritus. I noticed they picked up chairs, books and associated gear, but that pop cans, wrappers and other paper trash were still lying about haphazardly. I began picking up the trash, and one of the crew began to help in a hangdog sort of way. He brought an armful of trash to me, and handed it over apologetically. I smiled, and he smiled back, leaving with a wave of his hand. I trudged up to Mother's door, and she met me there with a trash bag in hand.

"After," she glowed, "it's been so exciting. Paul's article was in the paper yesterday, and the phone hasn't stopped ringing, and the reporters have camped out. I went to see Jocko, and he's doing well. It's so exciting!"

She went in with the trash and busied herself in the kitchen. I went into the living room and sat down to relative peace and quiet. I was tired, and nodded off. A bit later, my shoulder was being rubbed, and I turned to look and see what was bothering me. I looked into a pair of large green eyes. It was Soot. I didn't move, it was so unusual to have him doing anything interactive that I just sat there and stared back at him. He rubbed his whiskers into my shoulder and paused occasionally to see what effect it was having on me. This continued for several minutes and then the spell was broken as Paul entered the room.

"Hey After, did you read my article? They even used my name. Lots of times the editor will overwrite the writer's name, especially in an early effort."

"No Paul, I didn't, but the after effects of your article caught up with me on the front lawn a bit ago."

Soot scooted.

Paul sat down, visibly excited. "I haven't got a full time reporting job yet, but they did say I could go out and do a few local color stories!"

"That's good Paul," I murmured sleepily, "I'm glad I was of assistance, but I owed you anyway, for the work you did on that 'Green Frog' flyer."

"Have you read the story yet?"

"No, I didn't even know about it till I got home."

"I'll get it for you," he said and he raced out, bumping into the hat stand and excusing himself.

There was nothing else to do, so I turned on the TV and began watching the 10 o'clock news. It didn't take long; my story was the third, right after something the President had done and a ribbon cutting by the Mayor. The smarmy blond reporter was camped on Mother's lawn, talking about the 'reluctant hero', then there was footage of me running away, followed by me gasping for air. There was absolutely none of my interview, and all he said was that I declined comment on this case or any other cases. That was it, hardly a scoop. I was thankful for a few things though. I was not truly recognizable in the piece, so if it had been broadcast in Baltimore, the bad guys there would not be able to follow up on it. Also, the story was completely removed from why Felicity and I had even gone to Baltimore, so she wasn't even mentioned. I felt safe about that.

Paul returned with the paper, and we were front-page center there. No picture of me, just one of the burnt down shack. Jocko was mentioned, of course, as was Lieutenant Howard and Jocko's friend, Greg. Roy and Grits got a line or two. The rest was about me, where my office was located, and how I came to the aid of my friend on the force. Felicity was not mentioned, so once again, I felt good about the news not reaching Baltimore. I looked up at Paul and told him I thought it was a wonderful article. He beamed back at me, then said that this was my copy, he had several others. He then surprised me by taking the paper from me, then autographed the piece, right over where his name appeared.

"You never know, I might become famous," he said.

"You never know," I agreed. I didn't mention that even if one should become famous, it wasn't always a good thing!

That just about finished up the day for me. I had a lot of things to do over the weekend and decided that I would need an early start, so I trudged up the stairs, undressed and slipped into bed, thankful that things hadn't gone worse for us in Baltimore. I was going over everything that had happened the past few days and I thought I had a glimmer of an answer floating around near the periphery of my consciousness. It either wasn't ready to be held onto, or I wasn't willing to grab it and get a good look, for as my mind sent tendrils out to clutch at it, the nebulous thought wafted away in smoke, and I fell asleep.

Morning came as usual, and that is always a good start. I got to the bathroom before Paul had a chance to trash it. I showered and shaved, even threw a little salve on the few spots that needed more healing. A thought came to me that I might be a few days over on my rent. I also had to get my office telephone hooked up and get my answering machine on line. I felt that I needed to strike while the iron was hot. I also thought I'd run by the newspaper and place an ad for my services. My problem was that this all took money. I was reluctant to take from the thousand I had stashed in my sock, but I was able to rationalize it by calling it a loan to myself, and that I'd repay it right away with my new riches that were sure to come my way shortly.

With that resolved, I raided the sock drawer for three hundred dollars, got dressed in clean jeans, new socks, my new shoes and a nice button shirt, with all of its buttons. I had noticed that most of my shirts now had all of their buttons, and I suspected that Mother or the fossil had gotten tired of my threadbare looks and had decided to 'improve' me. People had been trying to do that for me all of my life, with very little success, but I rarely held it against them. It just takes some people longer than others to recognize a lost cause.

I grabbed another fifty bucks from the sock and went downstairs for breakfast. I was the first there, so I followed my nose into the kitchen and found Mother humming away busily. I greeted her and handed her one hundred and fifty dollars. One thing I like about Mother is, she doesn't say unnecessary things. She just looked at the extra money, smiled at me, and I knew we were square. I went into the front room and sat down, preparing my stomach for the goodies that were sure to be there soon.

It wasn't long before all of the other house members arrived. Even James deigned to share the morning with us. They all greeted me, congratulated me on yet another adventure, and we all traipsed into the dining room for breakfast. I asked Paul if he and Niki had anything going over the weekend, and he said that he thought they might hit a movie. That reminded me that I was to call Gloria about the very same thing, and I made a mental note to do so immediately after breakfast.

Ummm, that was a yummy breakfast, even James was impressed. He generally wolfed down whatever was on the table, and didn't comment one way or the other. He remarked about the exceptional taste today though. French toast with cinnamon and powdered sugar. Fresh blackberries and cream, fresh farm bacon, the thick type. Fluffy scrambled eggs, toast and marmalade. As you know, I don't drink much coffee, but it smelled even better than usual. I stuck to my skim milk instead. I also had seconds…well thirds actually, but why let anything go to waste.

Feeling suitably stuffed, I went to the phone and I fished the doughnut shop's number out of my billfold. I ran across the numbers I had scrawled from Felix's lock box as well. I have tons of pieces of paper in my billfold, unfortunately, none usually resembles money. I was determined to change that, maybe beginning next week. I found Gloria's work number, and called the shop. She answered.

"Hi Gloria, this is After."

"After!" she squealed. "I've been reading about you in the paper, and you were on TV last night. I told my 'rents about you, and that I know you. They thought it was way cool!"

"I take it that 'rents means parents?" I asked, in my uncool way.

"Yes." She giggled. "I keep forgetting how old you are!"

I was four or five years older, tops! I let it pass.

"I was calling to see if you were still up for that movie?"

"Oh yes, I want to see this French film. It's an old one; we can get in for a dollar apiece! I've always wanted to see it, and it's here in town!"

"Is it in French?" I asked, my heart sinking. I hate French movies, probably had a Country sound track too.

"Of course silly, or else it wouldn't be French! Don't worry, they'll have subtitles, or I can translate it for you. I know French, I've had two years of it in High School!"

Her enthusiasm was underwhelming. I had one year of Latin in High School, and the only thing that made it worthwhile was sitting behind Sissy Knowles, and watching her beautiful long hair. I never knew what the point of learning a dead language was. People told me that it would help me learn other languages, but I couldn't even keep up with English. Between words like 'rents and the unfortunate way people were misusing 'myself', I felt that even 1970's English was a dead language.

"OK," I said, "how do we want to do this, I don't have a car."

"I'll just come and get you! How about 6:30 tomorrow night?"

"That sounds wonderful."

"OK, I'll see you then, I need to get back to work now!"

"Bye," I said, and hung up.

That was taken care of. Now it was time for me to go run some errands. I went upstairs, brushed my teeth and what was left of my hair, and went back down, and then exited into the beautiful morning. I felt pretty good today. I wasn't any nearer to finding Felix, but felt that I was getting near to finding out why he was gone. I felt that those numbers could lead to a bank account, and if I could find out the status of that account, I might be able to discover the status of Felix. If there was no activity in the account, I was pretty sure that there was no activity with Felix either. On the other hand, if money was moving around, and it truly was two million dollars, then I was sure Felix was alive and well, but wasn't going to be found anytime soon.

With this on my mind, I managed to find the telephone company, and entered the building. It was located in downtown Hustle, which was comprised of two blocks of red brick and white stone buildings. There were parallel parking places along the main street and the places were generally only half full. The major shopping activity was in a little strip mall out by the supermarket, and at the local Wal-Mart. Most other businesses had closed in the past five years, so the locals told me. They all cursed the day Wal-Mart came to town, but managed to shop there enough to put most of the other shops out of business.

As usual, one of Hustle's finest citizens was manning the front desk. Instead of the bubble gum chewing switchboard running Niki at the Herald, this specimen was a geeky looking kid who was built like a stick with a black, frizzy haircut. He looked like a walking q-tip. I am not the best looking guy either, so I was totally willing to cut him some slack on that account. I stood there for well over five minutes as he busied himself reading something apparently quite important. I cleared my throat a few times, and I finally got his attention. He looked up, clearly annoyed that someone would enter a place of business and might require some assistance.

"What ya need?" he asked adenoidally.

"I need to get a telephone," I replied.

"They got them at Wal-Mart," he said, and went back to his reading.

"I guess I should have said that I need to have a phone line put in at my office," I said patiently.

He looked up again, favoring me with his manly look, "You gotta call a number for that."

I was astonished. "You don't do that here?"

"Nope, it's an automated number, or ya can do it on-line."

"What's on-line?" I asked, afraid of the answer. I envisioned myself crawling up a telephone pole to find a telephone line.

"By using a computer!" he half shouted, now clearly annoyed.

Ahhh, yes, I was caught up now. I have no need for a computer, so I have never been on-line. Just another of life's little pleasures that yet await me.

"So," I ventured, "Do you have the number here that I can call?"

"Nope, it's in the phone book somewhere." He went back to his reading.

I edged closer to him; he was reading a comic book! I got angry then and snatched the book from him, leaving him astonished and mouth agape. "Hey man, give that back to me!"

It was Wonder Woman, why wasn't I surprised? "The world will just have to wait for Wonder Woman to save it until after I get a few questions answered."

"Well, hurry up. I'm pretty busy around here."

"OK, for one thing, I need the number to set up a new phone line."

"I told you, it's in the phone book somewheres, maybe near the front."

"OK, get one and show me where."

"Man, we don't have any around here. I looked for one a few weeks ago, but there aren't any."

"Just what is it you do here anyway?"

"I don't know, man, you're only the second person to come in here since I've been here. A whole month maybe. I am supposed to help people with their problems when they come in. The other person was a pizza delivery boy, but he was in the wrong building. Some guys can't get a real job," he snorted in a superior manner.

I thought that was a pretty snobby thing for him to say. I know several pizza delivery people; they take their lives into their hands whenever they deliver. Never know when you're going to deliver to a crack house or a home filled with PMSing females. Either one could be fatal.

I tried again, "So, I call a phone number, give a person much like yourself my information, and then they are going to have some-one else come to the address, set up the line and I'm in, right?"

"That's how it's supposed to work. Actually, I've never seen any-body that does that. I don't really know how it works. Maybe it's already set up, and all they have to do is throw a switch somewheres." He leaned his head closer to me and spoke in a conspiratorial whis-per, "You know, everything is already wired. Everyone is already being bugged. Nowhere is safe. They come at you at night and stick computer chips under your skin. I check myself every morning, so far I'm clean."

I didn't know what to do, but it was definitely time to leave. I tossed the comic book back on his desk, and walked to the door, wanting to get out of there before some of whatever he had rubbed off on me.

I got as far as the curb, when I couldn't help myself. I went back in and said, "You know, they say that there is something in the blue ink they use in comic books that makes you more susceptible to hypnosis. That way they get you at night, and suggest that you don't really see where they inserted the computer chip under your skin."

I was gratified to see him turn pale, and toss the comic book aside. He then thought about what I had said for a few more sec-onds. I saw him go very blotchy, whereupon he got up, and raced to the rest room, presumably to throw up. I was hoping the govern-ment would turn off their surveillance cameras for that little scene. As I left, I couldn't help myself; I waved to all corners of the room, just in case!

I went back to Mother's and found the phone book. Sure enough, there were numbers to call; including all sorts of trouble numbers, new residence numbers and new business numbers. I wondered why they had more lines for trouble than they did for new business. It did nothing to allay my trepidations or assuage my fears. I was de-termined though, and I tentatively dialed the 'New Business' num-ber. It was busy. I tried again, and kept trying for five minutes. It finally rang, and a computer voice answered. It asked me for my existing phone number, and the area code I live in. I didn't have an existing number. I thought this was for new numbers.

I hung up and dialed zero. The operator was pleasant enough, but she couldn't help me. I told her that I had called the number and that they had asked for an existing number, which I did not have. She asked where I had called from, and I said that I had called from my landlady's house. She asked if I had gone to the local phone company, and I laughed, telling her just enough so she'd get the picture. She was quiet for a bit, then suggested that I just make up a number when I called. I laughed at her, then realized she was serious. I thanked her anyway, and went back to the phone book, looked up the 'New Business' number and dialed it. Amazingly, it rang and the computer voice answered again. I made up a number, gave them a few more bits of information and was asked to hold.

A real person came on the line and informed me that there was no such number and would I care to give them the correct one. I admitted my error, and said that all I really wanted was a new business number. She gave me a different number to call and hung up. I dialed that number, and a real person answered it as well. They took all of my information, and said that they might even have the line and jack installed by the afternoon. The real person then asked me how I got her number, as she wasn't aware that it was listed. I told her that I got it from a local phone book, that it was scribbled in pencil next to the 'New Business' number. I didn't want the telephone police to go after the operator who had given me that number. She wished me a good day and hung up.

I took a deep breath, and scribbled the number in pencil in the margin next to the proffered number. I was beginning to get paranoid myself, or maybe it was because I knew I would never get that number again. The phone company would probably have it disconnected at the earliest opportunity, knowing that it was out there where people needing new services might actually have access to it.

Next stop was going to be the electronics section at Wal-Mart. I got out of the house, took a quick look for Harold Gibbons' men, or a random telephone police truck. Seeing none, I ventured out and hoofed it to Wal-Mart. I know that there are loads of different phones and appliances to be had these days, but it hadn't hit home to me how many options there were. I started looking at phones. Some had built in caller I.D., some had speaker phone capabilities. Some were made especially for computers; others had various strengths of signal. Some were to hook onto cable, some to a regular phone jack. I was lost. I went up to the kid at the counter, told him what I wanted. He asked if I wanted a 'hold' button. I told him that I doubted I'd ever have more than one call at a time. He directed me to a forlorn little box at the end of the counter and sniffed that he thought this one would do me fine. It was the last of the 'old' phones.

I asked, "Do you still have any with the dials on them? You know, the dials that light up?"

He looked horrified and emphatically denied any association, past or present with such an anachronistic piece of junk. I paid $21.95 for my antique and got out of there as fast as I could. He was doubtless calling the phone police as I left, and I wanted nothing to do with them!

I got back to Mother's without incident, went up to my room, retrieved my answering machine and got back to the street where I had an enjoyable walk to work. I arrived at Roy's around one o'clock and found him sitting behind the counter, smoking a cigar and counting his money.

"Hey After!" he smiled at me. "The phone guys were here, did you order a phone?"

"Yup, us superheroes have to be contacted from time to time."

He had the graciousness to smirk at my joke and asked, "So, how did it go in Baltimore?"

I told him the story, and he was properly impressed. He was also relieved when I told him that I didn't think they could trace us, as we didn't write down our names, and Felicity had stolen plates.

"So, After, are you going to work tonight? Grits has a run and won't be back till the middle of next week."

I assured him that I would be working, and then I went in to hook up my phone. It took me awhile to figure out how to get the phone line going into the answering machine, and then into the telephone. I was also surprised to find out that both had to be plugged into an outlet, but I was gratified to realize that I could take my phone with me throughout the building, as it was cordless. I was suitably impressed with myself.

Roy called in to my office, "Hey After, I have your new phone number here at the counter."

I went to the counter and picked up a scrap of paper with my new business number on it.

"The phone man said that you are to receive your bills here."

I said, "That's right, I figured I'd stay here until you toss me out."

Roy laughed and said, "You know too much about me now, After, I'd just as soon have you where I can keep my eye on you!"

I thought that was fair, so I sat down and chatted with him a bit longer, picking up a few tips on antique glassware, and how to tell a repaired book from one that was still as fresh as the day it was bound. It was getting near three o'clock and I realized that if my phone was ever going to ring, I needed to get that ad in the paper.

I told Roy I'd be back at six, and made my way out of the Shoppe, and headed toward the Hustle Herald building. I saw Niki as soon as I entered. She was at the switchboard surrounded by four good looking chaps, none of which bore any resemblance to Paul. I sauntered up and waited for Her Honor to notice me. She finally turned her head while laughing at an off color joke and asked me what I wanted. She didn't recognize me at all.

"Have you seen Paul around?" I asked innocently.

"Paul?" she asked, equally innocently.

"Paul Grease, or haven't you seen him since your cousin left town?"

She recognized me then, blushed then got a mean look in her eyes. She realized that she wasn't fooling me, and the gloves were about to come off. Her lip curled back, and she said, "He's back in the Obit area, where he'll probably be till the day he dies."

I nodded, then said, "Maybe that's where he'll end up, but just think, he might actually go somewhere, he did make the front page two days ago."

"He did? Paul actually wrote an article on the front page?" She seemed impressed.

"He sure did, don't you read your own paper?"

"No one does," she replied haughtily. She then shooed the hangers on away and asked me, "Do you think Paul has a future?"

I looked her straight in the eye, and said, "Yes, but not with you." I walked away before she could stick one of her pointed fingernails in my eyes, and wandered back to the rear of the building.

I found Paul at a cluttered desk, and went up to him. "Hey Paul, how's life treating the new reporter?"

He squinted at me, then exclaimed, "Hi After! Did you say 'Hi' to Niki when you came in?"

"I said something to her, can't quite remember what. She told me where you are."

"She's something else," he said dreamily. "She's off to visit someone this weekend, some relative or other, but she said maybe we can go out sometime next week."

"I'm sure you'll have a wonderful time. Listen Paul, I know you used to work with Ads, could you steer me to someone who's really good at them?"

He looked doubtful, then said, "After, this is the 'Herald'....there isn't anybody good at ads here."

"Oh sure," I said, the truth finally realized. "Well then, how about someone who can at least take my order?"

"No problem, it's kind of dead in this department anyway."

I wasn't sure if he was making a joke or not, so I followed him to another nondescript desk, where two young men were working, and he introduced me to them.

They both knew who I was and seemed like friendly sorts; they shook my hand and asked if I was recovering from my ordeal of last weekend. I assured them that I was and inquired as to how I might go about placing a Classified Ad. It turned out that both were very proficient, and they both had ideas that we were able to use. I placed an ad for two weeks, and told them I'd be back later if I wanted to change it or renew it.

"You don't need to see us if you want it renewed," one of them assured me, "Just pay at the front desk, and tell them we have it on file. Of course you need to see us if you want any changes."

I thanked them and left, and as I was going down the hall, I looked back to say goodbye to Paul, but saw that Niki had gotten there first, probably to assess any damage I might have caused. Neither looked in my direction, so I left the building unscathed.

I still had enough time to get to Mother's, clean up and make it back to Roy's without any undue hardship. I got home just fine, spruced myself up a bit, and went down to supper. Meat loaf, mashed potatoes, beans, and salad were the courses this evening. I should have been gaining all sorts of weight on her food, but with all of my other activities, that just wasn't happening.

Paul was a bit late, and as he sidled into his seat, he looked at me and grinned. "I don't know what you told Niki, but she's never been friendlier. She's not going out of town after all, we're going to go out tomorrow and Sunday as well. I am in your debt again."

I smiled and didn't say anything. I was trying to get him away from that man-eater, but I had achieved entirely the opposite effect, as usual. I gave up worrying about it and went back to my eating. I was wondering why I had not heard from Felicity today, and asked Mother if I'd had any phone calls. She said 'No' and continued serving us our meals.

Dessert was cherry cheesecake, another personal favorite of mine, so once again, I was totally sated by the time I left the table. I felt that walking to work would only help matters, so I left the house, not moving all that quickly, but improving my pace after a bit.

Roy's was very busy when I got there, and he had to stay a bit, as there was really too much going on for a neophyte like me. I did

what I could to help, and it was a good half-hour before Roy felt
that things were enough under control to leave me alone.

He waved as he left and told me to call if I got busy again. It was
so unusual to be this busy in the evening, that I thought it a safe bet
that the rest of the evening would be uneventful. I think I probably
need to get more in touch with my feminine side, as my intuition
was totally off base again, as usual.

fifteen

I didn't hear my phone ring. It could have rung while I was dealing with customers, it may have been while I was assisting a couple who needed help carrying some items out to their car. There is a possibility that it rang while Roy was working, and that he heard it and ignored it. I'll have to ask him sometime. Anyway, I was cleaning up, and it was taking a bit longer than usual, owing to the busy evening we had had. I locked the front door, took the trash out back, and locked the back door as well. I swept up a few spots that used to have a few items, such as an old chest of drawers. Once those things left the building, there was always a residual of dust and dirt. It didn't take long for Roy to find another old piece, so I swept up whenever possible.

Anyway, I did all of this and went into my office to sit and relax for a bit. I had been wondering more and more lately about whom else had been in on my kidnapping run. Someone had to shoot Steroids, drive the car away, and come looking for me. I had thought that they shot Steroids to somehow help me, that the same shooter had shot the drug middleman at the fire to help me. I had thought that I had a secret benefactor. I was now beginning to rethink this. Perhaps Steroids and the Greaseball were shot for another reason. Maybe the drug guy was shot accidentally; perhaps I was the intended target. Things had gotten pretty hairy during that time. There was no good reason to kidnap me and then save me. Perhaps Steroids was going to die that night no matter what. He may have been doomed whatever he did.

There were really only three possibilities as to who the gunman could be. Roy was always around when things seemed to get hot. I was kidnapped from his Shoppe. He was there the night of the fire, and if he was involved, he would have known about the Greaseball's failed attempt at Mother's early in the case. He knew Felicia, and even set her up to talk with me.

The next possibility was Felicity. She knew that her brother had probably stolen two million from Harold Gibbons, either accidentally, or on purpose. He may have been trying to find a way to return the money, and Felicity dusted him for the dough. She was estranged from Felicia, and may have had an argument with her mother. It was her car I was kidnapped in, she had at least seen Steroids and the Greaseball at 'The Green Frog' the night that I met her and she was at the scene during the fire.

The third possibility was that Harold Gibbons was involved, either directly, or through his henchmen. He had a two million-dollar stake in the entire operation. He thought I was privy to something, and when his strong-arm tactics didn't work, smooth talk and money might. If he thought that I would settle for five grand when there was a potential for two million, he was blowing smoke. I tended to think Harold Gibbons was playing everybody, and trying to see what he could come up with. Subtlety did not seem to be his strong suit. Also, if he wanted me dead, he could have killed me outside Roy's and taken me somewhere to dump my body. He had already shown that he could pick me up and talk to me whenever he wanted. The fact did remain though that he had the opportunity to do all of these bad things, and that could not be discounted.

I tried to remove my emotions from my mental calculations. I tried to remove my good feelings for Roy and Felicity, and my negative feelings about Harold Gibbons. I am sure that you have been able to form your own conclusions, and you are probably correct. You have to realize that when you are actually involved and being manipulated, you can develop a blind eye to certain aspects. That was my sin, but I was beginning to see clearly now.

There was only one possible person that fit all of the potential slots, and it was up to me to prove it without getting myself killed. That was going to be the problem, and it required some thought. Thinking had not been my strong suit lately. Nothing had been my strong suit lately. Anyway, I was trying to think of a plan, and I repositioned myself in my office chair. That was when I noticed the little red light blinking away on my answering machine. Excitedly, I lunged for the machine. My newfound fame had already gotten me a job! I rewound the tape to zero and pushed the play button.

"Hi After, this is Paul! I was just checking to see if you got your phone working, I guess it is. I was also checking in to let you know that your Classified Ad is in tonight's paper. Don't be surprised if you get dozens of calls! See you at Mother's. Oh yeah, this is Paul if I didn't say so before. The guy at the top of the stairs. You know me."

I shook my head. That certainly didn't help matters. I rewound the tape again, and this time noticed that it rewound further than before. Quite a bit further as a matter of fact! Somewhat guiltily, I decided to see what messages Felicia had on her tape.

I pushed the play button.

"Hello mom, I have gotten a place to stow the money. I think I am in trouble though. Felicity and Harold Gibbons have both threatened me. Felicity says she wants some of the money or she'll tell Harold where I am. I am coming home, cleaning everything out and leaving. I'll be home this evening, and gone tomorrow."

The next call was from Felicity. "Mom, I know what you've been up to. I won't stand for it. Either you split the money with me or face the consequences. I'll be in sometime tonight."

That was it. I had no timetable to go by, although I assume Felicia had heard both messages, since the play counter had been set for Paul's call. I also knew that Felicity had not listened to those messages when she gave me the answering machine. That was a big mistake on her part.

I knew what I had to do, but wasn't sure if I had the stomach for it. It was going to be tricky. I needed to go home, get into my darkest clothes, find my lock pick set, and then wait until about two o'clock in the morning when 'The Green Frog' should be closed down. Mr. Harold Gibbons was about to have his business broken into by yours truly.

The warnings from the Lieutenant and Roy were screaming loudly in my head as I snuck quietly out the back door. I stayed to the alleys and off the road paths to get back to Mother's. I arrived safely and it was already half past eleven. I went upstairs, took a shower mainly to get any cologne or cigarette smells off of me. Several of our customers had smoked that evening. I didn't want someone to catch a whiff of a scent and realize they were not alone. I really didn't believe that Mr. Gibbons would have a guard at 'The Green Frog' at night, but there might be a delivery or something unexpected, and I didn't want to take any chances. I found my black jeans, somewhat the worse for wear, but tonight it wouldn't matter. I found a tee shirt and a black sweatshirt with a white logo. I turned it inside out to hide the logo and laid it to the side. I found my pick set. I got some dark socks and put them on, along with my new shoes, which were dark enough, and made well enough that they didn't squeak. I sat down and wrote a letter to Lieutenant Howard, explaining all that I was about to do. I told him of my suspicions and reviewed how I had gotten to this point. This did as much for me as anything else. It helped me to keep things clear in my mind, and also gave me a sort of icy calm that I was going to need. I placed the letter in an envelope, addressed it to the Lieutenant, but wrote on the envelope that it was not to be delivered until Saturday night. There was nothing else to do; it was time for some food and patience. I placed the envelope on my dresser.

I went downstairs, found a piece of chocolate cake, got a glass of milk and sat down to a nice, high-energy snack. I was wishing I had a gun right about now, and considered going back to Roy's and scare one up. I finally decided that if I was caught, I would be outnumbered, and I didn't want a death on my conscience, especially not my own death.

It was a little after one o'clock when I went back up to my room for a quick once over. I grabbed my picks and sweatshirt and headed out the door. Soot was waiting by the door as I left, giving me his most baleful look. I stopped, took a hard look at him, and told him he wasn't such a bad cat after all. He yawned at me, and walked away into the darkness, tail upright and stiff.

I opened the door and walked out into the night. Luck was with me, there was a crescent moon but it was obscured by a few clouds, it was as black as it gets in town. I made my way through the dark streets and alleys to the other side of town where 'The Green Frog' perched, seemingly waiting to snap up this little black fly. I got there well before two o'clock. 'The Green Frog' closed at one thirty on Friday nights and most of the parking lot was already empty. I was across the street and was perched several buildings down, nestled into a dark corner between the pools of yellow light afforded by the streetlights.

Cars were leaving with less frequency. The regulars were being assisted out by the bouncers. The waitresses got into cars or waited outside the door for their rides, the tiny red glows coming from the ends of their cigarettes. I didn't know if it was my imagination, or what, but my senses seemed much more attuned tonight.

It wasn't too much longer before Harold Gibbons' limousine arrived and the big guy himself got into the car. All of the girls were gone and it seemed deserted, but there was still one old blue Ford Escort in the parking lot. I decided to wait rather than take a chance. I waited another half-hour; it was nearly three o'clock when I decided that the car was just parked there. I walked carefully to the lot and snuck up to the front door, staying out of the lights as best as I could. I got my picks out when I was startled by a noise coming from inside the building.

There wasn't time to do much more than stand flat against the wall, next to the door, which opened my way. Joe, the bartender was coming out, and had a dolly with some empty kegs on it. He didn't close the door, and didn't see me, as he wheeled the empties toward a shed off of the parking lot. That made my problem a bit easier and I took the opportunity to slip inside the door. I saw that all of the chairs were upside down on the tables. There was a bucket of water and a mop, but the floor was already wet, so I figured that Joe was about done cleaning up. I went to the far side of the room where it was darkest, and crouched behind a large plastic plant in the corner. Joe returned quickly, taking the mop and bucket somewhere out of my field of vision. He returned, turning off all of the lights, then I heard him close the door and jiggle it to be sure it was secured tightly. I couldn't believe my luck, I had spent very little time outside and it appeared I had entered scott free. If there were any alarms, I hadn't seen any. I gave Joe five more minutes to return, just in case he'd forgotten anything, then I started to move around in the dark. There were a few sources of light here and there, mostly glows given off by machines, including one fairly bright light from a lighted wall clock singing the praises of a local brew.

By now I realized that I had neglected to bring a flashlight. That wasn't a disaster, as there were no windows in the building, but somehow I still kicked myself for attempting a break in at night without a light source. I wondered what else I had forgotten. I decided that I could chance some real light and went behind the bar, where a little searching brought me to a light switch. I flipped it on and had a look around. There was a door directly behind the bar, which I assumed to be the main office. There was another door near the plant I had hidden behind, and a third door behind the table that Harold Gibbons always sat at. I was willing to bet money that that door led to his private office, but I thought I'd check the other doors first.

I dismissed the restrooms out of hand, and went to the door at the far end of the building. It was unlocked, but only opened to an employee's lounge room. There were cubicles where the girls could freshen up and a few loose pieces of clothing strewn about. There was also an employee's rest room, but that was it.

I left that room and went back to the door behind the bar. It was locked, but proved to be an easy pick. It was a standard lock that you could get at any hardware store, and I was inside in seconds. The room was small, but surprisingly neat. It had two desks, a computer with all of the associated paraphernalia and file cabinets. I started at the nearest desk and went quickly through the drawers. It was a female's desk, with nail files, lipstick and such in the top drawer. There were no papers in that one. I went to the deep file drawer on the lower left and found business bills, shipping manifests and accounts payable. All this was for the legitimate running of 'The Green Frog' and nothing seemed out of place. The rest of the drawers were filled with extra paper, erasers, pencils and mailing items. It was a very tidy desk.

On my way to the second desk, I noticed a copier and made a mental note of it, in case I came across anything incriminating. The second desk appeared to be Joe's. It had liquor samples, some rags and a few bar glasses. It had catalogs for bar items as well as several books on 'Mixology'. I opened a few books to see if anything was between the pages, but I figured that if one desk in the room was clean, so was the other.

I moved on to the file cabinets. They were broken down into separate files. The first had to do with payroll, job applications and W-2 forms. It was well organized and of no consequence. The second was old bills, some legal papers dealing with the building itself and a few letters to and from attorneys regarding minor legal skirmishes with the local neighbors who objected to having a drinking establishment with scantily clad females in close proximity to their homes.

The room was a wash, which was reassuring, as I had a good idea where the real good stuff was anyway. I turned off the lights and closed the door, but didn't lock it, as I felt I might need access to the copier.

I turned off the lights from the bar, and let my eyes get accustomed to the gloom that reached back to envelop me. After a moment or so, I was able to negotiate my way across the floor to the mysterious door behind Mr. Gibbons' table. This lock proved a bit harder to pick, and I might have damaged it a little in doing so. It finally yielded itself to my charms and I opened it cautiously, prepared to flee at any sound of alarm. There was none, and I slipped inside, pulling the door behind me. I turned on the light, it was the motherlode. His desk was piled with bags of what appeared to be cash, there were other bags stashed behind it with what could only be marijuana. I was surprised to see it out in the open, but then I figured that under normal circumstances, no one would be allowed in here anyway. The room was really just one big safe. There were pictures all over the wall, mostly of Harold Gibbons with a multitude of scantily clad females. He had been in the nightclub business for a long time, as there were earlier pictures of him that showed him as a thinner, but still muscular man, with more hair and a definite attitude. There was another wall, his 'trophy' wall that had him posing with celebrities, including Dean Martin and another with Ronald Reagen. It was hard to know if Reagen was president at that time, as he has looked exactly the same to me for the past thirty years. There was even a picture of Harold with Lassie, complete with an autograph of Lassie's paw.

Somehow I was not reassured, and I confirmed the marijuana with one quick sniff in one of the brown bags. There were eleven in all, each a full grocery sized brown bag, with little individual Zip-Loc bags filled with pot, ready to be sold on the street.

The bags on the desk were randomly filled with bills, from ones to hundreds. I guessed each of the ten bags on the desk to have twenty thousand each.

This was good, but not what I was looking for. I would have to place a bug in Lieutenant Howard's ear when I got the chance. He could tell the proper person and let him deal with it in any way he saw fit.

I sat down in Harold's chair and began on the desk. The top drawer was filled with junk; including opened bills, old broken pencils, several pens and loose scraps of paper. I took a quick glance through it just to be sure, but it wasn't what I wanted. What I was looking for was evidence that he knew Felix, Felicia, or Felicity. I was also looking for something that would indicate that he had off shore accounts, such as the numbers Felix had left behind suggested.

I didn't find what I was looking for until the very last drawer. It was locked, but that was only a small problem for me. I am quite good at picking locks. It was a matter of minutes before I was in. This drawer was the only thing in the room that appeared to be organized. Files were placed with names of people typed on each. There were papers inside with other names, dates, type of drug shipped, who took the drugs, how they were transported and all of that. I was totally shocked to see all of this out in the open, and I was hoping I had not misjudged the local police, as I felt one of them must be on the take for Mr. Gibbons to allow for such openness. Then I realized just how sure of himself Mr. Gibbons was.

I rifled through the folders, finding one on Felix, another on Felicity, and even a thin one on me. I opened mine first, saw a slip of paper with a one thousand dollar expenditure for 'expenses'. There was also a picture of me from the first night I was there, sitting at the table. I figured that one of the waitresses must have taken it. They were certainly thorough. I was impressed.

I looked in Felix's folder next. There was a recent picture of him as well, standing outside 'The Green Frog' with a few other guys. He was smiling at the camera and seemed in control of himself and the situation. There were other sheets in the folder, detailing the drug runs he had made, the amount of money involved, as well as the people he had met for the transactions. There was an envelope in the folder, which I had to slice open. It wasn't marked, so I figured I could replace the envelope with a fresh one after I was done with it. It had a contract for Felix's demise in it. The hit was for $100,000.00. That seemed a fair sum to me, but there was no notice of its having been fulfilled. There were other notes on pieces of scrap paper. My name was on one, as being a possible accomplice of his. Felicia's was as well, as being a possible accomplice. I had assumed Felicia was in the clear, but after hearing the answering machine's message, it was obvious that she knew what Felix had done. She had basically hired me to find Felix, or lead her to the money. Whichever it was, it had cost her her life. I just wasn't sure by whose hand. That was about it for Felix's file.

I opened Felicity's last. There were only a few sheets of paper, but tons of photographs. There were pictures of Felicity as a young girl, sitting on Harold's lap. There were pictures of each stage of her life. There were pictures of Felicity at parties, and pictures of Harold and her that seemed to suggest that they vacationed together. These two were obviously very close. There was a picture of her, the

Greaseball, and Steroids. There was another picture of Harold sitting at a table with the three of them. This last picture was fairly recent, but did not seem to be from any place I had seen in Hustle. I assumed it was taken in Chicago, but had no proof. As near as I could gather, Felicity had been Harold's companion for quite a number of years!

I looked at the other sheets of paper. These were contracts. Apparently, Felicity had done a few jobs for Harold. She had done some early jobs for a few hundred dollars, but there was another job that involved a small time politician that had netted her twenty thousand. I was running with a very bad girl indeed. Then, I found the letter I was looking for. It was just a scrap of paper with some nearly illegible handwriting. As I've said before, my handwriting is terrible, so I can generally make out other bad handwriting.

The gist of the note was that Felicity was to gain my confidence, see if I was involved with Felix. If I was, I was to be killed quickly, if not, I was to be led along and see what I could dig up. Steroids and the Greaseball were along for 'support'.

I was almost totally caught up now, the only real question was the one I had started out with....was Felix still alive? No one seemed to know. I won't say that I wasn't upset to find that Felicity was involved. I won't say that I hadn't developed some feelings for her, and I won't say that I was looking forward to catching her and bringing her to justice. However, there were a lot of people dying in her proximity, and that had to be stopped, hopefully, before I was added to that list.

I grabbed the three folders and made my way back to the room behind the bar, where I copied everything I could. The pictures didn't turn out so well, but they were good enough. I felt I had some bargaining power if things went badly for me.

I found a clean envelope, and replaced Felix's contract in it. I took everything back to Harold's office and put them back in their proper spots, as best I could. I felt sure that no one would suspect anything amiss if they didn't realize that they had been compromised.

I gathered up my papers, turned off the light, made sure I still had my sweatshirt back on inside out, put my picks in my pocket and turned off the light, locking Harold's door as I left.

I threw the discarded envelope in the trash behind the bar and rechecked the office door; to be sure it was locked. I went to the front door and exited, only discovering at the last second that it had a tiny alarm on it. The red light went on and I knew I had to scoot. I was sure that things were still OK, as they would assume that it was someone breaking in, not breaking out of the building. I decided to take up my spot across the street and see who showed.

It was a very short time before a patrol car pulled up. An officer got out and jiggled the door lock. He went back to the car and radioed something in. Before he was finished, Harold Gibbons arrived in his big car. One of the henchmen got out with him and went to the door, repeating what the officer had done. The officer got out, had a short conversation with Mr. Gibbons and got back into his car. I didn't see anything suspicious, just a patrolman checking on a potential break-in. Mr. Gibbons and his man opened the door and entered. A few minutes later, another large car drove up and the other henchman got out. He went inside, and reappeared moments later, and began to prowl around the premises. A few more minutes and the first goon returned, hopped in Mr. Gibbons' car and pealed out of the lot. It was getting interesting, and I wondered just what they had discovered. No more police came by, and there was no activity at all for ten minutes or so. The next car to pull up was the old blue Escort, and I saw Joe get out and enter the building.

Another five minutes went by and Mr. Gibbons' car came back, pulling up to the door, and the driver got out. The passenger side opened, and lo and behold, there was my darling Felicity, going in to help assess the damage.

It was nearly four o'clock in the morning, and only a little more time until dawn would be breaking. I still had some things to do. I figured that all of the bad people were in one place, and that I could get around somewhat safely. I headed down the road to Felicia/Felicity's house. It didn't take too long, I was getting to know the streets fairly well, and my adrenaline level was peaking off the charts. I did make a slight detour. I had made an effort to discover where Jocko lived and had memorized his address in the phone book. I went to that address. I placed all of my copies of Mr. Gibbons' nefarious doings in Jocko's mailbox. I figured that if things went as planned, I'd be back to get them before anyone noticed. If not, between that and my letter to Lieutenant Howard, those two ought to be able to fit all the pieces together quite nicely. Hopefully none of the broken pieces would include me. The only problem was whether or not I would have any insurance if the bad guys caught up to me. I was counting on these papers to provide me with that much anyway.

I got past Jocko's and made my way to Felicia's. As far as I could tell, no one had returned her to the house, so I did a quick check all around and picked the simple lock on her back door. I got in and noticed that she had things fairly well packed. Boxes were labeled and stacked by the walls in various rooms. It seemed that Pastor James or someone from the church had been there, as some of the furniture was missing. It looked like the house was ready to go on the market. I was hoping that Felicity hadn't had time to take her gun. I wanted closure and confirmation, and finding a .22 revolver would do it for me. I started in her bedroom and found the few clothes that she had brought with her to Hustle in a small case by her bed. I opened it and found the revolver, along with Mother Teresa's deck of cards on the bottom of the case, under some of the clothes. I took the gun out and unloaded it. I wasn't sure how necessary this was, but I felt that it improved my odds. I replaced it where I found it, careful to wipe my fingerprints off of it.

I didn't like being in the house, and now that everything was confirmed, I was in a hurry to leave. I did want to check a few more areas out. I hadn't seen the bathroom since I had repaired the grout, and I was fairly certain that Felicity would hide anything important in her room or the bathroom. I looked everywhere in the bathroom, checking medicine bottles and inside feminine boxes. Nothing in any of those places. I went back to her bedroom. I pulled up the mattress. Nothing there either. I figured, like brother, like sister, and I checked under all the dresser drawers. Sure enough, there was the envelope with Felix's numbers in it taped under the same drawer. I took it.

It was time to go, especially so, as I saw headlights coming into the driveway and the first glimmers of daylight were appearing. I got out the back door and ran through the yard, away from her house as fast as I could go. I retraced my steps and picked up the papers from Jocko's mailbox. They had not been disturbed. I was trying to figure a safe place to stash everything when I saw Joe's blue Escort turning the corner in front of me. It appeared that a full-scale search was on for me, and I needed to disappear quickly. I dashed off between two houses, and saw the car drive by slowly, Joe looking right to left in an obvious searching mode. I knelt down behind a large Forsythia bush and waited until he left. He continued up the street. It was obvious that the streets were not going to be safe havens, so I cut out and raced through people's yards, occasionally causing a dog to bark. I was not really expecting to see many people up and about as it was Saturday, and no one was going to work just yet.

I found myself a few blocks from Roy's Shoppe, and took a roundabout path to the building, approaching it from the back side. A police cruiser was patrolling in a leisurely manner. I couldn't tell if the driver was just driving past slowly or if he was looking for something in particular. I was trying to get past the paranoia, but couldn't totally ease my mind that a cop might be on the take. Wouldn't it be a shame if it was the Lieutenant or his Sergeant? I was positive that Jocko was clean, and had never really doubted him in any case, but I wasn't sure he'd believe me if I told him I suspected a dirty cop.

I waited behind the dumpster until he had cruised on by. I snuck up to the back door, keys in hand and let myself into the Shoppe. I stayed very still, trying to sense if anyone was there. I needed time to think, and a place to do it. I knew that my purloined goods would not be absolutely safe anywhere, but I had a thought. I went to the stack of comic books and tore some pages out of several of them, inserting my copies into the missing space. I then replaced the books near the bottom of the pile, and wrote a note, stating that all books were to be held until further notice. I indicated that I had a buyer and to not let them go. I taped the note to the top comic book and felt that I had done what I could do. I wadded the torn sheets into a ball and deposited them in the trashcan behind Roy's counter, well under the rest of the trash.

My message light was blinking. I rewound the tape and heard Felicity speaking. "After, I don't know what you've done, but Mr. Gibbons has me and says that I am in deep trouble if you don't come forward. Please help me here, and he says that whatever you've done can be forgiven if you do what he paid you to do. Please call him at 'The Green Frog' at noon today. He says he'll deal with you. Please do it."

I didn't buy it at all. They didn't know what I knew. Felicity had lied to me for the last time, but I still had to find a way out of this mess. I needed to know about Felix. I needed to be able to live my life without looking over my shoulder. I needed Harold Gibbons, his henchmen, and Felicity in jail forever. Even then, I wouldn't be safe. I needed leverage. I thought that the papers I had stolen might do the trick, but I needed to be sure.

I dialed 'The Green Frog'. A man answered, "Hello."

I said, "After Coffman to speak with Mr. Gibbons."

He said, "Just a sec."

In just a few secs, Mr. Gibbons was on the phone, trying to sound in charge, but not scary. "After, what in the hell is going on? I thought we had a deal."

"The deal includes me living to a ripe old age. I am afraid I had to take out some insurance."

"After, After, After," he purred, "I never had anything unpleasant planned for you."

"Harold, Harold, Harold," I retorted, "I've been in your lower left drawer."

He gasped. I continued, "I wasn't interested in anything you had in any of the bags, they are intact. I did find several items of interest in some folders you had so very neatly filed away. You have the originals, but I have the copies."

"I underestimated you," he said softly. "It won't happen again."

"I understand that completely, and I don't want you to. If you give me some unmolested time to work something out, perhaps we could both come away happy."

"What's it gonna cost me?" he snarled. "Even I have my limits."

"How's twenty to life sound for limits?"

"OK, you have my attention. You have until noon, I'll be here waiting for your call."

"It's a deal, and you can tell Felicity to cut the bull, I saw her file too."

He laughed at that and said, "She's a corker, ain't she?"

"She is, at that," I said, and hung up. I thought I had bought myself some time, now I needed to know what to do with it.

I made another call; luckily, I remembered the number of the doughnut shop.

"Is Gloria there?" I asked.

"She's just leaving." the voice on the other end answered. "Hold on, I'll try to catch her."

I waited for a few minutes, then I heard Gloria on the other end. "Hello?"

"Hi Gloria, this is After."

"Hi After!" she cried. "Are we still on for tonight?"

"I sincerely hope so, but no guarantees. I am in a pickle again, and was wondering if you could bail me out?"

"Sure, whatever I can do!"

"Can you pick me up at the bowling alley in five minutes?"

"Sure, do you need anything?"

"Nope, I'll catch you up on things when I see you."

"Great, I'll be right there." She hung up.

The bowling alley was one block down the road. I wanted to be out of town, as I was sure Harold was going to be looking for me regardless of any deals we had made. I closed things up, trying to leave no clue that I had been there. I went to the front door and opened it a crack. Damn! There was Joe's car, and he was just getting out of it. I closed the door quietly and locked it, then raced to the back of the building. I opened that door, and saw no one. I got out, made my way to the storage shed, saw Joe coming around the right side of the building, and took off to the left side, expecting to be hit by a bullet at any second. I made it without incident, and found myself perched at a house across the street from the bowling alley. I prayed Gloria would be on time.

sixteen

There she was, turning the corner in her 'rent's Town Car. I saw no one else in the general area, so as she neared the building I stepped out and waved. She pulled over and stopped. I jumped in and suggested that she not waste any time in getting out of there. She took me at my word and took off, heading out of town.

"What can you tell me, After?" she asked, her face flushed with excitement.

"I can tell you that things have reached a critical phase in my case, that there are people trying to kill me, and that I have damaging evidence that will possibly save my butt, if I can figure out a way to get these people to deal. I don't think we'll be going to the movie tonight however."

"I understand, there's plenty of time for a movie after you're out of this situation. Where do you want to go?"

"I have no idea, out of town for starters, then somewhere safe for me to sit down and work this entire thing through."

"Let's go to my home," she decided. "It'll be safe there."

That was a good idea, and I let her have her way. I sat back and tried to clear my mind. I had no doubt that Mr. Gibbons was using this time to clear out his office. No doubt it was already clean. Calling the police would not help anyway. It would take too long to get a search warrant and there were some other things that he might be able to do to forestall the inevitable. No, I had to come up with something fool proof, and I wasn't sure what that would be.

We drove on for about ten miles, pulling into a nice long driveway, and up to a very large house. It was three stories, made of brick. It had gables and catwalks, beautiful gardens and everything was elegant and expensive. I must have shown my amazement, because Gloria turned to me and laughed.

"I guess it is pretty impressive at first glance, but it is way too much trouble, in my opinion. A small three bedroom would suit me just fine."

"Do you have brothers or sisters?" I asked.

"One of each, but my brother is away at college and my sister is a wild child, and is never home. She is worrying my 'rents to death. Speaking of which, we're in luck, they went out of town for the weekend, and we have the place to ourselves. You ought to be able to come up with your plan."

"I sure hope so, as I have no idea what that plan will be."

I had thought of several options, and discarded them, as I was basically sure that Harold Gibbons would be able to buy or bully his way out of just about anything. I thought about bringing the police in, and that might just have to do, although I knew Mr. Gibbons would be able to reach out from jail to get me. No, the only real option that I had was to make him think that I knew where Felix was, and how to get his money back. I could always claim that I got spooked when I realized that Felicity was in it with him. Then, I would trade him the papers for a few weeks to actually get to Felix or the money. At least Felicity would not have the envelope with the numbers anymore, and I wondered how the gun happy lady would handle that! I was hoping we could all strike a deal together.

I decided to try and work something along those lines, and was laying down some fairly good arguments when Gloria came into the room with some snacks and suggested I take a little time to eat and relax. I was glad to do so and ate a few lunchmeat sandwiches and drank some soda pop.

"What, no doughnuts?" I asked. "I thought you always gave me doughnuts when I find myself in a bind."

She grinned and came over behind me and started to massage my neck. I closed my eyes and enjoyed it; it could be my last neck rub ever. I was almost to the point of total relaxation when she stopped, and I felt her breath by my ear.

She whispered, "Don't open your eyes."

I kept them closed and before long I felt her sitting on my lap and she started to kiss me, first gently, then with more ardor. There was nothing else to do except give as well as receive, and I did my best to comply. We got into a little petting as well, when I suddenly stopped.

"No, this isn't right," I said. "It's too much like the condemned man's last meal. I'd rather be the one initiating this."

She sat back and asked, "Is it that other girl, that Felicity?"

"She never crossed my mind, you made me forget all about her, honest. However, it is time for me to see if my little plan is going to work."

It was nearly eleven o'clock, and I had yet to determine a meeting place. I had just about decided not to meet anywhere he would normally expect me, when I had an idea.

"Come on," I said. "It's time for me to take the initiative."

We got up, and I got my few things together. I took her hand, pulled her to me, and gave her one more long kiss, then held on for dear life. I smiled at her, and she smiled back. Everything was going to be OK, I just knew it. All of the sudden I felt that the money just wasn't that big a deal to Mr. Gibbons, getting his revenge was.

We got back out to the car and she drove me into town. "Where are we going?" she asked.

"I thought that we might go right back to Roy's, but I have a better idea. If something should happen to me, go to my office, find a pile of comic books, and look through them until you find some Xeroxed papers. Take those to Jocko O'Reilly at the Police station. He'll know what to do with them."

She looked worried. "After, what is going to happen?"

"I hope that nothing will happen, but you never know in a situation like this. They have four or five brains working against mine. I do have desperation and blackmail working for me though." I managed to smile weakly. She was kind enough to try and return it, but I could see tears in her eyes, so I looked away. This was no time for any sort of weakness on my part.

She continued driving, we were early, and I was counting on that. I didn't think Harold Gibbons was expecting a frontal assault, but he was a big boy with plenty of muscle. I had to be ready to hit on all cylinders, and catch him off guard. Then maybe, just maybe, we could get something accomplished. That something included me living to a ripe old age.

"Take me to 'The Green Frog'," I ordered. "No wait! I don't want them to see your car, drop me off a block away."

She gulped audibly, but I think she was impressed with the frontal assault option as well. We were almost there, and I reached down and squeezed her knee in thanks. I didn't want to look at her again. I gathered up my stuff, and when she stopped the car, I climbed out, ready to meet my fate.

She stopped just a block away from the club, and I was out of the car. She drove off immediately, and I didn't turn to look back at her. I walked the last block and was gratified to see Harold's car there as well as the other cars that his henchman had driven the night before. I saw no sign of the old blue Escort that Joe drove. Felicity's car was not there either, but I didn't expect it to be. I knew though, that she would be inside.

I walked up to the door, and opened it as if I'd owned it all my life. The guy who sucker punched me was sitting inside and about flipped when I entered. I could see that a lot had happened since I was there the night before. Tables had been moved and the door to Harold Gibbons' office was wide open, revealing an almost empty room, the pictures on the wall, and a bare desk standing mutely in the middle of it.

I brushed right by the guard, who seemed frozen in fear, or was it just dumb stupidity? I don't think the redundancy is an over exaggeration in this case. I waltzed into Harold's office and saw him, the other guard, and Felicity waiting by the phone.

I entered breezily, "I like what you've done to the place, but you didn't have to clean up on my account!"

The guard began to rush me, but was halted by Harold's beefy hand thrust in his face. "Let's hear what After has to say. Go get him a Chivas double, on the rocks. We might as well be comfortable."

The guard looked at me with contempt as he walked by, but I gave him a smile and a wink. His look became less sure of itself, and his step faltered a bit.

I didn't have a strong hand, but I had to play the one I was dealt, and a poker face would sure help right now. I hoped Felicity wasn't seeing through it. She had stood up when I entered, and had watched the bravado with a blank look on her face. Clearly, she hadn't seen this coming. She recovered somewhat and sat down again.

I looked around and didn't find a chair, so I went back out and brought in a folding chair, sat down and waited for my drink.

"I thought you were going to call at noon," Harold stated.

"I could, if you still want me to, but I'd rather have this over with by then," I said.

"Sounds fair to me," he agreed. "What have you got?"

My drink arrived, and I tried to be polite. I found a scrap of paper, placed it on the desk, took a sip, and placed the drink on the paper. Good, I noticed that my hand wasn't shaking at all.

The doorman came into the room. He told Harold that he had locked the door and would go back to wait. Harold nodded and dismissed him. The man closed the door behind him. Harold came over to me, then motioned for me to rise, so I did. He did a quick frisk, opened my shirt to check for wires and nodded that I could sit down again.

"If I had known we were going to do that, I would have brought my cards," I said with a leer at Felicity.

She grew pale, but Harold had just about had enough. He sat back in his chair and looked me over. He kept staring, and waited for me to fall off the chair, or do something else stupid. I took another drink, sat back and tried to relax, realizing that my back was soaked with sweat. I figured he'd discovered that during the frisking.

"This is what I have," I began after a suitable interlude. I have Felix's money just about tracked down. I might have it in a day; I might have it in a week. I don't have Felix, but could keep looking if you like."

"Why did you break into my office?"

"I discovered that Felicity was playing both ends against the middle, and I wanted answers."

This earned Felicity a hard look, and she began to look uncomfortable. "Go on," he muttered, shifting his seat so that he could look at both of us at the same time.

"Well, what I found here kind of set me to thinking that my future wasn't too bright, unless I had some leverage. I guess I found enough so that you were willing to talk to me today. Believe me, if I had wanted to ruin you, I could have put all the stuff out in the parking lot, called the cops and made off with the money."

"I'm still listening," he stated, and the hard look was being replaced with a more attentive one.

I took another sip of my drink, took my time and weighed the next words carefully. "I know that you can erase me at any time, so I decided to make myself useful to you. I knew that Felicity had a bank number with Felix's money in it. Did she happen to mention that to you?"

He looked startled, and glanced at Felicity.

She grew paler, and said, "I was going to tell you. We found it in Felix's box in Baltimore, although I didn't know it was a bank account."

"Yup, it sure is, and when I was going through your files last night, I noticed a whole lot more, just like it. I was wondering if maybe good old Felix wasn't set up by you or one of your employees."

"The little jerk just ripped me off, that's all there is to it!" Harold thundered. "He knew how to set up an account, as he'd done it for me several times."

"That may be, and it doesn't really change anything, as I am now the only one with that number."

Felicity looked angry. "You have no idea where that number is." she growled, a mean look on her face.

"Like brother, like sister." I waggled my finger at her. "You put it the same place he had hidden his box key."

Her paleness went all of the way to white at this and sat back, trying to hatch a way out of this, no doubt. I looked back at Harold, trying to let him know that I was dismissing her as irrelevant.

"So," Harold said, "You've figured out that Felicity was my insurance against you discovering the money and running with it. I guess your actions last night will attest to the notion that you won't run off with my money, should you find it. I'm still listening."

So far, so good. I had planted some doubt and bought some breathing room. Felicity was on her heels and I could concentrate on Harold.

"OK," I continued, "here's the best I can come up with. Take it or leave it. I'll give you all your papers back, forget all about anything I ever saw here, and find Felix's money for you. I might even find Felix, but I still have no idea what happened to him."

Harold grunted, still listening, I assumed.

"In return, I don't want any of your money, in fact, I want to give you your thousand back. I get to go on with my life and hopefully never see Felicity again."

He sat back and thought about it for several minutes, then asked, "Do you really think it's that easy?"

"No, but it's the best I could come up with. Besides, it isn't as if I was asking for a cut of the take or anything else. I am asking that we both return what is rightfully ours to each other. I think it's a fair deal."

"I think it's a fair deal too," he said. "It's just too bad that I don't deal fairly."

I looked up at him; all of the nice tones he had been using were gone, replaced instead by a hard-edged voice and the mean eyes. He went to his desk and opened a drawer. He reached in, and pulled out a stack of papers, then tossed a ripped up comic book at me.

"It's better to leave no stone unturned. One of my men managed to find these in your office this morning, while returning Felicity to her house. The two of them returned with these just before you arrived. Rather comical, don't you think?"

I couldn't move, I couldn't think. He had outplayed me, drawing a full house to my one pair. I just sat there, wondering why I was still alive.

"I do admire you though, you did very well, for an amateur. You see, I have had you followed from the beginning. I admit, you gave me the slip last night, and you have caused me some concern, and considerable expense. I had two of my friends working with me as well, but they were sadly, eliminated, quite possibly by you and Ms. Jeffries here."

"You think I shot those two creeps? They were working with Felicity, weren't they?"

"No, they were working for me." He turned to Felicity. "Sorry, my dear, but you don't come from a very trustworthy family." He continued, "Now I have no need for either one of you, as I have the bank account number." He pulled out a rather mean looking gun, and waved it back and forth between Felicity and me.

She looked back at him, and suddenly grinned, "You may notice that a few of those numbers have been changed. I took the precaution of making a few alterations and memorizing the different numbers as an insurance policy, just in case After decided to go for it all."

I chirped up at that point. "Actually, I wrote the numbers down on the envelope flap before I left her house one evening. You may notice that the envelope is missing its flap."

Harold was stopped there for a minute. He paused just a second too long, and Felicity had her .22 out. He turned to her, and she said, "Drop it Harold."

He dropped his gun, a stunned look on his face. I wasn't worried, Harold was disarmed and I had removed her bullets. I decided it was time to deal with Harold again.

"Mr. Gibbons, it isn't too late to deal."

He turned to me with a question on his face. Felicity just smirked. "What do you mean, After? It appears that our Ms. Felicity has the final answer, in the form of her trusty .22 there. I knew I should have had her frisked, but I thought she'd be gone before I had to deal with you."

"Things don't always turn out as you would like, Harold," she said. "I had no plans on killing you until you showed me that I was expendable. I thought we went back too far for you to do something like that to me. That's why I had to go back home, to get my weapon."

"We do go back a ways, my dear, we do," Harold said, sweat forming on his brow. "Remember who helped you get started in life, who gave you chance after chance, who took you in every time you needed a home."

"Yes," she said as she circled to the door. You took me in all right; you gave me a life all right. You put me on the streets as a prostitute when you got tired of me, you bastard. Then, when you needed dirty work, you got me as a cheap hit person. Now I'm going to shoot you, then I'm going to shoot After. It will look as if you two had a murder/suicide and I'll be out of here, with the numbers to Felix's account."

She had reached the door, and turned to face him. "I'm sorry it had to be this way. I'm sorry life turned out this way. I'm sorry you didn't keep me safe and secure as you promised. If anyone deserves the two million, it's me. I intend to take it and disappear from Hustle for good."

I took one last chance. "Pick up your gun, Mr. Gibbons, she doesn't have any bullets. I took them out of her gun when I took the envelope from her house."

He didn't pick up his gun, instead, he roared out something unintelligible and started to rush at her. She raised her .22 and shot him between the eyes.

He fell to the floor, dead instantly, limbs twitching slightly. I stared at her, totally at sea.

"I always check my gun before I leave the house. I also discovered that you'd taken the envelope. It doesn't matter, I've got it back now, plus tons of other numbers, thanks to you!" She paused looking at the door. I could hear noises coming from the other side as Harold's men were making their moves. She then said coolly, "Here's where it gets tricky."

The man that had been guarding the front door rushed in, stopping in cold surprise when he saw his boss dead on the floor, a bullet hole between the eyes.

He turned to look at Felicity, who fired her gun again, dropping him to the ground, a bullet hole where his right eye used to be. She looked at him dispassionately and said, "Getting sloppy, I was off by an inch." Then to me, "Stay here."

She looked out the door and apparently saw the other guard, as she fired off two shots. I took the opportunity to literally jump over the desk, and I grabbed Harold's gun as I hit the floor. It was one of those rare moments where everything was happening in slow motion, and I seemed to float in the air forever. I had time to reach for the gun and plan my roll even as I hit the ground. I sensed, rather than heard Felicity shoot at me. In my altered state I realized that she had shot five times; once at Harold, once at the door guard, twice at the other guard and once at me. If I could just get her to shoot again, and somehow miss.... I took off my shoe and threw it against the far wall, and stood up ready to cover her if possible. She didn't shoot at the noise, she was too good to fall for that, but her attention was drawn away from my position long enough that I now had the drop on her. I pulled the trigger back and was ready to shoot. She froze and said, "I guess we still have a little talking to do. I can still kill you even though you'd shoot me too."

"Put the gun down!" I ordered.

She sighed and tossed the gun onto the floor.

"Now, sit down. You have some explaining to do."

She sat down in the chair I had just vacated. She turned and tried to smile at me. "I know we can't do anything now, there's too much bad blood, but maybe you still feel enough for me to give me a running start. I admit that I wouldn't have done that for you, but you see, I am not a good person. You are, After." She gave me the big-eyed look, and for a millisecond, I almost fell for it. Then I remembered how she'd just chopped down three men without a second thought, and that she'd done contracts as well.

I said, "I need some answers, Felicity."

"OK," she replied, "what do you need to know?"

"Why did you kill those two henchmen? Did you know they were working for Harold Gibbons?"

"Not at first, but I figured it out and I had to find a way to get them out of the picture without Harold getting suspicious. The first guy was easy, he botched the job and he would have squealed if he'd been caught. I even told Harold about it afterwards. He thought that I was covering for you. I didn't argue. The second guy was easy too. After we kidnapped you, and you got away, I figured I could make it look like you killed each other, so I plugged him on the bank and went looking for you. Nothing personal."

"Apparently, there never was." I sighed.

"I was a prostitute, I am good at fooling people, I was a good one. Things might have been different with you, I hope you know that!"

"We'll never know, will we?" I said. "OK, what happened with you and your mother?"

"I got to town in late July. Somehow she knew I was coming. I didn't call her until after she'd discovered I was here. I didn't know she'd gone to see you. I never knew about you until I found you in Felix's apartment. Anyway, she saw me coming and I went up to her and told her I was glad to see her. The bus was coming just then, and I figured it was a good opportunity to take her out. You see, she was going to take all of Felix's money and run. Felix and I hatched the plan, and she got wind of it. She wanted a third of the money, and that was just unacceptable. I never owed her anything anyway."

"You killed your own mother?" I gasped.

"Why not, she killed Felix!"

I was flabbergasted. Felicia had killed her son? That was the one thought that had never occurred to me. I was shocked, and I showed it.

"Like mother, like daughter," Felicity said softly. "She was upset that he was going to take off. He had left the key somewhere, but she wasn't sure where. She drugged him when he returned home, and tied him up, to wait for him to tell her where the money was. He never told. She kept him tied up and cleaned up his apartment, looking for the damn key. She spent days at it, never untying him. She tore all the furniture up, then had junk men come in and remove it. She cleaned up the place, then she decided she needed help with him. I guess she hired you."

"You mean, Felix was alive when she hired me?"

"I don't think so. Right after I conked you on the head, I went to her house. He was still tied up, but I think he'd died about a day or two before. Mom never did take very good care of us. I took him out to the river, sliced him open, put some rocks in him and dumped him in. Messy work, not my style at all."

"So, as long as I was on the case, you figured I might come in handy?"

"Not really, I thought you were a loser, but I needed an excuse to get rid of Harold's goons. Then, when you got away from the kidnapping, I had to get out of town. I thought it was all over when you found me in Chicago. After, you actually turned out to be a pretty good detective."

"I'm not so sure, I didn't get it all until this morning, and I never would have found out about Felix."

We sat and stared at each other. She had no remorse; her once beautiful eyes were empty and cold. I wanted to ask her so much, but it was almost time to go. I needed to call Lieutenant Howard, and try to get him here to take care of this mess.

Instead, I asked her, "What about that fellow I was fighting the night of the fire?"

"I didn't mean to kill him, I was actually aiming at you. I mean, I didn't care if I killed him, but he just got in the way. I was a long way away and it was just speculation as to which one of the two you were. I couldn't get a bead on you when you started running to the house, and also, Roy, Grits and the other men from the house were running around, so I had to be sure who I had shot. I raced to him, saw it wasn't you, but he got a good look at me. I shot him in the head. I knew I had to get back to my car and pretend I was still a lookout! I drove to that farmhouse and called 911." She reached down to her knee and scratched it. I allowed it, as long as she didn't make a move for her gun."

"Gee, I appreciate you sharing that little item with me. By my count, that makes you responsible for six deaths recently."

She tried to pout, then broke into a grin. "Gosh, are you going to miss any of those nice guys?"

"That's not the point, we could have worked all of this out without bloodshed, and you wouldn't be going to jail for the rest of your life."

"Wherever I'm going, it won't be jail," she retorted, and scratched her knee again.

"I need to make a phone call," I said, reaching for Harold's desk phone. I knew the station number by heart and was prepared to dial it. I took the gun off of her for a split second while I was picking up the phone, and she went to scratch her knee again.

The rest of this happened so quickly that it is still a blur to me, but somehow, somewhere, Felicity had a second gun, either under her belt, or under her skirt. She had been scratching her knee to get me used to her fidgeting about, so when she did make her move, I wasn't ready for it. Anyway, I was preparing to dial, my gun wasn't on her, and she came up with what looked like a toy gun, but I knew it was lethal. I had time to duck, but I felt something slam into the right side of my head. I heard another shot; it sounded like a cannon. I was on the floor, trying to get my body to respond, but it seemed as if all systems were shutting down.

I sensed a presence over me and figured that this was it. I was going to die here on Harold's office floor. I turned to look at her for one last time, but it wasn't Felicity I was looking at. It was Joe, the bartender. He knelt down to me, a kind and concerned look on his face, and asked, "After, are you OK?"

He turned and spoke to someone and called out, "After's been shot!" I saw Lieutenant Howard, of all people come into my field of view.

The Lieutenant looked at me sharply, and went to the phone. That's the last I remember before I blacked out.

epilogue

I woke to the now familiar sights, sounds and smells of a hospital. I recognized my favorite nurse and turned to greet her, but got instantly dizzy. I tried again, much slower and saw many of my friends in the room, just waiting for me to regain coherency. They would probably have to wait years for that, but at least I could communicate.

"What's going on?" I slurred.

Several people started to talk at once. I could make out Lieutenant Howard, Jocko, Mother Teresa, Gloria, Roy and Pastor James. They deferred to the Lieutenant, always a wise choice.

The Lieutenant spoke for all, "After, you were shot by Ms. Jeffries, you were hit just above your right ear, luckily where the bone is thick. You suffered abrasions and a concussion, but the bullet did not penetrate. You'll be OK."

I felt my head; it was wrapped in a bandage, but didn't really hurt. I looked at everyone and smiled then asked, "Joe?"

The Lieutenant smiled at that and said, "Joe was trying to find you all day, he knew Harold and his men were planning to ambush you. Apparently you were always one step ahead of him. He's a good man, After. He got me into 'The Green Frog' just as the shooting started. I was almost too late, but once you got the situation under control, I just stood by the door and listened to what amounted to a confession."

"What happened to Felicity?" I asked.

The Lieutenant paused, then said, "I shot her as she shot you. She got that gun out so fast, all I could do was go for a chest shot. I'm afraid she didn't make it."

There was nothing to say to that. I would always wonder if she could have been something different and done better for herself had circumstances allowed. That was for later reflection though. As drugged up as I was, I was only capable of assimilating minor information at the time. I did feel a pang of regret, but it was far overshadowed by relief at being able to continue with my lifelong affinity for breathing.

Gloria came up and gave me a kiss and said she'd brought a book of French poetry to read to me. I guess I liked the idea, but we'd have to see. At least she'd be near me.

Roy then raised his hand as if he were in school and said, "You've got a ton of messages on your answering machine, so I guess you'll be busy when you're released."

That was good news, and I looked at my nurse questioningly. She said, "I think you'll be released tomorrow."

More good news. I was wondering how the Lieutenant knew to come looking for me. I asked him, "Did Joe call you or something? How did you know to look for me?"

The Lieutenant chuckled and said, "I'd like to say it was top flight police work, but Mother Teresa said your cat told her you were in trouble."

"Soot?" I asked.

Mother nodded and said that Soot had gone ahead and trashed my room again, but had come downstairs with my envelope to the Lieutenant in his mouth. It had been torn open and the letter was halfway out. She went ahead and read enough to realize the situation and had called him up right away.

Lieutenant Howard said, "I realized I couldn't enter 'The Green Frog' without a warrant, so I was trying to get one when Joe raced into the parking lot and told me what was happening. He let me in, and you know the rest.

I did, indeed, know the rest. I also knew that I needed some quiet, as my head was playing funny tricks on me. People came into and out of focus. They could see I was having trouble, so one by one, everyone left the room, until only the nurse, Gloria and Pastor James were left. Gloria made it quite clear that she was not leaving, as she sat in the chair next to my bed and opened her book of poetry.

Pastor James smiled and said he only needed a minute. He told me that Felicity would be buried next to her mother on Tuesday, and wanted to know if I would be present. I shook my head no. He then asked if I might desire to send flowers or anything?

I thought about it and then said, "Go ahead and order some from the supermarket. Jocko can get them for you. I'll take care of the bill later." After all, I now had what remained of the thousand dollars that I didn't need to pay back to Harold Gibbons, and I considered it money well earned. I also knew that there was two million dollars out there somewhere with no one's name on it.

The Pastor smiled and started to leave. I had a quick thought and called him back. "Just don't send petunias, they're allergic to them."

ABOUT THE AUTHOR

Vincent M. Lutterbie is a dentist living in Missouri. He deals exclusively with retarded and disabled people. He lives with his wife, and the occasionally visiting child. All three of their children are growing up and in college. He is active in local community affairs.

This is his first novel.

Printed in the United States
4632